SIFTING SANDS

Blood of
the Durit

Book 1

Sifting Sands

Angie Caedis

For Haley—

Thank you for being this book's biggest fan
before it was even finished, and for introducing
me to the wonderful world of fantasy.

PRONUNCIATION GUIDE

Names

Ren / Serehna	*wren / sir - wren - ah*
Mikel	*mick - el*
Olen	*o - len*
Harkin	*har - kin*
Rohan	*row - han*
Hassan	*huh - san*
Savi	*saw - vee*
Riat	*rye - at*
Kai	*ka - i (like my)*
Tariq	*tar - ique*
Vish	*vih - ssh (like fish)*
Silas	*sigh - lass*
Asha	*ah - ssh - ah*
Tian	*tee - an*
Coyir	*coy - yer*

PRONUNCIATION GUIDE

Gods

Hael	*hay - el*
Veles	*vell (like hell) - iss*

Daemons, Creatures, + Things

Daemon	*day - mon*
Mender	*mend - er*
Seer	*see - er*
Shade	*shay - d*
Torch	*tor - ch*
Berserker	*beh - zer - ker*
Weaver	*weave - er*
Durit	*dur - it*
Hekkriti	*heck - cret - e*
Turiden	*tur - eh - den*
Vitremi	*vit - trem - e*
Ricsin	*rick - sin*

PRONUNCIATION GUIDE

Places

Jahaer	*ja - hare*
Piro	*peer - o*
Denheir	*den - ear*
Tol Dena	*toll den - a*
Artolen	*are - toll - en*
Kohe	*co - hey*
Kupor	*cuh - pore*
Hira	*hear - a*
Merket	*mare - ket*
Varhit	*var - eat*
Letka	*let - kah*
Malneis	*mal - niece*
Raulik	*raw - lick*
Kalade	*cah - la - day*
Fiöl	*fee - ole*

Hael-blessed Daemons

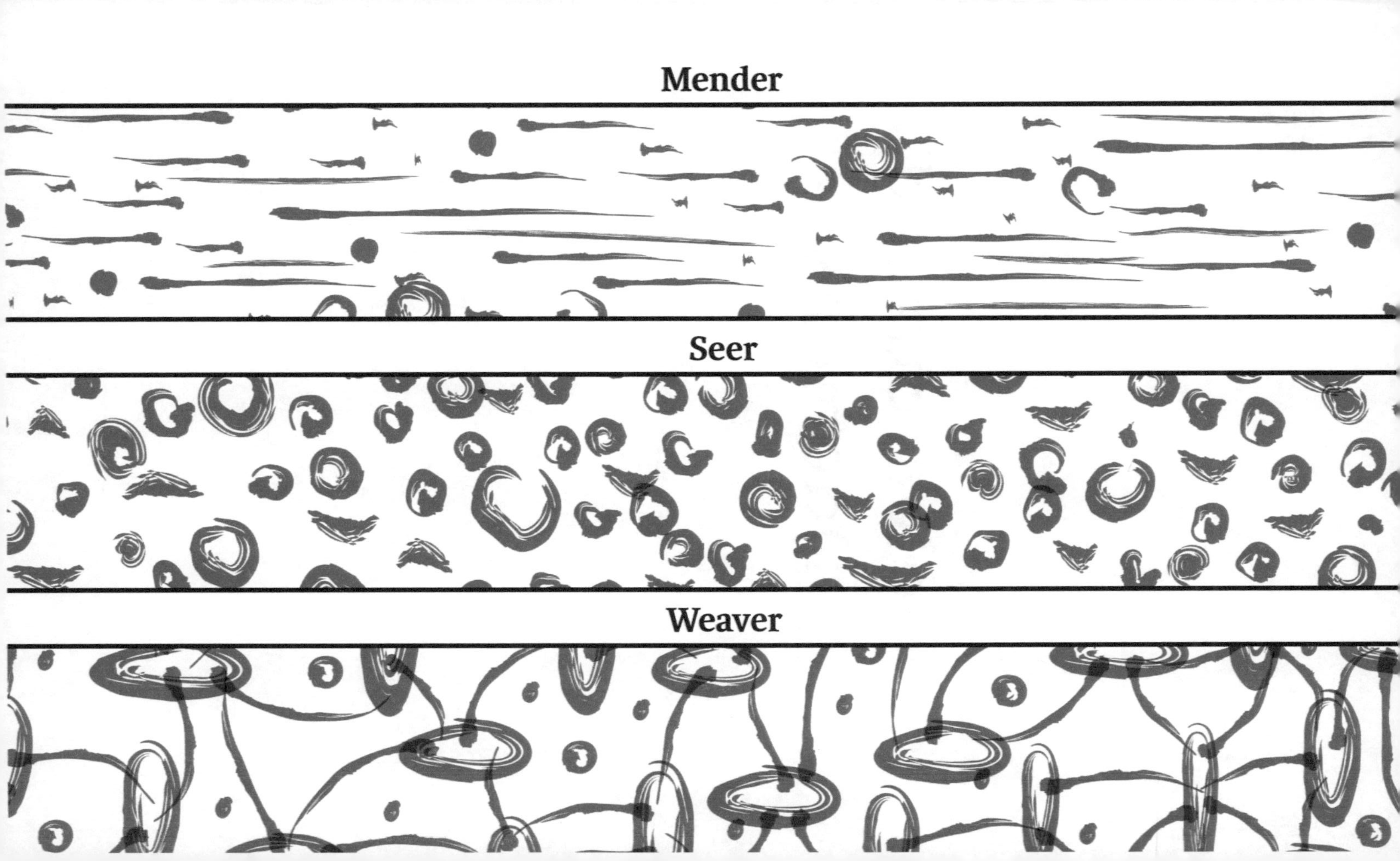

Mender
Seer
Weaver

Veles-cursed Daemons

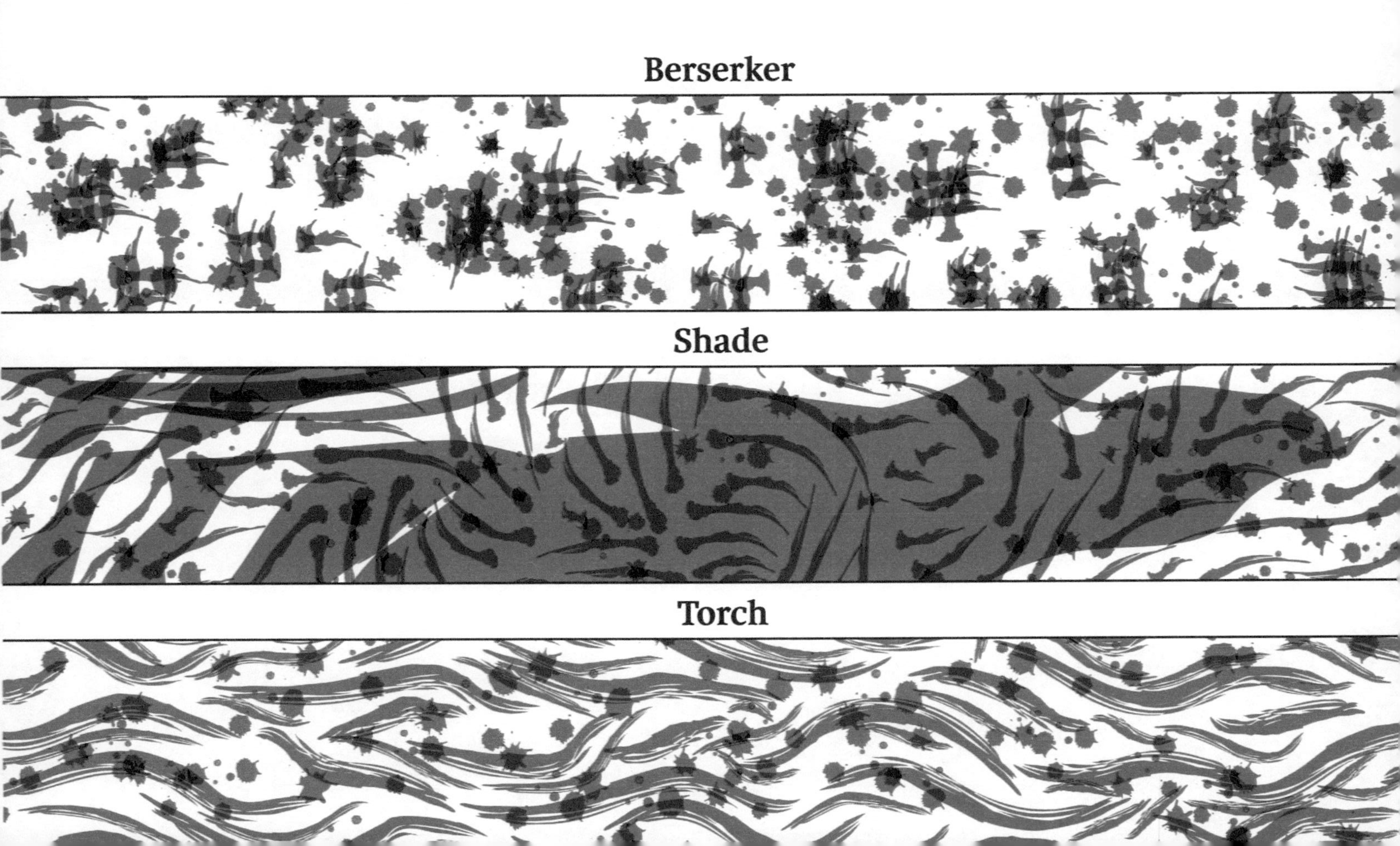
Berserker
Shade
Torch

Fate is a tricky thing.

*The faster you run,
the sooner it catches.*

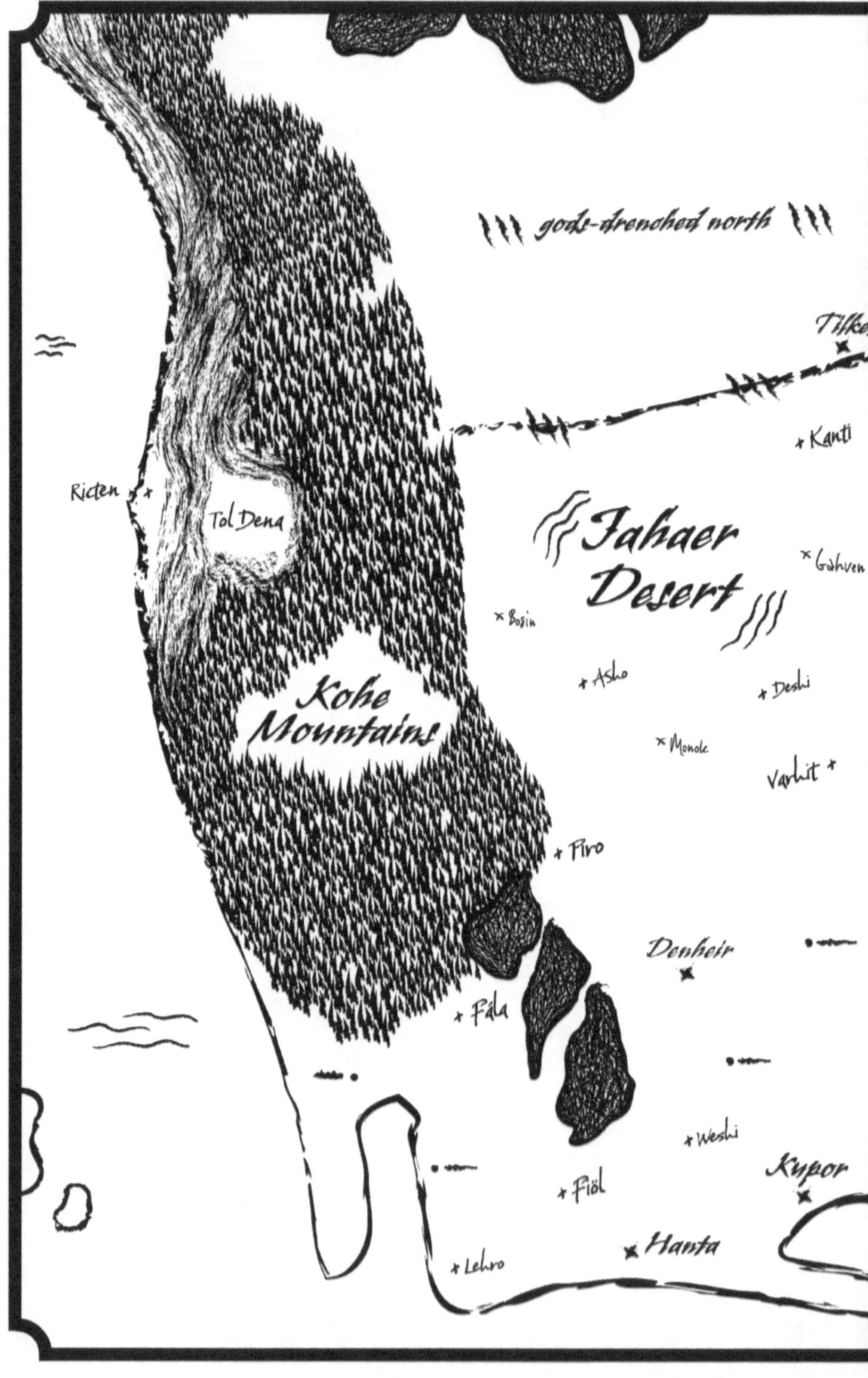

gods-drenched north
Tilke
Kanti
Ricten
Tol Dena
Jahaer Desert
Gahven
Bosin
Asho
Deshi
Monok
Varhit
Kohe Mountains
Piro
Denheir
Fala
Weshi
Kypor
Fiöl
Hanta
Lehro

Hefris
Lorent
Malneis
Koshi
Orfela
Artofen
Raulik
Merket
Hira
Triuken
Falo
Caen
iko
Madras
Letka
Torlena
Menda
Brunn Isle
Dolorit
eptiri
Brakt
Mün
Sefft
N
W E
S

Somewhere in the Jahaer Desert,
one hundred years after the Rebellion
ravaged the Continent...

CHAPTER 1

There's a wind sweeping through the canyon, sifting the sand around my boots. It's blowing my hair against my neck and peppering goosebumps across my skin. For a fleeting moment, I'm overwhelmed with the urge to cover my marks, but it fades like a dull ache. I don't know why, but there's no need for that here.

The sun is barely a sliver of light above the cliffside in front of me, peeking over the red rocks amidst the early morning gray. A chill runs across my skin. My body tenses. Every part of me is waiting. Listening. Something calls me forward, like a pull in my chest. But as much as I want to, I can't seem to move.

My gaze is locked on to the gaping chasm within the cliffside. The rock face is worn and crumbling. Dust trickles from its high-reaching ledges. It's just an opening in the canyon, a slot reaching into the bones of the earth. But as I look closer, I see there's more to it. I strain my eyes against the low morning light. The whip of hair across my face doesn't help. As I take a step forward, my left boot begins to sink into the sand. A familiar swell of panic fills my *stomach. I thrash, desperate to move, but the sand holds me tight. The more I struggle, the more I sink. My right foot catches, and my body sways. All of a sudden, the pull on my boots is stronger— faster. The faraway, budding panic is now a wild beast in my chest. Fear overtakes me, untamed and unable to be reasoned with. My arms flail for balance as I fight to yank my legs free.*

It's no use. It never is.

The desert has a mind of its own, and like always, it's decided it wants me. Time seems to slow, then stop, as I fall forward. Breath rips into my lungs, laced with the choke of dust and renewed terror. My body hits the sand and slips under the surface like it's nothing but water. Taken. Buried. Just as darkness eclipses me, a voice whispers against the shell of my ear.

"Where are you, Serehna?"

I inhale sharply as my body reels up, taking the woven blanket with me. My eyes blink rapidly until they adjust to the dim light of the tent. *I'm okay.* Breath tears through my lungs, and I let myself sit there and pant as I try to catch my breath. *I'm okay.* I force the mantra until my body starts to believe it. My head drops into my hands, and I take a few long, controlled breaths. Though my pulse begins to steady and my muscles relax, there's a lingering tension inside me still. I rake my hands through my hair. The strands are slightly damp with the sweat of fear and the heat of the desert that's arrived long before the sun has. Once again, a truly restful sleep has evaded me.

"You okay?"

I jolt at the soft voice as it cuts through the early morning stillness. Kora watches me from across the room. Her deep brown eyes are riddled with worry.

"I'm fine. Go back to sleep." I sigh.

She shifts against the mass of blankets around her until she's sitting cross-legged and facing me.

"The nightmare again?"

She looks at me with such sincerity that the truth of what plagues me almost slips from my lips. But she can't know. This torment is mine to end.

"Yes," I murmur. My voice is so quiet I'm surprised she even hears it.

"Was anything different this time?"

Small lines gather between my brows. *Was anything different?* My mind drifts back to the cliffside. How far did I make it down the canyon this time before I got stuck? Halfway? Definitely farther than last time, right?

My markings tingle with a phantom itch, but I ignore them. *The chasm.* My brow furrows deeper as my fingers tug at the loose threads on my blanket. Something *was* different this time. Something on the rock face. Were they etchings? Runes?

It was definitely something. I shut my eyes and try to recover any semblance of what I saw but come up blank. *Gods*, I swear. How long will that canyon plague my dreams? And who keeps sending me there?

"Ren? Are you sure you're okay?"

My focus snaps back to Kora. She's worried, but she shouldn't be. My burdens are my own. At fourteen, the only thing she should be worried about is growing up better than I did. And so far, she is.

"I'm fine," I huff, rubbing my hands through my hair once more. "But what's *not* going to be fine is when your sister wakes up and blames me for keeping you awake at this hour."

I'm trying to scold her, but the look on her face almost breaks my composure. She's cocked her head to the side like she's going to argue with me despite being half my age and half my size.

She's gotten so defiant since she and her sister joined the caravan a year ago. She started as a timid little thing, and now I find her constantly arguing with her sister about chores. Kora no longer wants to help with cooking and washing. She wants to go with me. She wants to scout and disappear into the desert for no other reason than I'm doing it. I won't allow it—*how could I?* I don't want my life for her, and neither does her sister.

When I look at Kora now, I'm not sure if I've kept her far enough away. There's a familiar fire in her eyes. I know I'm to blame for her new-found attitude, but I'd be lying if I said I wasn't proud.

"You know Kiara sleeps like the dead." Kora dares to roll her eyes at me, and I'm barely holding back laughter at this point. "Besides, she wouldn't—"

Crunch.

My body tenses.

"Shhh," I rasp, holding my finger up to her.

She freezes, and this time, we both hear the noise outside the tent. Breath chokes in my throat, desperate to hold the silence. Her eyes widen. Every ounce of teenage rebellion drains from her as the *shush* of footsteps across sand fills our ears. Someone's in our camp.

I yank my boots on quickly. I motion for Kora to wake the others before slipping a dagger out from under my pillow. As my fingers ghost the second one sheathed at my thigh, it's a breath of relief. My blades stay with me, always—and for good reason. You never know when someone might try to kill you on the gods-forsaken Continent.

I grip the hilt tighter as I hear our camels grunting and huffing outside. *Are there thieves stealing our supplies, or is this something else? Something more?* Murmurs and protests sound from behind me as Kora wakes the others. There are four of us in this tent.

Kora, her sister Kiara, and the only person in this life I currently call a friend—Mikel. He wakes up in a huff, but it's only a second before he mirrors my stillness. This isn't the first time he's woken up to danger, and it won't be the last. For either of us.

I nod to him, and he quickly shuffles over. He's already unsheathed his own weapon as he crouches next to me at the front of the tent. In his hand rests a curved dagger with a silver hilt. It's a beautiful thing with small plants engraved into the metal. It's the only weapon he has, the only one he deems necessary. I hope it'll be enough.

"How many?" he whispers.

I use the tip of my blade to peel back the tent's flap. I open it an inch before I pause. I can't see much of anything, not from in here.

"Don't know," I mutter. "But I should slip over to Zoah's tent before—"

Screams erupt from behind me as the tent pitches and tears. I look just in time to see knives slipping through the canvas walls like fehnári claws.

"Move, now!" I order everyone before barreling out of the tent.

My steps falter as I take in our camp with wide eyes. The sun hasn't yet risen, but I can still make out the dim desert in front of me. Five horses that don't belong rest with our camels. My eyes dart to the right where shadowed figures are currently slicing into Zoah's tent. I can barely hear the panicked yells amidst the hot blood pounding through my eardrums. *How did this happen? How did I let this happen?* I feel Kora latch onto my arm, and it rips me from my thoughts.

"Get to the camels. Now!" I yell.

I shove Kora forward, her sister in tow. I'm still frozen, watching them rush to escape, when a shape flickers in my peripheral vision. The glint of metal halts inches from me as Mikel lunges. He blocks the blow of the blade with his own just as it threatens to cut me down. He grunts as he forces the assailant back.

"Five!" I shout, quickly unsheathing the second dagger from my thigh. "There's five of them. We need to get Zoah and the others out of here!"

I'm moving before Mikel has a chance to reply. I hear the clash of metal behind me as I dart to the other tent. Zoah and his wife tumble from the opening and straight into my arms. They're shaking. The fear on their aged faces is foreign and cuts me to my core. This isn't a life they know. Theirs is a wandering one—*a peaceful one.* They welcomed me with open arms, and now they're paying the price. *Did I do this? Did I bring this to them?* I swallow back my emotions and usher them forward.

"Get to the camels. Go," I urge. "Kora and Kiara are already there."

A knife tears through the air, but this time, I see it coming. I duck and drive my body into the man, sending a harsh puff of air from his lungs. As we both fall to the sand, I catch a glimpse of the others rushing for the camels. Zoah. His wife. Their two adult children. *They're getting away. They'll be okay.* My relief is short-lived as the man underneath me lurches. His blade misses my shoulder by an inch as I roll off him with a grunt. He doesn't expect me to strike back, but that's just what I do. I stab my dagger into the meaty part of his thigh. He howls as I twist the knife. I know it hurts but it will only distract him for so long.

I yank the blade out and stagger to my feet. My gaze slips back to the camels. I can see Kora helping Zoah's wife while Kiara watches on in horror. Wild tears stream down her face. Everyone is frantic, desperate for escape. My stomach drops as I see one of the men stalking toward them. Two long blades hang at his sides, gripped in large, scarred hands. I suck in a breath, tightening my core before exhaling and whipping my arm forward. It's a motion I've practiced countless times. I know I won't miss. And I don't. No sooner does the knife leave my hand with a swift flick does it lodge in the back of the man's neck. He jerks, then drops. *Dead.* Something tugs in my gut, an uneasy heaviness that threatens to sink me into the sand. I didn't have a choice. There wasn't a choice. *Right?*

A firm hand on my ankle forces me back to reality. I've forgotten the man at my feet. He lunges, dragging me down into the sand with a heavy *thump.* My second blade slips from my grip. I feel the loss of it like an omen of what's to come. My attacker advances, hands digging at my clothing—pulling me closer. As he crawls on top of me, the grin on his face tells me it's now my turn to bleed. I fight to break free, kicking and thrashing. His knife slashes my forearm, and I wince against the feeling of cool metal under my skin. I can already feel the blood pooling from the broken flesh. As he pulls back to strike again, I wiggle my legs free. The heel of my boot flies high. It sends up a spray of sand before connecting with his nose with a vile *crunch.* Blood gushes everywhere. It splatters down on me like rain, but I don't relent. The shock and pain pull his focus, allowing me to slip from his grasp. I grab my dagger from where it's fallen and ram it up under his arm. There's no second-guessing myself. No time for guilt. This is kill or be killed.

Blood flows like a spigot as I yank my blade free. The man's body drops instantly, and the weight of him buries me. *Shit.* Panic chews at my nerves as I dig my hands against the dying man's flesh. His wheezing breath hits my neck with a sickening heat. Blood coats my clothes. *Blood.* More blood. *I did this.* Something foul takes root in my chest. I yell, voice cracking, as I thrash against the deadweight on top of me. Despite the pounding in my lungs and quiver of my muscles, I manage to roll him off. When I finally stand, I'm panting. It's been a while since I've had to fight like this—years, even. My body is screaming in protest. I should have known better than to let my guard down. Against my better judgment, I let myself get too comfortable out here. I won't make that mistake again.

Grunts and muddied breaths pull my focus across camp. *Mikel.* I dash across the sand as he fights off one of the men. My eyes flicker to the ground where another lies dead in the sand. That's three dead. Two left. I reach around my back and unsheathe the small dagger that rests against my shoulder blade. I might have gotten comfortable, but I still have enough sense to sleep armed to the teeth.

As Mikel shirks blows from his opponent, I see a figure emerge from behind the tent.

"Behind you!" I yell.

I flick my little blade too quickly, desperate to help Mikel. The dagger flies into the unknown man, lodging in his tricep. His eyes grow hateful as he turns toward me. The blow isn't enough to stop him, but it's enough to buy me time. As he yanks my blade free, I finally reach Mikel. We stand back-to-back as the two men circle us, eyes gleaming. My arm throbs. The cut I was dealt earlier stings against beads of sweat and prickling grains of sand. I can see the blood sliding down my skin in rivers of red. I clutch the last dagger I have, knuckles white with desperation.

"Looks like I need to sleep with more blades," I grit out.

Mikel chuckles darkly. "I guess it's too much to ask for a heads up next time?"

My spine stiffens. I swallow harshly. Words bubble up on my tongue like venom, but I don't let them free. Mikel knows better than to bring that up, but he's right. I should have prevented this. I grit my teeth as my gaze wanders over the men. They continue to pace circles around us, biding their time. Their clothing tells me they're not thieves or nomads. Aside from the red sand staining the bottom of their pants and coating their boots, there's little dust on them. Their faces are freshly shaven. Their muscles are taut and well fed. They're clearly from one of the cities, which means they're not here to steal food or supplies. They're here for something else.

"Slavers," I utter through clenched teeth.

"Fucking fantastic," Mikel grumbles.

Suddenly, one of the men stops circling us. The budding silence strums on my nerves. I turn to look, careful not to take my eyes off my opponent for too long. The man in front of Mikel has his head tilted as if studying my friend. He leans forward slightly. I hear the soft sift of sand as Mikel readies his stance. The slaver's brow pinches before his eyes go wide in delight.

"Hey, Harkin." He chuckles to the other. "We got ourselves a daemon."

Fuck. I take in a shaky breath. The hilt of my dagger beads with sweat from my palm.

"A Mender by the looks of it," the man muses.

The man in front of me raises a brow. "You don't say."

His gaze sweeps over me, and I know he's searching for a mark. He takes a step closer, then another. Mikel tenses against my back as his man closes in on him just the same. As my nerves buzz under my skin, I look for a mark of my own. The one I search for is not from the gods, but from man himself. I see no red swaths of ink banding across the man's hands. *Not Turidens.* My chest loosens, but not fully.

The circle around us grows smaller, and my skin prickles in anticipation. I clutch my blade tighter, feeling the skin stretching painfully across my knuckles. The slaver in front of me is staring like a starved man before a meal. His gaze slithers up my bare arms, but he doesn't find what he's looking for. I move my hands up in front of my face, pointing the blade toward him. I can only hope it blocks his view of the markings that run down the right side of my neck.

He chuckles as he looks at my single dagger. "You know how to use that thing, sweets?"

I clench my teeth, grinding the molars against each other. "Why don't you ask your friends?"

The smile fades as his eyes darken. He makes a clicking noise with his tongue, and it's only seconds before all hell breaks loose. Both men lunge forward. I meet mine face on, my dagger slashing the air to the right of his cheek. I yell as he grabs my bleeding arm and yanks me toward him. I bite through the pain of his fingers digging into my open flesh and strike my leg into his calf. While the kick doesn't take him down, it gives me an opening. He flails back, and I use the momentum to my advantage. I slash at him, but this time, I make contact. Flesh tears against my blade. He screeches as blood pours down his face. My hands are slick with blood as I send my boot into his stomach. He hits the sand, but my heart drops when I turn around.

The other man has Mikel pinned, hands constricting around his throat. Mikel's eyes flicker to me. They're bulging. Urgent. Fearful. He might have picked up some tricks from me over the years, but he wasn't built for this level of violence. His slender frame is buried under the man's weight. I can see the strength leaving him.

My eyes flicker to the camels. *There's still time.* The others are no more than blurs in the distance. My camel looks at me expectantly, its lead tied to a post. *If I go now, I can still make it.* My opponent is still down, sputtering as blood seeps down his face. I know what I should do. I've lived on the Continent too long to ignore the burdens of survival. Not everyone makes it. I owe my life to no one. My only ambition is to see another sunrise. My legs tingle, muscles jumping against the nerves. It only takes a second—a quick glance to Mikel. As I watch the life slipping from his eyes, my decision is made. I move without thinking.

I dive across the sand and tackle the slaver. We tumble, arms and legs flailing for purchase. My dagger gets pinned as he rolls on top of me. To my left, Mikel stumbles up from the sand. He's coughing and sputtering, breath finally returned to his lungs. His side drips blood from where he must have been cut earlier.

"Go! Get the others out of here," I struggle to yell.

The man shifts his weight on top of me, pinning my legs underneath him. As he moves to wrap his hands around my throat, I blindly reach for my dagger. I strain and stretch. The feeling of my fingers closing around the hilt is nothing short of relief. I slash at him wildly, my aim frantic and misguided. As he reels away, I manage to suck in a ragged breath before he barrels down on me once more. He digs his fingers into the gash on my arm, and I cry out in a muffled yell.

"Ren—"

"Go!" I scream at Mikel before I'm pinned back against the ground.

Rough fingers dig against my hand, and my blade is soon tossed to the side. I see the hesitation in Mikel's eyes. He wavers, unsure. He knows he can't save me. We both know it. His body is shaking. His tunic is growing darker with each passing second. He's losing too much blood. He can't mend himself fast enough to be of any use against these men.

A groan erupts from twenty paces away as the man whose face I sliced open finally gets back on his feet. Mikel looks to the man, and then to me. The look in his eyes is nothing short of devastation. He's the family I never got, the only person I trust with my life. The look tells me he feels the same. And now, I'm asking him to abandon me.

I widen my eyes at Mikel, silently pleading him to do what I couldn't. Tears line his eyes, but with a solemn nod, he finally listens. Solace rushes over me as he runs. I let a breath slip from my lungs. My head rests back against the sand. I can hear him getting on the camel—hear the sand sift and the animal groan as he kicks its side. *He's going to get away. He's going to be safe.*

"She ripped my fucking face open," a voice seethes from close by.

Any comfort I feel for Mikel's escape is snatched away as reality comes rushing back. I ignore the man I cut and stare at the one on top of me. His blue-eyed gaze is nothing short of feral. Cropped, blond hair frames his face. Thin lips pull into a predatory smile. My mind reels, scrambling for a way out of this. I'm stuck under his weight, pinned. I have no blades. It's two against one. Anything I can do is a wasted effort. I know I'm out of options. And by the way he's looking at me, he knows it too.

"Fuck," the bleeding man swears under his breath as he finally notices Mikel is gone. "The Mender."

"Leave him," the man on top of me orders. He pushes the side of my face into the sand harshly, exposing my neck. His grin grows from ear to ear. "We've got something better."

"Leave him?" The other man scoffs. "Do you know how pissed Rohan is going to be when he learns you let a Mender get aw—"

"Rohan isn't going to give a fuck about some Mender."

The man on top of me runs the tip of his blade across my skin, tracing the black markings that mar my flesh.

"We've got a Seer."

CHAPTER 2

They tell me it's a two-day walk to Denheir, and while I've never been there, I can't say I'm happy to get the chance to visit. The two men in front of me, who I now know as Olen and Harkin, didn't waste any time in beginning our journey. The blond one, Olen, seems all too eager to deliver me to whatever or whoever awaits us in the city. The other, Harkin, who now sports a new scar thanks to yours truly, seems like he'd rather leave me in the desert to rot. I can only assume he's not used to losing a fight, let alone to a woman, because he looks at me with hate deeply set in his eyes.

My blade's handiwork gleams against the sun, a reminder of the pain I've caused him. He almost returned the favor a few hours ago. I know I shouldn't have taunted him, but I'm left with little to wound since they bound my hands and took my blades. He would likely have slit my throat if Olen hadn't called him off like a misbehaving dog. Since then, I've kept my mouth shut. There's no telling how far I can push Olen, and as much as I'd like to find out, something tells me it's not a good idea.

It's been half a day since we left my ransacked camp. The sun hangs high overhead, and my feet ache in my boots. When I asked why I had to walk when there were so many horses, the men just laughed. With every twinge and throb of my feet, I call on Veles to swallow them whole. If the god of darkness managed to drag these men to the underworld, I might actually start praying to him. I glare at the back of my captors' heads as I shuffle along.

My hands are tightly bound with rope and occasionally pulled forward as Olen's horse finds a pace I can't seem to keep. The other horses, the ones whose riders we left face down in the sand, are tied to Harkin's saddle. They find their own comfortable pace on the other side of his horse, far away from me. They snort and huff from time to time, looking over with something akin to fear in their glossy, black eyes. *Do they know Mikel and I killed all but two of their riders? Or is it my blood that sets them on edge?*

Sand kicks up around me as the wind sweeps across the Jahaer Desert. I close my eyes and wait for it to pass. The soft *shush* of sand grounds me, at least for a moment. When I finally open my eyes again, the horses are still watching. I squint through the glare of the high sun, feeling sand and red dust grate against my skin as the wind continues to swirl. Some people say that animals can sense us daemons, but no one knows for sure. Our camels never seemed to be fazed by me, but horses? Horses are too smart to ignore the gift coursing through my veins. I glare at one of them, a massive black beast with white speckled throughout its coat, and I swear it glares right back. With a huff, it breaks eye contact and hurries ahead. I all but roll my eyes at the horse before my body lurches forward, tugged onward by the rope on Olen's saddle.

"How do you tell them apart?" Harkin asks.

"Hm?" Olen slips his gaze to his companion.

"The daemons." Harkin grunts. "How'd you know that one was a Mender?"

Olen sighs, like the answer is more of a burden than its worth. "They have different markings."

When something akin to surprise slides across Harkin's face, Olen laughs.

"What—did you think the gods marked them with no concern?"

"I mean, I just never—"

While Harkin stumbles over his words, Olen flickers his gaze over his shoulder. A wide grin grows on his face as he appraises me. I know what he sees; I don't need a mirror. I'm covered in blood, my own and his men's. Red dust is a second skin across my body and there's not a moment where I don't feel its sandy grit. The long strands of my honey-white hair have unraveled from my braid and cling to my neck, caked with blood and sweat. I look as feral as I feel, and the fire in my eyes doesn't help.

"Take the Seer, for example," Olen states, cutting of Harkin's ramblings. "Her markings are like small circles drawn with a leaking quill. The shapes fade and drip and drag into each other, but there's a distinct pattern there."

Harkin squints as he looks back at me.

"You need to learn this shit," Olen prods. "You're not any use if you don't know what we're looking for."

"Her marks are so small. How was I supposed to spot them?" he argues.

"It's your job," Olen spits back. "Figure it out."

Harkin mumbles under his breath, and I can only catch the words *smug bastard* before Olen's voice pulls my focus.

"But you're right," he continues. "Her marks are small." He looks me up and down, head cocking in contemplation. "How old are you?"

"Twenty-eight," I snap.

Amusement perks up his face. "A grown woman, and yet I've seen more marks on a child." He laughs, and something about the way it rumbles through his chest curls my hands into fists. "That afraid to use, are you?"

I bite my tongue, teeth gritting roughly against each other. My forced silence must bore him because he lets out a sigh and turns back around.

"What about the Mender," Harkin starts. "What did his marks look like?"

Olen takes a deep, steadying breath before answering. "Menders' marks are like lines of ink, but like all marks, there's disorder there. Drips and splotches and breaks in the lines. Menders' markings are tightly patterned across the skin. Theirs are the easiest to distinguish because they're so dense yet unmuddled. The opposite of a Berserker's, whose marks are chaos in themselves. Short bands of ink like hash marks that stretch across the skin, surrounded by lines and splotches, like the writer cared not where his dripping quill wept."

Harkin nods, but his brow stays furrowed. "And the color?"

I almost laugh when I see Olen's last ounce of patience snap. He presses his fingers into the ridges between his eyes.

"I've seen black and white," Harkin adds. "Is it a sign of age? Or skill?"

"The color is merely a reaction to the skin," Olen grumbles. "Lighter skin has darker marks. Darker skin has lighter marks. It has nothing to do with their skill or age. Do you really not know any of this?"

Harkin's face contorts into a frown, and I can practically see his mind working harder than it's able to. Olen's jaw clenches before he scoffs.

"Fuck's sake," he utters. "Remind me to send you on a scouting mission with daemons next time, and they can teach you themselves."

The two of them settle into silence once more, and I find my mind growing as heavy as my legs. The heat of the day is upon us and without so much as a drop of water or a moment's rest, I feel every lick of the sun's fury. I stagger and stumble but force myself to keep pace. I'm not weak, and I won't let them see me as such. My arm aches, though luckily, the wound isn't deep. They allowed me to tie it off with a strip of fabric before we departed, and the blood has long since crusted over.

The horizon shimmers against the desert's heat. One footstep, then another. I fall into a trance, letting my body lead me forward toward the unknown. My thoughts shift and swirl like the windblown sand around me. The others got away. I repeat it over and over in my head until I feel the truth of it settle into my bones. Mikel is safe. *Kora is safe.* My sun-warmed skin peppers in chills as I think about how this could have gone so differently. She got away before they could see her marks. I pull a shaky breath into my lungs and thank Hael for such a blessing. The god of knowledge might not have spared me this fate, but at least he spared her. If Kora sticks with Mikel, she'll be okay. He can teach her what she wants to know, mentor her on the uses of her gift. *She'll be okay. They'll all be okay.*

Arguing pulls my focus to the men ahead.

"We're not due back for another three days," Harkin presses. "Piro is less than half a day to the west."

I can hear the whine in his tone and find myself wishing my blade had struck lower. The parting gift I gave him gleams against the sun, flesh still wet and flecked with red. He winces as he talks, pulling at the damaged skin that runs from the top of his brow to his lower lip. I can't help but smile. There's no worse way to make it on the Continent than by bartering and trading someone else's life. Slavers can sink into the earth for all I care. Again, I wish my aim had been lower.

"And we'll reach Denheir tomorrow," Olen spits back. "We keep going."

A day. That's how long I have to rewrite the fate I've been dealt here. I'm not foolish enough to think I can take on whatever awaits me in that city alone.

My eyes trace the knots of bound rope that snake around my wrists. I flex my hands, testing the strength of my bindings for what feels like the hundredth time. I grit my teeth and raise my gaze ahead. I need another way—a quick window of opportunity.

I wrack my mind for answers, and like a gift from the gods, I remember it. Rubbing my arm against my ribs, I almost grin. The uncomfortable digging of metal against flesh is more than a stroke of luck. It's freedom. There's a blade, no bigger than my thumb tucked into the fabric binding my chest. I'd used it to spark the fire yesterday and tucked it away for no reason other than I'd been too lazy to carry it back to my pack.

Glee quickly dies out as I pull my bound hands to my chest. I twist and turn, but I'm unable to reach the blade. A low grunt slips from my lips. *I need another way.*

"Tomorrow? You want to ride through the night?" Harkin prods. "For fuck's sake, man. Two days in the saddle will have my balls in a bunch. Let's go to Piro."

Harkin complains like he's the one bound and captured, though I think I understand why. I've heard of Piro. It's an outpost at the base of the Kohe Mountains. One of the nomads I traveled with years ago told me of the place. More of a viper's den than a town. Full of thieves, drunkards, and anything you can pay for—women included. The man said he'd only passed through once and once was enough. There's a certain type of person that yearns for a place like that. Now knowing that Harkin is that type, I'm glad I had the chance to carve up his face.

"Come on," Harkin urges. "It's not like he's going to find out."

Olen doesn't even spare a glance his way.

Harkin huffs. "I think I'm owed compensation after what that bitch did to me."

"You mean what you *let her* do to you." Olen smirks. "I truly thought you were better with a blade. Besides, your compensation comes after we finish the job."

I grin as Harkin utters curses. The scar only further shows him for what I can assume he is—a brute. Shaggy brown hair sits atop his head, messy and sweat-soaked. It seems I'm not the only one baking under the sun. His wide cheekbones are framed by a short beard, and while it's trimmed, it's flecked with blood. His shoulders are boulders against his silhouette, and he sits so tall against his saddle that I'm surprised his horse can bear the weight.

He looks back at me, mumbling under his breath about the damage to his face. His heavy brow shades deep brown eyes that burn into me with pure hatred. I mirror the look until he turns back around. A flicker of pride swells through my chest as I stare at the man I bested. He's all but double my size, yet he'll wear my mark for the rest of his days. The satisfaction tastes sweet on my tongue.

"What does it even matter? We have a Seer like he asked," Harkin starts again. "The boss can wait a fucking day."

Olen tenses. The heat shimmering in the air looks like the anger is rolling off him in waves.

"Watch your tone." Olen's jaw clicks as he regards his companion fully. "He's going to want her as soon as possible. We have no time to waste."

My throat tightens like the rope is snaked around my neck and not my hands. I pick up my pace, straining my aching legs to get closer. This is the most they've said about my fate since we left camp. Any arguments or questions I've posed have been quickly silenced by the threat of a blade. But now, it seems their tongues have loosened amidst their arguing. I can only pray they let slip what I aim to know: who they're taking me to and why.

I've heard tales of slavers and the many places they sell their captives to. Merchant ships. Brothels. Outposts. I can only hope for the last of those outcomes. The very thought of the sea I've never seen, let alone sailed across, makes my stomach queasy. And the brothel? I'd carve anyone up if they so much as touched me.

I glare at Harkin as he continues talking. The freshly carved scar on his face should dissuade any madams and keep me away from that fate—at least, I hope.

"He doesn't know we have anything of value yet," Harkin continues to bargain. "For all he knows we picked her up in Piro."

Olen says nothing. He merely shows he's paying attention by tossing his companion a heavy glare.

"Don't tell me you're against breaking a few rules?" Harkin pushes. A slick smile dances across his face, pulling the marred flesh up like a grotesque mask. "You really that scared of the man? Big bad Ro—"

Olen flinches, and before I can follow the blade he threw, it lodges in Harkin's arm—right above where mine struck earlier. Harkin screams, then swears as he rips the blade free. He winds up to throw it back but halts. Olen has unsheathed the sword from his saddle and it rests at the base of Harkin's throat.

"Getting a prize like this to Rohan is more important than whatever drink or cunt you seek to sink into in Piro." Olen's eyes are blazing. "Don't forget who paid your bounty. Or maybe you want to go back to Tol Dena?"

I see Harkin visibly gulp before he tucks away the blade that's still dripping with his blood. He nods, far more feebly than I've seen any grown man. As Olen resheathes his sword, I can't stop the snicker that leaves my throat. Both men perk up at the sound, eyes darting back toward me.

"Something funny?" Olen prods.

He stops his horse immediately. The tension feels heavier than the heat as Olen dismounts. A black scarf is wrapped around his head, trapping his blond hair and protecting him from the sun and sand. His light blue eyes peer out from the fabric, seeming to track my every movement as he comes closer. Anger warms my chest at the sight of him. He's not small by any means, but he's smaller than Harkin. His frame is tall and lean. He looks more like some wealthy merchant than a slaver with his chiseled features and arrogant smile. I should have easily taken him down. The fact that I didn't makes me all the more eager for a do over.

Olen's gaze drops to my bound hands. He raises a brow at me as he steps closer. "You know, you're not exactly in any position to be getting on my nerves. You took out one of my men. I'm not feeling very friendly."

I stand up a little straighter. "Two men," I say.

A smile curls his lips. "You're a fiery little thing, aren't you?" His gaze slips down my body before finally rising to my face again. "You're going to make me rich."

Words spit from my lips before I can reel them in. "No," I seethe. "I'm going to make you suffer."

I rush him, knee driving into his crotch. Seconds later, I'm face down in the sand. I'd barely felt his hands tug the rope that binds me. The heat has me dizzy. Dehydration has my head throbbing.

Olen coughs from my assault as I brush the sand from my face. I struggle to get up, my tired muscles begging me to stay down. As soon as I get to my knees, the pressure of a boot on my back flattens me to the ground. I pant and spit out a mouthful of sand as I fight to regain my footing. He only forces his boot down harder. When I look up, he's grinning far too wide for my liking. He clicks his tongue against his teeth, a pitying sound, before he releases me. I immediately spring to my feet.

"You really think you could take me?" he taunts. "Huh, Little Seer?"

I flinch as his hand seeks to trace the markings on my neck. I try to find space between us, but the rope offers me no such indulgence.

"Why don't you give me back my knives, and you can find out for yourself?"

He merely chuckles as my eyes dart to the pack strapped to his saddle, *my* pack. I convinced him to take it with us. How? I don't know. But I wanted my things. There's something about growing up with nothing that makes you cling to what you do have. And while I lost three of my blades to the bodies resting hours at our backs, there are plenty more in my bag.

"Such a beautiful, violent thing." He smirks, grazing his knuckles against my cheek before I can pull away. "This is bound to be fun." With a shake of his head, he turns to mount his horse once more.

My mind races with ideas as he turns his back on me. *Could I tackle him? Choke the air from his lungs with the rope he dared bind me with?* My eyes slip to Harkin who glares at me like he can hear every murderous thought. I grind my teeth together as I see the moment for what it is. *Lost.*

Back atop his horse, Olen's hands yank at the rope, sending me stumbling forward. I grab onto his saddle for balance, and his horse pitches wildly at my very touch. It takes a harsh tug of the reins to calm it, though its eyes are still as wide and black as a bottomless pit as it watches me with huffed breath. I step back, finding my way to the end of the rope's length once more.

Harkin mutters under his breath, cursing my very presence, while Olen simply lets out a breathy laugh.

"Let's get you to Rohan first." Olen smirks. "Then we can see if you're still brave enough to ask for your knives."

CHAPTER 3

The sun hangs low on the horizon, a giant orb of deep orange that bakes me in my skin. After walking all through the night and all through the day, we're less than an hour from Denheir. Any hope I had of attacking these men in the dead of the night while they rested was foiled once Olen decided to push ahead.

Exhaustion hangs off my limbs with a heavy swell. If Olen's goal was to quell the fight in me by wearing me down, he's won—temporarily, at least. Everything hurts. My wrists feel raw from the constant rub of the rope against my skin. My lips are dry and cracked. Every blink brings the nasty scrape of sand that my eyelashes didn't manage to catch during this morning's high winds. My throat burns after only getting a trickle of water last night from Harkin. He spilled most of it down my chin. I know he did it on purpose.

The grueling pace Olen keeps us at grows the constant throb in my legs. I've been trying to keep up, and the few times I did fall, Olen merely shot back a taunting look before tugging me forward.

I'd forgotten how much hunger hurts, how much it gnaws at your sanity. Two days in this desert can feel like two weeks if you're not prepared, and they've guaranteed I'm not. They refused to let me grab a headscarf from my pack. I can feel the heat radiating from my scalp. The skin is tender and hot, brutalized by the sun. I'm in hell, but I know it's about to get so much worse.

Olen is whistling, a lively tune that seems to shoot pain across my temples. I know it's the sun—dehydration, not his incessant noise—but I throw him a nasty glare anyway. I put my bound hands up in front of my face, trying to block the glare of the sun that's shining like glass across the sand. I can barely make out the dark blob on the horizon. It's held my concentration for the past hour, wavering like my own strength, but it's there. *We're getting close.*

With each step I take, Denheir comes into view in pieces. I've never been to any place this far south, which isn't surprising since there's over fifty outposts and cities across the Continent, and I try to avoid them all. But, what I do see as we approach Denheir is familiar enough. A market lies ahead. The wall of tents is pitched so closely together it's hard to see anything else. But as the desert slips underneath my boots, buildings sculpted of sandstone and lumber begin to appear over the top of the market stalls. It's the only sign of civilization in the vast landscape in front of me, and the urge to run in the opposite direction is overwhelming. I don't need a vision to know that whatever fate awaits me there is not a good one.

The shrill tune Olen whistles gets louder the closer we get. His excitement is like knives against my skin. As we finally step into the market, my nerves are practically humming. My hands have grown clammy. My eyes dart from one vendor to the next. Some meet my gaze, look at the rope binding my wrists, and turn away quickly. Others stare, their heads titling to the side, minds buzzing with who or what I might be. None of them say anything. None of them intervene. Slaving is frowned upon in some parts of the Continent but there's no law against it. There are no laws at all. This land is one of chaos and self-sovereignty, no longer claimed by any tyrant or king. The Rebellion saw to that. The Continent answers to no one but itself. I just wish I could say the same right now.

Movement ahead has me tensing on instinct. One of the vendors steps out from his stall and into the road. He spits at the ground in front of me, mumbling filth under his breath. My gut clenches as I realize I have nothing covering my neck. *Ah fuck, he's spotted the marks.* My jaw ticks as I lock eyes with him. He's short, red-faced. His bald head glistens under the sun. Beady little eyes seem to gleam against the heat. I know that look too well. It's nothing short of hate.

I return the look hotly until something catches my eye and soothes the rage inside. *Yes.* My eyes dart to Olen before I step from the street, stumbling forward until I'm crashing into the wooden table inside the short man's tent. The commotion startles everyone; some scream, others cower in fear. The clumsy act sends a vicious ache through my hip, but I ignore it as my hands scramble across the table. My fingers graze the hilt before I'm yanked backward. At the last second my hand curls around the knife, claiming it as my salvation.

My ass hits the ground, and I know the clock is ticking. Ignoring the pounding of my head and the ache of my body, I maneuver to my knees. The man is swearing, cursing Veles, and throwing his hands in the air wildly. He doesn't stop with his howling until he sees the knife.

My eyes grow sharp and wild as I turn the knife to the rope binding me. Everything around me is a blur, a distant worry, as I work frantically. I struggle to saw through the layers of rope. The knife is dull, as pitiful as I feel in this moment. It's slow going, but I can't stop. One of the knots frays, and my chest swells. It's only when I feel the cool flat of a blade as it lifts my chin that I freeze.

"Ah, Little Seer," Olen coos. "Always the troublemaker."

I'm yanked up, and though I feel my bindings flex, the rope doesn't tear. Olen tosses my knife to the sand before inspecting my handiwork. He chuckles to himself as he turns my wrists. "A few more seconds, and you might have actually gotten away."

My jaw clenches at the taunting quirk of his mouth. "Can you blame m–"

"Seditious witch!"

The red-faced man is yelling once more, demanding that he be paid for the damage to his wares. My eyes flicker across the table, seeing his jars of honey and preserves have tipped over but are otherwise intact. *I should have hit the table harder.*

The man doesn't see Olen—not at first. He continues yelling until Olen's unnaturally blue eyes pierce into him. Then, the man falls silent. Sweat beads on his brow, and I see a glimmer of fear sweep across his face.

"I'm sorry," he mumbles. "I didn't realize—"

"For the trouble," Olen says gruffly, flipping a coin toward the man.

Olen turns away, heading to his horse. I look back toward the man, and my stomach drops. His hands are shaking, but he's no longer looking at me. He's looking at Olen. In this man's eyes, I am no longer the biggest threat. Sweat coats my palms. My throat grows tight and heavy. Something tells me that if I am to leave this market, to head wherever this path ends, it will be the death of me. My eyes dart through the horde of vendors.

"Please," I whisper.

A woman nearby meets my gaze as I take a step closer.

"Please, help me."

The woman stills. She's draped in yellow-hued fabrics, fringed in wooden beads. Freckles speckle her nose, and long, black hair frames her soft features. She looks behind me, and I hear Olen click his teeth in warning. Fear widens the woman's eyes before she drops her gaze. I look across the market. No one will meet my eye. No one will so much as look my way. My heart sinks before anger flares in my chest. *Cowards.*

Olen urges his horse to move on, tugging me forward. My feet stumble against the sand before I find my footing. Panic threatens to drown me as my lungs pull in breath after breath without relief. My gaze skirts around feverishly before locking on the only thing that can help me right now. Darting my hands out, I snatch it up before I'm jerked down the road.

Protests from nearby vendors spike the air before they're silenced into murmurs. Olen looks back at me but not before I hide my spoils. He cocks his head to the side, eyeing me cautiously, before shaking his head. He laughs, and I blink back frustrated tears as I glare at him. But I don't look away. I won't give him the satisfaction.

When he finally turns around, I quickly raise my bound hands to my mouth. Ravenous, I bite off a chunk of the bread I stole. It tastes heavenly, but I choke in an instant. My throat is too dry to handle anything but a lick of water. Olen snaps back around at the noise. He spots the bread before I have the chance to stuff the rest in my mouth.

"Guess I can tell Rohan you've been fed." He smirks.

I swallow the rest quickly and wipe my mouth with the back of my hand. My throat burns raw, but I still manage to spit out a response.

"Oh, yes, because you were planning to feed me. You've been so generous thus far." I sneer, wishing I'd been given a different gift from a different god. Nothing would satisfy me more than blasting fire at Olen's face right now. I know Veles would approve of such an act.

"I personally have no intention of feeding you." Olen smiles, though it feels anything but friendly. "But Rohan will want to make sure his new plaything is well taken care of."

"What?" My blood runs cold, and words tumble from my mouth before I can stop them. "If you think I'm letting anyone touch me, you're dumber than I thought." I feel the bread sour in my stomach, but I manage to keep it down. "I'll scar every man they send me. The madam will be begging you to take me back."

His brow raises at that. "What the bloody hell are you talking about?"

My mouth ceases to work. All I can do is stare at him.

"We're not selling you to a brothel." His laugh does nothing to ease the churning of my stomach. "We're not selling you to anyone."

Lines pit between my brows as I consider him. "I thought you were slavers," I utter softly.

His eyes flare wide in amusement as he eats up every ounce of confusion on my face. "No, Little Seer." He lets out another laugh as he leads us away from the market.

The buzz of the city falls quiet as we curve down alley after alley. I lose track of where we're going, feeling like I'm slipping through a maze of doorways and stone.

"Our boss is not in the business of slaving," Olen speaks up. "But we do hunt things for him."

My skin ripples with goosebumps, despite the heat that's still clinging to what's left of the day. "Hunt things?" I ask cautiously. "Things like what?"

Olen turns to me as we come to a stop, flashing a grin that's all teeth. "Things like you."

CHAPTER 4

Night has fallen, but the comfort it usually brings didn't come with it. The stillness in the room where I wait is anything but peaceful. My hands are still bound in front of me. I'm kneeling on the hard, stone floor, waiting—praying to Hael for some way out of this. The god of knowledge offers nothing to still my racing thoughts.

I shoot my gaze across the room at Olen and Harkin. They've been quietly standing guard since they dragged me, kicking and screaming, into this room over an hour ago. They don't speak. They don't move. The tension riding their shoulders has my heart hammering. They're waiting for something—*someone*. I debate forsaking Hael and praying to Veles instead. Dark gifts would be much more useful in this situation. They always are.

The door opens behind me, jolting me from my thoughts. I forcibly grit my teeth against the hazy mix of adrenaline and exhaustion that courses through my body. I don't know whether to fight or to melt into the floor and sleep.

As footsteps sound behind me, I keep my spine as straight as an arrow. I can't show any weakness. Nothing weak survives the Continent. In front of me, Olen and Harkin snap to attention as well. Harkin's eyes hover restlessly over my shoulder as he regards whoever has entered the room. His Adam's apple bobs before he shifts his gaze to the floor, not daring to draw it up again. *Gods. This isn't good.*

"Only one?"

The voice behind me is deep and curt. Resentful. Disappointed, even. The sound of it sends a chill up my neck, pebbling the sun-reddened skin. As the footsteps get closer, every muscle in my body seems to lock down and coil like a spring.

Olen nods and steps forward quickly. "There was one other. He got away…" Olen pauses, and the shell of a smile stitches into the corners of his mouth. "But I'm sure you'll find this one worth enough on her own."

Gritting my teeth, I fight every urge to let my tongue loose. I'm not an animal for sale or slaughter. And I will cut down whoever it takes to guarantee that.

As if sensing the rage flowing through me, Olen raises a brow. "Trust me, Rohan," he taunts. "She's worth more than gold if you can get her to behave."

My eyes are blazing and I feel the coppery tang of blood as my teeth pierce my tongue.

"Is that so?" the voice replies.

Someone steps up behind me, and I freeze. My breath catches in my throat as I wait for the thrust of a blade or a knee to the back. I wait and wait. Olen's eyes are bright, eager. Harkin hasn't looked up from the floor. I wait for pain to blossom among the stifled silence of the room. But it doesn't come. Instead, I feel a hand slip through my hair.

I tense, but then—for a moment—I relax. I feel like a child again. I'm sitting in my mother's lap. It's peaceful—the feeling of her spindly fingers playing with my hair. But just like the love I had then, the soft caress is fleeting. My scalp screams in pain as I'm yanked up by the strands. I whine and stagger against my tired legs as he releases me. It takes everything not to fall back to the floor.

"This little thing took out one of my men?" The voice laughs.

I clamp my teeth down on my cheek and blink the blur of pain from my eyes. "Two," I snarl, and he finally steps in front of me.

As I meet his gaze, my defiance almost wavers. I can see why Harkin, as big as he is, doesn't want to get on his boss's bad side. This man is clearly not someone you mess with. It's obvious enough just by looking at his tall, muscular build that he can handle his own in a fight. But it's not just that. There's a wild intensity etched into the harsh angles of his face. His sharp jaw and brow are framed by hair as red as flame. It's cropped at the sides, but the top brushes against his forehead, barely keeping out of his violent, green eyes. He's staring at me with a look so sharp I'm surprised he hasn't slit my throat for speaking out of turn.

Even so, I can't stop myself. I tip my chin up to meet his unwavering gaze. "Two," I repeat. "I killed *two* of your men."

His eyes grow a little more deadly at that. We stand in calculated silence, neither of us breaking focus. He tightens his gaze and takes a step back. He sizes me up, gaze raking over me from top to bottom. I lock my jaw down tightly as he begins to circle me. I know what he sees—or at least, what he thinks he sees. A young woman who has gotten caught up in something bad, something she can't handle. He sees the bloodied clothes, the matted hair, and the curves of my body and thinks I'm a fragile thing. But he doesn't see the skill I gained while sparring old friends, doesn't see the lean muscle under these clothes or the long scar that marks the worst day of my life. He doesn't see a threat, doesn't see the fighter the Continent forced me to be. But he will.

I keep my focus forward even though I feel my hackles rise as he steps out of my line of sight. My hands clench into fists to keep the panic at bay. I look to Olen, and the bastard is smiling from ear to ear. He flashes his eyes at me, and I imagine all the ways my knives could wipe that grin off his face. As Rohan comes to stand in front of me once more, a *tsk* slips out from behind his teeth.

"She's pretty, Olen. But this hardly seems—"

His words fall short. He tilts his head, and suddenly, his eyes grow wide. His hands are on me in an instant, brushing my hair aside and dragging his fingers down my neck. The touch is aggressive yet full of desperation and I squirm under his grasp. But it's too late. He leans in, and I can catch the whiff of tobacco on his clothes before he releases me. There's nothing in his eyes now but excitement.

"You brought me a Seer?" He walks toward Olen and shakes him—but there's no hostility there. He's almost giddy. "A godsdamn Seer?"

Olen's smile deepens. "Told you I brought something valuable."

Rohan slaps him on the back and lets out a deep sigh. When he finally turns back to me, another *tsk* slips from his lips. "Valuable, indeed."

I stare him down, eyes blazing, but there's a cold sweat spreading across my skin. It's accompanied by a deep discomfort inside of me, like bugs scurrying through the marrow. There's a reason I never stay in one place too long. It's the same reason I travel the desolate parts of the Continent, never to settle down and start a real life. It's why I prefer to be alone—why I should have never let myself get comfortable with Mikel and the others. Despite their origins from Hael, the benevolent god whose gifts some consider a blessing, the markings that mar my flesh are nothing but a curse. With them, I will never be safe.

Rohan gives me a predatory smile, and a shiver ripples across my skin. "What's your name?"

"Does it matter?" I snap.

Olen laughs from his place in the corner of the room. "Delightful, isn't she?"

Rohan's eyes are heavy with a heady mix of hunger and threat. He looks me up and down, then steps closer. "Don't make me ask again."

I can almost hear the enamel of my teeth wearing down as I grind them together. "Ren," I utter.

"Ren," he repeats, as if tasting it for himself. A smirk pricks the corner of his mouth. "Well, *Ren*. I'm Rohan."

He walks across the room and sits down at a large wooden desk. He opens a drawer and rifles through it before pulling out two brown leather pouches. He tosses one to Olen, the other to Harkin. The clink of coins echoes across the room.

"Bring me more like her and I'll see to it you get a bonus next time."

For the first time since entering the room, Harkin actually smiles. "Another Seer, you mean?"

Annoyance flares across Rohan's face. "*Yes*, another Seer—" He stops himself, brow crumpling in thought. "No. On second thought, bring me a Shade."

"Pretty rare, those," Olen remarks with a click of his tongue. "I'm guessing the pay will reflect that?"

"A Shade?" Hesitation spills across Harkin's face. "I heard one of them can kill a man without even—"

His words fail him as Rohan's eyes darken, his gaze nothing less than a promise of violence.

Olen lets out a breathy laugh before patting Harkin on the shoulder. "We'll bring you something good, boss. Don't you worry."

Rohan nods but as the men turn to leave, he stops them. "Olen."

The blonde looks over his shoulder, brow raising curiously.

"Stick around. I have some things I need you to do," Rohan adds.

A wide grin slides across Olen's face. "Anything you say, boss."

Olen and Harkin leave without another word, though I don't miss the smirk that spreads across Olen's face as he shuts the door behind them. Silence fills the room immediately. Like the dread in my stomach, I can feel the stillness gnawing at me.

I stand there, hands bound, and just watch. Rohan has started thumbing through a stack of papers, ignoring me completely. I rock on my heels and let my eyes shift to the door. I doubt Harkin is hanging around, not when he's already been paid. But Olen? Rohan's order has all but guaranteed he stays close. I can only hope that doesn't mean he rests just outside the door.

Either way, I have to try. The route we took to get here is fuzzy in my mind. We were on the main street, then cut through an alley or two. We walked a ways before we took a right. *Was it two more streets after that? Or three?* I should have paid more attention, but it doesn't matter much. As long as I'm running far from here, I'm heading in the right direction. I plant my legs firmly and get ready to bolt.

"Don't."

My gaze rips to Rohan. He hasn't even bothered to look up from whatever he's reading. His words hover in the air, and I swallow harshly against my dry and achy throat. My brow furrows as I watch him carefully. It'll take him too long to get up from his desk. I know it will. I tense my legs oh-so-slightly, getting ready to run.

Before I can, he looks up and shoots me a bored look. "Don't try to run. You won't make it past the door."

"You underestimate me."

He lets out a sigh before a deep bellow slips from his throat. "Tian!"

Barely a second passes before the door swings open. I spin around to see a beast of a man filling the threshold. He's a wall of muscle, and the scar that runs diagonally across his right, glossy eye tells me he doesn't go down easily. Even if I had my knives, a fight with him would be closer to death than I'd like to come.

"Need something, boss?"

"No, just wanted to show Ren how things are going to go from here on out. You can leave."

The man nods, making sure to glare at me before shutting the door behind him with a harsh *thud*. When I turn back to Rohan, his eyes are locked on me.

"Still think you can make it out of here on your own?"

I swallow the retort bubbling up my throat and keep quiet. This time, I do pray to Veles.

Rohan shoves his things into a desk drawer and leans back in his chair, getting comfortable. "Shall we discuss your future?" He smirks, revealing bone-white teeth. "Or have you already foreseen it?"

Heat rises to my cheeks. "My future?" I sneer. I step closer until my hands brush the smooth wood of his desk. "Let me guess. I'm going to be your little parlor trick? Tell your enemies I've cursed them? Or perhaps parade me around town so they know you can bring death to their door?"

He eyes me carefully before picking a gold coin off the desk. He rolls it over his knuckles with a rhythmic flick. "I find my approach to daemons to be a little less... outdated."

I try to stifle my laugh, but it slips from my throat with sick contempt. "You mean you won't pray to Hael? Won't beg him for protection so my presence may not taint you?"

He lets out a breathy laugh and rolls the coin back across his knuckles. "No," he says. "I think treating daemons as outcasts is a waste. Especially when there's opportunity to be had. An opportunity that benefits us both."

My brows furrow, and I find myself leaning over the desk. "Opportunity for what?"

His eyes glint wickedly, and he smiles. "Collaboration."

I can feel my stomach weaving knots as he stares at me with an insatiable hunger. It's as though he's the one who can see my fate and it's just to his liking.

"Daemons have special..." He rolls the coin across his knuckles once more. "...skills," he continues. "Every gift is useful. Every gift has its purpose. So why not use them to our advantage?"

"To *your* advantage, you mean?"

He ignores the hostility in my tone. "I have more than one daemon under my employment. They all reap rewards from the work I provide them. Gold. Status. Protection. There's much to be gained here, Ren."

"And is that what this is to be?" I argue, raising my bound hands high for him to see. "Employment?"

The coin falls to the desk with a clink as he stands. "It can be." He walks toward me, and I feel myself slinking away on instinct alone. "That depends entirely on your cooperation."

He withdraws a blade from the holster on his belt. It glimmers under the candlelight that flickers across the room. I tense, shifting my weight to the balls of my feet. As he gets closer, I raise my bound hands in front of my face. I inhale, steadying my heart rate for what's to come.

He simply eyes me, his eyebrow quirking in amusement. "As much as I'd love to see what you're capable of, there will be no fighting." His expression grows stern. "Now, give me your hands."

I refuse, keeping my guard up and watching every flicker of movement. He mumbles under his breath before darting his hands out and trapping my bound wrists in his grip. Before I can yank myself away, he's slashed the blade upward. My breath stills as I drop my head, watching my now-cut bindings hit the floor with a muffled slap.

A quiet laugh leaves his throat as he walks back to the desk. "Have a seat. It's not like you can go anywhere."

I turn to look at the door and weigh my options. I know that mountain of a man is still guarding my only escape. My eyes dart around the room. There are no windows. No other doors. The stone walls are draped in luxurious fabrics in rich hues of orange and red. Bookshelves line one side of the room, and their dark wooden frames gleam with polish just like the desk before me. There's not much to defend myself with, much less attack him with. Aside from books and furniture and a candlestick holder that might crack a skull if I use enough force, I'm out of luck.

"Sit," he orders, his voice a little less friendly now.

Hesitantly, I sit in the chair across from him. He grabs a jug on his desk and pours two cups. My mouth is salivating at the very thought of water, and I watch every drop spill into the cup like it's liquid gold.

He takes his time, then finally slides one across the desk to me. "Drink."

I don't like the way he's ordering me around, but I'm too thirsty to argue. I snatch the cup and cradle it in both hands, gulping the water down greedily. I'm almost choking as the last of it slips down my throat. He watches carefully as I set the cup down and push it back toward him.

"More."

His eyes flash with amusement but he obliges. I down the second cup slower this time, savoring it.

"Have you eaten?"

"No," I say quickly.

He eyes me like he knows I'm lying. "We can get you something to eat once we're done here."

Though his words offer comfort, I feel none.

"Fine." I huff, crossing my arms over my chest. As I lean back into the chair, I feel the uncomfortable, yet familiar, press of metal against my skin. I keep my face as neutral as I can, but inside, I'm beaming. My fatigue and fear is all but forgotten.

"What do you want?" I prod him.

His eyes light up like he actually believes I'll submit to the fate he's dealt me. I have to forcibly keep the smile from leaching across my face like a devil's grin. I shift in my seat, curling my hand up under my arm. My fingers tease the fabric of my tunic, drifting past the opening under my armpit.

"I want what everyone on the Continent wants," Rohan states. He takes a sip of water, his eyes never leaving mine. "Dominion."

"And you think I can get you that?" I scoff.

"Tell me, Ren. What do you dream of in this life?"

I look him dead in the eyes as I lean forward in my chair. My fingers press against metal and curl reflexively. "Survival."

"Hm." He smiles. "And what if I told you I could promise you a life where you never have to worry about anything. Not where your next meal comes from, not how you'll keep yourself safe—"

"Not wonder if men might raid my camp in the night and drag me across the desert?"

His gaze tightens on me, but there's a playfulness in his glare now. "Oh, come now, Ren. That—"

"Don't think by removing my bindings I've forgotten how I got here," I seethe. "Or what you are. Slaver or not, it all looks the same right about now."

Rohan smirks as he gets up from his chair. His sharp teeth seem to gleam in the candlelight as he leans across the desk, towering over me. "And don't think I've forgotten what you are." Before I can flinch, he grabs a fistful of my hair, yanking my head back. "*Mine.*"

Pain radiates from my scalp, rimming my eyes with tears. "I belong to no one."

My hand connects with his forearm, driving the tiny blade I'd kept hidden deep into his skin. He bellows, then swears before yanking me higher and pulling me out of the chair by the strands of hair wrapped in his fingers.

"You do, Ren," he growls, removing the blade with his free hand. "You're my property now. My prize. My peek into the future." His breath is hot on my skin as he leans in to me. "*Mine.*"

He releases me, and I immediately drop into my seat like a sack of flour. I kick back and scurry away, sending the chair clattering to the floor. I stand on shaky legs, fists curled in front of me.

He laughs as he casually makes his way around the desk, arm dripping blood onto the floor as he does. "Olen was right. You are a handful."

I swing at him wildly, the fury inside making me forget everything I've ever learned. My first punch goes wide, but the second one strikes true. I connect with his side, earning a grunt of surprise.

My luck is fleeting, and I hear the slap of him striking me across the face before I feel it. The sting seems to radiate through my skull, but I block it out, hurling myself toward him. I manage to throw two punches into his gut before I'm on the floor, coughing and sputtering. My face feels like it's on fire, and I glare up at him just in time to see the red, dust-stained sole of his boot. He kicks me in the stomach once, then twice more. As he presses his boot into my aching ribs, leaning his weight on the tender bones, the fight finally leaves me.

"Are you done?"

I spit the blood from my cut lip and glare up at him. "What do you want from me?"

"Other than for you to behave?" he taunts. "I want you to advise me."

Either he shook my head loose when he hit me, or his statement is as crazy as it sounds. All I can do is stare up at him blankly, stars flecking my vision.

"You're going to tell me the outcome of my plans before I so much as lift a finger. You're going to help me..." He pauses, rubbing his finger across his chin. "*Expand* this business of mine."

"What? Being a slaver not as fulfilling as it once was?" I scoff and lick the blood dripping from my bottom lip. There's a flurry of pain burning from my side with every breath I take.

"I'm not a slaver, Ren," he mutters.

There's anger in his eyes, but it quickly settles into something much more calculated, much more deadly. He takes a deep breath, running a finger along the blood that leaks from his arm. I wish I'd had a larger blade on me, wish I'd cut him from throat to gut.

"My ambitions are greater than what that trade could ever provide for me."

"What do you want?" I repeat, venom in my tone. I wince as the words leave my mouth, feeling every breath like a searing pain.

"Everything."

Something deep inside me recoils as I watch the way his green eyes darken. He smiles, as if sensing my fear.

"And now that I have you..." He hums, crossing his arms and looking down at me. "You're going to help me get it."

"I'd rather you break a few more ribs."

"Funny how you think you have a choice here," Rohan states coldly.

I scrape my nails against the floor as I push myself to my feet. "It doesn't matter if I have a choice or not," I spit. "I can't do what you ask of me."

"And why not?"

My body feels like it was pushed off a cliff, but I manage to hold myself up and meet his gaze. "It's not something I can call on when I feel like it," I huff. "I can't control it."

"Can't or won't?"

I flinch at that. "I—"

"You've heard the stories of Colak, yes?"

I nod slowly, warily. Everyone on the Continent hears stories of the Rebellion growing up, especially of those who served Milias Nayer. But usually, those stories are uttered in dark corners and not spoken plainly across rooms. Rohan has his eyes locked on me. There's a fire beneath the green hues, and I swear I can feel the heat from them licking at my skin.

"Colak could call visions at whim and used that skill to evade multiple attacks from King Achar." Rohan lectures me like I'm no more than a child.

My stomach is in knots. Colak was said to be the most powerful Seer since the origin of our kind. In the hundred years since the Rebellion ravaged the Continent, no one has been known to harness that kind of command over their gift—Seer or otherwise. *Rohan can't possibly think that—*

"You're going to learn to control it."

I laugh but quickly clamp down my jaw when I see he's not kidding. A moment ticks by, and I feel my heart beating a little faster. "And if I can't?" I ask.

He steps forward. My reflexes are too slow, my body too ravaged to do more than flail as he wraps a hand around my throat. Panic floods my eyes, the pupils growing wide. I squirm against his grip, but he holds me tighter. As his fingers squeeze, my vision peppers with black. I gulp against the lack of oxygen. My hands claw at his arms, nails drawing blood, but he only smirks.

"There is no alternative."

He drops me, and I collapse to the floor. My breath heaves in desperate bouts like I haven't tasted air in years.

"Tian," he calls casually, finding his way back to his chair.

The door opens quickly. I know who it is; I don't bother looking up.

"Take Ren to the room at the end of the hall."

Rough hands yank me up by my armpits. All I can do is slap my hands against Tian's skin as he drags me out. As I look across the room, it's like looking at the very face of death.

"And get her something to eat." Rohan smiles wide like a cat playing with a mouse. "She'll need her strength for tomorrow."

My strangled protests echo through the hall as I'm hauled away.

CHAPTER 5

My gaze is locked on the door. In the hours since I woke up, my focus hasn't wavered. I think if I closed my eyes, I could still see the grains of wood in perfect detail. My eye twitches, and I rub it quickly. It's been days since I got true rest. Last night was nothing but stolen moments of sleep. I tried to stay awake, anxious about the moment Rohan would barge in and yank me up by my hair. But again and again, my body betrayed me. First, my eyelids would flutter. Then my head would bob wildly, dipping to my chest before I shot awake, panic and fear ripping through me. My mind was so heavy with exhaustion last night that pain was an absent burden. But now that I'm conscious, it throbs with every breath I take.

I feel *everything*. My eye twitches again, and this time, I let it. Maybe a little rest would do me some good. It's not like he's going to slit my throat in my sleep—not when he's so adamant I'm of use.

I succumb to fatigue the minute I decide to close my eyes. The darkness behind my eyelids is almost peaceful. I take a deep breath, wincing at the pressure it puts on my ribs. I breathe through the pain and let my head rest against the wall behind me. Just twenty minutes. Or maybe an hour. *Once I've regained some of my sanity I'll be better prepared for—*

The door bursts open, and I shoot awake. My eyes blink rapidly. The grogginess blanketing me feels like I was asleep for days, not mere minutes. I expect to see Rohan, but it's the wall of a man, Tian, who fills the doorway instead. He doesn't utter a word as he steps into the room, but he does watch me, carefully—like I'm a wild animal who might lash out at any moment.

My eyes dart from him, to the door, then back to him. His caution fuels my own. I feel like a caged beast. Before I can even consider making a run for it, I catch a glimpse of something behind Tian. I swear silently as someone's shoulder peeks into the empty space of the doorway. Tian isn't the only one keeping watch.

The realization tugs me down like death's grip. There has to be a way out, a way to catch them off guard.

My pulse jumps as Tian drops a plate of food and a cup of water on the table beside the door. The clatter breaks the silence but does nothing to release the tension in the air. He turns away without another glance in my direction.

"You can't keep me locked in here," I object. "I want to see Rohan."

Tian turns toward me slowly. There's a severity to his glare that makes me scoot back against the bed. I don't want to admit I'm afraid, but there's something about Tian that makes barking demands seem like a bad idea.

"I'd be careful what I ask for, if I was you."

He shuts the door behind him without another word.

I hesitate, my feet curled up to my chest as I sit on the bed. His warning settles uneasily in my gut. After last night, I don't doubt that Rohan is brutal, cruel even. But still, I know he's the only way

I'm getting out of here. I can play his game, or I can make him play mine. Either way, I'm no closer to freedom while stuck in this godsdamn room by myself.

My stomach growls as I stare at the food on the table. It's more than they brought me last night, and I need it. Like sleep, it's been something I've been deprived of since my camp was raided.

I swallow thickly, practically salivating. I'd been too disoriented last night to even question if they'd poison me. But now? The new day brings renewed caution. I get off the bed slowly, groaning as I do, and examine what's to be my breakfast. A chunk of bread. A piece of meat that looks like the goat my mother—*Veles curse her soul*—would cook when she bartered well enough for it. I pick up the plate of food and smell it, then do the same with the water. There's no sweet tang of elleran berries or chalky whiff of frihn. Of course, there's more poisons that could easily be tainting what's in front of me, but I can't tell. I never cared for herbalism or botany. I much prefer my knives.

The pangs of hunger are threatening to knot my stomach, so finally, I succumb to it. I snatch up the bread and meat, wasting no time at all scarfing it down. Only when every spec of food is cleared from the plate do I drink the water. I gulp it hastily, swallowing every last drop and licking my lips to catch what's spilled. If I'm going to die from poison, I'm going to die satisfied and with a full belly.

I sit back down on the bed and wait. *How long did Mikel say most poisons took to take effect? Two minutes? Maybe up to fifteen?* I should have paid more attention. But plants and tinctures and funny smelling pastes that staved off infection were Mikel's thing, not mine. He would sit around the fire some mornings, thumbing through that big brown book he always carried while quickly jotting down notes. I always found it curious why he took the time to learn how to be a healer when his gift did more than remedies ever could. I never asked him why he did it. I should have.

I close my eyes and lay back on the bed as a deep sigh escapes my lungs. I should regret it. I should be boiling over like a vat of smelted ore, white hot with hate. But as much as I want to blame Mikel, I can't. I could have left him. I *should* have left him. If I hadn't grown so weak, so content with the comforts life pretended to offer, I wouldn't be sitting in this room, aching like a kicked dog. Again, I want to blame Mikel, but there's no one to blame but myself.

My hand traces my face gently, assessing the damage Rohan did. I try not to, but I can't help but wince as my fingertips brush the bruised flesh. *Bastard.* I grit my teeth and move my hand down to my stomach. I saw the bruises forming earlier; I don't need to look again. But still, I assess the damage. I lean back, groaning under the strain as I lift my tunic. My hand glides over the familiar curve of a scar, but I quickly ignore it and the ache it pulls into my chest.

Instead, I focus on the bruising. The light red has already bled into a sickly blue. By nightfall, I have no doubt my skin will be a blotch of deeply hued purple. I grit my teeth as I press my fingers against the bottom two ribs on my left side. A whimper escapes my lips, and I clamp my teeth into the inside of my cheek to stifle any more noise. Rohan's boot did some damage, but it could have been worse. I've been through worse.

I lean all the way back down and let out a torturous breath as my body fights against the rigidity of pain in order to fully relax. He's not going to let me go without getting what he wants. And even if I do manage to call a vision, he'll just want more. My mind spins in circles as I stare at the ceiling. I try to think about something else, but I can't. I keep hearing his voice like a waking nightmare that won't let me be. He wants my visions, but I don't know the first thing about controlling my gift.

Most daemons use their gift, honing it to their benefit—their call. Mikel was like that, always getting better when someone in the caravan needed healing. But there's danger involved in that. The more you use, the more you're marked. The gift bleeds into your skin, decorating the flesh like ink on paper. Veles-cursed daemons don't care. They wear their markings with honor, knowing those who see them will know the danger. But Hael-blessed ones? We aren't so easily protected by fear.

I close my eyes and let sleep drift over me like a warm blanket. For a minute, my heart races, thinking it's the lull of poison guiding me into nothingness. My skin peppers with goosebumps, but the fear subsides as quickly as it came. I close my eyes tighter and welcome it, knowing that whatever I have to do to get out of here, it will be much worse than drifting into the dark to meet the gods.

CHAPTER 6

"Get up."

I wake suddenly and with hands on me. My body moves subconsciously, fists striking hard and fast before I even open my eyes. I deliver two solid blows to the figure in front of me before I'm shoved off the bed and pinned to the ground with a boot on my back. This seems to be turning into a routine I'm not at all fond of.

"Not even fully awake and already misbehaving, I see."

I turn my head to the side and glare up at Olen. That cheeky grin is lodged deep in his face, and the sight sparks something foul in my chest. Hate would be too easy of a thing. I jump to my feet as soon as he shifts his weight off me.

"I guess I wasn't as valuable as you thought, considering you're still here. Already spent your blood money?"

"There's still plenty of gold to go around." He crosses his arms over his chest and beams a wicked grin. "I wanted to stick around for the show."

My brow furrows, but as I begin to speak, a mass overtakes the darkened doorway.

"He wants her. Now." Tian grunts.

"Well, well, well," Olen taunts. "Looks like the show is about to begin."

He nods to the door and—to his surprise and mine—I follow willingly. My body throbs. Every breath tugs at my bruised ribs, and my muscles ache from the trek across the desert. I know I don't stand any chance in a fight at present. All I can do is fall into step behind Olen and imagine where I would position the blade he more than deserves. *Middle of the back, near his ribs? Or maybe straight down the center, digging into his spine?*

My fantasies are cut short as Tian's thick fingers prod my shoulder, shoving me forward in order to keep up. We wind down the hallway, the narrow path only lit by a few candles. The shadows seem to slink up the walls like fingers, and for a brief moment, the ache of longing stirs in my chest. I swallow harshly, seeking to dislodge the burden of memories that threaten to flood my mind. Instead, I focus on where we're going.

The hall leads to a stone stairway, and I feel a chill permeating the air as we descend. The darkness creeps closer the farther down we go. The smell of wet stone and mildew seeps into my nose, and I stifle a choked cough. Our footsteps echo through the tight space, bouncing off the walls. A lone candle rests further down the corridor, lighting the way with a hazy glow.

We pass a few doors, but it's the one at the end of the hallway that catches my eye. It's large. Oppressive. I run my eyes over the dark wood and the metal latches that form a sliding lock. It's the type of thing you could slam your whole body into and, daresay, it wouldn't even budge.

Something that I haven't truly, deeply, felt in years snakes up my spine and clutches my throat. Fear is the weight in my boots, the growing labor of my steps. When Olen opens the door, that fear consumes me. My steps halt. My boots scuff against the ground. My hands press into the walls, fingernails scraping at rough stone. I try to retreat, but Tian is there, pushing me forward until my feet pass the threshold, and I'm trapped. As I stumble inside, I look up to see nothing but a single, wooden chair in the center of the room. Next to it, with eyes so bright they're like green shimmering pools, is Rohan. Olen slinks to his place in the corner, smirking at my obvious, flaring panic.

"Sit," Rohan orders.

I hear the door slam behind me and turn to see that Tian is gone. It does nothing to make this any better. My nerves feel like they're crackling flames as I shift my gaze to Olen, the lone chair, and finally, to Rohan. My eyes dart back to the chair, noticing something I missed before. There's a pair of iron shackles draped over the armrests—empty and waiting. My hand shakes softly. I look at Rohan, whose grip is now splayed against the back of the chair. He pats the wood with his fingertips. The soft drumming of it seems to pound through the empty room.

"*Sit*. Now, Ren."

My heart has fallen into my stomach. I can't seem to move.

"I could help her find her seat, boss." Olen leans off the wall but as he strides toward me, Rohan holds up a hand to stop him.

"No," he says firmly. "She'll do as she's told."

He taps on the chair, and somehow, my legs start working again. I feel like I'm walking to the gallows as I cross the room.

My feet take me there too quickly, and before I can rethink any of this, Rohan is shoving me down into the chair and clamping the irons around my wrists. The moment I hear the shackles *click*, my mind snaps out of fear's cloudy haze. My arms jerk at the restraints, rattling the chains again and again until my breath is a heaving beast in my chest. I feel every twinge of my bruised ribs, every ache in my bones, as I fight and scream and claw at the chair.

I still in an instant as Rohan's hands slither across my shoulders.

He leans over me, breath hot on my neck. "What do you say, Ren? How about a vision?"

I physically recoil, rattling the chains as I strain against their hold. I'm shaking—muscles weary, adrenaline threatening to pop my veins. But I don't stop. *I can't.* I thrash and grunt and tug until my wrists are sore, and my breath is no more than a desperate pant spilling from my lips.

Rohan lets out a sigh as he comes around the front of the chair. He tilts his head, appraising me. His eyes drift from my face and the bruise I know is there down to my body. Finally, he eyes my bound hands. He's enjoying this—and all I can do is bare my teeth at him.

"Wait," I murmur. "I'm seeing something..." I close my eyes, purse my lips together. "I see you in a dark room and... Yes. I see you getting your ass kicked by a woman and oh—" I pop my eyes open and shoot him a deadly glare. "Looks like you deserve it."

He only smirks. "Olen?"

"Yes, boss?"

Rohan keeps his gaze locked on me. "Leave."

Olen hesitates before doing as he's told. Disappointment lines his face. He looks to me with a distant, quiet smirk resting in the corner of his mouth as he passes. It's a small comfort to know that whatever is about to happen to me, he won't be here to witness it.

As soon as Olen shuts the door behind him, Rohan removes the dagger from his waistband. It's a brutal thing with a carefully crafted blade that looks as sharp as a maknen's tooth. It catches the candlelight flickering across the room and glints as if taunting me.

"What triggers your visions?"

I watch the blade carefully as he begins to clean his fingernails with the very tip of it.

"What?" I mumble.

He sighs but doesn't bother looking up from his task. "What do you do to call your visions? Is it a certain emotion? A response to—"

"I don't *do* anything," I object. "I told you, I can't control them."

He stops fiddling with the dagger and looks up at me. His face is void of any emotion I can read, and I flinch in anticipation as he lowers down to meet my eye.

"I knew a Seer once."

His voice drawls on, but my eyes are fixed to the blade he trails closer to my arm.

"Yanis was his name. He lived in the town I grew up in as a boy. He would charge a price of fifteen yenti to tell you about your future."

Rohan traces the dagger across my right forearm. The blade is barely a whisper on my skin.

"One day, I stole some money from my father and went to see Yanis."

I try to pull away, pressing back against the chair as Rohan draws the blade higher, but there's no escape.

"So I sat in his house, across the table from him, and asked what my future would bring."

The blade is at my throat now, dragging across my flesh as it travels to the other shoulder.

"But then he did something I never expected. He cut himself." Rohan stops the blade on my bicep, his eyes flashing to mine. "And you know what happened?"

My throat goes dry. I don't need my gift to see the future dancing in the emerald fire of his eyes. I feel the pressure of the blade before his words meet my ears.

"He called a vision."

I cry out as Rohan dips the tip of the dagger underneath my skin, carving out a small line of flesh. I'm still thrashing against the chains, flailing my feet wildly underneath me, as he finishes the cut and steps away. Sweat beads on my brow, slipping down my face like the fresh blood he summoned. My heart pounds. Rohan stands and waits. The blood—*my* blood— is dripping off his dagger as he stares at me.

"You think I've never felt pain before?" I snap. "Think I've never felt the sting of a blade against my skin?"

He says nothing, just cocks an eyebrow as if I'm some exotic, new thing he seeks to understand. But when he steps up to me again, fear steals my heart. I try to lurch away, but I can't.

He cuts deeper this time. Spit flies from my mouth as I curse him. My words do nothing to stop him, nor do they do anything to distract me from the bite of his blade. When he's done, he steps away. He watches and waits and when nothing happens, he tries again.

This dance of ours happens over and over until slick lines of blood drip from my fingertips. The ground is stained beneath me, and I feel every sliver of broken flesh like a new mouth breathing air. I lose my voice at some point, no longer able to scream and spew hatred as my throat cracks against the strain. But he doesn't stop. He tries again and again and again until there's little room left on either arm for more cuts.

My mind is numb, but my body? It's overwhelmed, bright with pain. I shake against the chair. Twitching. Weeping blood from every tear in my flesh. I lose track of time. My eyes flutter as my body begs for sleep—for nothingness—but I fight it. I raise my head, tears long-since dried on my face, eyes losing their luster. I stare at him, blinking slowly so he knows I'm still here. My gaze is weak but it's cold, unbreakable. There will be no visions for him—not now and not ever.

He all but smiles as he cleans the dirtied blade on his tunic. My vision wavers, growing dim at the edges. I grit my teeth and watch as his blurred form slowly slips away. Only when I hear the door lock behind him do I close my eyes and let myself slip into oblivion.

CHAPTER 7

Tian comes into the room to unshackle me at some point. I barely flutter my eyelids open enough to catch a glimpse of him before the door shuts again. The few candles lining the wall were snuffed out long ago; not even the smell of soot wafts through the chilled air now. Darkness is all that surrounds me. As I slip in and out of consciousness, the world is nothing more than a short-lived, heavy-lidded blur.

My body surrenders to sleep quickly and without my consent. In those brief moments awake, I can only manage to glance across the empty room. There are no windows. There is no light. My mind works slowly until I remember how I got here. I'm in a cellar, although *dungeon* seems more fitting. There's a bucket in the corner. I haven't had the strength or the need to get up and use it. There is no water or food, though I'm not surprised. We're past the point of being friendly. I am not a guest here; I never was.

I should get up—search every corner of the room for potential escape—but the very thought of pulling my body from where it's slumped against the chair feels like torture. Besides, I already know what I would find. *Nothing.* There is no furniture except for the chair. Nothing to fight off the man who has carved into my skin like it's his own except for the chains that rest at my feet.

The chair. My weary mind weaves scenarios of how I might use it to escape. *Throw it at Rohan and knock him unconscious. Smash it against the wall as a diversion and hide against the door, only to attack from behind when it opens. Break it and use one of its splintered legs as a spear.* Each scene ends the same amidst my foggy consciousness. Discovered. Caught. *Killed.*

My mind drifts in and out until I can no longer separate dreams from reality. I wrap the chains around Rohan's throat and tug, but he turns to ash in my fingers. My eyes flutter open and catch a gleam of white teeth across the room. Shadows drift up my skin, caressing my wounds like a lover's touch. Olen's voice drifts from the darkness, but when I peel my eyes open, no one is there. I pray for solace, protection against my own mind, but I find none.

I drift and drift and drift, until finally there is no thought left in me. My mind is a numb, hollow thing that can no longer discern the ache in my ribs or the sting of the damp, cellar air against my open flesh. I am nothing. *No one.* Just a withering mind. A broken corpse.

This must be death.

CHAPTER 8

I have no way to judge how much time has passed down here, but Tian has brought me food. Twice. It's a small comfort—to see his brooding, yet disinterested, gaze appearing in the dark and not the fiery red hair of the devil himself. Each time, the food is less than what will satisfy me, but I wolf it down without hesitation. I need my strength, but it never comes. Even now, an all-too-familiar ache returns to my stomach. I wring my hands together, squeezing my fingers until the skin is angry and red. Still, the thoughts circle me like vultures. And my pain remains ever-present.

The cuts running up and down my arms feel like ants nipping at my skin each time I move. The inside of my cheek is raw from abuse, but the bite of my teeth does nothing to quell the greater pain ravaging me. There's a shaking in my hands that no distraction will end. The infrequent stomp of footsteps in the hallway beyond unravels my nerves each time. Every distant voice churns my empty stomach. *When will he return? What will happen when he does?* I wring my hands again and the joints ache, begging to be relieved of my restlessness. But even as I wait in this room—carved and battered and shaken—not all is lost.

I haven't had a vision.

Whatever Rohan thinks he knows about Seers—whatever he thinks he knows about me—he's wrong. Pain is not the answer, though I doubt that will deter him. He will try again. I could see it in his eyes every time he dug that blade under my skin. He needs this—*needs me*. He will not give up, no matter how long it takes. And though I cannot control my gift, I am not naive. Sooner or later, a vision will come. There will be no stopping him when it does. He will have what he desires, even if he has to strip me of my flesh to get it. I know that now. But I don't plan on being here for that fate to take hold.

I roll my shoulders, biting back a groan as my achy muscles stretch past their limits. I stand behind the chair, ever ready. My eyes are pinned to the door. Tian should be coming with more food soon. *Will it be minutes? An hour?* It doesn't matter. I will not leave this spot until he does.

I wait. And wait. My eyes grow dry against my vigilance, but I do not waver. The rattle of chains echoes through the room as my hand cramps against its hold. The shakes come back, too. I fight against my body, praying for stillness until I finally settle. I swallow harshly, stifling any fear or hesitation I may have. I have to get out; there is no other option.

The grinding scrape of metal fills the silence as the lock slides away. My knuckles turn white, tightly gripping the chains I've removed from the chair. I trap my breath in my chest and wait. It feels like lifetimes before the door whines against the hinge. But when it finally opens, it's not Tian's worn, tanned face that greets me. I almost drop the chains as the candlelight illuminates his face.

Rohan eyes me curiously as he steps into the room. Olen is close behind. He saunters across the darkened space, lighting each snuffed candle with the flame of his own. I slink back against the sudden glare like a creature of the night. My eyes blink harshly, struggling to adjust. Shadows dance among the candlelight, lulling my mind to places it knows not to go. As my vision clears, all I can focus on is the object in Rohan's hand. I stare at the cup with a furrowed brow. He takes a step closer, and I flinch. The chains rattle behind my back and his eyes darken.

"Drop them."

My jaw clenches, but I don't move. I only grip my weapon tighter. Rohan sighs and nods toward me. Olen crosses the room quickly, too quickly. Before I can swing the end of the chain at his face, he withdraws a long dagger from his side.

"You know how this ends, Little Seer." He cocks his head and smiles. "But maybe you like having my blade at your throat?"

I scowl at him, holding my ground. "The only way this ends is with your body on the floor and that blade in my hand."

Olen's grin deepens as he takes a step closer. "If you want to play—"

"Enough," Rohan barks.

I can see the irritation roll off his face as he watches me, but he doesn't move. His green eyes narrow, as if deciding how much damage I could actually do.

"Ren, are you going to behave, or do I need to get my Torch?" Rohan asks.

My face pales, skin peppering with chills before I can fight the impulse. "You're lying. I've never even met a Torch."

His lips twitch up at the corners. "Shall I bring her down then?"

I swallow dryly and let the chains slip from my hands. As they rattle against the floor, a deep ache settles in my stomach. *A Torch?*

A chill rakes up my spine. He told me he had daemons working for him. He'd offered it up so casually a part of me hadn't believed him. *But if he's telling the truth… what other—*

"Sit down."

He nods to the chair, and bile creeps up the back of my throat. Though every part of me knows it's a bad idea, I do as I'm told.

My body tenses as he steps closer. Olen has settled back to his usual place in the corner, grinning like a wild dog. *How I would have loved to see those chains crack his skull.* When I look back to Rohan, I see his hand is extended out to me. I stare at the cup, then back to him.

"What is it?"

"Ale."

My face contorts in confusion. "Why—"

"If there's more than one way to loosen a tongue… Then there's more than one way to loosen a mind."

"You honestly think that—"

He doesn't wait for me to finish before the cup is pushed into my hands. The amber-colored liquid sloshes over the rim, dripping onto my pant leg. I watch it seep into the fabric amidst the splotches of dried blood.

"Drink."

I drink. The ale hits the back of my ragged throat with a mixture of relief and agony. I pull the cup away, coughing, but it's quickly shoved back against my lips. I sputter as the cup tips and more ale than I can possibly swallow rushes down my throat. I thrash, choking and desperate to pull it away, but a firm hand locks around my jaw and holds me steady. Only when the cup is drained, and I'm left gasping for breath, does Rohan relent.

"Fuck you," I cough, tears brimming my eyes.

He says nothing, just stares down at me with a sick fleck of amusement in his eyes. "Olen?"

"Yes, boss?"

Rohan looks at the empty cup, then back to me. He smiles. "Go get more ale," he orders. "It's going to be a long night."

CHAPTER 9

The room is spinning. Or maybe I'm the one spinning. I blink slowly. My body feels like it belongs to someone else. It's as light as a crow's feather, tingling like embers in a crackling fire. My vision wavers, growing fuzzy for a brief second before the room comes back to me. It's dark. There are only a few candles left flickering against the walls. It's cold, although my body is warm—skin pulsing as if flushed from a long day under the sun. I try to get up from the chair only to realize I'm on the ground, having already slipped from my seat. When I look up, Rohan is staring at me, anger streaked across those violent, emerald eyes. He's been staring at me like that for hours.

"She's drunk to the gods," Olen mocks from somewhere in the room.

Rohan doesn't flinch or even acknowledge him. Instead, he bears down on me with that bright, unnerving stare. He's waiting for something to happen. He'll be waiting long after he's dust in the ground if I can help it. My hands scrape against the floor as I try to pick myself up. I slip against the dusty stone, hands sprawling in front of me. I try again, cursing the gods under my breath as the room spins. Somehow, I manage to straighten my spine and meet his gaze before my legs wobble underneath me. I sway and fall against the chair.

"You're a bastard," I slur.

The weightlessness is slowly leaving my body, and in its place, rises a foul heaviness. My legs feel like they're buried under mountains of sand. My stomach sloshes with every movement I dare take. I lost track of how much ale he dumped down my throat long ago. The lingering taste of it tingles on my tongue as I lick my lips. A wave of nausea rolls over me. I swallow harshly, barely keeping it down. I try to think about something else—anything else. Early mornings in the desert. The chill in the air before the sun has had time to bake the sand and the world around it. How the tea that Zoah's wife, Nessa, made always seemed to slip under my bones and breathe life into my body. How I would die for some of that tea now.

"This is taking too long."

Rohan's vicious tone snaps my focus back to the room. My eyelids flutter open, and I find that he's still standing in front of me, waiting for something I hope never comes. His arms are crossed against his strong chest. I almost laugh at his arrogance. *As if the gods would cater to his will. As if this gift that curses my blood would listen.*

"The vi-isions-s don't answer to you-u," I try to say, although my words jumble their way across my tongue. "*I* don't-t answer to y-you."

I barely hear his response, barely hear the whoop of Olen's laugh. My blood thrums in my ears. It's like I can hear every drop rushing through me. My body feels like it's been buried deep underground—entombed. The world around me is too heavy.

Too close. Too much. I whimper as the sensation creeps up to the front of my head and throbs against my skull.

The room is a blur. I'm spinning, again. I force my eyes shut, but it only makes it worse. I'm spinning and falling and trembling in the dark of my own mind. I'm untethered. Adrift. I don't remember the last time I was this drunk. Maybe not since I lived in Artolen. *Yes, that last night we'd all spent together.* Someone—Chani, I think—had stolen a jug of rum from one of the taverns. We'd all passed it around, taking hearty swigs until our laughs echoed down the dark alley and our faces were wet and flushed.

My mind swirls in the dark as the memory takes hold. I can almost see their faces, my old friends—the ones I didn't seek out but needed so desperately back then. I see them smile and toss their heads back in laughter. I almost sob at the thought. The sound gets trapped in my throat and chokes out in a slurred mumble. They were so happy—*we*—we were so happy.

My chest grows tight, and I let the memory slip back to the dark corner of my mind where it belongs. I try to count the years since Artolen but my mind is heavy with burden. *Ten years? No*, eleven since I left what had become my home.

I keep my eyes closed as my head bobs and lulls on my shoulders. I wonder how many of them are still alive. I wonder if *he's* still alive, but I already know the answer. He'll be what—thirty years old now? A grown man, far from the reckless boy who taught me how to fight. *What would he say if he saw me like this? Saw me so weak?*

The thought slips through unchecked, the haze of ale crumbling the walls I've so carefully built. A flash of dark hair slithers from the shadows. Then a smile. Cunning. Mischievous. *Selfish.* I shake my head, but it doesn't do anything to rid me of my thoughts. My mind fills with the image of marked hands. Fingers dotted and lined with swaths of black, cursed by Veles. Even at nineteen, he'd had so many markings—so many more than the rest of us.

The hand in my mind reaches out to me. Bloody. Dripping. I feel the pain in my side, feel the break and tear of skin like the blade sliced through me mere seconds ago and not years. Pleading eyes—*desperate eyes*. Anger, so much anger. I can feel it pooling in the air like his shadows want to snuff out everyt—

My body is stumbling toward the bucket before I can open my eyes. I slump to the ground, both arms clutching it tightly to my chest as I retch with the last ounce of strength I have left. I shudder as my stomach empties. My palms are clammy as I grip the wooden rim of the bucket.

Olen snickers, but as I look up to curse at him, another wave of nausea overtakes me. I'm coughing and retching and shaking as my body expels every last drop of ale. Sweat coats the back of my neck, and I feel a bead of it slip under the collar of my tunic. I wipe my mouth before my head drops to rest on the bucket's edge. I try to steady my breath. It's quaking in my chest, threatening to turn into choking sobs, but I fight it with everything I have left. They can't see me cry. They can't see me break.

My body trembles. Every bruise I have, every cut, is alight with pain. *I'm weak.* That's all I can think as my body drapes over the bucket, crumpled and ravaged by sickness. I would take the blade. I would take the cut of the blade over this. That kind of pain is tangible—grounding. *But this?* I suck in a shuddering breath. This is helpless.

Two firm hands slide under my armpits and hoist me off the ground. I'm dragged across the floor, clothes snagging on rough stone until I'm back in the chair. I slump against it before my body begins to tremble. My muscles feel useless. This body is just a husk. I want the pain. I *need* the pain. I dig my nails into my palms but it barely phases me. I'm slipping into unconsciousness, and I'm grateful for it. Take me down into the nothingness. *Please.*

Something tugs me back to the room. A touch. My eyelids are too heavy, too tired to open. I raise my head off the back of the chair, and it falls forward. The touch stays. It holds my head up, caresses my cheek softly. Gently. Almost lovingly. I can't help but lean into the foreign feeling. As I do, my mind pools with inky blackness. He's there—in the dark. This time, I don't push the memory away. It's his hand caressing my face. It's his body that's leaning over me. His yearning that grips my soul and burrows there like it never left. Maybe it never did. I rest my face against his palm and feel the warmth of his skin. There's no blood this time. No pain. Just him. I feel one last caress of his fingers before my head snaps back.

The desert. I'm in the desert. I blink slowly, but the image in front of me is shifting, moving. I'm moving. My hands trace over a bundle of honey-white hair. It's the color of my hair, but it's not my hair. My eyes blink and refocus. I'm on the back of a mare. Her hooves sift through the sand, and her breath huffs from her nose quietly, yet roughly. She carries me up the dune until we're resting on top of it. The sun is high above the horizon, blanketing the endless sands in a lush, orange glow. I stare at it, revel in its beauty before another horse comes up alongside and pulls my focus.

My eyes trace over the black stallion and its peppering of white. The animal's head rears back as its rider brings it to a halt. I look up. Unfamiliar, gray eyes meet mine. The last thing I see is the mass of markings running down the center of his throat before I'm snapped back in a blinding flash.

My breath heaves in and out of my chest. I blink harshly until the foggy white of my gift dissipates from my eyes. I'm not in the desert. I'm in the cellar. None of that has happened yet. Which means...

Rohan is smirking down at me. His green gaze is alive, as wide as a predator's before a kill. Agony splits me wide open, baring my soul to the flames of my own resentment. I hate him. I hate what he's done to me. *What he's taken from me.* I try to move, to lash out, but I don't have the energy. My vision has drained whatever strength throwing up all the ale didn't already take. I can only sit and watch as my worst nightmare comes true. My stomach is empty and raw, but the look on Rohan's face makes me want to retch again.

"Not pain," he states.

He leans over me, and I clamp down my jaw to stave away the sickness curdling deep in my gut.

"Not drink." He tilts his head to the side, appraising me with hungry eyes. "But affection."

His hand reaches out, but before his fingers can brush against my cheek, I lurch away.

His smug grin only deepens. "Interesting," he taunts. "Very interesting."

CHAPTER 10

My eyes shoot open, but I don't move—not yet. I take in a slow, unsteady breath and dig my fingers into the bedding. *Bedding?* It takes me a second to realize I'm not tied to the chair or lying on the cellar floor. My body, every ache and cut, is cushioned by the soft bed underneath me, and it feels holy. But it's not right. I try to remember last night but my mind is a pounding drum inside my skull.

I blink until the room comes into focus. Light is streaming in from the window, spread across the bedding in warm beams of sunlight. Beyond that, a large chest rests at the end of the bed. It's all wood and brass and decorated with intricate carvings. It's well-made. *Expensive.*

As my gaze drifts further, my body tenses. Olen is leaning against the door, cutting an apple with a small knife. He hasn't yet noticed that I'm awake. Heartbeat now pounding in my ears, I let my gaze continue its sweep over the room. There's a wardrobe on the opposite wall, made of the same intricately carved wood as the chest. Curtains drape across the window in rich hues of orange, and the bedding wrapped around me has the same luxurious feel to it. It's a far cry from the room I was kept in the first night. It's certainly not a room for a prisoner.

There's a small bedside table next to me, and just as my eyes flicker to check on Olen again, my focus snags. The bedside table has drawers. Drawers for things, I realize. *Things like a weapon.*

I clench every muscle in my body, keeping deathly quiet as I shift my weight. My eyes are pinned to Olen as I lean across the bed, but he's intent, focused on carving away a chunk of apple. My fingers flex and strain for purchase on the drawer's handle. *Just another inch and I can reach it.*

I hold my breath and roll. The second I do, the bed creaks, and Olen's attention snaps to me. His eyes widen as I throw my body off the end of the bed and tear open the drawer. *There has to be something.* No one on the gods-forsaken Continent sleeps without a weapon nearby.

My heart stills. Resting in the shadowed back of the drawer lies a dagger. Just as my fingers graze the metal hilt, Olen's hand grips the back of my tunic. He shoves me onto the bed while I scramble for purchase against the sheets. My body alights with pain with every slip and thrash. I try to scurry backward but there's nowhere to go.

As Olen climbs on top of me, I feel the press of his knife against my cheek. The metal is cold and slick with the juice of his apple. "Little Seer," he coos. "Causing trouble, again?"

His other hand reaches into the drawer and retrieves the dagger. He holds it up in front of me, turning it in the sunlight as if to let me get a good look at what could have been my freedom.

"Now what" —he presses his own blade harder against my cheek as I squirm— "were you thinking of doing with this?"

I shoot him a nasty look though my tone turns sickly sweet. "Why don't you let me have it, and I'll show you?"

He laughs, tucking the dagger into his waistband before he gets off me. "As much as I would love to play, Rohan demanded you be kept in one piece."

Anger snarls in my throat as I shoot up from the bed and find my footing on the warm tile floor. I ignore the pain surging through every inch of my body and step toward him. "Funny how he was the one cutting me to pieces just the other night."

Olen shrugs before taking his place against the door once more. He glances down at his half-eaten apple, the fruit now resting on the tile. Annoyance ripples across his face before it's quickly replaced by a smirk. "You owe me an apple."

"Why am I in this room?"

"You know, that was one of the last apples we had. And another crate doesn't come in from Kupor for another month."

I stride across the room, kicking the fruit out of my way as I do. I don't stop until I'm up in his face, breath huffing in my chest. "I don't give a Demasken gem about your apple!" I yell at him. "Why did I wake up in this bed? Why care that I'm in one piece all of a sudden?"

He looks down his nose at me, cocky smile slipping across his face. He's a lot taller than me without my boots on.

My boots... I look down to find my boots are gone, and I'm barefoot. I'm also dressed in fresh clothes pulled from my pack and my skin is clean—cleaner than it's been in a while.

My eyes go wide as I take a step away from him and fold my arms across my chest. "Who bathed and dressed me?" I demand.

His smirk deepens, and I feel every drop of blood in my body chill like it's encased in ice. The way he looks me up and down makes me yearn for one of my daggers just so I can take his eye.

"Who—"

"One of the servants," he finally says.

I give him a clipped nod and step back until my legs press against the bed. I do nothing. Say nothing. He's watching me curiously, but I don't spare him another glance. All I can think about is why the hell I'm in this room. Rohan is far from a considerate host. I should still be in that cellar puking my guts out.

This is one of his games, it has to be. He's teasing me with an ounce of comfort, just to strip it from me later. He's cruel like that. He's only after my visions. Surely, he would do anything to—

Then it hits me. Memories spill through my mind like a tortured wail. My face goes ashen as I look over at Olen.

"Mm." He chuckles. "Remembering something, Little Seer?" There's a flicker of amusement in his eyes as he steps forward.

I recoil, fumbling backward against the bed. My eyes scan the room, but aside from the two blades he has on him, there's nothing useful. He holds his position in the middle of the room and does nothing but watch me. His smile is so wide it looks painted on.

My heart rate grows steadily in my chest. The ache of my ribs is ever-present. My lungs feel tight. I can't breathe. I dig my nails into my palms, leaving half-moon indents in the flesh. The urge to scream and claw my way out of here is only subdued by the constant throb of my body. I'm in no shape to take him on, not without a weapon.

I swallow harshly. "What are you going to do?"

"Me?" He laughs. "Nothing."

He takes a step back until he finds the door. As he opens it, my eyes dart behind him. The hallway is empty. Tian isn't there—as far as I can see.

"But now that you're awake..." Olen pauses, leaning against the doorway. "Rohan will be paying you a visit very, *very* soon."

The door clicks behind him. It's only seconds later that I break. Rage pours from me, cracking through my chest and into my lungs. My fists pound against the solid wood of the door. I yell and scream and curse; and even when my breath fails me, I don't stop.

CHAPTER 11

I've searched every corner of this godsdamn room, torn it apart. Aside from an assortment of fine men's clothing, a few books, and my pack—from which all my blades have been removed—there's nothing. That is, nothing useful to escape this nightmare. I did manage to find a salve that Mikel made me long ago, hidden in the bottom of my pack. It instantly soothed the cuts riddled across my arms but left a deep ache burrowed in my chest. *He's fine. Mikel knows how to take care of himself.* The only thing I should be worrying about now is my own fate.

I can't stop moving. My feet weave a path on the floor, taking me back and forth across the room. I've slipped my boots on, and there's a repetitive, light pounding on the tile as I pace. My hair is out of my face, tied into a loose knot at the base of my neck. I changed out of the clothes they put me in, too, swapping the loose linen pants for form-fitting ones made of hekkriti leather. I run my hands over the smooth, scaled texture that wraps around my thighs. The motion is a comforting one. There are two sheaths there. Though, both rest empty. My fingers twitch at the foreign sensation.

The pants are a weapon themselves in a way—an irreplaceable tool for survival. It was only last year that I took an odd job, deep in the west of the Continent, to scrounge up some coin. I had left Zoah and the others for three weeks with nothing but my pack and a promise to be back. Of course, Mikel hadn't believed I'd return.

The weeks passed. I had toiled and baked in the sun, hauled stones until my palms bled and my fingers ached to the bone. But I'd made enough money to see me through the next year. Luckily, there are still parts of the Continent that pay well for labor, especially when it comes to constructing outposts in the mostly uncharted west. Those that have the ambition to lay claim to those desolate, heaps of sand value speed and discretion over everything. They do not care who works for them or why. They turn a blind eye as long as you can help raise a town faster than someone can steal it out from under them.

My pockets had been fuller than expected, and the decision of what to do with the coin I had earned proved an easy one. I'd found a shop and treated myself to two things: a pair of pants and a harness with five sheaths for my blades. Both being crafted of hekkriti leather, I had little coin to spare after such a purchase. I have never come to regret it, though. It's an interesting material, the leather made from hekkriti lizards that dominate—*and I do mean dominate*—the upper parts of the Jahaer Desert. Scaly skin the color of honey and amber that almost cools against the sun's harsh rays. It's flexible but hard. Durable. It breathes among the desert's heat and holds up nicely to the slice of a blade.

It's gotten me through more than a few close calls, whether from the elements or those who have wished me harm. Which is exactly why I decided to put the leathers on today. I'm fighting my way out of here one way or another. I have no intention of staying put for whatever new horror Rohan has planned.

I dig my nails into my palms before shaking my hands out. *It's been, what? An hour since Olen was here?* The bastard made sure to lock the door behind him. I checked—multiple times. A deep breath loosens from my lungs as I brush my hands across the smooth cotton of my sleeveless tunic. I've dressed for a fight. Tight clothes—nothing to grab on to, nothing to drag me down. I eye the bag that rests by the door. I packed and repacked it twice. There's a large scarf near the top that will protect me from the sun once I've slipped back into the desert—back to the outskirts and the shadows where I belong.

My eyes flicker to the window. I'm two floors up. There's nothing but hard, knee-shattering earth below. No way to open it. Nothing to grab on the way down. I swallow the lump in my throat as I continue to pace. There's no way out of here except through that door. I try and try to remember something from last night but it's all a dark, foggy mess. *Damn the ale. Damn Rohan.* There's no telling how many obstacles are in my way once I get into the hallway.

I stop pacing and rake my hands across my face. My eyes snap closed as I try to calm the jumpy fluttering of my heart.

I just need to get out of this room, get through that door. One thing at a time.

Right as I start to find my center, the doorknob rattles, and my stomach drops. My eyes flicker open to a deadly green gaze that seems to pierce me where I stand. He observes me from the threshold, quietly.

Before I can form any sort of plan in my head, Rohan shuts the door behind him. It doesn't lock. The absence of a click is like music to my ears, but the joy is short lived as he steps closer. Panic grips me for a split second as my mind takes me back to that cellar.

I feel his knife in my skin, his fingers digging into my cheeks, prying my jaw open only to drown me in ale. It's only when I hear the thud of his boots against the tile that I snap awake. I have no weapon, but I don't care anymore. My hands flex at my sides, legs bouncing in anticipation. He does nothing in return, only gives me a once-over look and lets out a breathy laugh.

"You look like you're ready for a fight."

His gaze bores into me, amusement crinkling the corners of his eyes. He notes the pants, the empty harness—*which won't be empty for long if I have my way*—and the boots. He spends an unnecessary amount of time studying the bare skin my tunic allows, especially the freshly mutilated skin running up and down my arms. His smiles, as if reveling in his handiwork.

"I thought we were past this, Ren," he almost coos. "I thought you were done fighting the hand the gods have dealt you here. Thought you were..."

Broken, I think.

His eyes brighten. "...Finished."

I grit my teeth and take two steps to my left as he moves closer. He shoots me an amused grin but gets the hint. He's not getting anywhere near me, not yet. He stops and stays where he is.

My heart lodges in my throat as I realize he's blocking the door. I eye him up and down quickly. Solid boots. Loose-fitting tunic that's tucked into his pants. There's a scar peeking through the open collar, a slash across his collarbone. My eyes drift lower. One dagger holstered on his left side, a fancy-looking thing. The hilt is bright, shiny brass with intricate carvings. *The one he cut me with.* It will make a good start to my renewed collection.

"See anything you like?"

I scowl as my gaze shoots back up to his face. He's cocking an eyebrow, smirking at me.

"What do you want this time?" I all but snarl.

"Last night was..." His gaze slinks up my skin. "... enlightening." He hums.

His heavy stare turns my stomach, but I don't give him the satisfaction of shrinking away from it. "I'm glad you enjoyed yourself," I snap. "I just wish I would have aimed for you and not the bucket."

A dry laugh spills from his lips as he takes a step closer. I take one back in return. He's halfway across the room, and I'm slowly backing myself into a corner. *Not good, not good at all.*

"I thought for sure the pain would do it," he muses. "Then when that didn't work, I was sure loosening whatever mental blocks you had up would prove successful."

He quickly takes another step, then another. I feel my stomach knot as my back hits the wall. I have no where left to go. He seems to know it, too.

"But to think this whole time..."

He's closed what little distance remains between us in a few seconds. As soon as I feel his breath against my skin, something scared and feral crawls inside me.

"...All I had to do was touch you."

He brings his hand up to my face, and I duck. My movements are frantic as I slip under his arm and rush for the door. But it's too far away, and he's too close. I'm snagged by the arm and shoved toward the bed. My heart is pounding so viciously I'm afraid it might jump out of my chest.

I try to scramble away, but he lashes out for my neck. I thrash and claw but it's no use. He's bigger. Stronger. He forces me to sit on the edge of the bed, hand wrapped tightly around my throat. I can still breathe but my panic flares as he nudges my legs open and stands between them. Green eyes look down at me through heavy lids, like a hungry wolf. His other hand glides down my face, caressing my cheek in a way that makes my skin crawl. I swallow a swell of nausea. A chilled sweat breaks out across my flesh. I wait for a vision, but one doesn't come. My brow furrows oh-so-slightly before I mask the emotions from my face. As I try to yank away from Rohan's touch, the grip on my throat only tightens. I cough and sputter, but he holds firm.

"All I want is what's in that pretty little head of yours, Ren," he coos. "Just tell me what the gods have planned for the Continent—for me—and you can have whatever you want."

His thumb brushes roughly against my cheek, playing with the bruised skin. "Riches, power, *pleasure.*"

His hand glides to the back of my head, gripping my hair roughly. I feel his fingers loosening the knot, pulling at the strands.

"All you have to do is what you're told. Give me what I want."

My breath shakes in my chest. Of all the things I've faced in this life, of all the pain and suffering I've endured, it can't all have been for this. *This cannot be the fate that the gods designed for me.* A lone tear slides down my cheek, but before I can wipe it away, Rohan does it for me.

"Hush," he chides. "You'll find I can be very generous with those who prove their worth."

Another tear falls, and he watches it with wild amusement. He tilts my head back, one hand tugging my hair while the other circles my throat. He looks down on me, a beastly smile marring his face. I see it in his eyes then—among the dilated pupils and the green flare of his irises. I see there's only one way I survive this, only one way I see another sunrise. I allow one, final tear to slide down my cheek. There will be none allowed after this. It's the only way. I force out a wavering breath before I do what must be done. I let him win.

"Okay."

He tilts his head to the side, eyes practically sparkling in delight. "Okay?" His grip loosens, fingers unfurling from my hair.

I lock my eyes on him and nibble at my bottom lip.

Hael, protect me.

"You said you have other daemons working for you," I say softly. "I want to be treated the same." I find the courage in my voice as his hand slips from my throat. "And I want to paid for my gift. Paid *well*."

"Done." Rohan can't seem to keep the smile off his face. "Anything else?"

"I want my own place. I don't want to be locked in a room like some animal."

"We can make those arrangements once you've proven you'll behave."

His hands fall away from me, but he stays standing between my thighs. I swallow nervously, fighting the quiver in my tone.

"I want to learn." My breath is no more than a whisper on my lips. "I want to learn how to call my gift. I don't want it taken against my will." My fingers brush lightly against his leg, and I see the heat blaze in his eyes. "I want to give it."

He's as still as stone as I slowly stand. I let my hand graze up his thigh before my fingers curl into the fabric of his tunic. I anchor myself against him, patient and still like the well-behaved thing I know he wants me to be. "Affection, you say?" I muse.

He's watching me carefully, but with every second I can see his desire growing.

"Teach me," I whisper.

I'm standing on tiptoes now, as if desperate to reach him. My eyes grow wide, matching the hunger that's locked in his own gaze. Just when my lips are inches from his, I halt. I feel his hot breath, feel his heart beating where my fingers are splayed across his chest. Time ticks by slowly until I watch it finally happen. I watch his control snap.

He's pressing his mouth against mine roughly before I can take a full breath. The kiss is ravenous, untamed. I open my mouth and let his tongue dart inside as he devours me. A soft whimper slips from my throat, and just like I know it will, his body reacts. His hands are all over me, sliding down my leathers, cupping my ass and pressing me firmly against him. I push into him roughly, sending us staggering back into the wall. He spins us around until I'm pinned and at his mercy.

His mouth leaves my lips, dragging kisses along my jaw. I feel the flat of his tongue as he licks my neck, over the markings that symbolize his true desire for me. He grunts against my skin as my hands find their way to his pants, to the bulge that's growing there. I struggle with his belt as he bites and kisses at my neck, my throat, my chest. His hands slide up my tunic, groping my breasts. My ribs ache in protest, but I don't stop him. He's wild, like a starving beast tearing at fresh meat. His teeth nip at the skin on my shoulder, nicking the cuts he left on me days before. Fresh blood flows. He licks it clean. I moan. My hands tug at his waistband desperately. I find what I'm looking for and let out a breathy laugh as my hand frees it. *Gods, this is going to feel good.*

"Rohan," I moan in a whispered breath.

He growls and pulls away in order to look at me. I take in his blown pupils, the wolfish grin on his face, and can't help but smile back.

"Rot with Veles."

I watch his eyes widen as I push his own dagger into his flesh. The movement is swift and unyielding. His stomach offers little resistance. I take a moment to enjoy the fear and panic that flickers through those vile, green eyes before I yank the blade free.

Before he can stop me, I'm ramming it into him once more. I don't waste a second as I rip it out and push him off me. He's clutching his stomach and sputtering in pain as I snatch my pack and rush for the door. He stumbles after me, curses flittering among his ragged breath, but I'm already gone.

True panic sets in now.

My head whips to the left, then the right. *No one.* The hall is empty. A blessing from the gods, but I don't wait around to test my luck. I can already hear Rohan banging against things, trying to drag himself after me. Once more, I look from left to right. I take a deep breath and make a decision.

"Hael, guide me," I utter as I dart to the right.

I pad down the hall as quietly as I can. I look behind me, spotting the trail of red marking my path. My gaze drops to the dagger in my hand, still coated in Rohan's blood. I smile. The look is ripped from my face as a figure steps out of a doorway at the end of the hall. *Shit.*

I shift on my feet and slip to the left, down another path. My heart pounds faster as I see stairs ahead. Yells erupt from behind me. Boots pound stone. Voices collide against each other until I don't know where they're coming from. Amidst it all, one thing sends a chill down my spine. Rohan's voice booms through the house. He's still alive, but I knew that. It wasn't a killing blow. *My mistake.*

I'm stripped of my caution as his voice grows louder. I hurl myself forward and into the stairwell. My feet slide over the slick stone steps, and I slam into the opposite wall as I reach the bottom. Breath rips through my lungs. I can still feel every bruise on my ribs, every cut in my flesh, but I don't stop. There's a light to my left. *Sunlight.* It's streaming in through an open doorway, and I swear it's sent from the heavens above.

I'm sprinting down the last stretch of the corridor when a figure steps in front of the exit. I don't stop. I can't. I won't go back to that cellar. Not now. Never ever. The things he will do to me are not things I can live through. It will be worse than any blade, any hunger, any pain I've ever faced. He'll strip my soul bare until I'm nothing. *I can't stop.*

I barrel forward, colliding with the figure. It's not something they expect—the blade in their neck, the life I take from them. I drive us forward, into the daylight. Breath chuffs and wheezes against the crook of my neck. My gut clenches. I pry their hands off me, shoving them away. Their body drops like a deadweight at my feet. I'm sprinting away before I can look at their face. I don't want to know, and it doesn't matter. All that matters is what comes next. Getting out of here. Living for another day.

The yelling and commotion is heavy on my heels. Chaos floods the air around me, but I force myself forward, away from it all. I'm running with such desperation that my legs feel like they'll crumple underneath me. My stomach swells like a giant wave, and its emptiness is the only thing that keeps me from throwing up. My fingers scrape across the side of a building as I round a corner too quickly. Dust billows as my boots skid. I feel my nails break and split against the pressure. I bite back the pain and take in a sharp breath as I'm brought to a sudden stop.

There, in the middle of the street, tied to a railing, is a horse. Not just any horse. Memories of things that haven't yet come to pass spill into my mind. A honey-white mane. A soft, impatient whinny. Strong legs trekking across the sand. The mare. *My* mare.

My eyes dart across the street but no one is around. I can hear yells in the distance. They're getting closer. I approach on silent feet, making my way to the front of the horse with hands raised peacefully. The horse watches me with a cold, assessing eye, huffing softly.

"Easy there," I utter, daring to step closer.

She neighs and stomps but doesn't pull away as my fingers brush against her face. I take a deep breath and look the horse dead in the eye, almost pleading with it. "You don't know me, but we're going to go on a little adventure. You and I."

I untie the reins from the railing and grab the pommel of the saddle. The horse rears its head back but stays put. I swallow as I glance down the alley I came from. Four figures have rounded the corner and are looking across the courtyard with weapons drawn. My blood chills as I see a mess of blond hair catching the high afternoon sun like a glinting coin. Olen turns and locks his gaze on mine. He grimaces, raising his dagger as he runs for me.

I hoist myself up onto the saddle and nudge the horse roughly. My stomach lurches as we take off. The shouting gets louder as more men spill into the courtyard. I don't dare look back as I hurtle down the street, gripping my thighs against the saddle to keep from falling off. It's not the speed of my escape, but the sting in my back that makes me pull in a sharp breath and almost slip from atop the horse. I grunt in pain and fall forward, barely catching myself on the horse's neck. I prod us onward with my boot, gritting my teeth through the searing pain that's a skewer in my flesh.

The escape through the city is a blur. Market stalls and vendors whirl past in a frenzy. People jump out of the way. Some make a desperate attempt to shelter their wares from the melee, but it makes no difference. The horse doesn't falter, doesn't rear back against the chaos or deviate from the path forward. And somehow, neither do I. We make it out of the city but even then, I don't risk us stopping. They'll be coming for me now. *He'll* be coming for me.

Only when Denheir has faded into the distance do I grimace and sit up. One look over my shoulder confirms what I already know. Olen's dagger is wedged deep in my lower back, in the tender flesh of my side. *The bastard has good aim.* My teeth grind against each other as I reach my hand around and rip it free. I regret it instantly, first feeling the searing pain, then the steady flow of blood sliding down my skin. Still, I don't let the horse stop. We have a long way to go—especially when the destination is far from here. *North. I need to go north.*

I grunt in pain with every bounce atop the horse but fight through it. I won't die, not today. I've seen too much of my future for this to be it.

I press my fingers against my back, trying to stop the life from seeping out of me as we venture forward across the endless sands. It's only when the sun starts to dip toward the horizon that I feel my adrenaline crash and my mind slips into dazed numbness. My eyes close before I can stop them.

CHAPTER 12

It's been hours, or days. I really can't tell. All I know is I watched the sun set last night and didn't see it rise. Now, it clings to the horizon once again, a fiery ball sinking into the earth. I hear the sands sift underneath me, hear the horse drag us both forward. To where? I don't know. *Away.* That's the only goal—take me far away.

I swallow, but my throat is scratchy and dry. I cough against the feeling and lick my lips but there's no moisture there to spare. My eyelids flicker heavily though I manage to hold them open long enough to look around. Nothing. No one. The horizon is a glimmer ahead of me, hazy against the heat of the sinking sun.

I try to sit up from where I'm hunched over in the saddle and instantly regret it. Pain shoots through me like fire. My fingers paw at my back, at the fleshy part of my oblique that feels like it belongs to someone else. Crusted blood falls away from the tear in my tunic. I wince as I blindly assess the damage. Grunts and moans rumble against my parched lips. I only pull away when fresh blood coats my fingertips. *Shit.* I need to find a Mender. Gods, even some outpost healer would be better than letting it fester until my back is nothing but a mess of rotted, decaying flesh.

I fumble for my pack. How I managed to secure it to the saddle in my delirium without dumping the whole thing, I don't know. My fingers hunt for the tin of salve, and it takes me longer than it should to find it. My hands are shaking, but I manage to scoop some of the black cream out before stuffing the tin safely away. I feel every muscle and nerve in my body protest as I arch back and rub the salve over the wound. It burns. *Gods, does it burn.* Muffled cries try to spill from my lips, but I bite down hard, stifling the noise. The salve has never felt like this. I tell myself it's a good sign, *a sign of healing*, when I know it isn't.

The world spins for a minute as nausea rolls through me. I lean over and tilt my head off the side of the horse like I might puke. The feeling passes but not for long. I'm swaying, and I force myself to grip the reins with white knuckles.

I will not fall off this horse. I will not die here.

My vision speckles black as I lift my head. I want to slump back over the saddle and sleep but stop myself when I see that the barren horizon in front of me has grown darker. My brow pinches, and I lean forward to get a better look. It comes together in blurred shapes I can't seem to understand. One large mass. No, two. The one on the right moves away. I lose it as my head bobs wildly. The world is spinning again. I mumble something incoherent, my own words lost to me.

Like a tumbling boulder, my body slumps forward. The horse startles but settles as I curl against its neck. The wind flitters by, brushing the silky, honey-white mane against my cheek. My eyelids droop heavily, and then fly open with a distant panic.

Those are people.

I try to pry myself up but can't. From the corner of my eye, I see a silhouette of black against the horizon. It's walking, getting closer. My heart picks up its pace, but I fail to do anything about it. Slurred mumblings drift from my lips as the heat and the pain continue to ravage me.

The person gets close enough to where I can see the shape of them now. Broad shoulders seem to block out the sun. Nothing but the flash of hazel eyes is visible among the draped swaths of beige and tan that shield them from the heat. I try to search those eyes, looking for a hint of danger, but my eyelids flutter once more, and darkness swallows me. I feel like I'm sinking into nothingness, and yet, I'm really sinking. My husk of a body snaps awake in panic as I realize I'm sliding off the saddle.

I fumble against the reins, scrape my hand against the pommel, but it's too late. The deep rumble of a voice is all I hear before the sand greets me in a rough embrace. It swallows me whole. My body sinks into its curves and crevices like Veles himself has sent for me.

The voice around me gets louder, then splits in two. I'm a boneless heap in the sand as the sun stops shining. I force my eyes open to find someone standing over me, blocking out the sun with those broad shoulders once more. They lean closer, hands reaching for me, as the darkness closes in and everything, at last, goes black.

CHAPTER 13

Distant, murmured voices. I hear those first.

The muddled chattering of their words seems miles away. I'm dreaming, or at least I think I'm dreaming. Everything is black, but slowly, memory trickles in. *The desert.* I was in the desert with a gaping hole for a side thanks to Olen. I'm hurt. Or maybe I'm dead.

What I feel next dismisses the notion. Numb, tingling limbs. Achey and tired. Then the soft throb of pain that grows steadier the more I acknowledge it. Not dead. Alive. Very much alive.

Something cool prickles on my brow, then slides down my cheek in a slick drop. I try to move, but everything alights in fresh pain. I wince and grit my teeth, forcing through it as my fingers grip something soft. My mind spins, trying to piece it all together among the onslaught of pain and ache. I remember the voices just as they quiet around me. Everything goes silent.

My eyes shoot open. I wince, bracing against the daylight that slams into my vision. A wet towel slides off my forehead and onto my lap. As my eyes adjust, I see it. The figure. I thought it was a dream but it's not—*he's* not. Broad shoulders roll back as a heated gaze meets mine. He stalks the short distance across the tent, and I see it for what it is. A threat.

I reel away, fumbling for something—anything. The glint of silver lying on the small table to my right appears like an answered prayer. I dive for the knife, shoving away from the mess of blankets I've been carefully tucked into. My back roars in pain, flesh ripping, but I stretch past my discomfort to reach it. Just as I curl my fingers around the hilt, I find a sword angled at my throat. My breath stills as I look up at the man, feel the force of his gaze and the slight prick of the blade against my neck.

"For fuck's sake, Hassan."

A woman slips into view, coming to stand behind the glaring man. My gaze passes between them quickly, my body not daring to move. The sword's blade still rests at my throat and my own weapon is still clutched in my hand.

"She just broke her fever and has no idea where she is."

I eye her curiously. There's something in her hands, supplies of some sort. Bandages. Tinctures. She's a little older than me by the looks of it. Maybe somewhere in her thirties. Her short, brown hair is shaved on one side, revealing a long scar that runs from the back of her skull to the tip of her ear.

She swats the sword away and glares at the man next to her. "How would you feel if you woke up with a blade at your throat?" she argues.

"*She* reached for a blade first," he stresses. He makes sure to send a deathly glare at me before addressing his companion once more. "She shows up dressed like a warrior, bleeding, and then lunges for a weapon the minute she wakes. We don't know who she is." I see his jaw muscle ripple under the strain of how hard he's clenching his teeth. "We just know *what* she is."

I tighten my grip on the knife.

"Gods above, you're as bad as the Turidens," the woman grumbles. "Are you going to suggest we kill her just because she's a daemon?"

The hand gripping my knife shakes. There's little I truly fear in this world, but mention of the Turidens sends a nervous shiver up my spine. They're glorified murderers—zealots who hide among the masses and seek to return any daemon they encounter back to the earth. Our presence to them is a blight on the Continent. I hope to never come across one ever again, but if I do, I won't mourn the blood I spill.

"Daemons are not to be trusted, Savi," the man argues. "I think you of all people would understand that."

"You don't know her."

"And neither do you," he spits back. "Which is why we should be rid of her."

"And what do you—"

The woman's words muffle in my ears as I reel up like a swarm of locusts. Everything else in the tent falls away. It's just me and *him*. The knife slips through the air fluidly, guided by my practiced hand as I find my target. I catch his eyes widen just before we collide. The man staggers backward, evading my blow at the last second. Unfortunately, the only result my efforts provide is a bloody nick on his forearm.

The clash of metal rings through my eardrums as he finally raises his sword. My body trembles against the pain and ache of my wounds. I try to parry the man's blows, but my strength gives out, and his sword makes quick work of the small knife curled in my grip. My wrist flexes against the pressure of his strike. The force shoots a prickle of fiery nerves through my hand that I can't bear.

I drop the knife, losing it in the tangled mess of blankets at my feet. My heart thunders in my chest, eyes wide and feral. I already know I've lost. The prick of his blade against my chest is an odious reminder.

As I raise my gaze to meet my opponent's, I see my own hate mirrored in his eyes.

"*Enough*," he grunts. "I am in no mood to clean your blood from this tent."

I move to step forward, pressing against the threat of his blade. My body protests; it feels like fire is seeping from my flesh. My brow furrows, knotted in pain as my eyes flicker uncertainly. I blindly reach a hand around my back. My fingers are coated with blood as I bring them up to my face.

"Hael, help me," the man grumbles. "It would have been less trouble if we'd left you to die."

The woman I'd all but forgotten about mumbles a curse before turning toward me.

"Ignore my cousin; he can be a real prick sometimes." She considers me—taking in my ragged breath, hands curled into fists, blood still dripping off my fingers—and sighs. "We're not going to hurt you," she offers. "Don't let Hassan's lack of manners make you believe otherwise."

I hold her gaze steadily. Her eyes are softer than her companion's—than Hassan's. Where his are all anger and heat, hers are playful. Kind, even. I can feel my pulse pounding under my skin as time ticks away slowly. Every instinct is telling me to rush them, to run. But something else flickers among the unease rolling in my stomach. It goes against everything I learned growing up on the Continent. For some reason, I trust her. My head dips in a curt nod before I uncurl my fists.

"Good." She smiles. "Now let me check your bandage. I'm fairly certain you ripped your stitches out."

I stiffen as she approaches, and she notices. She moves slower now, like I'm an animal backed into a corner. She offers another smile, and I have to remind myself that as stubborn as I am, I can't reach the wound to clean it myself. I swallow dryly as she guides me to sit. She quickly eyes Hassan and without even a word passing between them, he leans down and snatches the fallen knife out of my reach. Every movement of the woman's is careful and deliberate, like she knows I might take back the trust I lent her any minute. Gingerly, she reaches for my back, and I lean forward to give her better access to the wound. My teeth bear down as the cut flares with pain.

"I'm Savi," she says as she rolls up the back of my tunic and begins to work. "You've already met my charming cousin, Hassan..."

She chuckles and gestures to the man, but I don't bother looking up. My eyes are fixed on the blanket. I track every tug and press of her hands. The entire time, my body stays rigid. Friendly or not, my trust only goes so far.

"Ren," I offer, my voice nothing more than a gruff whisper.

"Well, Ren," she starts, "whatever happened to your back, it's not pretty."

I flinch as she peels the damp, blood-soaked bandage away. The air flow is equal parts bliss and torture against my skin.

"What happened?"

The question is simple enough, though I can't help but feel the weight of it. "Dagger," I say flatly. "Ran into some bad people in the city."

Not quite a lie.

She's fumbling with fresh bandages, but her words come too slow, too casual. "What city?"

She's just as nervous as I am. For good reason. Strangers can become enemies just as fast as this desert can turn on you. *Kill or be killed.* I take too long, struggling to think of what cities are nearby. But I don't know where I've ended up or how long it took to get here.

"Denheir," I admit.

Her hands still for a second. I hold my breath, body poised for a fight. I keep my head low, but my eyes shift across the room to Hassan. His gaze is locked on Savi's as a silent conversation seems to pass between them.

Finally, Savi resumes her tending. "Wild place, Denheir," she mumbles. "Doesn't surprise me that you ran into some trouble."

I wait for more, but it doesn't come. Just as the tension in my body starts to unfurl, Hassan shifts his weight and snatches my attention. When I meet his gaze, that sneering face has only gotten more hostile.

"What are you?"

His words cut into me and I can't keep the scowl off my face.

"A woman," I spit out.

Savi laughs as her fingers gently tug at the cord stitched into my back. Every light touch feels like the press of a hot ember, but I don't flinch—not while he's watching. He's not as amused as his cousin, not even a little bit.

"What kind of *daemon* are you?" The word rolls off his tongue like a curse, like saying the very thing might bind him to Veles.

"You can't tell?" I taunt.

His upper lip twitches. "I have never bothered to learn what the different markings mean," he says, waving a hand toward my neck. "It doesn't make a difference what your curse is." He sneers. "Just that you have one."

"So why bother asking?" I snap. My gaze narrows on him but the heat in my eyes wavers as Savi wraps a fresh bandage across my wound. I flinch.

"I want to know what I'm dealing with. Want to know what kind of danger I've brought into my camp."

"Oh, would you fuck off, Hassan," Savi grumbles from behind me.

I feel the gentle tug of my tunic falling back into place before she stands.

"She's not some cursed creature."

Savi casually hands me a canteen as she glares at the man across from us. I barely listen to the words spitting from her lips as I snatch it with greedy hands and drink. The water is warm, but the moisture coating my throat has me feeling reborn.

"She's a person, just like you." Savi shoots a mischievous look my way. "Only more badass because she can see into the future."

I stop drinking, water dribbling off my chin. There's no hungry desire in her gaze. No hate. No fear. Only delight. I'm still staring at her as she turns back to Hassan.

"So, stop being such a dick, or I'll be the one to tell you the future." She shoves her cousin roughly. "And that future will be my arrow up your ass."

She shoots me a wicked grin. Hassan scoffs, rolling his eyes. It's the most docile he's looked since I woke up, but I don't dare let myself think he's accepted my presence here. I size him up quickly as he stalks out of the tent. He's tall and broad. I've taken down men his size, but my eyes catch on his arms, bare and on display in the sleeveless tunic he's wearing. Thick muscle cords his biceps. There's an assortment of scars marring his tan skin—some old, some fresh. His wavy, dark brown hair flows to his shoulders. Down his back, sheathed diagonally, rests a sword. My teeth grind together as I remember how it felt to have it pressed against my throat mere minutes ago. *How would he feel—I wonder—to be on the end of my blade, instead?* My gaze tightens as I catch one last glimpse of those harsh, hazel eyes. He shoots me a vicious look before slipping from view.

"Finish that water." Savi smirks.

I wipe the venomous look off my face, but it's too late. She caught me staring down her cousin like I might toss a blade into his back. *I might, but she doesn't need to know that.*

She nods to the canteen. "We found a well nearby so there's plenty to go around."

Savi looks at me steadily, and there's something I'm not used to swimming behind her eyes. Silence beats for a second, and my skin itches against my own uncertainty. I wait for the smile to fall from her face, for hatred and anger to finally emerge from the kindness on display, but it doesn't. Restlessness stirs my limbs.

"How about I bring you some food in a bit, and you can tell me how you ended up here?"

All I can manage to do is nod. Her frame disappears behind the tent's flaps but my voice races after her. "Savi."

She pops back in, brow raised.

"Thanks."

Her head tilts, and a smile quirks up the corner of her lips. "Get some rest," she says. "I'll be back soon."

CHAPTER 14

I had enough rest under Rohan's watch, and I don't plan on making the same mistakes twice. The minute Savi left the tent, I chugged the rest of the water and began searching for my things. It didn't take me long to find my pack. They didn't take my blades, a fact that settles my uneasy feelings—momentarily, at least. I've sheathed Olen's dagger in the front part of my harness, the blade he graciously threw into my back. The larger one I stole from Rohan is sheathed at my thigh. I can understand why Hassan was wary. Not a lot of nomads wear their weapons so brazenly. Most confine their blades under layers of scarves and tunics, feigning innocence until the need to prove otherwise presents itself. But some of us don't have the luxury of looking harmless. Some of us need to be a threat in order to stay alive.

I pull my pack closer and take inventory. I still have Mikel's salve. My fingers barely graze the tin before the aching twinge in my chest forces me to push it away. I know Mikel will have gone back to our ransacked camp to scavenge supplies for the others.

It's something he would do; helping others is his nature. I can only hope he stayed with them and wasn't reckless enough to follow my tracks. *If he comes looking for me and Rohan finds him...*

I swallow harshly and continue digging through my bag. I found some extra bandages in the tent and added them to my things. The canteen, too. It's empty now but will come in handy if I can find that well Savi mentioned. I rifle through the rest. There's clothes and a small amount of coin that I'm surprised Olen or Harkin didn't steal.

I still as I touch the last item that rests at the bottom of my pack. My fingertips run over the cool metal, feeling the raised line of shadowy pigment that I know runs through it. *Think of it as a good luck charm. A piece of me that's always with you.* The words spear my heart as memory bubbles up. I drop the ring and look up as I hear rustling from the front of the tent.

Savi saunters in, two plates balanced in her hands. She stops, quirking a brow as she looks over my holstered weapons and the pack that rests at my feet. "You were going to run off without eating anything?"

There's a moment of silence before a rumbling laugh leaves her chest. She shakes her head and sets the food down.

"And here I thought we were going to be friends."

My words catch in my throat. I stare at her, then the meal. Steam wafts up from two wooden plates in a heavenly cloud. There's a small bowl of stew and a hunk of bread on each. She looks at me expectantly, amusement still flecking the hazel eyes that match her cousin's. With a breathy laugh, she gestures toward the food. "Well, go on. Eat something."

I hesitate before the shuddering grumble of my stomach makes the decision for me. I grab the plate and manage to sit down before all civility leaves me. The minute the bowl touches my lips, I'm devouring every drop. The stew is warm and rich, filled with small pieces of meat and vegetables. I force myself to pull the bowl away and take a breath before I drown in my fervor.

"I haven't seen anyone that hungry since Kai got food poisoning and couldn't eat for two days." She laughs. Savi sits on the pile of blankets across from me and begins eating her own stew. "He was so ravenous I swear he ate a week's worth of rations in a single day."

I tear off a piece of bread and chew silently. Her eyes drift to my open pack, and my body stills when I notice the bandages peeking out.

She shoots me a teasing look, clearly seeing the guilt riddled across my face. "I would have given you those if you'd asked."

"I—" My breath falters in a tangle of excuses in my throat.

She levels a careful look at me. "We're not all the same, you know."

There's nothing rough in her tone, nothing stern or demeaning. It's then that I see it in her eyes, the thing I couldn't place earlier. Compassion.

She bites a chunk of bread, smiling again. "So, tell me," she mumbles between bites. "You show up covered in blood..."

My eyes wander down my body and stop at the dried red that's caked on my tunic. It's Rohan's blood, but she doesn't need to know that—not when the back of my shirt is stained with my own.

"...fitted with Kupor-made blades, which—no offense" — she holds up her hands — "are definitely not yours."

I smirk, thinking how much I cost Rohan by stealing his dagger—Olen's, too. The weapons forged in Kupor are some of the best on the Continent. Quality metal with intricate engravings that distract for only a moment before the perfectly honed blade slips into your skin. Kupor-made blades are the only thing that kills as greatly as it costs. I enjoyed ramming that blade into Rohan's gut, probably more than I should have. It almost made everything all right. Almost like retribution paid in full. There is nothing more shameful than having your own blade turned on you. *I hope he feels that shame now.* It's only when I remember how his voice bellowed after me that the smile slips from my lips.

"Although those leathers look like they were tailored just for you."

Savi's voice is distant as my thoughts drift and my stomach churns. I feel Rohan's blade, the one safely strapped at my thigh, sliding under my skin. I feel every cut he inflicted across my arms like I'm still back in that room. I feel the damp chill of the cellar, the strain of the darkness as it floods my vision.

"Who knows... maybe you're more than capable of dropping some coin on a couple of blades. But something tells me you're not some rich merchant..."

It's like I can still taste the ale on my tongue.

"...not with those markings on your neck. Again, no offense."

I feel the rough stone floor under my sweating palms, hear the clank of chains. Nausea roils in my stomach, threatening to slink up my throat. I feel like I can't catch my breath.

"You okay?"

I realize I've stopped eating, and my whole body has gone rigid. A phantom feeling—the touch of Rohan's strong, unyielding hands—has tightened around my throat. I manage a deep breath, shaking myself from my thoughts. "Fine," I utter, though I can't meet her gaze.

She watches me curiously as I force myself to finish the stew. I pause every so often to dip the bread into the warm liquid. It's the only noise that fills the tent for a long while. As I bring a spoonful to my mouth, I feel the heaviness of her words before I hear them.

"What happened?"

I can't bear to look up and meet her gaze. My fingers drift absentmindedly over the unhealed cuts that cover my arms. Mikel's salve helped a great deal, but the skin is still red and angry. It's not deep enough to warrant stitches but with the way Rohan sliced me up, I know it'll scar.

"Just got caught up in something I shouldn't have. That's all."

I swallow the half-truth down with my last piece of stew-soaked bread. She says nothing, and I make a point to focus on the food, finishing the rest quickly. I keep my eyes low. I know what I'll see if I look up. Pity. Disgust. Anything she could feel for me is too much, too personal. It won't change what has passed or what is to come.

Savi shifts, and I'm relieved, thinking she's grown bored of my silence and will leave me be. My heart drops into my stomach as she reaches across the blanket. I flinch, fingers grazing the hilt of my dagger, but all she does is take the empty plate from my lap.

"It's okay. You don't have to tell me now." Savi collects the dishes and gets up to leave, but not before giving my pack a lingering look. She bites down softly on her lip as if debating the words that are about to slip. "I understand if you want to leave," she says. "You don't know us, and by the gods, my cousin made sure to fuck up a first impression."

She lets out a deep breath and her gaze momentarily hardens. "But you're in no shape to travel, and we're days from any outpost—unless you want to go back to Denheir. But judging by..."

She stops herself, and I reluctantly meet her gaze.

"I doubt you're eager to go back, is all I'm saying."

The mention of Denheir makes my skin grow hot and clammy. It all flashes through my mind once more. The cellar. The chair. Rohan's boot crashing against my ribs. My teeth dig into the inside of my cheek.

Savi is silent, like she's just bared witness to every horror racing through my mind. My jaw locks. I don't know what's worse, a stranger's pity or the fact that Rohan broke me in a few days' time. I'm stronger than this, or at least I thought I was.

Savi hovers in the doorway, her eyes fixed on me like she wants to say more. But before she can, I pull my eyes from her and drag my pack closer. I'm fumbling for nothing but a distraction when her voice finds me.

"Travel with us for a few days—longer if you want," she adds. "Give yourself the time you need to rest and heal. You can trust us. I promise."

The word rings in my ears. *Trust.* Trust is earned, not given. But she's right. I'm in no condition to travel on my own right now. Although the food in my belly has given me strength, every inch of my body still thrums in pain. Whether I move or just breathe, the ache and the sting is there, a constant reminder of my condition. This desert is unkind. I can't defend myself, not in this state. Even pointing that knife at Hassan made my body scream in protest. I grit my teeth and realize all I'm able to do is what she asks of me. Stay and *trust.*

I nod, and a smile I'm beginning to get familiar with dances across her face. The joy pulls high into her sharp cheekbones.

"Good," she states. "We're on a job but need to resupply in Hira first. It's almost a week's journey. Once we get there, we can see how you're feeling."

I take a deep breath and nod again. *A week?* I can do a week. It's not like I'm unfamiliar with traveling with strangers. It's been the story of my life since my first mark showed up, and my mother, *Veles-curse-her-soul,* tossed me onto the street like a vermin infesting her home. But the streets had been kinder to me than they were to most. I'd had *him* after all.

I stop my mind from slipping into dark, familiar corners as I look back at Savi. There's one thing I've come to learn about surviving the Continent. It's not about making friends. It's about keeping your enemies few and far between. Considering how I just left Denheir, I'm in no place to be reckless now. I can manage a week on my best behavior. *Right?* All I need to do is keep to myself, rest, and be ready to leave once we get to the city.

Hira. My mind wanders. I've heard of the place. Though it's smaller than other major cities like Artolen, it's a trading hub. It'll have everything I need in order to head north. But where do I go from there? *Raulik, maybe?* It's not far enough north, but it's a start. *How far is far enough? Will Kanti even be safe for me?* I'll have to look at my map later, see where the hand-drawn outpost markings fade into blank swatches of nothing. That's where I need to go—into the nothing, the nowhere. The untouched sands where not even a fool would venture. Only a desperate one. Rohan will never find me there.

My chest flutters with a dash of hope before a nagging thought stops it from growing. "You said you were on a job," I ask, my gaze tightening. "A job doing what?"

There's a hesitation to Savi's response that sets me on edge. I study her face, my fingers tingling in anticipation. *Can I unsheathe a blade faster than she can react?*

Finally, she answers. "We're tracking a bounty. They were last seen somewhere near the southeastern ridge of the Kohe Mountains, heading into the Jahaer."

My stomach drops, but I keep the uneasiness from slipping across my face. *Bounty hunters.* I'm all too aware of the unfamiliar weight of the dagger strapped to my chest and the one that rests against my thigh now. They're heavier than the blades I'm used to. The draw won't be as quick or fluid. I size up Savi, just as I did her cousin. She's about my same height, but she's stronger, I can just tell. Her body is lean yet packed with muscle. She's solid and powerful. I look at the scar running from the back of her head to her ear, but this time, I see it in a new light. It's brutal, but old. There are no others that mar her flesh. None that I can see. She's obviously learned from whatever mistake found it carved there. I see no blades on her, but that doesn't mean they're not there.

When I look back up at her, there's a smirk curling the corner of her mouth. One predator admiring the other.

"We're leaving in the morning at first light. If you're not up, I'll come and wake you." She looks me over, just as I had done to her a few moments ago. "Just promise me you won't slit my throat when I do."

I can't help but smirk back. "Maybe throw something at me first," I offer. "I tend to... wake violently."

"How could I forget?" Savi laughs. "This tent is yours for the night. I'll make my miserable cousin share his with me."

She turns on her heels to leave and slips from view before I can respond. I watch the flap of the tent flutter behind her. The sun is setting. Another day has passed since I left Denheir, but how long ago was that? *Two days? Three?* How long will it take Rohan to find me? Maybe he'll cut his loses and hope another Seer crosses his path.

I lay back on the bedroll and sigh. Pain immediately shoots through my back, making me wince. I grumble and swear, trying to find a more comfortable position. Everything hurts, and I finally accept that tonight's rest will not be a pleasant one.

I leave the dagger strapped to my thigh but loosen the harness and slip it from my shoulders. As kind as Savi seems, I can't trust her. I yank the dagger free and tuck it close to my side. My fingers grip the hilt, and somehow, I feel better. My breath begins to settle into a rhythmic lull in my chest. But soon enough, noises from outside the tent rip me back to consciousness and ruin any chance of peace. It's the sound of taunting and laughter. Bright, drunk voices dance through the night. I can hear the crackle of a fire. The scrape of a pan.

I try to focus my mind and decipher how many people might be out there, but I can't keep track of all the voices. I sigh and force myself to close my eyes, fingers still locked around the dagger. The noises outside begin to lessen and fade as my mind drifts. I think of the desert—of the stories Zoah's son used to tell about his travels to the farthest corners. He'd spin wild, dark tales about the northern part of the Jahaer Desert. In all my years of wandering with no clear direction other than away from the cities I once called home, I'd never made it up there. I always stayed far, far away—even before I heard the tales Maurit told around the fire. That part of the desert is old, filled with things best left alone.

But Maurit had brought all of the drunken rumblings and rumors I'd heard to life, shining light on those places so rarely touched. He told of creatures that burrowed under the sand, ready to strike. Creatures that lurked in caverns and crevices. Things that made hekkriti lizards look like stray dogs. He said he'd walked through places that seemed to want to keep you there. Places where you could feel the magic of the gods in the earth. He said there were people out there, too, living among it all—if he is to be believed, that is.

Part of me thought I'd never see those places, never be foolish enough to tempt my fate. *But now?* Now, I may have run out of places to hide from the world. I have too many enemies and not enough friends, it seems. Maybe I'm best out there in the nothing, with only beasts to keep me company. After all the blood I've spilled, am I not a beast, too? Maybe the gods are calling me to that unholy land. Maybe they're calling me home.

My back throbs. I toss and turn to get comfortable, but it's no use. A chill breaks out over my skin. The cuts across my body and the gash on my back feel like they're on fire, but I surrender to the fever. I shrug off the blankets and feel the cooling touch of the wind as it picks up and drifts into my tent. I'm unsettled, drifting halfway between sleep and reality. Tossing and turning and tossing some more.

I groan softly, opening my eyes to see that the sun has finally settled under the horizon. Fatigue pulls at me, giving way to distant, wild thoughts of what may be lurking under the very sands I sleep on. Chills pebble across my skin as the wind becomes a steady companion in the night. My body settles, pain subsiding.

Finally, sleep comes—but not before the image of sifting sand fills my mind. I can almost feel the shiny, black claw of the beast as it breaks the surface and threatens to pull me under. Everything fades away into nothing, and I sink into a delirious sleep with a pounding heart and sweat on my brow.

CHAPTER 15

Breath rips through me as I jerk awake. I feel nothing but panic as I curl my fingers around my dagger and thrust upward. I hear the laugh before my eyes fully adjust to the low light of the tent.

"Shit," Savi utters. "I'm glad I decided to throw a pillow instead of tapping you on the shoulder." She saunters over and offers me a full canteen. "Otherwise, I might have a new scar right about now."

My heart is still thrashing as I take the canteen from her. I don't drop the dagger as I lift the water to my lips and drink. It takes me a moment to remind myself where I am. *Back in the desert. Not Denheir. Not that cellar.* It's hard to shake the nerves that are running rampant through my body, but the look on Savi's face helps. She's amused, unaware of the nightmare she pulled me from.

The canyon, *again.* I'd barely made it a step further this time before I'd been sucked under the sand. But it didn't end there, not as it usually does. I fell and fell and fell until I was in a dark pit of nothing. The darkness licked at me, sent chills up my spine. I waited for his voice, but it didn't come. He didn't come.

Savi clears her throat, pulling my attention. A few beads of water slide over my lips and drip onto the blankets as I look up at her. I'm clearly not a morning person; at least she knows that now.

"Sorry for the..." I mutter, gesturing around me. "Old habits."

The amusement slips from her face. It's replaced by something rigid and all too knowing. I look away before she asks a question I'm not willing to answer.

"Are we leaving now?" I ask as casually as I can.

She reaches down and grabs the empty canteen from me, not at all fazed by the blade still held firmly in my grasp.

"Not yet, but soon. I wanted to wake you so you could eat and meet the others before we head out."

Uncertainty slithers through my stomach. For a moment, I had forgotten that it wasn't just Savi here. There are others. *Her cousin.* I grit my teeth, doing a poor job of mustering a smile as she turns back to me.

"And how many of you are there?" The question comes off stilted and cold and I regret my words instantly.

Savi just raises a brow and smirks. "Why? Still looking to fight your way out of here?"

I open my mouth, but she cuts me off.

"There are six of us." She smiles. "And you're not captive here, Ren. We just want to help."

I wonder how Hassan feels about being included in that promise. Peeling myself from the cocoon of blankets, I feel the stitches in my back stretch in protest. My dagger sheathes across my chest with a soft *shush*, and I tap the one at my thigh to make sure it's still there. The gesture is subtle, but I know Savi clocks it. If she's asking for trust, I'll offer it the only way I know how—with reservations.

"Come on," she says, letting out a breathy laugh. "Everyone is eager to meet you."

I raise a brow but follow. When I step out of the tent, I take in a deep, cleansing breath. The sun hasn't fully risen, seeping soft light over the desert. I begin to rub my arms, staving off the night's lingering chill. The gnarled flesh under my fingertips is a cruel reminder of how I got here in the first place.

My eyes snap down to my bare skin and the cuts covering them. Something foul churns in my gut as I stare at the mutilated lines of flesh. Before I can slip back into my tent to grab something to cover up, Savi reaches out to me. Her touch is gentle, ghosted against my shoulder. She looks at me with a flicker of compassion that threatens to soften my hardest edges. The feeling sways my gut uneasily, and I lurch away.

"We've got more than our fair share of scars around here," she offers. "You're in good company."

I nod silently, rolling my shoulder as if I can erase the kindness of her touch. She leads me to a small fire amidst the spread of their camp. My eyes wander, scanning for threats. Unlike Zoah's camp, where we only had two tents to share between us, I count four large tents spread across the sand. Off a ways rests a slew of camels and horses. Luckily, I see my mare among them. Something in my chest settles a bit as I follow Savi the rest of the way. *I can leave whenever I want*, I remind myself. I'm not a prisoner here.

That comfort is quickly snuffed out as I glance across the fire and see Hassan. He's eating, but that doesn't stop him from glaring at me while he does so. I shoot back a heated look of my own before Savi's voice pulls my focus.

"Everyone, this is Ren," she announces. "In case you were too busy playing cards to hear what I said last night" — Savi's gaze pierces two men sitting across the fire. Her brow raises as they beam wicked smiles back at her — "she's going to be joining us along to Hira."

As everyone's attention locks on me, I look them over one by one. There are five people sitting around the fire. All men. I stand up a little taller, my fingers brushing the dagger at my side. The two men Savi scolded are still grinning wildly. They sit there whispering to each other, plates of food forgotten in their laps.

"That's Kai." Savi gestures to the one with long black hair. It's pulled back into a messy bun like he just rolled out of bed.

He nods at me before resuming his breakfast. "Nice blades," he mumbles through a mouthful, smiling all the while.

My eyes dart past his face to the two curved swords strapped to his back. Their holsters cross each other, raising the hilts just above his lean, muscular shoulders.

"Thanks," I say steadily.

The other grinning fiend shoves Kai back playfully, giving himself an unobstructed view of me. "I'm Riat." His gaze runs down my leathers, a roguish look glinting in his golden-brown eyes. "That hekkriti leather?" He whistles. "Didn't know it could look that good. But then again I've never seen it on a goddess before."

"For fuck's sake," Savi utters. She shakes her head and throws the empty canteen at him. "Leave her be. She doesn't need any of your nonsense."

"I was just being friendly." Riat gives Savi an innocent look before winking at me.

I let out a soft laugh and let my eyes run over him in return. His skin is tanner than Kai's, though the mischievous spirit they both boast makes them seem like brothers. Like Kai, his hair is pulled back into a bun. The deep brown locks are pulled taut, and the sides are shaven down to the skin. For a moment, I think I spot a marking near his ear, but it's just a fresh cut from a clean shave. He has eight small throwing knives sheathed along his belt.

Interesting. My eyes catch on the scar that curves from his cheek through his full lips. His smile only deepens at the attention.

One of the other men quickly breaks the moment between us. "You're a daemon?"

I turn toward the voice, blood running cold. My body tenses into a knot of anxiety as I look at the man speaking to me. He's much larger than the other two. My gaze drops to his massive hands as he works steadily to sharpen a blade. My fingers practically flex against my own weapon in anticipation. But the look on his face isn't filled with hate like Hassan's. There's a serenity crinkled in the corners of his eyes. It catches me off guard, and I stand there silently, trying to make sense of the calm aura that's attached to the boulder of a man in front of me.

"My aunt was a daemon." A faint smile drifts across his face. It's careful, like he can see the tension riddled in my shoulders.

I open my mouth but still can't find the words. I look at him, but this time, I ignore the bulk of his muscles and the numerous scars carved into his dark skin. I ignore the blade he's sharpening and the two others sheathed at his waist. Instead, I take in his soft brown eyes. I take in the neatly trimmed facial hair and the small gold jewelry decorating his ears. I take in the man in front of me as he is—not as the threat he could be.

Finally, I'm able to speak. "What gift did she have?"

"Berserker," he answers. The slight curve of his lips has dipped into a full smile now. "As a kid, all I wanted was to be like her. Man..." He sighs. "...Could she fight. It didn't matter their size or how well they wielded a blade. She took down whoever and whatever. Utterly invincible."

He lets out a breathy laugh and goes back to sharpening his blade. "She always told me it didn't matter how big your opponent was or how outnumbered you were. The tides can always turn in your favor; you need only be relentless in the desire for your next breath."

His eyes search my own. I fidget amidst the depth of his stare.

"Something tells me you know exactly what I'm talking about."

My mouth grows dry as I swallow down emotions I refuse to name.

"That's Tariq," Savi chimes in.

I nod, unable to speak. He nods back before returning to his knife.

"And that," Savi says, pulling my attention again, "is Vish."

I follow Savi's gesture across the fire to the man sitting next to Hassan, careful not to look at my new enemy in the process. Vish looks up from his journal, but no greeting slips from his lips.

The silence between us makes my muscles twitch. Unlike the others, I see no weapons on him. He's the smallest of the group but his eyes are as sharp as daggers. He watches me from under thick brows. I can tell by the way his eyes scan over me, brutal with focus, that he's trying to figure me out. He chews up every bit of me and spits it out. But he's not looking at the daggers or Rohan's handiwork or even my marks. No, there's something more calculated about the way he's sizing me up. I can barely keep myself from shifting on my feet as his scrutiny gnaws at me.

I look over him once more, double checking for weapons. *Nothing, not even a small knife at his waist.* All I see is the gold ring on his left hand and the journal on his lap. Thick, black hair trails down his back in a tight braid. A few strands have slipped free, framing his angular face in wispy pieces. The others are like me—draped in blades, decorated with scars. But not him. Sweat breaks out across the back of my neck.

Vish's gaze narrows on me. "You're a Seer, yes?"

I don't flinch. I don't break away from his gaze. I simply stare back into those dark, unnerving green eyes of his. "Yes."

"How interesting."

I watch the rigid flex of his jaw as he continues to observe me. His eyes are locked on my markings now. "Unusual to come across someone with your gift," he comments. "Not many Seers left on the Continent."

My fingers rap against the leather of my harness. The steady drum of it quickens with the beat of my heart. "I wonder why that is," I grit out.

The implication of my words hangs in the air unanswered. His fingers tap against his journal, almost nervously. "Where are you from?"

I eye him curiously and look him over once more. He's wearing a long tunic, sleeves billowing past his wrists. The neck is high, protecting him from the sun's growing rays. Nothing about him is threatening, but looks can be deceiving.

"North," I offer coldly.

Vish tilts his head. "A Seer from up north." He mutters the words, almost if they're just for himself.

His gaze is fixed on me so intently I swear his pupils flicker and pulse. The stare he gives me is vacant. My brow furrows as I wait for the unsettling moment between us to break. He looks at me for only a second longer before his face shifts. Something akin to surprise settles in his eyes before it's shaken loose. He blinks repeatedly, as if coming back to himself.

"Ren," he offers. "Is that short for anything?"

A deep, empty ache fills my chest. "No," I lie. "It's just Ren."

He looks me up and down once more before pulling his journal closer. He mutters to himself and flips through the tattered pages quickly. He says no more, offers no explanation. I can't help but feel as though my sum of enemies just went up by one.

Savi clears her throat, and as I look back at her, there's an uncomfortable heat on her cheeks. "Okay, well...." She lets out an uneasy laugh. "You've already met my cousin, Hassan."

I let Savi's words float in the air, untouched for a minute. Hassan is still glaring at me, and I can feel the pressure of it like his blade is once again at my chest. The tension grows until it's an inescapable heat under my skin. My heart pounds as I stare at him, and he stares at me. I know I shouldn't care, but the need to wipe that look off his face swells inside me. I grit my teeth and flash a feline smile.

"Yes." I tilt my chin up before letting a scoff slip from my breath. "Unfortunately, I've met the ornery old goat."

It's louder than I meant it, and a deadly beat of silence hangs around the fire. It lingers like a plague, and just as I think I've made a grave error, laughter rips through the air.

Kai is cackling so hard, his plate clatters from his lap. Though he tries to hide it, I see a secretive smile slip from Tariq.

"Oh, gods. This is going to be good," Riat snickers, eyes flashing devilishly.

Hassan's jaw clenches. "I would watch your tone, *witch*," he rasps. "While Savi may be the one offering you protection, I'm the one in charge here."

I step closer to him, unsheathing the dagger from my thigh with a quick flick. Everyone around me tenses. If Hassan is concerned, he doesn't let it show. He stays seated, glaring hotly.

The anger pounding through me is loud enough to block out any sense I have left. "And what makes you think I need protection?"

His eyes flare in response. He stands quickly, despite muttered objections from Vish. I hold my ground, and the grip on my blade grows tighter with every step he takes. He's taller than I thought he was. His muscles seem to flex and ripple under his tunic as he stalks around the fire to reach me. I plant my feet in the sand and raise my dagger steadily as we come face to face.

"Are you really this foolish?" he baits me.

I raise the blade a little higher, now level with his throat. "I've dealt with far worse things than you."

He doesn't draw his weapon, nor does he make so much as a move for me. Instead, he watches me with those angry eyes until I can feel sweat coating the hilt of my dagger.

"Hassan," Savi barks.

"What's it going to be, *witch*?"

He doesn't back down, only takes a step closer so that my blade now touches his throat. I glare at him, but I know a bad call when I see one. The wound in my back is burning—still angry despite whatever Savi did to fix me up. There's a vicious twinge along my ribs where Rohan's boot made contact, and my arms are screaming where the barely healed skin is pulling against the strain of my muscles. I might be able to take Hassan on a good day. *But today? Today is far from one of those days.*

It's with clenched teeth and hate in my heart that I lower my blade and resheathe it.

Nothing happens for a heartbeat as Hassan and I continue glaring at each other.

"Well, *that* was tense," Kai states, eyes as wide as his smile. He leans forward and scoops another ladleful of food onto his plate. "Anyone want seconds or...?"

Savi is shaking her head, a flitter of curse words spilling from her mouth. "Kai, fix her a plate before you inhale the rest of it. *Please*," she orders before turning to Hassan.

She gives him a stern look, raising her brow. "Ren is my guest, cousin. And while I don't doubt she can handle herself, I have no problem stepping in to remind you how we treat our guests."

Hassan brushes past me, bumping my shoulder on the way. "I'll remember that when she's gotten us all killed, *cousin*," he seethes. He's stalking across the sand toward the tents when he yells back, "Or maybe she'll do it herself."

"Bloody hell," Savi grumbles.

Kai offers me a plate, and while I know I don't deserve it, I take it eagerly. He grins at me, a whisper laced under his breath. "It's not often someone gets under Hassan's skin. I think you'll fit in just fine."

I open my mouth to tell him I don't plan on staying, but he's slinked back across the fire before I have a chance. I let out a soft sigh and start eating.

"Ren, you'll ride up front with me," Savi tells me. "We'll scout the way, and you can tell me all about yourself."

It's a demand, not a request, but I don't argue. I simply nod and scarf down the food as politely as possible, which is hard since my stomach feels like a bottomless pit lately.

"Oh, come on, Savi," Kai drawls. "It's like you're trying to keep her from us." He's already finished his second helping and is digging around the pan for thirds. "I want to get to know her, too. She's clearly a badass. I seriously thought she was going to *stab Hassan*." He laughs incredulously and shakes his head. "Which, I mean, let's be honest. Aren't we all wanting to do that from time to time?"

Savi raises a brow. "I'll pretend I didn't hear that."

"So can she—"

"She's riding with me because I know what pests you'll be to her," Savi states, cutting him off. "An hour with you, and she'll be begging for Hassan's company."

"Maybe you should ask *her* who she wants to ride with," Riat interjects.

"She doesn't need your—" Savi starts.

"We don't bite, I promise," Kai interrupts.

Riat wiggles his eyebrows at me. "Unless you want us to."

"They're like fleas, I swear." Savi groans. "Little pests that you can't get rid of." She lets out a deep sigh and waves them off with her hand. "She's riding with me today. End of story. Now go finish packing. We're leaving soon."

The two men grumble before moving from their seats in the sand. Kai scoops up one more bite from the pan, barely scurrying out of reach as Savi tries to smack him with a rag. He snickers under his breath as he and Riat slip out of sight. As the sun begins its ascent over the horizon, camp itself seems to wake up. Tents are taken down. Horses and camels are watered before we set off. Packs are secured to saddles. Everyone has a part to play, and I take it all in, unsure of my place among the group I've found myself with. Though I know she has things to do, Savi hasn't left my side. She either wants to keep me company or wants to keep me far away from her cousin. As she pats my shoulder and looses a deep breath, I almost feel like it's the former.

"They're an odd bunch, but I promise you, they're good men and loyal to a fault." She smiles softly, gazing across the patch of sand that's now a flattened mess of tents and packs. "Even Hassan."

I try to not prickle at the mention of him. As my eyes drift across camp, I can't help but search for the brooding figure I know I'll find. When I spot him, I all but bristle. He's talking to Vish while loading gear onto various horses and camels. It's only when I see my own pack in his hands that I spring into action. Just as my boot sinks into the sand, Savi stops me with a gentle grip.

"He might be an ass, but he's honest. Your things are untouched and accounted for. I promise."

I swallow harshly, fury alight in my eyes as I watch Hassan strap my pack to the mare I stole in Denheir. Once again, my mind tells me to argue, but something deep in my gut has me believing her.

"So, Hira..." I ask without looking at her, unable to pull my gaze from Hassan. "What's it like?"

"You've never been?"

I shake my head. "The cities are..." My silence hovers in the air. As I raise my gaze to meet hers, I know I don't need to say anything more.

"Yeah," she breathes. "Well... Hira is special. The markets are unbelievable. It's close enough to the coast that they have smoked fish. The best you can get on the Continent without being on the water. And the blades—" She shoots me a knowing look. "They're not Kupor-made, but I think you'll be pleased with the selection."

I smile at the thought of replacing all the knives that Rohan took from me. I should have enough coin for at least one, maybe two blades depending on how well I can barter for them.

The sun warms my face as I look out over the desert, and for the first time in days, I don't feel dread slinking up my skin. It's only a moment, however, before it's replaced by something stronger.

"Why are you doing this?"

Savi cocks her head at me. She opens her mouth but closes it abruptly. She thinks hard, like she doesn't quite know the answer herself. "Because I know that look on your face all too well."

A tiny flicker of panic takes root. I feel myself tensing, trying to rebuild the walls I must have let down somehow. She merely watches me unravel and the depth of her gaze only unnerves me more.

"What look?" I utter briskly.

"Whatever happened—" She stops herself.

Savi's brow furrows before a soft smile drifts across her face. It's then that I notice it. Underneath it all—under the warmth and the beauty and the way her whole face seems to light up when she talks—her eyes hold a gentle sorrow. It burrows deep in my chest, like it knows my own.

"Sometimes you need someone to remind you that you're not alone... that there's more to the Continent than hate and violence."

I can only stare at her as unsaid things cling to the back of my throat. She seems to understand, simply offering me a smile and nodding to where the others are packing up the last of the gear.

"Come on," she offers. "There will be plenty of time to talk."

As I follow, each footfall feels like I'm stepping into something new. Despite the ache in my muscles and the sting of my cuts, I let myself smile, too. Something good is coming and I don't need a vision to sense it. I can feel it in my bones.

CHAPTER 16

I forgot how good it feels to travel, to move across the sand with a destination in mind. My body rocks gently as the mare carries us across the desert. I reach down and scratch her neck, prompting a grateful huff from her. She's rather pleasant, considering I'm not her owner and she's far from where she should be.

"What's her name?"

My head whips toward Savi, startled as I remember it's not just me out here under the baking sun. I give her a hesitant look before clearing my throat. "I, uh—I don't know. I found her in Denheir."

Savi dips her head and smirks, saying nothing but everything all at once.

"Okay, fine." I laugh. "I needed to leave quickly, and she was right there so I... *borrowed* her."

The fiendish look only deepens on her face. "I think *stole* is the word you're looking for."

My cheeks redden as I let out another laugh. "Yes, okay. I stole her. But she doesn't seem too upset about it."

"Not at all." Savi smiles.

Her horse nickers as it matches pace with mine. I don't miss the way its eyes widen or how its ears flatten against its head as it looks at me. *Damn skittish thing.* I'm not even doing anything, just existing. My eyes catch on the thin strips of leather braided through its black mane.

Savi gives it a loving pat. "This is Teak," she beams. "Been with me through everything. Saved my ass on more than one occasion."

The horse huffs as if in agreement. Savi laughs and gives it another pat. I smile to myself and stare out at the desert before me. The moment settles between us like she's an old friend—like we've been here before. There's an uncanny twinge in my chest. I don't let myself think too hard about what that means.

We've been riding for almost an hour now, though it feels longer. The silence and the sand stretches on like it's the only thing to exist in this moment. I can barely hear the faded pitch and lull of voices at my back. We're far ahead of the others; Savi made sure of that. When we set off this morning, she was quick to direct us to the front of the caravan. We've been keeping a steady pace ever since. With the way Hassan was glaring at me when I emerged from my tent, I don't blame Savi. Distrust is all I see when I look into her cousin's harsh, hazel eyes. The heat of Hassan's gaze feels like a threat in itself, and I can't seem to look at him without my hands itching for daggers. Luckily, we made it through the rest of the morning without any weapons being drawn.

I glance back and find the others are still bobbing shapes against the late-morning haze. Something aches heavily in my chest at the sight of camels lugging gear across the desert. I force a deep breath, but memories flood my mind before I can stop them. I think of the way Zoah's daughter, Elphi, always sang softly in the mornings, humming to herself as she loaded gear onto her camel. Or Kiara—

how she always wrapped Kora's headscarf with love and precision so that she wouldn't feel the sun's hot rays on her scalp. No matter how hard Kiara tried, there was always a stray curl or two that popped free and brushed Kora's plump cheek. I can all but see Mikel's face staring back at me. The knowing look he'd give me when I was in a mood. The way his puff of curly brown hair gleamed almost golden against the sun. My stomach clenches as happy memories are replaced by the last ones I have. The way Mikel's eyes pleaded with me. The blood coating his tunic, staining the fabric so dark it almost looked black. I shut out any more thoughts before they threaten to unravel me. *They're all fine. They have to be.*

I shift uncomfortably in my saddle. My tailbone aches, and my body seems to grow stiffer with every mile we travel. A deep breath leaves my lungs with a heavy sigh. It's louder than I mean it, and Savi peers over at me from the side of her eye. I don't know if she's keeping me isolated from the others for my benefit or theirs. Either way, I'm grateful for it.

The quiet of the morning has helped me make sense of the last few days—or try to, at least. My mind is an incessant chatter of what if's and how's. Every worrying thought brings a new one. Savi has seemed to sense the tension I carry, keeping any conversation between us brief and casual. But I've let intrigue and uneasiness fester for too long. I can feel her questions brimming like a boiling pot. Her gaze lingers as I untie the canteen from the saddle and drink.

"You should name her."

My eyes slip to Savi before I take another sip. "Huh?"

"Now that she's yours," she adds, gesturing to the animal I ride. "You should name her."

"I've never named a horse." I wipe some water off my bottom lip with the sleeve of my tunic and shrug. "What would it even be?"

Savi eyes me, then the horse. She stares at us both for what feels like an eternity before she smiles. "Mirage."

"Mirage?" My brow furrows at that. "Why?"

She stares again, but this time her focus is solely on me. I feel the weight of her gaze, like she's eager to find something I'm not willing to show.

"Because you both look like glimmers on the sand. Like ghosts."

I look down at the horse, at the honey-white hair that matches my own. Her body is even lighter in coloring—the palest shade of sand. And the eyes... ice blue. Odd and unsettling. My focus catches on the speckling of red against her flank. Blood, *my* blood. It's the only sign of the horrors that brought me here. Savi is right. The horse looks like a ghost—a nightmare trekking across the sand with elegant strides. Something tightens uneasily in my gut. That's how I must appear to her, too. And to the others. As a mirage. A ghost. An omen of things to come.

I let out a deep sigh and pat the horse's flank. "Mirage it is," I mutter.

Savi smiles. "Good. Now, there's another thing we should discuss..." Her smile wavers as she glances behind us.

I follow her gaze and regrettably catch Hassan's attention. Even at the distance he keeps, I can still see the hate simmering in his eyes. I roll my own and look toward the others. Unlike Hassan, they pay me no mind. Riat and Kai seem to have Tariq locked in a debate of sorts. I stifle a laugh as he lets out an exasperated groan that even I can hear from a distance away. He shakes his head at the pair of troublemakers, but I see the smile he tries to hide. Vish, surprisingly, isn't staring at me like he can unearth my secrets with a mere look. His nose is buried in his journal, scribbling away at the pages as his camel trots along.

"My cousin doesn't like strangers... clearly." Savi scoffs.

I reluctantly look back to Hassan and see his gaze hasn't wavered.

"So the only thing left to do is make sure you're not a stranger anymore."

My focus shifts to Savi. She's still smiling, but there's a sober look across her face now. I shift uncomfortably in my saddle as I pull my gaze away from hers. "What do you want to know?"

She chews on the question, and every second makes me wish I'd sink deep into the sand, never to return again. Every step, every beat of silence, drags me further into my own restlessness.

"Where did you grow up?"

My heart skips a beat. As much as I don't want to talk about that place, I can't help but feel grateful for such a simple question. It's better than answering the ones I know she really wants to ask.

"Merket," I say. "But I left when I was twelve."

Her brow bunches. "That's a small town in the east, right? South of Artolen?"

I nod but my chest tightens. The emotion feels traitorous and I clench my teeth to push it away. "Yes. I lived there for a while, too."

"I've heard Artolen is a wild place," she offers.

"It can be."

She must think I'm going to say more because silence stretches between us. I weave my gaze into Mirage's mane, focusing on the varied hues of honey and sand that almost shine against the sun. But most importantly, I keep my mouth shut.

"What made your family migrate there?"

"They didn't come with me."

The words are too quick to roll off my tongue. I watch her try to piece it all together, at least what she thinks she knows. Her expression drops slightly. "You moved there by yourself... at that young age?"

I stay silent as she works the rest of it out.

"What happened to them, your family?" Her voice is soft and quiet, as if I'm a thing that might break.

I'm grinding my jaw, longing for anything other than where I know this conversation is going. The urge to prod Mirage, nudge her into a full sprint, gnaws at me. I have to tighten my hands around the reins to stop myself. My grip locks down on the straps until my knuckles are bone-white.

"My father died when I was six," I say flatly. "He owed someone money... you can imagine the rest."

"I know that pain—"

"Don't." The word is clipped, sharp.

Savi's mouth opens, but I don't give her a chance to speak. "He was better off leaving this world before he saw what was to become of it," I mutter. "Of me."

"And what about your mother?" Savi asks softly.

"She was alive when I left for Artolen."

The lines between Savi's brow have grown into deep valleys now. I don't dare look at her, only peek from the corner of my eye to see if she's still watching. She is.

"How did you end up on your own?"

I let silence fill the space between us, hoping the sound of hooves dragging through sand will calm me. It's naive to think it would. "Do you know anything about daemon children?"

If fire wasn't practically burning through my veins right now, I might feel bad for the way Savi flinches at my tone.

"Not much," she admits, stiffening atop her horse. "Just that your gifts appear when you're children."

"Mm," I grumble. "And what do you think happens when those gifts appear?"

"I—"

"The markings start off small," I say, cutting her off. "A few dots or a line. Nothing more than a smudge of ink." Something foul stirs in my chest. I shift in my seat, letting the jolt of pain from my back ground me. "There are few places on the Continent that desire daemon children," I continue. "Grown, we can be used, forged into weapons, or simply killed. But as children?"

My tongue clicks against the back of my teeth. I let my fingers run across the leather harness I put on over my clothing. I stop at the hilt of my blade, trailing my fingertips across the carvings. "Not many want to take the life of a child, not even one they deem as tainted."

I make the mistake of looking at her and catch the sadness woven into her face. The sight churns the grief and fury inside of me, and suddenly I can't stop the words from flowing.

"My markings appeared when I was eight. I didn't know much then, didn't know how superstitious my mother was or what was going to happen when I showed her." I laugh to myself, a sickly noise, as I think back to that day. How curious I had been. How I had watched her face turn ashen.

I pull away the scarf shielding me to reveal my neck. "Three little marks." I sneer. "That's all it took."

I run my fingers across my skin. The markings have grown over the years—despite my best efforts. Three markings have turned into a column racing down my neck. I tried to stop it from happening, but it didn't matter. There was never any escaping this fate.

"She tossed me to the streets like a token of bad luck. But it was for the best. I found my way in the world... eventually."

Savi says nothing as I fix my scarf, tugging the fabric back into place and covering the markings once more. I feel the weight of everything I've laid bare like a wet cloak across my back. It feels like all the Kohe Mountains have crumbled, burying me in the dark of the earth. For a while, all that can be heard is the huff of our horses and the distant voices that flitter across the sand.

Finally, Savi speaks. "My family was killed by—" Her hesitation draws my focus. "A group of men," she continues. Her voice is quiet but steady. "We lived in a small outpost out west, near the mountains."

She stares out across the desert and shakes her head, as if shaking away bad memories. I can see her pain, feel it rolling off her. Part of me wants to reach out and squeeze her hand, but I don't.

"They came in the night, took whatever they could find, burned the rest." She looks behind us and swallows harshly. "Hassan arrived three days later. He was looking for my father but found me instead. Beaten, bloody, and..."

She turns to face me, looks me dead in the eyes. Her expression no longer carries its brightness, nor its carefree joy. Every part of her seems clenched, held together tightly like if she lets go a wave of emotions might drown her. "It was over ten years ago, but I still can't shake the memory of it. As hard as I've tried."

The memory of my own darkest day flickers to life. The harsh stone of the alley. Shouting in the distance. Blood, so much blood. A phantom pain tingles across the scar on my stomach. I have to forcibly clench my hands into fists to keep myself from patting the old wound. It's as though my mind is convinced fresh blood still flows there.

"Hassan taught me how to take care of myself," Savi continues. "He taught me how to fight. How to make sure nothing like that ever happened again."

Her gaze hovers on mine. It's filled with pain and something else, but she doesn't shy away—doesn't let it consume her. In that moment, I understand. We are not the same, but we've both been scarred by the same world; molded into something stronger in the process. I don't need to offer sympathy and neither does she. This was inevitable. The gods had planned our suffering like threads woven in a tapestry long before we arrived here.

"Hassan's like that—protective. Honorable," Savi states. "Everyone here owes him some debt, not one he imposes but one others feel compelled to fulfill. He saved Kai's life in Fiöl after a job went south. Helped Tariq bring in the men who killed his aunt. Stopped Vish from—" She stops herself, pursing her lips together. Silence beats between us, hovering against unsaid things. Savi sighs. "We've all seen the bad the Continent has to offer. Hassan carved a place for us, brought us together. That's all I mean to say."

I let out a deep breath, mind racing with everything I've learned. I try to find her version of Hassan amidst the one I've met, but I come up short. *Can such compassion really dwell in someone with so much hate? With such disdain for what I am?*

I shake away the heaviness of my thoughts and quirk my brow at Savi. "So you're saying the ornery old goat isn't a complete ass?"

My lips quiver into a faint smile just as hers do. She lets out a soft laugh and it all but melts the tension and pain dampening the air between us.

"Oh, he's still an ass," she confirms. "But he's a good person, too."

Against my better judgement, I toss a glance over my shoulder. Hassan is no longer glaring at me but looking east across the desert. The sun lights up his skin in a golden hue, only broken up by the dark scruff of his face. I let my mind wander, and for a brief moment, I see him how Savi must see him. As a protector. A leader. Not a threat. My heart seems to skip a beat as his gaze snaps to mine. Hesitation flickers across his face, like maybe he's seeing me differently, too. But the moment passes as quickly as it came. The scowl slips over his face once again, and I'm quick to mirror it. Something uneasy flickers in my gut as I turn away and nudge my horse forward.

"How many days to Hira?" I ask.

Savi lets a *tsk* roll from behind her teeth as she contemplates it. "Four, probably five."

Guilt hangs heavy in the back of my throat. Savi rambles on about the journey. She tells me how Kai and Riat will insist we stop at every outpost for food and a pint of ale. She tells me that they've all been together for years. She tells me that Tariq was the latest addition to their band. Tells me how he saved Riat's ass in a tavern brawl years ago.

She goes on and on, but I'm not listening, not anymore. I'm thinking about what Savi shared with me. The pain and suffering she endured. *The loss.*

Dread slithers up my sweat-coated spine and seems to whisper in my ear. *Rohan.* He'll be coming for me. My blood seems to thrum, anticipating the threat like he's already at my back. I try to push away the memory of his knife digging into my skin or the harsh grip of his fingers in my hair. But as I do, it's only replaced by the image of him turning that violence on someone else.

My eyes dart to Savi. I eye the scar marring her skull, the beaming look that's now returned to her face. *What will happen to her if Rohan finds me here? What will happen to the others?* My heart patters unsteadily.

I turn my face toward the sun, beckoning the bright rays to strip me clean of my thoughts. It works. I'm quickly preoccupied with black spots peppering my vision. I blink the sun from my eyes and focus on the horizon in front of me. The only thing that matters now is that I move forward, away from the devil at my back.

My eyes flicker to Savi once more. She's laughing, still deeply engaged in the stories she thinks I'm listening to. I nudge Mirage forward, increasing our pace. I need to get to Hira. I need to go north. The more distance I put between me and Denheir, the better.

"...I swear, I really thought he'd learn his lesson after that. Have you ever been to the Brunn Isle?"

I blink a few times, letting myself find the way back to the world in front of me. "Uh, no. I haven't."

"It's an amazing place," Savi raves. "You have to go at least once, just to try the ale..."

She carries on but her words fade into the background of my thoughts once more. I stare out into the desert, into the blank expanse of nothing that I so desperately want to disappear into.

Five days. I just need to survive the next five days. *And if Rohan finds me before then?* I clench my teeth and push away the thought. I can only hope my suffering does not bring anyone else's with it.

CHAPTER 17

"We'll rest here for the night."

Savi slips from the back of her horse, boots splashing against the hot sand. We've been traveling for hours, and the sun now hovers over the horizon, prepared for its nightly descent. There's still plenty of light, enough for us to set up our tents and share a meal. But in an hour, all that will be left is darkness.

I glance at the nook Savi has selected for our camp. We're up against a crescent-shaped outcropping of rocks. They're scattered all over the desert here, like small islands in an endless ocean of sand. It will provide some protection from the wind or a sandstorm if one runs up on us in the dead of night. I don't let myself think too long about how this position corners us and leaves us vulnerable to other types of threats. I'll save those thoughts for tonight when I'm clutching a dagger to my chest and feigning sleep.

"Here," Savi beckons me. "Take this and hammer it into the sand. We'll need to tie up the horses."

I barely have time to grab the wooden stake and small mallet from her before she's gone. Savi moves across the empty camp methodically: mumbling to herself as she decides who and what will go where. She quickly claims a spot for herself, dropping her pack with a plop. She then moves to a new spot and digs out a place for the fire. Only when she turns to me do I remember she gave me a task. She raises a brow, and suddenly, I feel like a child shirking their chores.

I drop my pack in an instant and begin hammering the stake into the sand. It takes more than a handful of strikes to do so, and once I'm done, fresh drops of sweat pepper my hairline. Mirage snorts as I tie her reins off, and I make sure to give her a soft pat before loosening the saddle. As I let it drop to the sand, a flicker of unease fills my gut. *If something happens, if someone comes in the night...*

I loose a heavy breath and stare at the saddle at my feet. Mirage nudges my shoulder with her nose, breaking my critical gaze. I sigh and give her a loving scratch.

"I know, girl," I utter. "You need to rest, too."

I ignore the gut feeling that this is a mistake and leave the saddle where it lies. If something happens in the night, well, I've ridden bareback before.

I give her one final pat before approaching Savi's horse. It gives me a nervous whinny as I do. Teak's hooves stomp into the sand. It's glossy, black eyes widened. *Shit.* Whereas my horse doesn't seem at all bothered by my daemon blood, Savi's horse is eyeing me like I might be Hael himself.

I sigh and tie the reins off as quickly—albeit cautiously—as I can. The last thing I need is Savi's horse running off because I spooked it. It lets out another fretful whinny before I finish the knot and step back, hands raised in surrender. It snorts and stomps until it decides I'm far enough away to no longer be a threat.

Sighing, I sling the strap of my pack over my shoulder and head toward Savi. Before I reach her, a loud voice carries across the sand.

"Once again, Savi," Tariq shouts atop his camel. "You've found the perfect spot."

"Don't say that just yet." She laughs. "I haven't checked for scorpions."

I have to suppress a laugh as I see Tariq visibly shudder.

"I'll forget you mentioned those cursed things," he grimaces.

The others trail closely behind, and I find myself stiffening at their approach. It was easier being with just Savi all day. She'd gotten the hint after our talk of families—I wasn't in a chatty mood. But now, as the others join us, I can only imagine the unasked questions that have been eating away at them all day. I'm a new face—a stranger amidst them, after all.

Riat and Kai both ride horses, sauntering toward camp side by side. They're laughing and swearing, seemingly in a heated discussion about stewed meat. The details of such a topic, I can't quite hear. Vish rides a small camel behind them. He tucks his journal into his pack quickly, eyes darting to me. My gaze tightens on him before it slips to the two camels that follow. They're riderless, packed high with supplies and gear. I wonder how much they've brought with them on this job, how often they find themselves out here for days on end, maybe even weeks.

My eyes shift once more until all I see is him—*Hassan*. He brings up the rear, which surprises me. I took him for the obnoxious leader-type. The one that always needs to be first. My eyes narrow on him, squinting slightly against the low glare of the sun. He's atop a large brown horse. Its mane is loose, but some small strands are braided with the same leather I saw on Savi's. My focus locks on two small sheaths fitted to the horse's saddle, occupied by small blades. Of course, the sword he had pointed at my throat yesterday is still strapped across his back.

As he stops his horse at my staked post and slides off the saddle, his heavy gaze meets mine. It's nothing short of a miracle—rather, Savi's carefully crafted distance—that we haven't spoken since this morning. That distance hasn't seemed to help though. I still feel the tension between us like a threat from the gods. He barely takes his eyes off me as he ties up his horse and unloads his gear. His ever-present glare gets under my skin more than I'd like it to. He's watching me like I'm going to gut the nearest person as soon as he turns his back. It has me so irked that I might just ram my dagger into his stomach to prove a point.

"Ren, do you know how to build a fire?"

Savi's voice pulls me from my growing fantasies about stabbing her cousin.

"Yes, of course."

"Mind getting it going while we set up the tents?"

I'm about to respond when Hassan stalks past with an armful of supplies. I don't have time to step out of the way before he smacks his shoulder into mine.

"Asshole," I say loud enough for him to hear.

He doesn't bother turning back around, just shoots a retort over his shoulder. "Stay out of the way, *witch*."

Savi sighs next to me. "Go start the fire. I'll talk to him."

"No, it's fine," I snap. I know my hostility is misplaced, and I regret it instantly. I turn, offering Savi a tight-lipped smile. "It's fine. I'll get the fire going."

I turn on my heels and head toward the middle of camp before she can say anything more. I don't need her to fight my battles. Not that this is even a battle. It's one guy with an attitude problem. *I can handle one guy.*

I huff as I lower myself to my knees in front of the pit Savi dug. There's a small pile of sticks next to it that she must have brought with her. The tension loosens from my shoulders as I get to work. At least I won't have to walk around for an hour searching for scraps of dead bushes to use as kindling. We were never this prepared when I traveled with Zoah. But then again, we weren't bounty hunters out on a job. We were a band of outcasts, looking to find solace away from the world.

Thanks to the piece of flint I always keep in my pack, it takes me little time to get the fire going. I let out a deep sigh as I sit back and watch the flames grow. They billow and flare, licking at the sticks. The heat of the day is slowing slipping away, but it still feels too hot to be this close.

I get up, stretching my back and legs. A groan slips from my lips as I do. I feel every bruise, every cut, and every tense muscle. I take a deep breath and work through the strain. It's almost cathartic: the pain releasing across my body. Every shudder of it reminds me that I'm here, that I got away.

I close my eyes and rub my fingertips over a kink in my neck. It's been years since my body has taken this much abuse. I've been spoiled, too used to Mikel fixing me up.

The corners of my mouth flick up into something almost resembling a smile as memories flood my mind. He'd always said I was too reckless, too stubborn to do things safely. I found his suggestions for caution boring and unreasonable. Why take the long way around the canyon when I could simply scale down the rocks? Why put up with the greedy bastard of a blacksmith when I could simply *persuade* him to give me a better deal from the end of a blade? Surely, Mikel had to see the practicality that often accompanied my so-called recklessness?

A smirk dances across my lips now at the thought of all those injuries that followed my more zealous ideas. Broken arms. Bloody knuckles. A knife wound here and there—superficial, of course. All those times, Mikel would be sure to patch me up. He'd swear under his breath, admonishing my foolishness, knowing I'd do it again and again.

My heart aches at the thought, and the amusement slowly slips from my face. Mikel is not here, nor will he be here to patch up my reckless mistakes again. He is long gone, no longer burdened with the problems that seem to follow me. I wince as I feel a twinge in my ribs. Now the only cure for my wounds is time. If only that didn't feel so precious right now.

The bustle of camp pulls my focus from my aching muscles. Tents go up quickly thanks to Savi and Tariq. They work in tandem, pulling the canvas taut before staking it into the sand. The rest of the things—pots and pans, food, and other supplies—are strapped to the backs of a few camels.

I watch Riat and Kai shove each other like teenagers with too much energy as they unload everything. Vish and Hassan have wandered off a short distance away. They're huddled together, speaking in strained, hushed tones. Vish shakes his head as he pulls the journal from his pack. He says something to Hassan, who only pushes the journal away in response.

I watch the two for a while, but it's the tension rolling between them that keeps my focus. If it weren't for their murmured voices, I would swear they were arguing. Vish's mouth moves too quickly. Words fly from his lips and his brow furrows into a deeply set ridge. Hassan throws his hand up, gesturing toward camp. Vish levels him a careful look before pushing the journal back toward him. They must be charting the course for the next day. Or maybe they're tracking their bounties.

My brow furrows at that. *How did it all work? How did you track someone across the desert when all you had was endless sand?* I've never thought to track anything, always heading away from anyone or anything rather than toward it.

I'm still considering the thought when Vish catches me staring. His eyes are keen, perceptive. He tilts his head, gaze raking across me. He mumbles something to Hassan, and it's only when those hazel eyes snap to mine that I look away. I move my feet before I can think, heading for where Savi and Tariq have finished setting up the tents. As I head over, I see they're drinking from a dark bottle.

"Fire's done."

Their gazes raise to me quickly, though the looks on their faces are laughably different from those I just got from Vish and Hassan. Savi pulls me in by the shoulder like we've been friends for years.

"Good." She smiles. "Hassan will shut right up once he sees you're pulling your weight around here. That ass values few things more than hard work."

Tariq chuckles before taking a long pull from the bottle. I get a whiff of it as it leaves his lips. It's rum—rich and potent. My mouth is practically salivating at the thought.

Tariq must see an eager glimmer in my eyes because he smirks before offering it to me. "You drink?"

I let out a breathy laugh. "You ever met a daemon who didn't?"

The liquor slips past my lips smoothly. It's hot, but I don't care. Compared to having ale shoved down my throat, the warm burn on my tastebuds is like nectar from the gods. I take one more swig before I push the bottle back into Tariq's hands. I need to stay alert. *No getting drunk. No letting my guard down.* No matter how comfortable I feel around Savi, I don't know her—or them. It's something I have to remind myself while I look at Savi.

She offers me a bright smile as she grabs the bottle and downs a hefty amount of rum.

"Hey, save some of that for the rest of us."

Savi is quick to hold the bottle out of reach as Kai sidles up next to her. "Last time we gave you rum, you took off all your clothes and wanted to dance around the fire," she quips.

Riat laughs as he wraps an arm around his friend. "And don't forget he drank the whole bottle before we could have any."

"You're acting like I'm some kind of drunk." Kai pouts as he crosses his arms over his chest.

"With rum, you are a drunk." Savi chuckles. "And you're not getting any tonight."

Kai flashes his eyebrows at her. "Oh, yeah? You gonna stop me?"

They both freeze, staring at each other silently until finally, Kai lunges. They're all flailing arms and rambunctious yells as Kai fights to steal the bottle. It's only when he manages to rip the rum from Savi's grasp that the chaos settles. They're both left panting, smiles buried in their cheeks.

"*Fine*," Savi grumbles. "But the minute your clothes start coming off, I'm having Tariq tie you up in your tent.

"Kinky." Riat snickers.

A surprised huff slips from Tariq's lungs. "Nope, absolutely not." He laughs. "I'm going to bed early—before any of this nonsense occurs."

Savi seizes the opportunity to snatch the bottle back from Kai. "No one is getting crazy tonight," she states before taking a swig. "We don't want Ren to think we're a bunch of debauchers and ruffians."

A deep hum ripples from Riat's throat. "But that's exactly what we are." He turns toward me, flashing his eyes. "She'll find that out sooner or later."

Tariq sighs, rubbing his hands across his face. "Gods help us," he mutters.

"Riat, you're looking a little thirsty there, my friend," Kai teases. "Here, have a drink." He steals the bottle from Savi mid-sip before tossing it to his friend.

"Why you little sh—"

"Getting started early, I see."

Hassan's voice makes me tense. My gaze locks on him as he and Vish join the group.

"Oh, come on," Savi jeers. "We were just having a drink before we get dinner going."

He levels a look at her that is anything but amused. "We're working a job, Savi," he chides. "Just because you picked up a stray doesn't mean we can forget we're out here for a reason."

"Hassan—"

"A stray?" I cut Savi off and cover the distance to Hassan in the blink of an eye.

Vish quickly retreats like I might kill them all on a whim.

"You don't like daemons. I fucking get it, okay? But remember that I didn't ask to be here."

His nostrils flare. "And yet, here you are."

"Yes, and I know you can't stand it—breathing the same air as a *witch*," I snap. "Maybe you were right, maybe you should have just let me bleed out and die. You would have saved the both of us a lot of trouble."

"Maybe I should have," he growls. "Because I have a feeling you're more trouble than you're worth."

"Hassan..." Vish takes a hesitant step toward us. "Let's talk abou—"

"Did you even ask her how she got here?" Hassan's gaze snaps to Savi. "Or how she got those cuts? The knife wound in her back?"

His focus is solely on his cousin, as if Vish or I aren't even here. "Did you ask her anything at all, or were you too eager to make a friend that you overlooked the danger you've put us all in?"

"Easy," Tariq says. His eyes dart between the two cousins carefully. "Hassan, you're taking this too far."

"Am I?" he argues. "Because I know the kind of men who live in Denheir. I know those cuts on her arms aren't from some tavern brawl. And I know the panic in someone's eyes when they're running from something."

"My friend, remember what I—"

Vish puts a tentative hand on Hassan's shoulder, but it's quickly brushed off. Hassan clenches his jaw and turns his venomous gaze back on me. "Who are you, really?" He takes a step closer, all but pressing his chest against mine. "Because you're not some poor, innocent girl who got caught up in trouble she didn't cause."

His gaze bears down on me, and I feel anger pool in my skull, dismissing all rational thought.

"Tell me, what did you do to deserve a knife in the back?"

"*Nothing*," I seethe. I swallow my fury down bit by bit, but it still manages to creep up my throat until it's all but fire on my tongue. "I'm just trying to survive the fucking Continent." I push my hands against his chest, shoving him away. "And I'll gladly take down anyone who gets in my way."

The *hiss* of Hassan's blade against its sheath drives me to bad habits. I draw both of my daggers. I only hesitate slipping them into flesh when I feel the press of a sword at my throat. Hassan's breath is hot against my face. My fingers twitch as I press my blades into the loose fabric of his tunic. He can slit my throat, but I'll make sure he bleeds out just as fast.

He grits his teeth and keeps the threat of his blade on my neck. "Explain yourself. *Now*, witch. Or my hand just might slip."

My heart hammers, pumping adrenaline through my system. Even if I made the first move, he has me in a bad spot. And as much as I hate backing down, I'd rather not die today. I flare my eyes, signaling a truce I resent having to ask for. It's a silent agreement that I rely on as I slowly lower my blades. He waits until I've sheathed both before the sword leaves my throat. He doesn't bother putting it away though. It hovers at his side, curled in a steady hand as he watches me, waiting for my answer.

My gaze tightens murderously before I give it. "The nomads I was traveling with had their camp raided," I start. "We thought they were slavers but they were looking for daemons. They brought me to Denheir. I got away. The end."

Vish slips his way closer, eyeing me carefully. "Why were they looking for daemons?"

"Why does anyone look for daemons?" I scoff. "Are we not weapons or corpses for the Continent?"

Vish's mouth tightens into a stern line, and I all but roll my eyes.

"They wanted daemons to work for them," I concede. "The man in charge, he—"

"What man?" Vish prods.

"Why would they want daemons to work for them?" Hassan presses.

Fiery red hair fills my mind. Then, green eyes looking down on me. A rough hand against my cheek. I feel sweat slick across my skin. "It's—he..." I all but shudder. "He wanted me to advise him. When I refused..."

I choke on my words. I'm deep in the cellar once more, trapped in my mind as the darkness closes in. I'm clawing my way out, dragging myself from my thoughts when Vish's voice breaks the spell.

"What—" Vish starts.

"Speak, *witch*," Hassan grumbles.

It's only through gritted teeth that I find the words. "He thought he could force them out of me, thought that they answered to him."

Vish's eyes widen knowingly, and I force myself to look away.

"Force what out of you?" Kai asks, peeking over Vish's shoulder. His brow is scrunched in confusion.

I steel my face against any emotion. "My visions." I swallow harshly and somehow find it in me to stand a little taller. "He thought a blade would do it, but..."

Hassan's eyes roam across my arms, and even though they're covered, I know he's thinking about the scars. The attention is too much. I pull my gaze down to the sand.

"I guess my tolerance for pain wasn't what he expected. He had to get... creative."

Silence. I look up to see Kai's face has gone pale. Vish is staring with an unexpected mournfulness that grates my nerves. I don't need the pity, nor the shame that hangs heavy in the air. I don't dare look at the others for fear I'll pull a dagger out of sheer frustration.

"How did you get out of Denheir?" Hassan asks, much too demanding for my liking. "How did you get away?"

I let the question linger for too long, and silence hovers around us. It's so quiet I can hear a breeze blowing through camp, whipping against the tents. I think of Rohan, of his hands gliding up my skin. I think of the heat of his lips trailing up my neck. I think of the way his eyes flickered wide in pain as I plunged that blade into him. But most importantly, I think of the weight of the other man, quickly shoved aside as if his life meant nothing. My throat grows tight, and I can't seem to raise my gaze from the sand. I swallow my guilt, for it has no purpose.

"I have my ways."

Hassan goes to protest, but Vish immediately intervenes. He steps between us, turning his back on me as muffled whispers leave his lips. Hassan's eyes flicker with heat, but he stays silent.

"Trust me—"

Vish's voice comes and goes in hushed pieces.

"... time with her..."

"—I need to be sure."

I step forward, desperate to hear more, but Hassan's eyes snap to mine. Vish follows his gaze, quickly turning around and stuffing any final words he may have behind closed lips. He looks me up and down slowly, brows pinching as his eyes lock on my markings. Without another word, he walks off. I'm left standing there, lips pursed and jaw clenched as I watch him retreat into the sea of tents.

I turn to Hassan for answers, but he offers none. He merely scoffs, fury stifled under his breath as he steps past me.

"Show's over," he grunts. "Get dinner going before we lose the light."

The others linger, hesitation weighing them down into the sand.

"*Now*," Hassan barks.

He stalks after Vish, then quickly slips into the tent and disappears from view.

I stare after them for far too long as the others meander away and resume their tasks. It's only when Savi looses a breath from somewhere behind me that I'm torn from my daze.

"Want another drink?" she utters, extending the bottle of rum toward me. "I think you could use it."

I take the offering without a word, pulling in two long gulps before handing it back. The urge to finish the whole bottle burns in my chest. I don't want to feel, don't want to deal with whatever situation I've found myself in. All I want is to forget the past week. But I know inebriation's enticing haze won't be the relief I hope it to be. It will only coax the devils from the corners of my mind and weaken my defenses. I lick my lips, getting every last drop of rum. It will be my last taste for the night.

My eyes find their way back to Vish's tent. I pick and sift through every memory—every last word and lingering look the strange man has given me. There's something in his gaze, a knowing I can't seem to place. I'm sure I haven't met him before, but with the way he looks at me, it feels as though he's met me. The unfounded suspicion is a knot in my gut.

Savi has long since left my side. I can hear her scolding Kai about stealing bites before dinner is ready. The minutes tick by. Sand swirls around my boots. Finally, I relent. My body aches as I trudge across the sand. The others greet me when I join them, but I can only offer a shell of a smile.

I fall into a familiar routine though this camp is not my own. I help Riat lay blankets around the rim of the fire. Then, help Savi plate the food. Every task is done without thought, for my mind is a distant tempest. It's only when Hassan and Vish emerge from the tent, expressions drawn tight, that I snap out of my fog. I don't trust them and I know the feeling is mutual.

The smartest thing to do is lay low until I'm strong enough to leave. I need to stay out of trouble, for I'll surely find it here. But as Hassan's piercing gaze meets mine, I can't bear to look away. I glare at his stupid face, daring him to be the first to back down. He doesn't. The moment is only broken by Vish, who leans close to Hassan and whispers furtively. I watch Hassan's jaw clench. He offers me one last, heated look before I'm utterly forgotten.

CHAPTER 18

"So there I am—blood leaking from my face, two of his men crumpled at my feet, and more gold than I know what to do with."

Rum spills onto the sand as Riat waves the bottle in the air. He's been telling this story for gods-knows how long, and he's lost more rum than he's drinking at this point.

"Veles damn us." Savi groans. "What did you do that time and how did I not know about this?"

"I didn't do anything." More rum splashes into the sand, dampening the corner of the blanket that Riat and Savi are sitting on. "I was trying to play a hand of cards, and you know... you get to talking. I was telling them about this woman I'd been with the night before." Riat blows out a heavy breath and chuckles. "Wild little thing. Had me doing all sorts of unmentionable acts to her."

Tariq laughs quietly to himself, asking the gods to please spare him the details. Kai only smirks.

Savi rolls her eyes at him. "Let me guess." She sighs. "One of their sisters?"

Riat lets a devilish smile flicker across his face. "Wife."

"Fuck's sake," Savi says. "One of these days, we're going to roll into town, and you're gonna to be struck dead."

"Savi, please," Kai says, speech slurred from all the rum. "You're interrupting the story, and I don't know what happens."

"I'm surprised you weren't there," she challenges him. "Usually if there's trouble, you two are deep in shit together."

"Kai was busy that night." Riat smiles. "Doing his own... things."

Kai's brow furrows before his face lights up. "Oh. Yes." He blushes, biting his bottom lip softly as if a memory flooded his mind. "Septirí is a... great city. I was... otherwise preoccupied."

Riat only snickers. "So the bastard accused me of lying. Said there was no way I'd taken his wife to bed. Said I was full of it." He looks at Tariq from across the fire with a raised brow. "I may be a lot of things. But a liar? *Never.*"

He takes a quick swig of rum, spilling most of it again. "So, I told him everything. What we did. About the little birthmark on her thigh. All the things she moaned for." He's grinning from ear to ear now. Riat leans forward, eyes gleaming wildly as he finishes the story. "He didn't take it well." He chuckles. "Once the fighting had truly started, I'd already taken down two of his men. He was nothing more than a quivering leaf in the wind by the time I got to him. Though he had the balls to tell me I better watch my mouth next time I came to town. I told him his wife rather likes my mouth."

Muttered curses drift from Savi's lips just as the air is filled with raucous laughter. Kai and Tariq are in fits—both well and drunk by now, despite Tariq's earlier assertion that he'd be missing the fun.

"I swear, you're the biggest rake on the Continent." Savi is shaking her head at him like a mother scolding a child.

He only beams proudly before leaning past her to look at me. "*Reformed* rake," he ensures me. "Those days are behind me. But old habits have made me quite... *skilled* in those areas."

He winks and another wave of laughter erupts around the fire. I can't help but join in as it spills from deep in my belly.

"Riat, don't embarrass yourself." Savi leans over and snatches the bottle from him before taking a swig. "We all know you couldn't handle a daemon woman, let alone one as spirited as Ren."

A breathy laugh escapes his throat, waving Savi off. "Oh, piss off." He laughs. His lips quirk up into a wild grin as he locks his gaze on me. "What do you say, Ren?" His eyes sweep down my body before meeting my gaze once more. "Think I could handle you?"

I have to suppress another laugh as he turns on his charm. It's not half bad, but it's not going to work. I've seen the act he's putting on too many times from men across the Continent. The cockiness. The exaggerated seduction. I'm sure one heady look is all it takes for younger women to fawn over him. Plus, he has other things going for him. The scar gracing his full lips. That playful heat in his eyes. The danger he seems to emanate. Some women like a man that needs to be tamed, and Riat? He's like a wild dog barking at the door. A cute dog, but a dog nonetheless. I don't doubt he has any trouble finding a woman to warm his bed most nights. But I'm not some nice girl from an outpost, and I certainly don't share my bed.

I cock my head at him as a smirk curls the corners of my mouth. "You know they say you can tell a lot about a man by his weapons." My eyes drift along his body, down to his belt where his knives rest. "Mm," I mumble from deep in my chest. "Let me see?"

He unsheathes two blades quickly, flashing me a wicked grin. I pretend to give the small throwing knives careful consideration before letting a *tsk* slip from the back of my teeth.

"Such little things." I wince and give him a bored look. "Pity."

Tariq's laughter is so loud, I'm afraid it might send the rocks above us tumbling down. The others join in quickly. I even see a slight smile flicker across Vish's face. The slip of emotion feels like a victory considering he's been looking at me stone-faced and solemn all night. The only one who doesn't react is Hassan. I shoot him a sideways look as Savi and Kai continue to tease Riat. Hassan hasn't said a word. He won't even look at me now. And while I know it shouldn't bother me, it does.

"Okay, boys." Savi laughs. "I think that's enough of that for tonight." She steals the bottle of rum from Riat and corks it.

There's a collective groan between Riat and Kai, but they ultimately surrender. They pick themselves up from the sand, wobbling slightly as they follow Savi to their tent like baby geese. I watch them meld into the shadows, slipping from the light of the fire. The night is silent in their absence. Only the crack and pop of flames are left to fill the air. It's not long before Tariq offers the rest of us a good night and heads to bed himself.

I haven't had any more rum, despite whines and protests from Riat and Kai, but now I wish I had something to stave off the chill. I pull at the draped scarf that's fallen off my shoulders, but it does little to warm me. Just as I scoot closer to the fire, a quiet conversation reaches my ears. Hassan and Vish sit across from me, words passing almost inaudibly between them. The flames illuminate them in flickering shadows. I don't miss the hardness and hesitation etched in their faces. Vish whispers something, widening his eyes at Hassan.

"You have no idea if it's—" Hassan's voice rises but is quickly cut short by a harsh look from Vish.

The smaller man's gaze darts toward me. Once more, I feel like I've been caught witnessing something I shouldn't have. Maybe it's the fact I'm an outsider here. Or maybe, just maybe, it's the habit these two seem to have with whispered conversations. There's a secret here; one they keep from the others, and now—one they keep from me as well.

I stare, my focus constantly flickering between them. I rest my gaze on Hassan, silently challenging him to acknowledge my presence. He doesn't, although the twitch in his jaw tells me he's well aware I'm here. I barely restrain my irritation as Vish turns away and mutters something else. I might as well not be here at all. I'm merely a shadow to them—a nuisance. Either way, I'm sick of it.

Just as I shift to leave, Hassan beats me to it. He's on his feet and stalking toward his tent—the one he still shares with Savi since I'm staying in hers—without so much as a glance in my direction. I bite back whatever frustrations I have and loose a deep breath before settling deeper into the sand. It doesn't matter how tired or cold I am right now, I'm not heading to my own tent until he's safely in his. It's childish but I don't care. If he wants to ignore me, I can do the same.

I crack my neck and get comfortable. There's no telling how long I'll be waiting until the coast is clear. I'm sure Hassan has some bullshit routine of slinking about camp before bed to ensure everyone is safe. No matter that there's enough weapons between everyone to fill an armory—or that, aside from Vish, everyone is built like a mercenary.

I stifle the grumble that threatens to trickle from my throat as I look across the fire. Unsurprisingly, Vish's eyes are on me. But he doesn't look away when I notice. No, he keeps staring. He's quiet. Motionless. *Critical.* He looks at me without so much as a word, but his eyes might as well be damning me where I sit. His focus eats away at my lingering animosity until I can't bear it any longer.

"What?" I snap.

He takes his time answering, and it has my blood boiling.

"Where were you, before Denheir?"

The question is anything but casual. There's a rigidness to his tone that sets my spine straight. He's not making small talk. He's collecting information, assessing if I'm still a threat. Part of me considers acting like one just to garner a reaction but somehow, I keep my daggers sheathed.

"Jahaer," I say flatly.

The side of his mouth perks up, like he finds my petulance amusing. "The desert is a big place," he offers. "Hard to find anything out here, especially if you don't quite know what you're looking for."

My gaze tightens on him, but I say nothing as my mind tries to decipher his words.

"You were traveling with nomads, you say?"

I grit my teeth when he presses further.

"Not usual for a woman to be off on her own, especially one with gifts such as yours." He pauses, watching me carefully, as if reading every flicker of emotion on my face. "How long have you lived out here?"

"Long enough to know how to handle myself," I snap.

"Hm. Yes, it appears so."

Silence finds its way between us once more. I take a deep, steadying breath to calm myself. I almost miss Hassan's silent hostility as Vish watches me. Anything would be better than that discerning stare of his. He presses his fingertips together roughly, steepling them. His eyes never leave mine, not for even a second. He shatters the silence and the last of my resolve in an instant.

"What was the name of the man in Denheir?"

My skin prickles. I ignore the phantom feeling—the memory of his touch drifting across my arms, my neck, my jaw. Somehow, I force myself to relax back into the sand, feigning disinterest. "What does it matter?"

"I want to know what we're up against now that you're traveling with us," Vish replies.

"My presence here is temporary," I bite back.

"Is it?"

I hesitate, words pilling on my tongue but unable to make the journey past my lips. *I am leaving, right?* A few more days, and I should be healed enough. The bruising on my ribs should no longer cause a constant ache when I breathe. My cuts are closing— no longer pulling at the skin. And my back? It still feels like a fire blazing through my very flesh every night, but there's no infection. As long as I keep to the outskirts and avoid anyone, there should be no need to test my strength in a fight just yet. I need to head north before I lose the head-start I've gained on Rohan.

So why is it, despite knowing all this, I'm struggling to find the words? Something stirs in my chest, some once-lost feeling. I let myself ruminate on things I shouldn't. Riat and Kai's laughter. The kindness Savi shows me. The palpable affection these people feel for each other. I shove everything down into the deepest parts of myself. There's nothing for me here.

"Ren."

I inhale sharply as I come back to the moment. "I'll be long gone before he ever crosses paths with you," I clip.

The words feel like sand in my mouth. Doubt lingers in my chest. Rohan could show up in the morning, for all I know. It's only sheer, dumb luck that it was Hassan and Savi who found me nearly dead.

Vish's lips flatten into a harsh line, as if he senses my uncertainty. "Be that true, I would still like to know what to expect." His eyes cut into me, and the urge to shrink away is overwhelming. "We don't run into many people out here. But the ones we do are sealed into our memories forever like carvings in stone. It's hard to forget even the most ordinary. But coming across a daemon? A Seer, at that?" He leans forward, elbows on his knees. His steepled fingers press against his beard as his lips purse in contemplation. "It's uncommon. Memorable, even. I would hate to mention you to the wrong person. But if I don't know with whom to avoid telling such tales, my tongue may just slip."

My jaw grinds, and my fingers tingle for my blades. "I prefer my threats spoken clearly," I snarl. "Not veiled in favors and good nature."

"It's not a threat." He leans back and rests his hands in his lap, not far from where his journal rests. "It's an agreement of sorts. You trust me, and I look out for you."

I force myself to take a deep breath before I do something I regret. My hands splay against the sand, far away from my daggers. "Rohan," I state through clenched teeth. "His name is Rohan."

Something flashes across Vish's face. It's gone in an instant but not before I clock the recognition there. He knows Rohan—knows him or knows of him. I'm certain of it. My stomach twists.

"I see."

His clipped words only cement the unease deeper into my gut. Before I can say anything more, he's on his feet. His brow crumples as he shoots me a lingering look.

"Douse the fire," he utters. "And get some sleep."

He's gone seconds later. I watch him stalk across camp before slipping into his tent. All I can do is stare across the empty sands while my mind swirls with unfriendly thoughts. *He knows Rohan.* It's a vicious reality that leaves me with so many questions. *Does Vish know him by reputation? Or is it something more personal?*

I turn toward the now-dwindling fire and let my gaze burn into the smoldering flames. A numbness creeps over me as I sit there. I lose track of time, only bothering to get up and kick sand over the fire once the last lick of orange is stolen by darkness.

The night wraps around me with an unkind chill as I make the way to my tent. The entire time, all I can think about is Rohan and how he will find me—if others don't lead me to him first.

CHAPTER 19

I'm currently sandwiched between my two biggest problems—what lays behind me and what is to come. Vish rides ahead, and my focus lingers on his back. He didn't say anything to me this morning, which was a welcome reprieve after last night—despite the nagging dread that our conversation left settled in my gut. *He knows Rohan.* I know I should be pestering him for answers, but my mind keeps bouncing from one thing to another.

According to Savi, we're four days from Hira. The minute it's in sight, everything changes. I can barter for supplies, food, and more blades. I can plot a course north. Most importantly, I can disappear. Vish is right, the Jahaer Desert is a big place. Unless Rohan has enough men to search every grain of sand, there's a good chance I can lose him.

I shift my focus back to my immediate problems. It's the one behind me that has me the most on edge. Hassan brings up the rear of the group, and while he's still giving me the silent treatment, he's no longer ignoring me. Vish must have told him about Rohan this morning because I can't even take a sip of water without Hassan being on high alert. Even now, as I turn around to look at him, he's glaring at me like he knows everything I did in Denheir.

My mind spins, churning out scenario after scenario of how the next few days might play out. It could be nothing more than stilted conversation and sideways glares until we reach Hira. *But if Rohan finds me...*

I try not to let my mind go there but it's an impulse I can't shake. If he finds me, will Hassan hide me? Or will Hassan happily hand me over? As I pull my gaze from his, I know the answer.

Savi raises her hand at the front of the group, and our caravan halts.

"We'll take a short break here," she yells back. "Everyone do what you need to do before we leave. We won't be stopping again until we make camp."

I hear Kai groan in front of me, followed by some snarky comment from Riat. The boisterous conversation between the two of them fades into the background as I dismount and stretch my back. Riding is different with Hassan's band. Zoah never had anywhere important to be. With him, we were just wandering. Sometimes we would set course for an outpost or town to resupply. But most of the time, we were just trying to make a life in the desert. We'd camp for days on end before eventually moving on to the next place. It was almost nice: settling into a routine, easing into calm mornings by the fire, late nights swapping stories. But it was that aimless, easygoing way of life that lead me here.

Before Zoah, I'd never allowed myself to stay with a group for that long. Maybe a few months here and there in between taking odd jobs and making my own way. *But two years?* I almost shatter my molars from how hard I'm grinding my teeth while thinking about it. Two years is too reckless, even for me. I let myself pretend I could simply live without consequence. I got comfortable. Happy, even. I was foolish to think it could last.

I'm stretching my legs when Hassan barrels past me. I almost lose my balance, having to rest a hand on Mirage's saddle to steady myself. The disturbance earns me an irritated whinny. Murmured curses slip from my lips as I stare after him. He doesn't bother looking back, and I use the opportunity to send a vulgar gesture his way.

Riat catches me, snickering loudly. Hassan instantly whips back around, accusations rippling off his furrowed brow. I savor it—the fact that I manage to get under his skin. I shoot him a sickly-sweet smile and watch the emotion blanche across his face. His jaw clenches before he turns toward Vish.

Smirking to myself, I rummage around in my pack. I find a long scarf, the edges of the tan linen worn and faded, and drape it around my shoulders and head. The bearable morning heat has given way to an afternoon sun that already looms high overhead. In a few hours, it will be an unforgiving kiss against any bare skin it finds. I tuck the tail end of the fabric over my shoulder and adjust the panels that cover the sides of my face.

As my fingers find their way to my neck, I linger. The skin is uncovered, bare. Something stirs in my gut—shame or sorrow, or both. I used to be more careful. *When did that change?*

An ugly voice in my head rears up. I got comfortable. I forgot what the Continent is capable of—what its *people* are capable of. My teeth clench against each other as I yank another swathe of fabric from my pack. I re-wrap my head, covering my neck, head, shoulders, and even the lower part of my face this time. When I'm done, I don't need to see myself to know that the markings are well hidden. The only visible thing is the rigid glint in my eyes. There was a time when this was all I let the world see. Maybe it's time I return to that.

"Impressive."

I turn away from Mirage and find Riat, Kai, and Tariq are all watching me. Tariq is eating something wrapped in cloth, savoring it. The sight of the crumbling baked good makes my stomach grumble, but I don't dare ask for any. Instead, I pull my canteen from my saddle.

"Seriously," Kai continues. "I can't wrap my head for shit. The sun always gets me."

Riat slaps him on the back and laughs. "He's not lying. One time, we were out here for weeks tracking a bounty. When we got back to town, he was the color of chri berries."

I let out a soft laugh and shake my head. I can picture it, Kai's ivory-white skin baking under the sun and growing a vibrant red. My mouth opens and the offer to teach him lingers in my throat. But as I look at him, at the smile beaming brightly and the mischief in his eyes, something uneasy washes over me. *This is exactly what happened with Zoah.*

The realization is like a slap to the face. I look at Kai, and I see Mikel. I see Kora. I see the people I let myself care for, the people that I let myself get weak for. I snap my mouth shut, stifling any words. *These people are not my friends. I'm not staying.* The reminder is a punch to the stomach. I pull the fabric away from my mouth and take a deep swig from my canteen, drowning the words I wish I could say.

"Why don't you have more markings?"

Before I can say anything, Tariq has thumped Riat upside the head.

"*Ow,*" Riat emphasizes, rubbing the back of his head. "What was that for?"

"For being nosy." Tariq states. He shoots me a sheepish look, and I remember what he said about his aunt. As I take in the soft look in his eyes and the contrite grimace on his face, I wonder what intolerance he bore witness to growing up.

"What's the big deal?" Riat argues. "It's an honest question."

"It's rude."

"How's it rude?"

He's still arguing, but Tariq has already busied himself with more important things. He's enjoying the last bite of his food, and I have to fight back a laugh as I watch the burly man be so content with a baked good.

"Daemons always have loads of markings. So many you can spot them a mile away," Riat says.

"You've known a lot of daemons?" I ask, genuinely curious.

"Eh, not really," he answers. "You're the third one I've ever met." He crosses his arms over his chest and purses his lips. "First was this old man out in Kalade. A Mender who fixed me up a few times. Had markings that went straight down his face, *over his eye.* Even the eyelid was covered." He whistles softly, as if impressed. "The Mender was a good guy. But the other? *Fuck.*" He laughs. "The second I met was this devil of a Torch. Nearly seared me like a chunk of meat. Bastard, she was." He looks at me with that seductive flint in his eyes that I'm all but growing used to. "You're by far my favorite. Sweet and easy on the eyes."

"Hm." I chuckle. "Sweet, huh?"

I saunter up to him, letting my eyes drift up until they lock on his all-too-eager expression. He's grinning wildly, waiting for whatever scandalous thing he thinks is going to happen next. I flash him a smirk before I sweep his legs out from under him. He drops quickly, but before he can get up, I have him pinned.

"How's this for sweet?" I drawl.

I'm pressed on top of him, dagger at his throat, while he pants underneath me. He's staring at me with wide, blown pupils, utterly speechless. Tension prickles up my spine, and I look up to see all eyes are on me. Hassan and Vish have stopped talking. I watch as a crumb falls from Tariq's gaping mouth. I linger for a second longer before I chuckle and roll off of Riat.

"You should be better prepared." I smirk as I stand up and brush the sand from my clothes. "You never know who could be a threat. Despite being sweet and easy on the eyes."

Riat is still in shock as I sheathe my blade. The silence around me shatters as Kai bursts into a fit of laughter.

"Gods above," he wheezes. "I would pay to see that again." He shoots me a fiendish look, brow raised high. "Me next?"

My smile deepens as I strap my pack back to the saddle. The whole time, Riat stays down in the sand, watching me with wide eyes.

"I think I just fell in love," he mumbles.

He's up on his feet a second later, leaning against Mirage, who is less than enthused about the intrusion. The horse stomps the earth, sending up a puff of sand, but Riat doesn't relent.

"You and me." He licks his lips, eyeing the dagger holstered at my thigh, the one that was just pressed against his throat. "We could have some fun."

A sharp laugh leaves my throat. "Not going to happen."

"Oh, come on," he croons, slipping his hand over mine where it rests on my pack. "Just think of all the things we could—"

"Everyone done fucking around?"

The joy is ripped from my body the instant I hear Hassan's voice. As he shifts his gaze between me and Riat, I swear his anger only grows.

"Riat," he barks. "Need I remind you we're here to do a job?"

Riat sighs, shooting me an irritated look before reluctantly turning toward Hassan. "I was just being friendly. It's not like we're tracking—"

"Vish has picked up the trail," Hassan spits back. His eyes hover on me, the glint in his hazel eyes like a golden fury. "Stop trying to fuck the witch and get ready to leave."

"I have a name," I snap. I'm stomping up to him, getting in his face, before I can stop myself. It's a miracle my blades are still sheathed. "Unless you'd rather I address you as *the goat* from now on?"

His jaw clicks as he leans into me. "I don't care what your name is. Especially when all you do is cause problems and distract my men."

I hear Savi mumble under her breath, but she keeps her distance. Everyone does, as if they know no good will come from this.

"Do you ever get tired of being such a foul, angry beast?" I quip. "It must be tiring to lead such a life. To always be such a miserable ass. To pretend you're better than everyone. Never feeling *anything* but hate." I spit the words and wait for them to cut him down.

But he doesn't flinch, doesn't even widen his gaze at me. He just stares, deep into my soul like he's trying to take root there. I shiver on instinct, the intimacy of his focus too much to bear.

Luckily, Vish steps up and breaks the spell between us. "The bounties are due west, only a few hours or so. We need to leave now, or we risk losing them."

"We're not heading to resupply?" Kai asks.

Hassan keeps his eyes on me as he answers. "No."

Dread swells in my stomach. "What about Hira?"

Hassan's gaze tightens before turning toward his band, ignoring me completely. "We're leaving to intercept the bounties now. Once we have them, we'll hand them over at Varhit."

"Back into the desert?" Riat grumbles. "I thought we were heading to the coast?"

"Varhit is closer. We'll rest there for a few days before we pick up a new job." Hassan throws a stern look to Riat before drifting it toward Kai. "You will have plenty of time to spend your take on drinks and company there."

The group talks quickly. Savi reminds the others who the bounties are—how violent they might be, what their offenses are, what to expect. Tariq and Kai give an update on supplies—how much food we have, what we have in terms of restraints, how long until we run out of water. Their words are lost on me as the sand stirs behind Hassan. The grains glitter against the sun before giving way to a flash of black. A lump lodges in my throat. My hand grows clammy as I slowly reach for the dagger at my side.

"Don't do anything foolish," Hassan orders everyone. "These men are far from the worst we've brought in. No one try to play the hero. We take them down quickly and efficiently—as a team."

"Sounds boring." Riat scoffs.

"It's a job," Hassan stresses. "It's not—"

Hassan's eyes catch on me as I pull my blade free from its sheath. My hand is shaking. I stare at the space next to his boot, eyes wide and unwavering.

"What are you—"

"Don't move," I utter.

His brow crumples roughly. His gaze shifts from my face to the dagger in my hand, then back up to my face again. Like the idiot I know he is, he takes a step toward me.

"What—"

The sand stirs, and my heart jumps in my chest. I chuck the dagger at Hassan before he can even finish his sentence. Only when I see the blade pierce shiny, black scales do I loose a breath.

Hassan's eyes are wide, but they only grow wider as he looks down at his boot. The snake writhes at his feet, struggling with the last spasms of fight it has left in it. My dagger is a spike through its head, and I watch as black blood seeps into the sand around the creature.

"*Veles below*," Kai utters, stepping up to both of us. He reaches down toward the snake but Savi quickly lunges forward and slaps his hand away.

"Are you out of your mind?" she seethes. "Those broken scales can rip your hand open easier than any blade."

Kai grimaces before taking a cautious step back. The others crowd around, staring at the dead thing in the sand. Tariq gets the heebie-jeebies and quickly retreats to his camel, mounting so that his feet rest far from the sands below. Riat dares to poke the snake with one of his knives. Savi is exasperated, and I hear her mutter something about unruly children. But I can't focus on any of it. All I can do is look at Hassan. His eyes haven't left mine for even a second. There's wild disbelief carved into that rigid face of his.

"That's a vitremi," he states flatly.

I grit my teeth, biting back a scoff. "I'm aware."

He quirks his head slightly, eyes raking across my face. "That would have killed me."

My eyes roll before I can stop them. "Again, I'm aware. I've lived in this desert for most of my life, you know."

It's rare to see a vitremi, but this isn't the first I've encountered. I remember one night, years and years ago, when I was making my own way in the desert. I had a small, old camel that could travel no more than ten miles a day and a raggedy tent. It was a pitiful way of life, but it was all I had. That night had been unseasonably hot, and I wandered out into the open desert in desperate need of a lick of a breeze against my skin. My bare feet had carried me up a dune, my mind too tired to remember there were much worse fates out here than the heat.

I felt it before I saw it. The sharp, cool touch of scales against my ankle. Even now, the memory chills my blood. I had lurched away at the sight of the Continent's deadliest snake at my feet, one that is said to be touched by Veles himself. But it didn't strike, didn't sink those sharp, black fangs into me and fill me with a poison that only a quick Mender can remedy.

Instead, it had slithered closer, gliding across the top of my bare foot before slipping under the sand. I ran back to my tent with my heart in my stomach and the vow to never step foot in these sands without boots again. Looking down at the creature now, I can't help but wonder if it's the same one. My stomach grows uneasy at the sight of the slaughter caused by my own hand. I tear my gaze back up to Hassan before regret can burrow.

He says nothing, but his eyes continue their scrutiny. He's searching my face for something. For what, I'm not sure. Silence rests unsettled between us, only broken by the sound of him yanking my blade free. Blood drips off the tip, and though I'm far from squeamish, I find myself looking away. Again, uneasiness stirs my gut. I've killed many creatures out in the Jahaer, either in self-defense or in order to not starve. But something about seeing that dead vitremi feels like I killed a part of myself.

I hear Hassan wipe the blade against the sand to clean it. When I finally look back, he offers it to me. I take it without a word, resheathing it quickly.

"You didn't let it kill me."

My eyes snap to his. I look for a flicker of amusement on his face or a touch of irritation. There is none. Nothing but pensive severity rests in his expression. My heart seems to squeeze and choke when I realize what he's implying. I pull in a deep breath and force myself to hold his gaze.

"You may wish for this desert to take me, to drag me down to the underworld so that you may be free of my very presence, but that sentiment is not shared." I grit my teeth and step toward him.

His chest is mere inches from my own, and I can hear his breath still at my approach. I watch the muscles in his jaw clench, watch his eyes flare uncertainly.

I burn my gaze into him and drop my words to a whisper. "I am not the devil you wish me to be," I utter. "Your hate is yours alone."

His throat bobs before I pull myself away. The others mumble, and Savi steps up, but my pace is determined. I pass her quickly, hauling myself onto Mirage. As I settle into the saddle, I don't look at the others—don't dare turn to see if Hassan's gaze is still locked on me. Instead, I look at my hands. Though my skin is clean, it's as though the vitremi's black blood is hot on my fingertips. Something like panic swells in my throat. My blood pumps wildly in my veins. I dig my nails into my palms and pray the feeling goes away.

Soon enough, the others load up and we're off. Vish leads the way, keeping a rigid pace ahead. I should be thinking of the bounties, of what the encounter will bring, but my mind wanders to what is to come after. There's a residual pounding in my chest and a heaviness holding my breath hostage. We're heading deeper into the desert, further from the cities. My brow furrows, trying to remember where Varhit even is.

It's west of the coast, but how far deep to the west?

Didn't Zoah mention it was a few days ride from where we were camped? Which means we're heading north, but not north enough. We're heading back to where Olen and Harkin found me. Back to where this all began.

My throat bobs as I swallow the nagging ache there. Something tells me this detour isn't a coincidence. And whether it be by the gods' design or someone else's, I'm not sure I'm ready for what it brings.

CHAPTER 20

I pull my headscarf down and take on the onslaught of heat from the sun. The rays prickle against my now-exposed scalp, but the renewed air flow against my neck is like a breath from the heavens. Sweat slips down the back of my tunic before I can stop it. We've been traveling for hours on end, not daring to stop for fear of the bounties gaining too much ground.

As I stare ahead at the endless desert, I can't help but wonder if this is how Rohan feels right now. Uncomfortably hot. In desperate need of dismounting his horse if only to stretch his legs for a minute. Anxiously awaiting the moment his prey is in sight. There's nothing but sun and strung-out anticipation. It's the hunt. But the purpose of the one I find myself on now is lost to me. I have no coin to be gained, no justice or revenge to seek. All it is to me is a grueling, monotonous trek across the sand, made worse by the tension that festers in my bones and the realization that every second here is delaying my escape north.

I risk a glance behind me. I look past Hassan and his hardened gaze. It's only a distraction. His annoyance at my very presence here won't prevent what's to come. So I ignore him and look toward the horizon. I look for a shadow, a flicker of movement—any sign of my impending end. But like the many times I've checked the sands at our backs, there's nothing and no one. It's a temporary relief. One of these times, there will be something out there. *He* will be out there.

"If you're thinking of leaving, be my guest."

My focus rips from the horizon to meet Hassan's glare. I don't bother answering him before I turn away. A clicking noise sounds from his cheek as he urges his horse forward. Before I know it, he's sidled his horse up next to mine. I keep my gaze locked forward, pretending as if he doesn't even exist.

"You've checked the horizon nearly a dozen times since we set course," he says. "If you're having second thoughts, better you leave now before it gets too dangerous for you to handle."

A vicious scoff rips from my throat. "You honestly think I'm afraid of what's to come?" I shake my head and mumble obscenities under my breath. "I've been in danger my whole life. Tracking bounties hardly qualifies as trouble."

"Is that so?"

I see the corner of his mouth twitch up before he stifles it. "So why are you acting as skittish as your horse?"

I look down at Mirage. The mare is nipping at Hassan's, whinnying in irritation as the beast gets too close for her liking.

"She doesn't like you," I say flatly. "Seems she's a good judge of character."

I don't catch what he mutters under his breath. As we move across the sand, his question itches at my throat.

"I'm watching for him," I mumble.

I keep my face flat, eyes fixed on where Tariq and Savi are up ahead. They're talking loudly, excited about something, but I'm not watching, not listening—not really. Instead, I let the world around me unfocus and blur at the edges. If I truly look, see the camaraderie between them—the happiness there—it will only hurt. I need not be reminded of what has been taken from me so many times.

"What makes you so sure Rohan will come for you?"

My heart slithers up into my throat but I don't respond. *I was right. Vish did tell him.*

"You must think you're pretty special," Hassan grumbles, "to think one man would chase you across the desert."

My head snaps to attention. "It has nothing to do with me," I spit. "As far as he's concerned, I work for him now. I belong to him." I grit my teeth and drag my vicious gaze away from Hassan. "Unlike you, I don't think I'm Hael's gift to the Continent."

I wrap the headscarf back into place, shielding myself from the sun once more. I'm happy to block Hassan from my view in the process. We ride silently, tension plaguing the space between us. I try to focus on the steady hoofbeats underneath me, but his words grate my nerves. *The ass.* He thinks he knows me, but he's wrong.

The caress of fabric against my cheek startles me as a breeze flutters by. In an instant, it all comes rushing back. Not fabric, but fingers stroking my cheek. Rohan prying the vision from me, taking it with a stolen touch. Not just any touch, a touch I imagined as someone else's. I gulp against hot air, throat dry, but I don't reach for my canteen. The scratchy burn is a far better reminder that I'm alive than the soothing flow of water. I press my fingertips against my temples, stifling the slight shake in them and rubbing my tension away. The sleeves of my tunic slip down and flutter in the breeze.

"Your arms—"

I shoot Hassan a sharp look as he struggles to find the words.

"How did he...?"

I tug my sleeves down, hiding the broken skin. My hands grip tightly against the reins and Mirage tenses under me. "Please spare me the illusion that you care. We both know you don't."

The venom in my tone hits its mark, and his face takes on the same guarded tension I know mine currently holds.

"You're right," he mutters. "Forget I asked."

Just as he pulls back on the reins to create distance between us, Kai's voice shouts from up ahead. "Hassan!"

My eyes snap to Kai's outstretched hand, following it to a glimmer of movement below the sand dune we've just crested. As I see it clearly, my heart kicks up a notch. Up ahead are two men on camels. They're cloaked in dark tunics, faces shielded from the sun. I can't tell how old they are or how much of a threat they might be. But I see the moment they realize they're no longer alone. Legs kick and reins snap as they take off. It's only seconds later before chaos erupts around me. The others take off, and without hesitation, I do the same. I have no part to play here but it's the thrill of the moment that has me racing forward.

Hassan speeds past, tucked against his horse as it races down the dune. Riat is next, followed by Tariq. The pair move as a unit, spreading out to the right of Hassan, attempting to separate the fleeing men. It works. The bounties separate without concern, fraying whatever allegiances they had and leaving their individual fates up to the gods. I watch the scene unfold like orchestrated chaos. Hassan intercepts his target first. He overtakes the man quickly, the camel no match for his horse. It's a quick flash of bodies and sand as Hassan leaps off his saddle and tackles the man off his own. They hit the ground in a flurry, and I lose them in a spray of sand.

A yell rips my focus across the desert. Riat and Tariq have trapped the other man between them. The bounty's gaze darts back and forth between the two men, eyes wild and desperate. Savi is close behind. She's unstrapped the bow from her back and is currently nocking an arrow. Her thighs clench against the saddle as she barrels down the dune. She holds steady all the while, aiming right at the man's chest. The man has nowhere to run, but still, he does.

In a rush, the bounty drives his camel toward Riat. The animals panic. Curses slip from Riat's lips as he maneuvers out of the way, dodging the swipe of a sword as the man barrels past. Savi looses an arrow, and it lodges deep into the bounty's arm. He yells, body sagging yet still determined. His fingers wrap around the arrow's shaft, splitting it in two. He barely turns to look over his shoulder before blindly throwing a knife. It flies toward Tariq, who swats it away. It was a poor throw, but I don't miss the flecks of blood that rip across Tariq's forearm. The bounty is heading straight toward me, and I do the only thing I can think of. I draw both daggers from their holsters and charge him.

Mirage huffs wildly underneath me, but she doesn't hesitate. Sand kicks up behind us. The heat blazes down on me. But all I can focus on is the way the man's crooked teeth pull into a brutal smile. He thinks this is going to be easy. I can't help but smirk as I copy Hassan's own move. I lunge from my saddle and tackle the man as our animals pass. We hit the ground in a heavy thump and I instantly feel the air rip from my lungs. My body aches but I don't heed its warning. I roll.

The sword slips from the man's grip. It's a miracle he didn't slice me open on the way down. If he was a better swordsman, I would be paying for my recklessness now. His weight drives us into another roll, and I fight the urge to thrust the blade into him. I don't think

Hassan or Savi would appreciate me letting their bounty bleed out. I grit my teeth and drive my knee into the man's groin instead. He grunts and coughs. I quickly shove him off me, finding distance between us. My back throbs as I stand.

A cool trickle slides down my skin, and I have a feeling it's not sweat. I grit my teeth through the pain and resist the urge to pat the growing wet spot on the back of my tunic. *Savi is going to be pissed.* The thought tugs a smile on my face, stirring memories of Mikel and similar scoldings I've received. I sheath one of my blades and point the other at the man below me.

"Stay down," I bark. "This isn't my fight, but I will gladly draw blood."

The man grimaces. He spits into the sand as he struggles to his knees. "Stupid whore," he utters. "You're going to pay for that."

The bounty's hand slips to his side, but it's too late. A blade spins through the air, reaching the man before he has a chance to pull the dagger hidden in his tunic. A wild howl echoes across the desert as Riat's knife lodges into his hand. Blood drips from the mess of broken flesh and tendons.

The pained howls continue as Tariq settles at my side. He points a blade at the bounty's neck before he can attempt anything else. I take a deep breath and let myself feel every ache across my body. My ribs could have done without me smacking the ground, that's for sure.

I sheathe my blade across my chest and bite back the pain. Sand kicks up around me as Riat saunters over. In a swift movement, he yanks his knife from the man's hand. Curses spill from the bounty in rapid succession. His words for me were tame compared to the filth pouring from his lips now. Riat merely chuckles and tosses his bloodied knife in the air. It flips twice before he catches the hilt in perfect timing. He looks to me and winks. Savi lets out a sharp laugh, and the world seems to spin a little slower once more.

"Always the showoff," she taunts Riat.

"I wanted to prove these *little things* can get the job done."

He shoots me a devilish look and a wide grin. I shake my head with a laugh and look over just in time to see Hassan send his fist flying into the other bounty's face. Blood and sand sprays everywhere. The man rears up with a blade, but he's quickly deterred as Hassan lands another blow. The dagger flies from the bounty's hand and splats in the sand. Kai simply stands there, already dismounted from his horse and looking rather amused as he watches the scuffle from a few feet away. It's clear Hassan doesn't need any help. He hasn't even bothered unsheathing the sword from his back, relying on his fists instead.

"Still think I'm the showoff?" Riat baits Savi. He gestures toward Hassan and lets out a breathy laugh. "Looks like I wasn't the only one looking to prove something."

I pull myself up onto Mirage's saddle, ignoring the throbbing in my back. Riat and Tariq quickly bind their bounty, and I find my gaze wandering back toward Hassan. He has his man pinned face down in the sand. Arms flail, and the man's yells muffle against the ground. Hassan quickly pats him down. There's a flash of a small blade as he pulls it from the bounty's tunic and chucks it across the sand. It takes Hassan no time at all to bind the man's wrists and haul him up.

The man struggles at first, but it's clear there's no fight left in him. Blood drips from his face, and his gaze is locked onto the sand. Hassan mumbles something to Kai before pushing the man toward him. Kai laughs as he leads the bounty over to the others, but my gaze doesn't follow him. I watch Hassan's chest heave as he works to catch his breath. Pieces of his wavy brown hair stick to his forehead as sweat beads there. The muscles in his arms almost swell from the blows he just delivered. There's a cut across his plump lips, and as the blood drips, he wipes it away with the back of his hand.

Something in my stomach flutters uneasily. My cheeks flush without permission as his gaze catches mine. Just as his brow quirks up, I rip my eyes away. *Gods.* I force a heavy breath from my lungs, trying to rid myself of whatever just came over me. It's nothing, really. I shake my head and grip the reins tighter. I can find him attractive. It's not a big deal. It doesn't mean I want him. I would *never* want him.

My molars are still grinding into each other as Vish sidles up next to me. He's stayed back, letting the others do their part. It makes sense, considering his part came long before the chaos began. I shoot him a careful look, expecting to find the same harsh scrutiny from last night. But he's not even looking at me. His eyes are locked tightly on the bounties.

"It's hard sometimes," he says softly. "To hunt men just because others have told you to—because others have deigned them a problem or threat."

His words instantly sober me. Hassan is long departed from my thoughts as I remind myself what the situation is here. My shame burrows its way into the deepest dregs of my soul. I look at the men—the bounties—now captured and bound only a few dozen paces from me. *What did they do? What will happen to them after they're dragged back to the cities? Will they pay off their debts? Be killed? Or will their fate be something worse?*

I feel a chill ripple across my sweat-locked skin as I think about the place I've only seen in my nightmares. Death is rumored to be kinder than a cell in Tol Dena, a place where your body is said to rot slower than your mind. My skin grows hot, and my thoughts rise to a violent buzzing in my ears.

What if Rohan put a bounty on me? The back of my throat seems to close up as dread climbs my windpipe. I stabbed Rohan. I stole from him. *Gods*, I killed the other. Just like these men, I have done harm—committed offenses. When will it be my turn to be hunted? And when I am, will these people be the ones who come to collect?

"Why do you do it?"

The words slip past my lips in a strangled breath.

Vish's brow arches slightly as he pulls his gaze from the bounties. He observes me for a while, but I can't meet his gaze. The quiver of worry washing over my face isn't something I can let him see.

"Every path to freedom is riddled with suffering," he says. "One must choose the path they're willing to take."

His words swirl around my mind, creasing deep lines between my brows. As I turn toward him, he's already gone. I watch him head off toward the others, repeating his words in my head. I try to find answers among them, but the solace I seek isn't there. *Suffering.* Always, there is suffering.

I watch Hassan spit blood into the sand. It seeps into the earth, disappearing like an offering. His eyes flash to me for a brief second before pulling away. *Which path of suffering am I willing to take?*

I look behind me, at the desolate sands. It's empty. Quiet. Lonely, even. To my right, more sand. And in the distance, the silhouette of the gorge that separates us from the coast. I could go now, leave behind this path I've somehow chosen. My eyes drift back to the group in front of me, the small band of rogues who would be better off without me—and I, them. I almost believe it, but there's doubt flickering in my chest.

Savi waves me over, beaming a bright smile like a beacon across the sand. A second later, Kai is at her side. He wraps an arm around her shoulders, chatting happily into her ear. Savi says something to him before both of their gazes slide to me. They look at me curiously.

Kai cocks his head to the side, the shell of a smile dancing across his lips.

As I watch them watching me, I feel like I've been here before. There's a flicker of knowing in the back of my mind that I can't place, not entirely. The familiarity creeps up my neck and seems to tingle the markings on my skin. I shudder at the feeling. I stare ahead, feeling like I'm watching this life through glass.

The illusion is shattered when Kai gestures for me, calling me to join them. In that moment, I know what path to take. Whether I'm ready to face the suffering it brings, I'm not sure. I gently nudge my heels into Mirage's side and tug the reins. She takes me across the sand, away from the life I knew before, away from my better judgement, until I'm too far gone. As I reach the others, I'm met with a look I'm beginning to know far too well.

"For a second there, I thought you were going to leave." Savi smirks. She gives Mirage a loving pat as I dismount.

Kai takes a long sip from the flask he's pulled from his belt. After he wipes his mouth, he looks at me expectantly. "She would never do that," he scoffs. "She's one of us now."

My heartbeat stills, and I wonder, for a brief moment, if I made the wrong choice. This suffering has the potential to hurt much more than any blade or strife. I would know, I've faced it before.

"We'll make camp here."

Hassan's voice cuts through my thoughts, and I find myself tensing as he joins us. For some reason, I can't look at him. Tariq, Riat, and Vish are close behind, although Tariq's focus doesn't leave the bounties for more than a few moments at a time. I can practically see his muscles twitching in anticipation of a fight. But the men stay where they are—bruised and bloody, sweaty and panting in the sand. Judging by the look in their eyes, I'd say they don't have any intention of doing something foolish right now.

Not that they're going anywhere. They're bound with thick ropes, the ends of which are gripped tightly in Tariq's hand.

Hassan's eyes drift across each and every one of his men. His brow raises when he notices the small cut on Tariq's arm. "Problems?" he asks.

Tariq smiles softly and chuckles. "Not any that Ren couldn't manage."

Hassan's gaze cuts to me, and I swear there's surprise behind those harsh, hazel eyes.

"Seems you're not the only one that can jump off the back of a horse," Riat snickers. "And I much preferred watching her do it."

Savi rolls her eyes, laughing under her breath. She opens her mouth to say something but stops. Her gaze widens when she notices my tunic. With a quick motion, she spins me around. I don't need to see my back to know it's bad. The groan that leaves her lips tells me everything I need to know.

"Gods above, Ren," she chides. "You'll never heal at this rate."

I look over my shoulder, noticing everyone staring at the bloodied patch of fabric stuck to my back. As Hassan's eyes meet mine, his jaw clenches.

"Savi will patch you up once we get settled." He clears his throat as he looks away. "Riat. Kai—help Tariq get those two sorted for the night. I want their bindings staked into the sand. I'll have no repeat of what happened in Fiöl."

Riat begins to mumble something but shuts up when Hassan gives him a stern look.

"Savi," he continues. "You and Vish get the tents up." Finally, he turns to me. His eyes linger as if eating up every emotion on my face, every lick of sweat and sun. He raises a brow curiously. "Think you can manage to get a fire going?"

It's more than a question of my skills, or my injury. I know that. There's something unsaid snaked in his prodding tone. He wants to know if I'll make the fire tonight. The night after. Maybe a week from now. He wants to know if I'm staying, and oddly enough, he's giving me a choice.

I let out a sigh and roll my eyes. "I managed it last night, didn't I?"

His face lights up before the emotion is quickly snuffed out. "Good." He nods. "Seems you'll be of some use around here after all, witch."

A ghost of a smirk tugs at his lips, and I almost laugh at the momentary slip in his steely facade.

I step up to him, tilting my chin defiantly to meet his gaze. "Let's just hope I can find use for an ornery old goat."

I push past him, smile tugging at my lips as Savi and Kai's laughter flutters after me.

CHAPTER 21

The wind is whipping violently across my face, but it's nothing new. My heart hammers as I stare at the chasm up ahead. I can see it clearly now. I've made it closer this time. At least fifty paces. But the chasm isn't some gaping split cut into the cliff face by wind and time. No, it's been carved. The chasm isn't a chasm at all. It's a doorway. The dark opening is so high that I have to tilt my head up to see the top.

It towers in front of me, like a void leading to another world. Intricate carvings run up and down the sides of it, marring the red rock face. They look familiar but I can't decipher what they are with the wind whipping my hair across my face and blanketing my vision. As I take a step closer, my stomach locks in anticipation. I don't sink. My brow furrows as I look down. Slowly, tentatively, I take another step. Then another, and another. I'm so close now that I can see someone within the chasm—the doorway. It's like they're waiting for me, like they have been for a while.

The figure hovers among the shadows, seeming to blend in with them like they're a part of the darkness itself. My skin prickles. I stop dead in my tracks as a black tendril of smoke appears in front of me. Curiously, it curls up my leg and reaches for me. Fear has me locked in place, unable to move. It moves higher, snaking around my wrist as if trying to burrow under the skin. My eyes widen as the shadow slithers up my arm, turning my veins black in its wake. My throat is an achy husk as I swallow. Something isn't right. I'm frozen. I can only move my eyes, tracking the shadow and the destruction it wrecks on my body.

Blackness pools under my skin, spreading like tar. The shadow stops, hovering above my chest. My breath heaves in wild bursts, though I still can't find the strength to move. Suddenly, the world shifts. Darkness swells in one quick burst, flaring in front of me, bleeding into my very soul. I stagger away, limbs flailing. Panic seizes my chest as that sinking feeling I know all too well overtakes me. The sand tugs at my boots, cementing me in place but it's too late; I'm already falling backward.

My body crashes into the ground at the same time that the breath leaves my lungs. Sand sprays around me. The shadow is there, hovering. It blocks out the sun, growing closer until finally, like a wave, darkness spills over me. I barely blink before the world is gone.

"Find me, Serehna. It's time."

I jerk awake. My daggers are already drawn and slicing through the air. There's nothing and no one here—only the tricks of my mind. *It got worse. How could it get worse?*

I'm shaking, and my breath is ripping through me so violently I think I may be sick. My grip slackens, and the daggers fall from my hands, plopping onto the blankets soundlessly. I stare at the tent wall and fight to remember every second of what just happened.

It's a doorway. But where is it? The carved walls slip back into my mind but it all seems too far away. I can't get a clear picture.

I dip my head into my hands and let out a sigh that sounds more pitiful than I'd like it to. As I close my eyes, the shadow comes back. It's rushing over me, stealing my last breath until I, too, am nothing but darkness itself. I inhale sharply as my eyes rip open. *Fuck.* My hands are shaking again, and I squeeze them into fists to try to get them to stop. It doesn't work. All of a sudden, the tent feels too small. Too dark. I quickly grab my daggers, resheathing them before untangling myself from the blankets. I'm out of the tent in the next second.

The first breath of fresh air soothes my racing heart. I take in a second, holding it in my lungs like it will rid me of all terror. Slowly, I let it out. The desert is still dark. Not even a flicker of daylight crawls up the horizon. Morning is still a while off but I can't go back to sleep. I can't risk closing my eyes again and falling back into that terror. Who knows if my tormentor will slip into my mind once more.

I let out a deep sigh as I make my way through camp, careful to keep my footsteps silent. I nod to Tariq as I pass the fire. He nods in return, giving me a soft smile before turning back. He's on guard duty and I glimpse a sleeping Kai next to him. The bounties are fast asleep as well, their bindings staked deep into the sand.

I make my way past the last tent and keep going. Only when I get far enough away from camp do I let another sigh pass my lips. I run my hands through my hair and stare up at the moon. Its orange-hued rim radiates out into the dim light, and I find myself growing a little calmer. I tilt my head up and let my focus drift to the many stars that speckle the sky.

"Hael, guide me," I mutter to myself.

I drag my thumbnail down my neck, passing over my marks, before nodding and raising the digit to the sky. The act sends an unsteady tug through my gut, like it does every time I try to pray. I shake off the feeling as I stare at the horizon. The canyon is the only thing that fills my mind.

Heaviness swells in the back of my throat as I accept the truth I've been avoiding. Someone has been manipulating my dreams for months. It was clear what this was from the start, yet all I've done is play dumb. I know a Weaver's work when I feel it. *How many times did Chani practice on me? How many times did she send me into a wild, fantastical dream in order to bring me joys the days in Artolen would rarely provide?*

But this is different. This has purpose. And as much as I wish it was Chani who tortures me now, I know it isn't possible. Her blood spilled the same day as mine—though she was not as lucky. My chest twinges, but I don't allow grief to dig its claws any deeper. Instead, I rake my hands through my hair and let out a heavy breath. Whoever this Weaver is, they want something from me. They're pushing me toward this canyon, toward *him. But, why?*

Sand shifts in the night, pricking up my ears. My body stills as an icy chill overtakes me. Someone is behind me. Both of my hands splay across the hilts of my daggers in an instant, stripping them from their sheaths. It's a quiet action, one I've rehearsed a thousand times. When the footsteps crunch too closely, I turn, blades ready and eager.

"Finally going to kill me?"

I freeze. Hassan stands across from me: arms folded in front of his broad chest, eyes glinting with a potent mixture of amusement and annoyance. My mouth is agape, and I close it slowly as I resheathe my daggers.

"You should know better than to sneak up on me."

"I didn't sneak up on you," he says. "If I had, you'd be on your back with my sword at your throat."

I roll my eyes and huff, though I can't ignore the treacherous feeling squirming through my insides. It's that feeling alone that emboldens my tongue. "Only in your dreams will you ever get me on my back," I taunt.

His eyes flare, something deadly sparking amidst the hazel there. "Are you sure?"

I freeze as his tongue teases his split bottom lip. He steps closer. I can practically feel the tension rolling off him. The nearer he gets, the more my body seems to hum in anticipation. He stares at me with darkened eyes, and I swear there's a hint of cockiness under all that brooding of his.

My breath hitches as he takes yet another step, so close now I can feel his breath hot on my skin. It's like heat from a fire compared to the early morning chill. His eyes grow heavy as his hand ghosts over my neck and makes its way up to my jaw. I expect to flinch away, but Rohan and his horrors are far from my thoughts.

"What are you—"

Hassan's fingers trace my skin gently, and, for a minute, I'm lost to the sensation. Heat flushes my cheeks. My breath hitches as his thumb tugs over my bottom lip. I'm dizzy, floating on bated breath. The next thing I feel is the cold press of a blade against my neck.

"I thought you told Riat to always be on guard." He smirks. "You're easier to distract than I thought, *witch*."

The word slips from his lips in a gruff breath that sends goosebumps across my skin. I want to feel rage. Shame. Something that makes sense. He used my own trick against me—a trick I've used many, many times. *Veles below*, I just used it on Riat. *On Rohan.* I should be thinking of ways to catch Hassan off guard, how to kick his legs out, or draw my own blade. But I'm not.

Instead, I find myself leaning into him. What I feel is worse than anything I could have prepared for. It's the uncanny feeling of lightning before it strikes. Anticipation. Curiosity. *Desire.* My skin is practically buzzing with it as I look up at him. The blade is long forgotten. His fingers hover against my jaw. I watch his eyes darken. For a brief moment, he leans in, too. Everything else slips away. All sense of reason. All animosity.

Right as my lips part, I see a flicker of panic spread across his face. Before I know it, he's pulling away, taking the threat of the blade with him. The moment of silence that follows stings more than I wish it to. I swallow harshly before anger floods my core.

"Did you come out here to bother me?" I snap. "To ruin my peace?"

His eyes are stern again. Whatever I saw in them—or thought I saw in them just moments ago—has vanished.

"No." Hassan sheathes the knife at his waist and looks out across the desert. "I couldn't sleep."

"Hmph."

I nod and follow his gaze, though my heart still patters uneasily. A muted gray cloaks the sky as the last breaths of night linger. I can only make out dim shapes across the sand. Dunes spread far and wide. The mountains that tower far to the west are like bleak shadows. I try not to think of what awaits me there, if and when I'm left with nowhere else to flee.

Sleep is still heavy in the air, permeated by a cold silence that usually feels peaceful but only unnerves me now. I think of the beasts that prowl the Kohe Mountain range. I think of a dank cell in Tol Dena, ready and waiting for me. None of the apprehension I feel compares to what clutches my chest when I think about the canyon. It's a desperate, dreadful ache—one that tells me the gods will not be so kind if I ignore this tug of fate.

A chill rakes across my skin. Unease pools low in my stomach. I wrap my arms around myself, wishing I had put on more layers before I left my tent. I should go back inside, but I don't. Something keeps me tethered here, next to Hassan. Somehow, despite the hate I know he holds for me, I feel safe by his side. In this moment, I understand what Savi said. Hassan looks after people; it's his nature. Against my better judgement, I feel myself relaxing next to him. It's wrong. I hate the feeling—but not as much as I wish I did.

Hassan and I stand in silence. As the minutes tick by, it becomes a bearable stillness. A deep breath looses from my chest. I stare at nothing but the barren desert ahead as I let my eyes unfocus. The dream comes back to me, and I let it, despite the anxiety that builds in my chest. I can still feel the wind whipping through the canyon. Feel my boots sinking into the sand.

I close my eyes for a moment and picture it. A doorway in the face of the cliffside. Carvings—no, *markings*. *Yes*. Markings carved into the rock face. Old. Older than anything I've ever known or seen. Desperation fills my chest like a rising tide. I need to get there, to reach the place that plagues me. It's the only way.

A feeling of urgency buries in my chest, too strong to ignore. I hear it again, now. That voice—*his* voice. It haunts me even in the waking hours. I was never supposed to hear it again. I told myself I would no longer know that voice, nor the darkness of his eyes, nor the slink of his shadows. After the day he let me lie bleeding, I was done. But here I am, plagued by the only person as stubborn as I it seems.

"Why can't you sleep?"

I'm startled back to reality by Hassan's voice. I open my eyes and look across the desert. The sand is no different than my dreams, but the energy, the energy is different. Muted. Flat. It's not like that inescapable pull I feel when I'm standing in the canyon, staring at that chasm.

I take in a deep breath and stare at the horizon, like that place will appear before my very eyes. Hassan's gaze is heavy on my skin as his question remains unanswered.

"It's of no concern to you," I finally mutter.

He scoffs and looks away. "You're right. It's not."

I turn to glare at him. "And why can't you sleep?"

It's his turn to refuse my question but surprisingly, he doesn't. "I don't like this situation," he states. "I don't like the target it might place on everyone here—on the people I care about."

Guilt seeps deep into my bones like a poison-tipped arrow. I open my mouth to speak but he stops me.

"It's not your fault."

My brow furrows but he doesn't give me a chance to speak.

"You didn't put yourself in Rohan's path. You didn't ask to be—"

He stops, and I turn just in time to see his jaw tick. The look in his eyes is pure rage, but I can't help but feel it's not for me. As our eyes lock, his gaze softens. I swear I see that look again, the one I think I'm imagining. It threatens to cut me down for reasons I can't—*won't*—admit. I avert my eyes and let the words tumble from my lips. "Everything will be fine once we get to the city."

He shifts next to me, but I refuse to meet his gaze.

"We'll go our separate ways. If Rohan is tracking me, I'll lead him far away." I practically choke on my words. "I'll be gone, and the people you care about will no longer be in danger."

He's silent, and I risk a glance. His face is riddled in tension. He's staring at me like I've pulled a blade on him. But he doesn't say anything, he just stares at me for a while before he turns toward the horizon and lets out a sharp breath.

"You're right. Everything will be fine once we get to Varhit."

It's then that my heart swells with something foul. It's a resentful, bitter thing that I know was my own doing, but I let it spread into my veins like venom anyway. Without another word, I head back to my tent.

CHAPTER 22

The arguing has gotten worse. After traveling all morning, I thought the bounties would be too tired to try to talk their way out of this. But as I hear their voices shouting at Hassan behind me, I know they're far from through.

"I'll double the reward if you drop us off in Deshi."

I hear Hassan scoff. "With what coin?"

"You don't know who you're dealing with," the other bounty growls. "It'd be a mistake not to take the offer."

Riat pulls at his horse, leaving my side and falling back to where Hassan and Tariq flank the bound men.

"Hm, let's see," he taunts. He pulls two pieces of parchment from his saddlebag and squints his eyes dramatically as he reads. "Emeric, you're wanted for quite a hefty gambling debt, and Lias..." He looks at the second man, eyebrow raised. "Looks like you're wanted for doing something questionable to a donkey."

The man's face pales, then reddens, before he sputters his words.

"Only kidding." Riat laughs, cutting him off. "Just like Emeric, you don't seem to know when to quit once you're down a hand. And with this kind of debt?" He whistles. "Man, you must be pretty fucking bad at cards."

The two men argue and throw insults at Riat, which he happily parries back and forth. I let their voices fade behind me as I trudge forward on Mirage. My spine is in desperate need of a break, not that I'll be getting one anytime soon. Now that we have the bounties, Hassan has made it clear there's no time to waste. The sooner we get to Varhit, the sooner they all get paid.

I do what I can to stretch my back, twisting until I hear a satisfying crack. Just as I turn to do the other side, Vish comes to an abrupt halt ahead of me.

"We're being followed."

The heat from my body is gone in an instant, replaced by a cold, bottomless dread. *He's found me.* I stare at the back of Vish's head, hoping I misheard him. When he continues to stay unnervingly still, I know I didn't.

"I don't see anyone." Kai turns to look behind us, frowning in concentration.

I risk a glance back, and to my surprise, the desert appears empty for miles.

"He's careful," Vish offers. "But I've caught a few... *glimpses* of him today." His lips tighten into a thin line. I can tell he's worried. He's trying not to show it, but I see the flicker of it wrinkling the corners of his eyes. Even though I've only known him a short time, the man is always undisturbed—as flat as a stone wall. To see him even slightly uneasy is unsettling. My stomach clenches, and I can't help the panic that seeps into my voice.

"You've known someone was following us all day, and you're just now mentioning it?"

Vish doesn't bother looking at me, his eyes are still fixed on the horizon. "I had a feeling someone was trailing us, yes. I noticed yesterday but wanted to be sure before I alerted everyone."

"So, you waited until they were close enough, to... what... exactly? See if they were friendly? Let them get close enough to where our escape is pointless?"

I ride up next to him, causing his camel to groan unhappily as Mirage gets in its face. "Why don't we make camp right here and wait for them? That's what you want, right?"

Panic is the only thing I feel. It's raw and irrational and seeks to consume me. The cellar's chill creeps up the back of my neck. Hands paw at my skin. The words are spitting from me like fire, and before I know it, I've drawn my blade.

"It's clear you know Rohan," I spit. "So what's the plan here, hm?" My hand shakes against the weighty hilt of my dagger. "Let your old friend catch up so you can finally be rid of me? I'm sure you'll fetch something shiny for the troub—"

Vish's face contorts with an anger I've never seen before. "You have no idea—"

"Enough!" Hassan pushes his horse between us. "Rohan isn't taking you," he barks. "And no one is trying to get rid of you either." He shoots me a heated look, eyeing me then the weapon clenched in my hand. "But drawing a blade every time you're scared isn't helping."

"I'm—" I choke back a retort and swallow the shame that threatens to burn across my face. He's right and I hate it.

I slowly slip the dagger back into its holster. As my eyes dart to Vish, I fight the urge to say something more. The adrenaline pumping through my veins is drenched in anger and fear. Nothing good can come of it. I grit my teeth and swallow it down. Trust is a thin line between us all, and in this state, I'm all too ready to snap it.

Vish stares at me with that infuriatingly calculated gaze of his. I can see the wheels turning in his head—analyzing me, the situation, all of it. Finally, he nods to the horizon. "It's not Rohan," he offers. "Not unless he's dumber than the last time I came across him."

"When did—"

"Our shadow is alone," Vish adds, quickly cutting me off. "And no one would track a group alone unless they're stupid. Or desperate."

Hassan's jaw ticks as he stares at the barren sands between us and whoever is out there. "Or dangerous enough to not care about being outnumbered." He takes in a sharp breath before turning to Vish. "You're sure he's alone?"

The man gives a quick nod. "Yes, I would have sens—" He pauses. Something flares in his gaze as he looks at Hassan, to me, then back to Hassan. "Yes, he's alone. On horseback."

The rest of the group has circled around us. There's tension heavy in the air. The two bounties are arguing under their breath, likely planning their escape for when chaos inevitably breaks out. Riat runs a finger along his blades as he glares at them. The bounties shoot him dirty looks, but Riat's point has been made. They stay put.

"What's the plan?" Savi asks. "Keep going to Varhit and hope he's not stupid enough to try something, or wait for him here and get it over with?"

"Maybe he's lost?" Kai asks. "Needs directions?"

A gruff laugh slips from Tariq's throat as he raises a brow at Kai. "And maybe he's going to offer us all the rum we can drink and a plate of roasted pig."

"I'm just saying," Kai argues. "Why assume his intentions are bad?"

"You live on the same Continent as the rest of us, right?" I mutter under my breath.

Hassan rubs his palm across his face, dragging beads of sweat away with his frustrations. "Vish, what do you think?"

I watch Vish twist the gold ring around his finger. He's silent, but his eyes seem to sharpen, taking in everything around us. He's so focused, I swear his pupils constrict into slits before he blinks and turns back to Hassan.

"We break for the gorge. If we reach it in time, we can lay in wait and catch him off guard. Handle him however you want then. We should be safe to travel the rest of the way to Varhit."

"How are we going to catch him off guard?" Riat chuckles darkly. "There's nothing out here but sand. And the gorge?" He gestures loosely to the wall of red rock that lies in the distance. "What do you expect us to do? Leave everything and climb it?"

"There's a smaller pass that cuts through, not too far from here. It's manageable. Safer to travel. If we can get there fast enough, we can hide and wait for him to enter. Ambush him."

"How the hells do you know that?" Riat asks.

Vish's gaze darts away uneasily before he finally answers. "I've been through here before. Long ago."

"And you remember some random canyon?" Riat challenges. He shoots Kai a ridiculous look but his friend only shrugs.

"Makes sense to me."

"Right..." Riat grumbles.

My heart skips a beat. *The canyon.* Pieces of the Weaver dream flood my mind until the picture comes into focus. A deep canyon. An entrance carved in stone. I still my breath and shake the thoughts away. No, it can't be here. I can't be this close. I'm chewing the inside of my cheek loosely in my teeth when Hassan urges his horse forward.

"Get moving," he urges everyone. "We stick to Vish's plan. I want to see who we're up against."

Tariq let's out a breathy laugh. "Seven against one? I'm not worried."

Hassan looks at Vish, no doubt noting the same quiet distress I see in the man's eyes.

"Be prepared for anything," Hassan orders. "And anyone."

CHAPTER 23

It takes about three hours to get to the small pass in the gorge. To both Riat's and my surprise, it's exactly where Vish said it would be. Once we make it far enough into the mouth of it, tucked out of sight, we dismount and get ready. According to Vish, our pesky little friend has gained ground. Whoever he is, he'll be here soon. How Vish knows that when I never so much as glimpsed the man following us, I don't know.

I can feel the blood pounding through my veins as I take long, desperate gulps of water. It does nothing to calm me. At the end, all I'm left with is an empty canteen and ragged breath.

"How do you know he'll take the bait?" I nag Vish.

He's sitting on a nearby rock, elbows resting on his thighs. He's far from comfortable. I can see the tension stiffening every muscle in his body. He's like a snake poised to strike. Vish shoots me a sideways glance, not bothering to turn his head. "If he doesn't, we'll know soon enough."

I mutter my skepticism under my breath and turn away. I don't know how long we've been waiting, but I can't handle much longer. It feels like my nerves are eating me alive—feasting from the inside out. My legs practically twitch underneath me. I need to do something.

My eyes sweep around, searching for a distraction. Riat and Kai are busy watching over the bounties. I notice one of the men getting under Riat's skin. I can't hear the taunt, but it has Riat throwing his hands in the air. Kai is quiet, peeling an apple while his friend paces. He knows better than to intervene. Riat has been in a foul mood since we got here. He's nervous. They all are.

Kai's eyes dart to the mouth of the canyon every few seconds as he eats. Tariq is nowhere to be seen, having wandered off ages ago. He was eager to find a vantage point to confirm we hadn't somehow stepped into a trap. It's not likely, but I'm quickly learning that no one here likes leaving things up to chance. The soft rustle of leather and parchment rips my focus back to Vish.

His hands still against his journal—like a child caught doing something they shouldn't. I eye the bound pages, then meet his gaze. There's something hesitant swimming behind his green eyes. He closes the journal with a *thud* and stuffs it back in his pack like he can't risk me getting even a glance at what those pages hold.

I shift away, tearing my gaze from the man and his secrets. Vish will offer me nothing but more worry, and I cannot bear any more. My eyes scan the canyon for a lick of distraction. I almost groan when I realize I'm left with only one option. I loose a deep breath and head over to Savi who, unfortunately, is with her cousin.

Whereas the others are tucked into the curve of the canyon, hidden from view, they're both standing near the opening. Murmured conversation passes between them swiftly. My presence remains unknown as I approach their backs.

"What's going on with you?"

"Nothing," Hassan grumbles.

"*Nothing?*" Savi mocks. "Since when do you and Vish argue? Don't think I haven't noticed. Or the others, for that matter."

Silence.

"Is it Ren?"

My feet halt in the sand. Hassan stiffens.

"No." The word is no more than a grunt.

"I see the way you look at her."

"She's a burden we should be quick to rid ourselves of. Nothing more," he spits back.

My stomach lurches. A deep ache hits me like a blow, but fury quickly takes its place. I want to yell at him. I want to throw every blade I have. But I don't. For once, I'm smart. Instead, I listen.

"Why won't you—" Savi stops herself. She merely stares at her cousin, shaking her head. "You know what? Never mind. You're an idiot."

Hassan's jaw clicks, but he says nothing.

"If you won't admit it to yourself, fine. Forget Ren. There's still something you're not telling me," Savi pushes.

"You're paranoid."

"Am I?" An unfriendly laugh leaves Savi's throat. "I know all your tells, cousin. You're not as good of a liar as you think."

I hesitate, keeping my distance a few feet behind them. They still haven't noticed me. I should have announced myself long ago, but curiosity has stripped me of any courtesy.

"It's safer if you don't know," Hassan mumbles.

I can practically feel the strength of the inhale that Savi takes.

"So you are keeping something from me. *Motherfucker.*" Her hand whips out and smacks him on the shoulder.

"When you need to know, I'll tell you." He grunts. "For now, just *trust me.*"

Another laugh slips from Savi, this one equally as unkind. "Oh, is that all? Just trust you're not doing something that's going to get us all killed?"

He takes a step closer, fist curling tightly at his side. "You know I would never put anyone here in danger—let alone you." He takes in a deep breath, but it does little to settle the tension he holds. "I can't tell you this, not yet. Not until I've worked things out with—"

Hassan stills as he notices something in the corner of his eye —me. His gaze flickers across the sand, and I freeze. Words form on the tip of my tongue but it's too late. His eyes are blazing, locked on me with such intensity that I want to sink into the earth.

Savi notices the alarm stitched across his face and turns to find me. "Oh. Ren, do you need—"

"Eavesdropping?" Hassan barks, cutting her off.

"No, I was just—"

"What did you hear?"

As my gaze tightens on him, I ignore the ache in my chest. "Enough."

He hesitates. Something flashes across his face before a snarl curls his lips. "We took this little detour because of you. You know that, right?"

"Hassan—" Savi starts.

He shoves his cousin's hand away and steps toward me, closing the distance quickly. "None of us care if a lone rider is trailing us. We don't have enemies scouring the Jahaer. But you?" He gestures to me with disdain dripping from his lips. "You pissed off the most notorious man on the Continent. For all we know, he's already placed a bounty on you for whatever it is you did back in Denheir.

And if Vish is right, he'll have every mercenary south of Tilket bleed this land dry just to bring you in kicking and screaming."

"What are you... right about wh—"

"You think whatever happened to you in Denheir is bad?" Hassan is breathing down my neck, fury spitting from him like fire. "You don't know what he's truly capable of. What danger you've put us all in."

"And you do?" I shout, smashing my hands against his chest. "How could you possibly know what happened? What I've been through?"

"Because he left Savi to die!"

Everything stops. The heat claws at my neck, suffocating me. My heart no longer pumps in my chest. I look to Savi, but she's pulled away, unable to meet my gaze.

"What do you—" My throat grows dry, no longer capable of putting words together.

"How do you think she got that scar?" Hassan rasps. "Who do you think sent those daemons to burn everything to the ground?"

"Daemons?" My brow furrows as I try to understand, try to fill in the blanks where they seem so vast. *Savi's story.* I take a step back, heart pounding in my chest as the reality I'm faced with takes shape. "The men who attacked you..."

Savi finally turns to face me, but what I see has me stumbling over my words. Pain is etched deep in her eyes, replacing the brightness I thought always lived there.

"...they were daemons?"

She swallows harshly and nods. "Two Torches and a Berserker," she says. She takes a deep breath and shoots her cousin a vicious look. "That was not your story to tell."

Hassan's face drops, and for the first time since I've met him, he actually looks sorry. "Savi, I—"

"It's fine," she says sharply. "But what's not fine is taking the past out on Ren. I thought we were past this shit."

"It's okay. I understand." I try to offer her a smile, but it falls flat on my face. My heart aches for Savi, but even more, it aches that because of me, I've brought old devils to her door.

"Ren, you have to know, this changes nothing."

Savi's words cut me deep. She's sincere, I can see it in her eyes. But that only makes this harder.

I pull in a sharp breath, and I swear it cuts through me, shredding my heart to ribbons. "Hassan is right. I'm only putting you in danger by being here."

As I move to slink away, to run from the pain around me, Hassan yanks at my wrist. "Where are you going?"

I step into him, so close I can practically whisper in his ear. "Touch me again, and you'll lose a hand."

He allows me to shake his grip from my skin. But he doesn't take his eyes off me. "Where are you going?" he repeats, his voice gruff. "You shouldn't leave now."

"A walk," I utter through clenched teeth.

His gaze tightens. "Be quick about it. Our shadow could be here any minute."

I can't help the scoff that leaves my lips. "You mean you wouldn't be glad to be rid of the *burden* if I managed to wander off?"

I turn before he can say anything, stalking off into a slot in the canyon. Only when I've slipped myself from view do I let my frustrations burn through me. *Gods.* I slap the canyon walls, and rage and pain sting in tandem. Suddenly it all makes sense, but not for reasons I enjoy. *Savi.*

I force a deep breath through my lungs. I should have understood, should have seen through her words. But how could I have? Not when she's been nothing but kind to me. Fury courses through me as my mind shifts to Hassan. Of course he hates daemons, hates *me*.

I find myself bunching my hands tightly into fists and immediately stop myself. This wasn't my doing. I did not ask for this. I did not make Rohan what he is. I did not put Savi through her suffering. Hassan can be angry at me, he can hate me for what I am. But that doesn't mean he deserves *my* anger, *my* attention.

I shake my hands out, desperate to rid myself of the tension but it doesn't work. I'm still a tightly bound ball of rage and venom when I find a secluded nook in the slot canyon to relieve myself.

My brow furrows as I pull my pants back up and tie the waist. *I should have worn my leathers.* The thought echoes through my mind like an omen.

I grit my teeth as I look down at the linen pair of pants I have on. The fabric billows at my thighs and is cinched at my waist and ankles. It gives me enough movement without the threat of getting overheated. But the reason I wore them today is now my biggest concern. The fabric is light and breezy, perfect for trekking endless hours across the scorching desert. *But in a fight?* A blade will cut through without any effort.

I rake my hand through my hair as I head back to the others. I wasn't expecting to be fighting any of Rohan's men today, and being unprepared for what awaits has sweat prickling my brow. I check my blades as I walk. My fingers tap my chest, feeling the holstered dagger underneath the fabric wrapped over my torso. Next, my hip. A deep breath leaves my throat as my finger strokes the hilt of the blade tucked into my waistband. Its presence is a fleeting comfort. Two blades feels pitiful compared to the amount I used to carry on me. But—it's all I have, and I'll need to use them wisely. No throwing. Only calculated strikes. The blades can never leave my hands, *ever*.

The path widens as I make my way back to the main canyon. I wandered farther than I meant to in my anger. Hassan will likely chastise me when I return. Rage simmers in my chest at the thought of seeing him again. I believe Savi when she says nothing has changed between us. But Hassan? I'm sure he will continue to indulge the grudge that the markings on my skin conjure.

Stop.

The tickle of disturbed air on the back of my neck keeps my feet from venturing forward. My body stills, and it only takes a second to splay my fingers across the hilt of the dagger that's tucked into my pants. I spin around and face the threat at my back.

Nothing.

My brow furrows as I drop the grip on my weapon. I rub my hand against the back of my neck, trying to quell the uneasy feeling that lingers there. The skin prickles against my fingertips, erupting in goosebumps once more as the feeling grows stronger. The slight *ssshhh* of sand hits my ears like a crashing wave. It snaps everything inside of me awake, but this time when I turn, I'm thrown against the rock face before I can even unsheathe a blade.

A groan of pain leaves my lips as the breath is flattened from my lungs. I gasp, staggering away from the canyon wall. I can feel every place that will be bruised tomorrow. My ribs ache, still not fully healed. I try not to think about the wound on my back but the burning swell of tissue is hard to ignore. All the pain blinks out in an instant as movement stirs in front of me. My dagger is unsheathed from my hip within seconds. But as I turn to aim it at my attacker, I feel my blood run cold.

Gods, I'm in trouble.

He smiles, cocking his head to one side as he looks me over.

"Sorry about that, love," he smirks. "I would never throw a woman around, but something tells me you know how to use that." His eyes drop to the dagger in my hand before looking up at me again.

Rage and fear swirl dangerously inside of me as I take a step closer. It's stupid, but it's my only option. He's currently blocking my path to the others, and there's no way I can take him on myself. Not if I want to survive. Not in the state I'm in. Not with what he is.

My hand slips up under my tunic and pulls the second dagger free. I tighten my grip on both, holding them defensively in front of my face as I take another step toward him.

"I *do* know how to use these," I utter through gritted teeth. "So unless you want your guts all over the ground, best if you get out of my way."

His gray eyes flash playfully as his smile widens. "You're a brave little thing, aren't you?"

He takes a step forward, but this time, I can't fight the instinct to back away. He takes another, and I retreat again. Anger flares in me as he smirks. I'm getting farther away from my escape, and that just won't do.

I ignore every instinct that tells me this is a death wish and lunge.

Just as I make contact with him, I'm thrown against the canyon wall once again. This time, I'm ready. I bounce off it, ignoring the biting pain that shears through my shoulder, and roll. I find my legs under me and spring forward. My daggers slice through the air, nicking the empty space where his throat had been moments before. His hand grips my arm and yanks, throwing me down into the sand, but not before I slice. He grunts in pain as the blood drips down his arm. I keep the grip on my blades as I crawl forward, trying to pull myself up. My stomach drops as my ankle is tugged backward and I'm dragged across the sand.

I scream, thrashing and kicking until my boot makes contact with his groin. He grunts and buckles, giving me just enough time to get to my feet. With sweat beading my brow and my body aching, I lunge once more. I know I should be running, but all common sense has left me now. I'm nothing but pent-up rage and adrenaline. My body connects with his, sending a splash of sand around us as we hit the ground. I scramble on top of him, pinning my thighs against his side as my blade presses into his throat.

"What do you want?" I rasp through ragged breath.

His eyes drift down to where I'm straddling him. "Right now?" He smirks. "I could think of a lot of things."

I lean next to his face and press the blade harder against his skin. My other hand pushes down on his chest, holding me steady above him.

"The only thing that's going to happen is—"

Everything around me disappears. A cold tingle races up my spine with an agonizing slowness. It's happening, and I can't stop it. My eyes begin to fog over with white, and before I slip under, the only thing I can think of is that I'll probably be dead when this is over.

I stalk toward the tent, throwing the flap open wildly as I slip inside. My blood feels like it's on fire. It's going to consume me. Breath heaves in and out of my chest. I want to scream. I want to take everything in here and destroy it.

Somehow, I force myself to stand still. I drag my eyes down the far wall of my tent as rage and something I refuse to name claws inside my chest. It's too much, and I can feel every ounce of it coursing through me. I close my eyes and breathe. All of the emotion I've been forcing down over the last few days is ready to burst. And when it does? I don't know if I can handle it.

I open my eyes and let my gaze unfocus. I try not to feel anything. It's a wasted effort, but I try anyway. It's then that I hear someone step inside the tent. My hands tighten into fists and every ounce of restraint I have left snaps.

"Get out," I seethe.

"Not until you talk to me," he shoots back.

I spin around to face him and immediately realize it was a mistake. I ran into this tent for a reason. Seeing him in front of me—it only makes my mind spin more.

"I don't want to talk to you."

He scoffs and steps forward. Something flutters through me as he closes the distance between us. I look away, but his hand quickly finds my jaw and pulls my gaze back to him. I try to shake away from his grip, but he tightens it.

"I'm the only one you can talk to."

I grit my teeth as I stare up at him. "What do you want, Silas?" I snap.

He cocks his head at me, a ghost of a smirk slipping across his lips before he leans down. "You."

His lips meet mine, and the fire in my veins burns hot.

I gasp, reeling back as I pull my hand off his chest. My eyes blink, the milky haze slowly leaving them as the world as it is now comes back to me. It's then that I truly look at him. The short, white hair that falls into his gray eyes. The markings that decorate his skin. The teasing smirk that's etched across his face. My brow furrows, and my heart seems to stop for a second.

"This just got a lot more interesting," he snickers.

He flashes his eyes at me before I feel his weight shift. I panic, realizing both of my hands are at my sides, daggers held loosely. Before I can react, my body is flipped off his and pinned. He hovers over me, his hips pressed roughly into mine. He lets out a breathy laugh as his hand finds the markings on my neck. He trails his fingertips across my skin gently.

"A Seer," he hums. His eyes light up as he wraps his hand around my jaw and forces my gaze to him. "That was some kiss," he says. "But I can't help but wonder what happens next."

My whole body stills. *There's no way...*

"You saw—"

"Your vision?" he finishes. The smirk grows deeper on his face and he licks his lips. "Yes, love."

That's not possible. I thrash underneath him, only managing to pull my face free of his grip. "How?"

He leans closer, his breath teasing the shell of my ear. "I think the better question is: when?"

"Get off of me!"

My arms beat against him, but it has little effect. He sits back, his weight still pinning my hips down. My dagger appears in his hand, and I still.

"This is quite the blade," he murmurs, turning it over in his hand. His eyes flash back to me. "Is it yours?"

I ignore him, my eyes desperately searching for the other dagger. *There.* It's resting next to his thigh but close enough to grab. I dart my hand toward it but he's faster. He knocks it out of reach before leaning back over me. A frustrated yell rips from my throat as I thrash under him. He taps his blade—*my* blade—against my cheek.

"You just don't know when to submit, do you?" His tongue clicks as he shakes his head at me.

"I bested you once," I spit. I lean up so the blade presses further against my cheek. It bites into my skin, drawing a bead of blood. "Hand me a blade and give me a chance to do it again."

"Did you, though?"

As soon as the breathy laugh leaves his lips, my face falls flat. I look him over, staring at the markings running down his face— the ones I had originally spotted. The lines and splotches form columns across both cheeks, connected by a small band of them running across the bridge of his nose. My eyes dart to the ones I hadn't seen earlier. More markings line his throat. Every inch of skin I can see is covered. Again, my eyes shift, this time to the hand holding the blade against my skin. More markings. They decorate the top of his hand, breaking out across his knuckles then to the fingers themselves. The sight sets a deep ridge between my brows.

"Why didn—"

"Drop the blade."

I watch the smirk slip off his face as the point of a sword levels against his throat. My eyes flash up to Hassan. I never thought I'd be grateful to see those angry, hazel eyes. His jaw is clenched tightly as he holds the blade steadily at my attacker.

"I said, *drop the blade*," he barks again.

My attacker does as commanded, however reluctantly and with a huff of annoyance. His eyes flicker to me as Tariq hauls him up.

"I didn't know Seers had their own personal bodyguards," he taunts with a feral smile.

I rush to my feet, ignoring the protesting ache of my body as I retrieve my daggers. "Do you have chains?" I ask Hassan, sheathing my blades.

He raises an eyebrow at me. "Yes, why?"

My eyes burn into the man at the end of Hassan's sword. He's smirking, not at all fazed by the two men that hold him captive.

"You're going to need something stronger than rope to bind him," I state. "He's a Berserker."

Tariq stiffens his posture immediately, tightening his grip on the man. He yells over my shoulder, and I turn to see Kai rushing off just as Vish joins us. Hassan doesn't take his gaze off my attacker. His eyes are alight with fury. I'm surprised his knuckles haven't burst from the flesh with how tightly he's holding his sword.

"Did he hurt you?"

The daemon only laughs.

"I'm fine," I grit out.

Tariq raises a brow at me curiously. "You're fine?"

I swallow harshly. "Yes."

"You sure he didn't break your arm or something?"

Ignoring Tariq, I stare at the man in his grip. The questions running through Tariq's mind are the same ones running through mine. He could have broken my arm. He could have snapped me in two. But he didn't. I search his face for answers, but all I find is the unnerving delight that dances in his eyes.

"He didn't..." I start, but my mind is still reeling. None of this makes sense. My fingers run across my dagger as my brow pinches. "He fought me without his gift."

I turn to look at Hassan, and he looks as confused as I feel.

It's Vish who speaks up. "Hassan, we need to get him chained so we can question him."

"On it," Kai calls, quickly passing us and making his way to Tariq.

They bind the Berserker quickly, snapping his wrists into cuffs. Chains dangle from both sides which Tariq and Kai use to tug my attacker forward. The clank of metal sends a shiver up my spine. I look away before thoughts of the cellar can flash through my mind. Finally, Hassan lowers his sword.

"Tariq. Kai. Take him back to the others. We'll make camp in the canyon tonight."

They both nod and pull the daemon forward. I step aside as they pass, but the daemon's eyes lock with mine. Something burns hot over my skin, and I quickly drop my gaze to the sand. He chuckles under his breath as Tariq and Kai lead him away. My heart is hammering, and I try to still it with deep, steady breaths.

"You okay?"

Hassan's voice jolts me from my thoughts, and my hand curls around my dagger instinctively. The concern etched across his brow has me equally as flustered.

"I'm fine," I utter.

There's a heaviness in his gaze that tells me he doesn't believe me. He takes a step forward, and it's an effort not to take one back.

"Why didn't he kill you?"

My mouth opens, but I don't say anything, not for a while. I try to find the answer. Try to give myself a reason to believe that I simply fought well, but I know that's a lie. I'm barely healed. He had every advantage he could have had. *He's a fucking Berserker for Veles's sake.*

My blood boils as the fight plays over in my mind. *Gods*, he didn't even pull a weapon of his own. All he really did was push me around as I struggled to hit my mark. He was barely trying. It's like he was toying with me.

My teeth hurt from how hard I'm clamping down on my jaw. I let out a sharp breath and look back up at Hassan. "I don't know."

CHAPTER 24

His eyes haven't left me since I began setting up camp with Savi. The constant attention is a heat on the back of my neck. As I finish securing the last tent against its post, I toss a quick glance over my shoulder. Gray eyes clash with mine as a smirk curls his lips. I drop my gaze to the shackles binding him and my stomach rolls. Tariq and Kai staked his chains into the sand. *Will that even hold him? And if he breaks free, how many of us will it take to truly overpower him?*

My stomach only knots at the possibilities. Even the bounties know this is a bad idea. They quieted the moment they saw him. There have been no arguments from them since—not even an uttered complaint or a cocky bribe. They took one look at the Berserker and saw him for what he is—a threat. His mere presence is a danger to us all. Yet he sits there quietly, smiling.

I shake off the dread creeping up my spine and head over. I stayed away long enough to settle the pounding in my heart and the ache in my body, but my mind is a whole other story. *I need answers.*

The entire walk across camp, his eyes track me. The closer I get, the more I feel my nerves prickle under my skin. By the time I reach my destination, I'm practically buzzing. Hassan is ignorant to my approach, far too busy glaring down at the daemon and barking questions.

"Why were you following us?"

The Berserker ignores Hassan completely, legs splayed out in front of him, hands placed casually in his lap. He looks comfortable, and I know the small act of defiance has Hassan's blood rising. The bounty hunter's jaw is locked tight as his attention swivels to me. "You shouldn't be—"

"Mm, hello Seer," the Berserker coos. His eyes roam up my body before landing on my face. "Come to show me how the rest of that vision ends? I'm dying for another taste."

Hassan bristles next to me.

"He asked you a question." I ignore him, gesturing to Hassan.

The Berserker only smiles. "How about a question for a question?"

My brows raise at that but Hassan steps forward, fists balled up. "She's not answ—"

"Fine," I chirp, cutting Hassan off. "I'll go first. Why were you following us?"

The Berserker shifts in place, and the chains binding his wrists clank as he sits up. He lets out a deep breath and chuckles. "I wasn't following you."

"Bullshit," Hassan barks. "Our tracker noticed you days ago."

"Your tracker, huh?" The Berserker takes a long look around camp. "They must be good if they could spot me. I was keeping my distance."

"So you *were* following us," I prod.

His eyes flicker back to me. "What's a Seer doing with a bunch of bounty hunters?"

"Answer my question, and I'll tell you."

He chuckles under his breath. "Fine," he says, relaxing back into the sand once more. "I *was* following you. I was planning to raid your camp tonight. I'm running low on supplies."

I don't know what Hassan was expecting, but it certainly wasn't that. He's even tenser than before, and with the way his gaze is burning holes into the daemon, I'm surprised he hasn't drawn his weapon.

"Now..." The Berserker pins his gaze on me. "Why are you hanging around these desert dogs?"

My mouth quirks up, but Hassan has bristled again. The Berserker will be lucky to leave our camp with all his teeth if he keeps this up.

"I was attacked by thieves on my way to Varhit. They're letting me tag along until we reach the city."

He smirks, like he can see the lie written across my face. "Is that so? Who knew bounty hunters could be so accommodating." He throws a darkened glance at Hassan as he lifts his hands, rattling the chains around his wrists. "Guess that doesn't apply to everyone."

"*She* didn't attack one of us," Hassan fires back.

The Berserker raises a brow. "One of you? I thought she was just *tagging along.*"

I ignore him, but uncertainty rests heavy in my gut about where I belong in all of this.

"It's my turn," I state firmly. I crouch down and get face to face with him. "What are you doing out here? Why are you so desperate for food that you'd be willing to attack a caravan that vastly outnumbers you?"

"Do you outnumber me?" The fire in his eyes seems to burn a little brighter as the words leave his lips. "Do you think any of them could stop me if I wanted to tear you apart right now?" He lets the question settle between us before he leans in close, dropping his voice to a whisper. "Want to find out, Little Seer?"

All of my resolve seems to slip from me in an instant. Suddenly I'm back in that cellar, Olen's eyes piercing me from across the room. I shoot backward on my heels, eager to get away, but the Berserker lashes his hand out and snakes it around my wrist. Darkness floods his eyes in an instant. All I can do is stare into the black pits of his gaze as his grip tightens, constricting my skin and veins until I feel like I might pop. This is what I expected in the slot canyon. This is the terror I anticipated when I saw those markings on his face. The bones in my wrist flex, ready to snap.

"Let her go."

Hassan's sword is pressed against the Berserker's face. A drop of blood drips down his forehead from where Hassan's heavy hand is slowly forcing the blade's tip into his flesh. The Berserker doesn't flinch. He keeps his focus on me, and I watch as the inky blackness dissipates from his eyes, revealing the whites once more.

As soon as he lets go, I fall backward against the sand. Hassan's blade stays firm against the Berserker's forehead. I watch as more beads of red slide down his brow. He blinks away the blood drips as they slide over his eyelid. All the while, that feral smile only grows. He knows he scared me, and he likes it.

"What are you doing here, truly?"

He stares at me for a while before letting out a deep sigh. "Fine, here's the truth." His gaze darts up to Hassan, and he raises his brow expectantly. "Can I get a little room to breathe?"

Hassan only holds the blade steadier. The Berserker scoffs and looks back to me. "I may or may not have made some enemies in Piro..."

I merely tilt my head and put my hands on my hips, waiting for more.

His mouth quirks at my irritation. "I had to leave quickly—without my things—before it got posted."

My brow furrows at that. "Before what got posted?"

Hassan takes a step closer, maneuvering the sword to the daemon's throat. "He means before the bounty got posted." He whistles, and it only takes a second for Savi to jog over.

"He talking?" she asks.

Savi's gaze moves from the sword to the blood pebbling down the daemon's face before shooting me a *what-the-hells-has-my-cousin-been-doing* type of look.

"He says he was going to raid our camp tonight. *And* that he's got a bounty on him in Piro," Hassan mutters.

Tsk. Tsk. Savi's tongue snaps behind her teeth as she shakes her head. "Damn, man. You really picked the wrong people to mess with."

"He's going to need the boot chain and everything to be staked in two places," Hassan orders. "He almost snapped her wrist just now."

"Gods abov—"

"I wasn't going to hurt her," the Berserker groans. "I just wanted to see if it would happen again."

Hassan looks between me and the man, his brow furrowing deeply. "See if what would happen again?"

A wicked smile breaks across the Berserker's face. His eyes are glued to me. "You didn't tell him?"

"What is he talking about?"

I try to answer Hassan but the words tangle in my mouth.

"Ren?" Savi questions.

"I–I had a vision. It was nothing."

The Berserker raises his hands up to his heart, mock anguish playing across his face. "*Ren...*" My name on his lips is nothing more than a taunt. "I'm hurt," he teases. "Did our kiss mean that little to you?"

"Your what?" Savi balks.

"You kissed him?" Hassan thunders quickly after.

"No—*no*." My eyes dart between Savi and Hassan as I desperately search for the words. "I had a vision, and he saw it. I don't know how. But, I... we—"

Hassan's face is pulled into a violent grimace whereas Savi is barely holding back her laughter.

"It's not—*no*." I shake my head, cheeks flushed with heat as I pull my gaze away from them. "Nothing happened. I–I'm going to go start the fire."

I'm gone before I can make things worse. I don't dare look back over my shoulder, quickly stalking across camp. My cheeks are red with shame as I weave my way around Tariq and Riat who are securing the bounties for the night. Riat tosses a flirty comment my way, but I ignore it and keep going. I pass the fire pit and still keep going. I keep my head down until I've hidden myself away behind the flaps of my tent. Only then do I drop down into the plush array of bedding Savi has given me and scream into a pillow.

"Veles wreck me," I moan as I flip onto my back and stare up at the tent's roof.

The vision comes back to me in pieces, the draped canvas tugging at the memory. He had been—*will be*—in my tent. The Berserker. *Silas.* I grit my teeth as that smug look of his flashes in my mind. He was the cause of all that anger I felt in the vision—I know it. I was ready to cut him down with a blade one minute but the next...

That anger had morphed into something else so quickly. Into something... different.

My fingertips drift across my bottom lip, all but feeling the burn of that kiss again. I inhale a sharp breath and stop. *Gods*. I run my hand across my face and groan. It has to be some kind of trick. He did something to cause this. *Can daemons affect each other's gifts?*

I wrack my mind for an answer, but there's little knowledge there to sift through. I've come across a pitifully small amount of daemons in my life, considering I am one.

I flip back onto my stomach and bury my face into the pillow once more. There has to be another explanation. There's no way *that* could be in the future.

I grit my teeth and let a deep grumble loose from my lungs. I've never tried to change the outcome of a vision before, but I'll be damned if I let this one happen.

CHAPTER 25

The fire crackles and spits in front of me. Food scrapes across plates as we all eat, but aside from that, it's silent. It's like the night around us is hovering on bated breath. Everyone is hesitant—guarded, even. Everyone, except him.

Gray eyes find me from across the fire, and I hold their gaze with a violent steadiness as I eat. I'm not afraid of him. Technically, I am; but he doesn't need to know that. I try not to think about the way his hand wrapped around me like a snake with a desert mouse, but I can still feel the phantom touch of it. I twist my wrist, testing the ligaments just to be sure everything still works. There's a dull ache but nothing more. I've kept my distance since then, busying myself with the fire for far longer than I needed to. It did little to quell the nerves raging inside me.

No one has ever been able to see my visions. Not even Mikel. There were a handful of times over the past two years where a vision would ravage me like a fever. And even when he would wrap his arm around me in the midst of one, desperate to comfort me, nothing had happened. I try to make sense of it all but I feel like an outsider in my own body. *Have I been able to do this the whole time? Or is it him that's causing this?*

I asked Savi if they were able to get any more information out of him. Other than telling them his name, he was tight-lipped. But I already knew his name, since I had heard it slip across my own tongue. *Silas.* I grit my teeth and shake away the memory before my mind slips back into that tent. I hate that of all the visions it could have been, it had to be that one. Even more, I hate that he saw it, too. He got a peek into my mind, and every smug glance from him is a constant reminder.

I watch as he lowers the cup of rum Kai gave him. I don't know why Hassan allowed it; he certainly doesn't deserve it. But maybe Hassan is hoping a slightly inebriated Berserker is safer than a sober one. I'm not too sure if any option is safe. I watch as a drip slips across his bottom lip. He darts his tongue out, licking it up in a slow flick before flashing his eyes at me. *Gods.* I tear my gaze away and lift my own cup to drink.

"You all right?"

"Fine," I mumble into my cup.

Hassan looks across the fire at Silas and then back to me. "We're increasing guard duty tonight," he states. "Tariq and Kai will take the first shift. Then Savi and Riat. Then me and Vish."

I stop drinking and turn to look at him. "So everyone but me?"

"It's safer if you kept your distance."

My brow furrows deeply, and I can't help the scoff that leaves my lips. "Why? I don't need to be protected from him." I slam my cup down into the sand, sending rum spilling from the top. "And since when do you care about my safety?"

His expression hardens before he turns away from me. "I don't," he utters through clenched teeth.

"Good," I snip back. I tip my cup, downing the rest of my rum. "Then you'll have no problem letting one of the others rest so I can take their shift tonight."

He snaps his head back toward me, hazel eyes flaring in warning. He's waiting for me to back down, but I don't. I simply uncork the bottle of rum and slosh more into my cup. "Well?"

"Unbelievable," he grumbles. He steals the drink from my hand and gulps down every last drop of rum. "Fine." He tosses the empty cup into the sand and stares across the fire. "You can take Vish's place. He needs his energy to navigate our route tomorrow."

A smile tugs across my face before I can truly understand what I've done. *If I'm taking Vish's place, that means...*

My gaze snaps to Hassan, but he's busied himself in a conversation with Tariq. I glare at the back of his head, wondering if he paired me with him in order to supervise any interactions I have with Silas. I shake my head and find the rum bottle once more. There's a good amount left, and I gulp it down in one go. It burns the back of my throat, but I push through it.

Riat and Kai call to me from across the fire, egging me on. They pester me to join them for a drinking game, but I wave them off. My focus drifts back to the unrelenting gaze I'm becoming all too familiar with. I don't care that Hassan will be there tonight. I'm going to figure out why Silas can see my visions, even if I have to risk finding out how the last one ends.

CHAPTER 26

I feel Hassan's presence before I hear him. The soft rustle of the tent flap being pushed back only seems to add to the anxious fluttering in my chest. I didn't sleep well—not that I expected to. There were too many thoughts sifting through my mind before I closed my eyes. The nightmare that followed only made everything worse.

I stare up at the tent's roof and wait for Hassan to say something, but he doesn't. He hovers at the tent's opening, as if unsure whether to come all the way in. It's too dark to see more than his faint, shadowed figure and for a second, my heart drops. *What if it's not Hassan?* My hand slides under the pillow to where I've hidden the dagger that's usually sheathed across my chest. I try to keep quiet but the soft *shush* of blankets in the tent is clear.

"I know you're awake," he says gruffly. "Get up."

My heart settles at the familiar voice but only before I let my irritation get the best of me. "Were you just going to stare at me until I said something then?" I toss back at him.

I lean up on my elbows and glare. I know it's too dark for him to see, but I glare, nonetheless. He mumbles under his breath before stalking back out of the tent. His shadow lingers just outside its entrance as if that will hasten me. *Gods, why did I ask for this?*

I quickly slip into fresh clothes, but as I put on my leathers, I slow down. My hands roam over my body gingerly. I can't see the bruises from yesterday's fight, but I can feel them. I grimace as I tug the pants on, feeling a rather nasty one along my hip. Savi re-bandaged my back, though the throbbing ache from the first few days has returned with a vengeance. Maybe by the time we make it to Varhit I'll be healed and without any new injuries. Doubtful, but I can always hope.

A chill slips across my skin, and I decide to drape a few extra layers over my tunic. My fingers graze one of the scars on my arm as I wrap myself. The skin is raised, scabbed over and rough. I know it looks worse. I have no doubts now that each and every one will scar. He went too deep for it not to. The flash of memory sends a deep roiling through my stomach. I march out of the tent before I can think about it anymore.

Hassan looks me up and down as I finally appear. Even in the dark of the early morning, I don't miss the way his jaw seems to lock. "Took you long enough."

I scoff as I push my way past him. "That eager for my company?"

He says nothing but quickly falls into step behind me. The light of the fire reaches out into the night as we approach, flickering long shadows across the sand. Savi leans back against the canyon wall, bow draped across her lap. Next to her, Riat draws small circles in the sand with one of his knives. They both stiffen, then relax, when they see its only us.

"This seems wildly unfair," Riat whines as he gets up and brushes himself off. "Out of everyone, I should have been paired with Ren."

"*Gods damn me,*" Hassan mutters under his breath. "And why is that, Riat?" he says louder now.

Riat's smile widens as he saunters up to us both. "Because she clearly prefers my company to yours." He slides an arm around my shoulders.

I let out a breathy laugh as I pat his hand. "While I won't argue with you there," I tease, "I think I'd only distract you."

"That's *precisely* why I think it's a good idea," he argues.

"You'd last three minutes before—"

"Are you two done?" Hassan snaps.

One of the bounties flinches awake at the sound. He opens one eye, spots us, and grimaces before nodding off again. Riat meets Hassan's heavy glare with a smile.

"Damn, boss. What sand crab pinched your ass this morning?" Riat pulls me in closer and drops his voice to a whisper only I can hear. "Or maybe it's a certain Seer that's got him all riled up..."

He pulls away before I can say anything, laughing under his breath as he heads back to his tent. Savi mutters something to her cousin and leaves soon after.

I'm still chewing on Riat's words as stillness settles over camp once more. Hassan and I stand silently, staring out at the darkened tents long after Savi and Riat have disappeared from view. The tension flowing between us is heavy against my skin. I turn to find him watching me from the corner of his eye, and something uneasy flutters inside me. I no longer know if I can endure the next few hours alone with him. As a gruff chuckle sounds from behind me, I remember that we're far from alone.

"I was wondering when you'd come pay me a visit."

I turn to find Silas looking all too eager. He seems utterly unconcerned that his hands are bound to his ankle and that his chains are staked into the sand in not one, not two, but five places. I have to hand it to the others, they're thorough. The flames dance against his light eyes, providing a harsh contrast to the pitch-black that pooled in them earlier. The blood drawn by Hassan's blade has dried, though it's now smudged against the dark markings on Silas's face. He looks feral—a devil against the ominous flicker of firelight. He's a prisoner in every sense of the word, but I can't help but feel like he's the one in control here.

I shudder as I break eye contact. Despite my hesitations, I sit down. We rest on opposite ends of the fire, but the distance doesn't feel far enough. I force myself to meet his gaze though I instantly regret it.

"I have some questions."

"More questions?" He chuckles to himself before gesturing his bound hands toward me. The movement is constricted, and his chains clank loudly against the still night. "You know the rules, love. Ask away."

"What are you doing?" Hassan whispers roughly. He sits down next to me, too close. As his thigh brushes my own, something inside me panics. I fight the urge to scoot away, and instead, do the only rational thing I can think of—ignore him.

"How did you see my vision?"

Silas purses his lips, amused. "That's your first question?" He smirks and rests his hands on top of his thighs. "I have no clue. That was all you, love."

"Stop calling me that."

"Okay, *Ren*," he taunts. "My turn."

He drops his gaze to my lips. As if he summoned it himself, the heat of that future kiss burns hot in my mind. I try to snuff it out, but when he looks back up, I know he sees right through me.

"Why didn't you tell your friend here" — he gestures to Hassan dismissively — "about the vision?"

"Why do you care?" I snap.

He grins. He's getting under my skin, and I'm making it too easy. I straighten up and mask the emotions on my face as best I can. "It wasn't important. Why bother him with it?"

I know I said the wrong thing by the way his eyes light up.

"Not important?" he prods. "If it's not important, then why are you here asking me questions about it?"

I bite my tongue. This feels like a mistake. But something is tugging at me, nagging me that he knows something, so I play his little game. "You already asked a question," I state plainly. "*My turn.*"

He nods, but that devilish grin stays stretched across his face. I take my time picking the next question. He's going to keep asking things I don't want to answer; I can tell by that smug expression I so desperately want to wipe off his face. I'll need to get my answers as fast as possible.

"Have you ever seen another Seer's visions before?"

"No," he says. He beams at me from across the fire, crinkling the markings on the bridge of his nose. "Just you, love."

I grit my teeth but say nothing. He takes his time with his question, and for a second, I think he's grown tired of our game. But as his voice carries across the desert like a chill in the night, I know this is far from over.

"You look tired. Like you didn't sleep at all." He leans forward and strands of white hair fall in front of his eyes. "How many thoughts of me kept you awake?"

Hassan's fist curls next to me, but I barely notice. I'm too preoccupied with the fluttering in my stomach and the heat spreading across my chest. "None," I lie through my teeth. "A thought of you is hardly worth the effort."

"Hm." A close-lipped smile spreads across Silas's face. "You lie so pretty, Ren."

"I don't usually gag prisoners," Hassan growls. "But for you I can make an except—"

"Why didn't you use your gift on me?" I blurt.

The sly grin slips from Silas's face as more words tumble from my lips.

"You could have easily overpowered me, you said as much yourself." My brow pinches, and I'm practically leaning over the fire, desperate for the answer. "You let me best you. Why?"

The moment passes between us in silence. He's staring at me, solemnity locked in his hardened gaze. "I have no intention of killing you, love," he admits. "And a real fight with me only ends one way."

My thoughts swim uneasily as he watches me from across the fire.

"You sure are a cocky bastard," Hassan quips. "Do you really think those marks on your skin mean you can best anyone in a fight?"

Silas's gaze darts to Hassan, but the playfulness in his eyes is long gone. "Want to find out?"

"Do *you*?" Hassan's gaze is unflinching as it locks with Silas's. "It's funny how out of all my men, you chose to attack a woman. *Alone.* Doesn't seem like much of a fight for someone who's so confident in their abilities."

My face contorts into a grimace at the same time Silas's feral smile returns.

"Are you saying little Ren can't hold her own in a fight?"

Hassan's jaw clenches, but before he has a chance to speak, Silas beats him to it.

"You think she's weak because she's a woman?" Silas mocks. "It's clear to me she can wield those blades as well as any man."

"That wasn't my—"

"Ah, but that's what you meant. No? Implying that attacking her was the easier fight." Silas leans forward. I can tell by the smirk on his face that he's relishing Hassan's fluster. "Did you not stop to think that maybe I chose to face her and her alone for a reason?"

"Oh, I'm sure you—"

"Both of you, shut up!" I snap. My eyes drag back and forth between the two of them as they fall silent.

When I'm convinced they will stay that way, I turn my gaze on the fire. I let the image of hot embers burn into my eyes until the corners grow dry. I try to settle myself in the silence, but something stirs in me like a snake slithering from the sand. My eyes flicker to Silas only to find his gaze waiting for me.

"You said you had a reason," I say, though my voice is low and hesitant, "a reason for attacking me in the slot canyon."

He watches me, head tilting like he's trying to read every flicker of emotion I'm hiding from my face.

"What was it?" I ask.

I watch the reflection of the fire dance in his eyes, waiting for the moment he opens his mouth. Hassan sits next to me in silence, though I can feel his body poised and tense against mine. I swallow dryly, my hesitation only building when Silas shoots me a sly smile.

"You're not going to believe me."

"Bold of you to assume I believe anything you say," I scoff.

He flashes his teeth at me. "So why then—"

"Veles damn you," I curse. "Just tell me—"

"It was a feeling."

My own words rest heavy on my tongue, utterly forgotten now.

"I was going to wait until night fell," he hums. "It was clear you were all waiting for me. I was going to bide my time and take what I needed once you fell asleep." His eyes linger on me in a way that has me shifting in my seat. "Something told me to walk into that slot canyon. Some force greater than my own common sense."

My throat clenches tightly, and though I want to force a snarky comment from my lips, I cannot.

"A feeling?" Hassan practically rolls his eyes. "Will you have me believe this is some daemon thing? A connection between the two of you that the gods themselves designed?"

Though I know the comment is meant to belittle Silas, I can't help but feel the burn of it.

"You really dislike us, don't you?" Silas replies. He shoots me a quick look before turning back to Hassan. "Tell me," he continues, "do you even know how daemons came to be? Do you know where our gifts come from? Do you know anything about us at all, or is your hate blind and without care?"

"I know enough." Hassan's words are cold and drag across my skin like shards of ice. "You're not the first I've met."

Hassan won't meet my gaze though I can tell he knows mine is fixed on him. There's a forced rigidity set in his features. His lips are pulled taut, jaw locked. His body is tightly wound, stiff with restrained rage. I can't help but think of Savi, and though I don't want to, I understand his anger.

"Both of you, stop—"

"Please," Silas taunts, cutting me off. He raises his hands up to Hassan in offering, clanking his chains once more. "Share with us what you know. I'm sure Ren is dying to hear about our kind from someone who so clearly respects us."

It's a miracle Hassan hasn't snapped his own fingers with how hard he's clenching his hands. "Your gifts come from the gods," he blurts. "Veles bestows dark gifts, gifts that have the power to take life. Those who bear his mark are said to have tainted souls."

The words leaving Hassan's lips are nothing short of venom; though Silas listens on with a sick satisfaction lighting his eyes. He snickers. "Hear that, love?" he calls. "My soul is dark and tainted…" His eyebrows wiggle before he levels an indignant look at Hassan. "No wonder some are afraid to fight me."

Hassan ignores the jab and continues. "Hael daemons are said to have better use for their gifts. They can help people, bring balance to the chaos Veles weaves." He finally looks at me, but as I meet his gaze, his eyes swim with hesitation. "Though, anything the gods touch is to be regarded with caution."

I turn away, severing our gazes from one another.

"That's all?" Silas laughs. His chains clank as he finds a more comfortable position. "You only know what gossip and fear swirls about the Continent. You know nothing of legend. Of fate."

"I know what I need to," Hassan retorts. "Knowing daemon bedtime stories does nothing for me."

"No?" Silas leans forward, his eyes glimmering against the dwindling fire. "Let me tell you a story, and maybe you'll change your mind."

Hassan says nothing. Silas's eyes dart to mine, his gray irises alighting with mischief. I haven't heard tales of the Origins spoken since I was in Artolen. My mother had never shared them with me. Maybe if she had, I would have known better than to show my marks to her. It wasn't until years later, after stumbling upon more like-minded company, that I learned how I'd come to have this fate. As Silas's voice begins to drift across the fire, my skin peppers with goosebumps.

"In the beginning, two gods ruled over the world. Great, powerful beings. Brothers. They watched over the world, weaving fates from high above like artists upon a loom. The eldest brother, Hael, brimmed with knowledge. He gave the people awareness and intelligence. Brought them compassion and health. He kept the Continent in the light, ruling over the day. Years went by, and the land flourished. But the youngest, Veles, found his brother's rule lacking. He gave the people raw emotion. Wants and desires. Passion and fury. In the dark of the night, he ruled with strength and fear, shaping the Continent in his own image. The land bled and the land lost. Hael quickly saw what his brother was doing, saw the chaos he was weaving into the world. He urged him to stop. Hael urged Veles to bring peace to the night, to carve a space in the darkness for the light itself. Veles agreed. He promised to change, promised to do better for his brother. Years passed, and the land healed. But on a day where the moon bled halos of red into the sky, Veles visited his brother."

Silas clicks his teeth before leaning closer to the fire. His eyes flash brightly as he looks between Hassan and me. "Depending on which retelling you believe to be true, Veles either tried to kill his brother with his shadows *or* he used the bare strength of his hands." Silas grins. "I think we know which version I prefer."

He hums to himself as he begins again. "So, Veles attacked his brother in the dark of the night, strength filling him as he wrapped his hands tightly around Hael's neck. His eyes pooled black, blacker than a starless sky, until Hael's neck snapped in his hands. Except, Hael's neck didn't snap. Though Hael did not boast dark gifts like Veles, the eldest was too powerful for his brother to best. And though rage coursed through him at his younger brother's betrayal, Hael could not end him. He pitied Veles, pitied the hate and jealousy churning through him. Hael loved his brother, but even more, he loved the world they had created. So as punishment for his brother's treachery, Hael took Veles's hands. He cleaved them—split bone and spilled blood. It rained over the world, and before either brother knew what had happened, Veles's blood soaked into the earth. Hael banished his brother to the underworld, forcing him to watch what he had left behind in perpetual darkness.

"But as Hael looked after the Continent, he realized his brother's blood had tainted the land. People drifted through the world bearing his gifts. They were glimpses of his anger, his strength, his darkness. The land, once more, bled. It was unnatural, unbalanced. So, Hael took a blade and cleaved his left hand. He offered it to the land, seeking to bring light to the dark. His blood poured into the earth, blessing the Continent with gifts of healing, dreams, and sight. The land found balance. Gifts passed through the earth as the years went on. Now, the gifts of the gods mark the smallest of souls, and when those souls perish, the gods' blood flows back into the earth, only to be passed on endlessly." Silas sighs contently, leaning back against the sand as far as his chains will allow.

"Basically, when one daemon dies, the earth creates another. The flow of blood is unending, pumping through the very sands we sit on like a vein." He smirks. "Our presence on the Continent is as inevitable as the gods themselves."

The story settles deep into my bones. Only the *snap* of the fire or the steady beating in my chest reaches my ears. I feel at peace, lulled by the magic of Silas's words, of the origins of my very being.

"And what, pray tell," Hassan spits, "is the moral of that story? That Hael cursed this land when he couldn't do what needed to be done?" His lips curl into a sneer as he glares at Silas. "Or maybe it's that Veles and those cursed by him are nothing but death bringers."

Silas rolls his eyes though I can see the anger set in his jaw.

"The Origins speak of the bond between Hael and Veles," I chime in. "It's the balance. One is not complete without the other. The world needs light and dark. Knowledge and desire. Suffering and joy. That was why Hael spared his brother. Why he bled for the earth. He knew there was no life—no balance—without the two together. The night is not truly dark without the day."

Silas looks at me curiously, his mouth perked up into something more genuine than his usual smirk. "Is that what it means to you, truly?" he asks.

"I—"

My words are quickly cut off by a bitter laugh from Hassan.

"Whatever way you seek to spin it," Hassan remarks, "Veles sought to kill his only brother for the sake of power and greed. And Hael, out of weakness, chose to spare his life and damn the Continent." He turns and levels a firm gaze on me. "The only lesson to be learned is that Veles is a conniving bastard and love can be your greatest weakness if you give it to those who seek to destroy you."

My mouth gapes open before I manage to snap it shut.

"By the gods. That's what you got from it?" Silas laughs. "I'd rather think someone wasn't loved enough as a child."

"What I got from it is that those whose veins run black—those cursed by Veles—will bleed the Continent until there's nothing left."

"And what of you?" Silas prods. "Are you spared from judgement because the gods haven't touched you?" He raises his hands, and the clank of chains is all but defeating in my ears. "Look around," he demands. "You sit here comfortably while three men are chained because you deemed it so. Though none of them have caused you harm, you find it in yourself to play with their fates."

He clicks his tongue behind his teeth, shaking his head. "And you say I'm the monster?"

I move my lips to speak, but nothing comes out. All I can do is stare across the fire at Silas, repeating his words over and over in my head. As I look into his eyes, see the fury and the adamance there, everything clicks into place. *That could be me.* I could be the one bound, set to seek punishment because others deemed it so. How many times did I fight and steal—even kill—in the name of survival? How many times did others seek to control or confine me due to my nature? Due to the markings on my skin? The blood in my veins? All of a sudden, the fire feels too hot, the canyon too crowded. I get up too quickly, startling Hassan.

"What is it?"

I can't look at him. All I can do is shake my head again and again. But the thoughts won't quiet. The hypocrisy of what I've allowed is blaring inside me. "This is wrong." I blurt.

"What are you talking about? What's wrong—"

"*This* is wrong," I urge. My hands gesture wildly toward Silas. "We've bound him, *captured* him." My voice shakes, unsteady and frantic. "Why? What right do we have?"

Hassan furrows his brow. "He attacked you."

"But he didn't hurt me," I argue. "He could have killed me. But he didn't."

"It doesn't matter. He admitted what he was going to do. For all we know he was going to gut us all when he raided our camp."

"But you don't know!" My voice is unchecked and travels loudly through the canyon, a cry against the stillness of the early morning. I'm going to wake the others but I don't care. "For the gods' sakes. We don't even know if he has an actual bounty on him."

Hassan stands up to face me, but I reel away as he tries to steady a hand against my shoulder. "He's dangerous."

"Why?" I yell. "Because he's a daemon? Because he's trying to do what he can to survive?" Tears fill my eyes, but I refuse to let them fall. "Do you know what I've done in this life to stay alive? The things I've had to do to make sure I saw another sunrise?

Hassan rests both hands on my shoulders firmly, and it's only then that I realize I'm shaking. I try to still the vicious, desperate breaths heaving in and out of my lungs but it's no use.

"This is different. *You're* different." His voice is soft, almost caring, but it does nothing to settle me. "Whatever you did, it's nothing compared to whatever he—"

"I've taken life."

The confession slips out before I can stop it. I see the shock flash across Hassan's face, feel his grip loosen on my shoulders. It's all the confirmation I need to pull away from his temporary embrace. Whatever he felt for me—or didn't feel for me—it's gone. He'll never see me the same. The only thing I can think to do now is make it worse.

"I killed two of Rohan's men when they raided our camp. Another when I escaped Denheir." My throat feels tight and strangled but I force the words out. "They weren't the first. Nor do I doubt they will be the last."

Everything stills around me, and surprisingly, so do I. It's like my own words, my own admission, has shaken me steady. My breathing grows calm. The tears have all but been blinked from my eyes. There's no regret lingering inside of me, only simple truth. I did what I had to do, like I've always done—and I won't apologize for it. Not to Hassan, not to anyone.

I look to Silas, and though I expect to see a dripping smugness resting there, all I see is the faint glimmers of approval. As the smile begins to quirk up the corner of his mouth, I look away. I swallow the swell of emotions at the back of my throat and turn to Hassan.

He's said nothing. I don't want to care. I don't want to want his acceptance, but I feel its longing ache. The look on his face is worse than what I could have imagined. Gone is his anger and resentment. Gone is the brazen attitude and sharp glares. All that's left is a blank stare. Unreadable. Shell-shocked.

I pull my gaze away before I can see something that shatters me further. Only then do I catch movement flickering in the dark behind him. *The others.* I've woken everyone up. They heard it all. I can tell by the ashen stillness of their faces. Everyone knows who and what I am—just another murderous daemon, though I can't blame Veles for my proclivity for violence.

Shame lurches in my chest but only for a second. It quickly shifts to something darker.

Who are these people to judge me? They don't know what it's like to live like the Continent always has a knife ready for your back.

I step around Hassan and keep my eyes low as I head to my tent. I pass Savi, and when she doesn't say anything, an unwanted ache grows in my chest. They all stay silent as I pass. No one says anything. No ones utters a lone word to quell the desperation and pain I fell inside. Not Riat, nor Kai, nor Tariq.

But when I pass Vish, he steps forward. My gaze flickers up to him, hot and violent. Whatever he has to say, I don't want to hear it. But he only looks at me, eyes solemn and soft, and nods. I frown as I look away, a mixture of conflicting emotions threatening to strike me down. I slip into my tent, strip from my clothes, and fall onto the blankets. Tears line my eyes, but I do not let them fall. I stare into the dark, listening to the murmur of hushed voices until silence finally swallows the night. My muscles relax, tension unraveling like the final threads of hope I had that this time, things would be different. I barely close my eyes before exhaustion takes me.

CHAPTER 27

Camp is awake—bustling—but I don't stir from my tent. I've been awake for hours, but it's the unknown that keeps me behind these canvas walls, fully dressed and packed but unable to so much as peek outside the tent flaps. I don't know what to expect once I leave my hiding spot, and the anticipation is eating me from the inside out. If I don't move from this tent soon, they'll either leave me behind or come check on me. I don't know which is worse.

With a deep sigh, I grab my things and step into the sunlight. The canvas flaps flutter against my back as I take in my surroundings. Camp is all but cleared out. Tents are flattened and packed. The fire has been smothered. The bounties are waiting by the camels, already tied to the saddles. The only thing that remains is my tent.

The realization dances uneasily in my stomach. I mask the emotions on my face as someone spots me. *Savi.* One look from her, and the lingering hesitation I've been feeling all morning reaches new heights. As hard as I try, I can't read the expression on her face as she walks over. It's only when she's feet in front of me that a soft, careful smile slides into place.

"We were wondering when you'd wake up."

I don't know what to say, not when her face is masked as carefully as mine.

"Bet you were," I mutter.

I take my time looking around again, but this time, I notice we're being watched. Hassan and Vish stand on the other side of camp, faces stern and guarded. Words pass between them, and I watch as Hassan's face twists into a scowl at whatever Vish just said. The two bicker back and forth, eyes never leaving me. It's only when Vish stalks off in a huff that I manage to pull my gaze free. They're either annoyed I woke up so late or mad I woke up just in time. Only one way to find out.

"You're getting a late start." I nod toward the gear strapped to the various horses and camels. "Hassan can't be happy about that."

Savi tilts her head, a ghost of a smirk pulling at her lips. "It was his idea."

I must look as confused as I feel because she lets out a small laugh and pats me on the shoulder. "He thought you should rest after..." Her smile wavers. Hesitancy tightens her face before her usual cheerfulness reappears.

"He just didn't expect you to sleep until almost midday," she finishes, smile now fitted back into place.

I try to find the answers I'm desperate for but between Hassan's blaring gaze and Savi's calculated cheer, I can't find any. The only thing I now know to be true makes me all the more unsure. *They waited for me.*

My eyes flicker across camp, looking for something to settle me, or distract me. The only thing I find is the bounties standing by the camels, looking more agitated by the minute. I watch one swat a fly away while the other groans about the heat.

"How long will it take us to get to Varhit?" I ask.

Savi hesitates. "Plans have changed. We'll continue through the canyon and make our way to Hira."

My brows knit together tightly. "I thought you said the bounties were due in Varhit?"

It's then that something slips across her face. I barely catch it, but it's there. It pulls at the edge of her mouth and wrinkles the corners of her eyes. *She's nervous.* I step toward her, eager to pull forth the words she won't speak, but she backs away quickly.

"I'll help you pack up the tent. Once we're done, Kai saved you some breakfast."

She slips inside my tent without another word. The heat of the day hangs off me heavily, but not as heavy as the weight in my chest.

"There's still something you're not telling me."

I cast a look across the canyon and find Hassan's eyes locked on me.

"It's safer if you don't know."

"So you are keeping something from me..."

"When you need to know, I'll tell you..."

I replay the conversation over and over again in my head. Each time, the words become a little clearer than they did the time before. Hassan has plans he's keeping from his crew—from Savi. But maybe she's no longer in the dark about whatever secret her cousin keeps.

I step inside the tent where Savi is currently loosening the ties that hold the rough canvas to its posts. As I watch her work, the reality of where I am and how I got here hits me like a bucket of cold water. *I don't know these people.* They're strangers. They track people down for a mere sack of coin.

My thoughts drift to the bounties outside, then to the Berserker. No matter how hysterical I was last night, there was truth to my words. *Who is to say these people won't turn on me if a bounty with my name exists in the next town? Would the good nature they've shown over the past few days spare me? Or would it be stripped from them just like this camp has been from the desert?*

I step up to help Savi with a newfound sense of caution. I try to catch her eye, desperate to see something to dispel my heightened distrust, but she won't look at me. She keeps busy, loosening the last tie before slipping out of the tent with a bundle of folded blankets under her arm. As I watch her go, I can't help but replay the conversation between her and her cousin one last time.

"...I can't tell you this, not yet. Not until I've worked things out with—"

Dread creeps across my skin. *What plan has Hassan made? And with who? And why do I get the gut-wrenching feeling that somehow, I've gotten myself mixed up in it?* My stomach drops until I feel it all but sinking into the sand itself.

It takes Savi and I no time at all to take down my tent and pack the rest of my things onto the caravan. The entire time, silence permeates the air. She offers me nothing more than stilted looks that I know are meant to be polite but feel more like a slap in the face. Seeing her put on an act when I'd gotten so used to her carefree laughter and breezy attitude is worse than anything Hassan could say or do today. I'm tightly wound, ready to snap by the time I throw my pack over my shoulder and slap the dust from my hands.

Kai is waiting for me with a bundle of wax paper when I finally make it over to my horse. He's smiling, seemingly undisturbed by what I revealed last night. I see no hesitation lingering in his eyes, nothing to show there's a deeply rooted secret he must keep from me. He simply teases me about sleeping like the dead and tosses the honeyed bread at me.

But Mirage? She's acting as agitated as I feel. She stomps and whinnies as I approach. As I move to her flank, I understand why. Silas stands a few feet away, his hands shackled. The chains trail down his body and are connected to a lone metal cuff around his left ankle. It fits snugly around his boot, creasing the fresh leather. My gaze tightens as I take in his appearance for longer than I should. He's better dressed than I would expect a daemon on the run. His pants are cinched at the waist with an assortment of holsters, loops, and straps. I count four—*no*, six spots for blades. They hang empty off his hips. No weapons, at least none that I can see. Though, I'm sure Hassan had him searched. My eyes drift up his torso. His tunic is loose but like his boots, it looks new. My gaze hovers on the deep, open collar of it. His chest is muscular, taut. But that's not what catches my eye. The chaotic Berserker marks decorate his neck and trail far down his chest, past where I can see. I can't help but wonder if his whole body is covered like that.

"Enjoying the view?" He shoots me a wicked smile and takes a step closer. Mirage rears her head back, whinnying loudly. Only when I brush a comforting hand against her neck does she settle.

"Your horse doesn't seem to like me," he chirps.

I pull away from his attentive gaze as I strap my pack to the saddle. "Good."

Two hard tugs of the saddle's straps, and I'm ready. I check for my daggers instinctively. The smooth scale of my leathers teases my skin as I dance my fingers across the blade sheathed at my thigh. I make my way up to the one strapped in the harness across my chest. Whatever today brings, I'll be ready.

"You look nervous."

I grit my teeth before turning back toward Silas. "And you seem surprisingly calm for someone in chains," I blurt.

"A temporary setback."

He grins, and I watch as his eyes slowly drop to the dagger holstered at my thigh.

"Is it true what you said last night?" His eyes flicker up to mine. "You killed Rohan's men?"

I search his face for any judgement but there is none. His expression is steady, almost eager. I swallow harshly and nod.

"Hm," he coos. "Maybe I wasn't the only one holding back in the slot canyon."

He takes yet another step, and I feel Mirage bristle under my touch. I stroke my fingers through her mane gently, but my mind is elsewhere. Silas is a mere breath away. He's taller than Hassan, and I have to tilt my head to reach his gaze. His gray eyes burn like an icy heat and I feel the intensity of his focus prickle across my skin.

"I'm surprised your friends haven't fit you with chains after your little declaration." He takes in a heavy breath, as if savoring our proximity. "But maybe it's only a matter of time before you join me."

"Not going to happen," I snark.

"Are you sure about that, love?" His mouth curls up into a sinister grin. "Your hunter over there sure likes playing the good guy. What do you think he sees now that he looks at you? Do you think he imagines all the men you've killed? The trails of blood you've left behind? Do you think he wonders if he'll be next?"

I hesitate, and Silas lets out a breathy laugh, taunting me further.

"When he finally sees you for what you are—for what you've done—I want you to remember one thing..." He leans in close, and his breath whispers against my ear. "The gods don't weave fates for the dead. Virtue doesn't mean shit if you don't survive."

My eyes widen as his words cut deep. I hear the chains clank against themselves before I feel his hand curl around my waist. His eyes fall to my lips and for a moment, I'm lost to the world. I forget everything, all reason. Despite the anger flaring in my chest at the truth of his words, my mind spins with the thought of that future kiss. I lean in, giving over to the tug of what my vision promised. It's only when I remember the black filling his eyes and his strength as it crushed my wrist that I snap out of it.

I stagger back, shoving him away. "Stop it," I rasp. "Whatever my vision showed, it's not happening."

His lips curl into a devious grin. "We both know it doesn't work like that."

He moves toward me but halts his steps when my hand slides to the hilt of my dagger.

"I mean it, Silas."

"I don't doubt it, love. But some things are stronger than sheer will."

"Like what?" I argue.

"Fate."

In an instant, the space between us erupts in a flurry of wings. Black feathers rustle against the air, and I reel back as a crow swoops toward my face. It soars past, circling us, before finally landing on Silas's shoulder. It perches there, tapping its feet to get settled. Then—it looks at me.

Silas chuckles, raising a brow at the alarm spread across my face. "Ren, meet Coyir. Coyir, meet Ren."

"You're telling me that this crow is your pet?"

A loud *caw* breaks the silence, and I have my answer.

"Gods." I let out a breathy laugh and shake my head.

Silas runs a finger along the bird's beak, almost lovingly. "Coyir has been with me for years. Crows are very loyal creatures..."

His eyes grow dark as he turns to look to where Hassan quickly approaches. "Unlike humans," he mutters.

Hassan barely looks at me, and that's all it takes for last night's anger and shame to simmer through my blood once more. I turn my back on the two men, pretending to busy myself with my pack. The bird crows loudly as Hassan settles between us.

"I see I should have tied you to one of the camels," Hassan grunts.

"It's not like I'm going anywhere with these." The chains clank as Silas shows off his restraints. "I don't see why you insist I must walk," he continues. "Chain me to my saddle and tie off my horse to the Seer's…"

I risk a look over my shoulder and catch Silas's gaze harden toward Hassan.

"…unless you enjoy making daemons suffer."

Hassan doesn't entertain the taunt with a response. He simply stares the Berserker down, eyes shifting between him and the crow that's perched on his shoulder like death itself.

"I guess it's in your nature," Silas taunts. "One doesn't simply decide to be a bounty hunter for their love of people."

Hassan pushes into Silas's personal space, shoving him back a few paces. Coyir flies off in a flurry, and I lose the sight of the bird high in the sky.

"You have no idea why I do it," Hassan seethes.

Silas takes a step forward, but Hassan already has his sword drawn. The metal gleams against the sun.

"I hunt bounties to keep people safe and to make sure people like you get what they deserve."

"People like me? You act like you know me so well. Now, why is that?" Silas muses. He takes a step closer, letting the tip of the blade press against his chest. "Because I'm a daemon?"

Again, he takes a step. Hassan's hand holds steady, and the sword digs through the fabric of Silas's tunic. I watch the blood blossom into the woven threads.

"Because I can sense the rot in you," Hassan states. "I've dealt with enough thieves and murderers to smell their stench."

A sadistic grin breaks across Silas's face. "Careful, hunter. Wouldn't want the lady here to know you think ill of her." He cocks his head to the side, eyes lighting up. "Or have you forgotten her confession last night?"

Hassan flinches against the words, but before he can do anything hasty, I shove his hand down, lowering the sword. "Enough," I state. "We're wasting daylight."

A stilted pause settles between the three of us, and for a moment, I don't think either of them will relent. Finally, Hassan pulls away. He sheathes the sword across his back, but his eyes never leave Silas. "Stay away from her," he orders.

My spine stiffens before anger rears its ugly head. "I can handle myself—"

"It's hard to keep away when you've seen what the future holds." Silas smirks, his eyes darting to me. "Isn't that right, love?"

My gaze narrows on him. "Hardly."

"Stay. Away. From. Her," Hassan repeats as he yanks Silas by his chains.

He leads Silas across the sand toward their horses, practically dragging him. Silas shifts against Hassan's hold, managing to turn around to flash me a knowing look.

"Remember what I said, love," he calls back. "Survival."

I stay where I am, long after Hassan has tied Silas to his saddle. I stare at them—at nothing—and my eyes strain against the high sun.

Virtue doesn't mean shit if you don't survive.

My brow furrows, and I try to deny the swell in my chest but it's there. It won't budge. There's something about Silas that reminds me of someone. He knows what it's like to live on the outskirts of this world, to be judged by the very blood that flows inside me. I look at Silas and can almost imagine him in Artolen. I can imagine him running around the city with a wide grin on his face and mischief in his eyes. I can imagine him swiping a loaf of bread after I admit I haven't eaten in days. Silas understands survival, maybe even understands me. Just like *he* did. All Silas is missing is the shadows. It's on instinct alone that I seal off unwanted memories before they have a chance to take hold.

I force a deep breath from my lungs, and I hoist myself up onto Mirage's saddle. She mirrors the sentiment, huffing loudly. As I watch the others start off down the canyon, heading to Hira for reasons undisclosed to me, I feel a prickle of energy in my veins. It's apprehension and fresh adrenaline. It's the threat of the unknown. It's the inescapable feeling that this day, or the one that follows, will change everything. It gnaws at me, but I nudge Mirage forward despite it. My eyes clash with Silas's as he walks next to Hassan's horse.

Fate is a tricky thing. The faster you run, the sooner it catches. I can only hope that this time, the gods grant me their favor for what's to come.

CHAPTER 28

I don't know where to look. It seems wherever I do, I'm met with things that unsettle me. Leading us down the empty, dry riverbed that winds through the canyon is Hassan. He hasn't relaxed since we set off hours ago. His shoulders are bunched tightly, and his eyes seem to constantly sweep for threats. No matter how many times he scans the path ahead, there's two places his eyes inevitably end up. Me and Silas. Every time he turns around and those stern, hazel eyes land on me, I pretend I wasn't staring—waiting for the moment they did. Questions are all I have, and his silence isn't doing me any favors.

When his eyes find mine once more, I tear my gaze away. The desert heat pebbles sweat on the back of my neck, and I gingerly pat my headscarf to mop it up. Those around me are silent in our trek. Nothing meets my ears but the rocks kicked and shuffled amidst the pack animals' hooves. My eyes creep up the canyon walls, and I'm forced to tilt my head back to take it all in. I can barely make out the top of the gorge. It's much too high to climb. The canyon seems to cradle us, its imposing structure the only thing as far as the eye can see. Dust and sand trickles from the orange-tinged rock face, stirred by a trailing breeze. The sky is a far-away thought, seeming unreachable above the high canyon walls.

My eyes shift to the withered riverbed under our feet. Thankfully the Jahaer doesn't see much—or any—rain, else we would be swept away with nowhere to go. The arid landscape is parched, and there's scant plant life marking the trail we follow. It's desolate here, an unfriendly reminder of what this desert does to living things.

I stare ahead, letting everything around me fade into nothing. The canyon from my Weaver dreams is a constant tether for my thoughts. I think of where it could be, if I'm getting closer or farther away. My mind swirls. *What if it isn't even real? What if this isn't a Weaver's doing at all?* It could be a cosmic joke from the gods, some punishment from not using my gift. *Madness.* I press my fingertips into my temple. *Who is to say not using your gift can't do as much damage as using it too much?*

"You've been quiet today."

My head snaps to the left, heart pounding in my chest. We've been riding in silence for so long, I all but forgot Tariq was even there. I offer him an attempt at a smile though the result is tight-lipped and resembles more of a scowl.

"As compared to my usual chattiness?" I quip.

He laughs, and the genuine warmth that spreads across his face helps the smile form on mine. "You're definitively not as talkative as Riat or Kai," he offers. "But I thought, at least for a moment there, you were warming up to us. I was getting used to that sharp tongue of yours."

I open my mouth but shut it almost instantly. There's nothing I can say that will settle the ache his words bring to my chest. He's right. I was finding my place in the group. It felt like, maybe, I had found somewhere on the godsdamned Continent that I might belong. Zoah's caravan was a temporary fix, an opportunity to be with people while still keeping my distance. *But this?* This felt like Artolen did. It felt like what I imagine home is supposed to feel like. But Artolen didn't last, nor would this have. I swallow harshly and pull my gaze to the wide canyon in front of us.

Tariq sighs softly, as if understanding the conflict etched across my face. "Things haven't changed as much as you think, you know."

I look at him from the corner of my eye, curiosity piqued.

"It's hard to see past his anger sometimes, especially when it gets the best of him..." Tariq starts. "But Hassan is fiercely protective of those he loves. He'll do whatever it takes to make sure his people are safe."

My gaze wanders to Hassan. He's wrapped a tan scarf around his head, covering all but his eyes. It's exactly as I remember him from that first day. Piercing eyes against the hazy sands, a towering figure that seemed to block the sun. So much has changed since then; at least, I thought it had.

Tariq's words stir inside of me. *Am I imagining the coldness that Savi seemed to wake up with? Has anything really changed since last night?*

As if sensing the attention, Hassan turns his head and meets my gaze. The apprehension in those eyes answers all my questions for me.

"Why tell me this?" I snap at Tariq. "I'm leaving once we get to Hira. There's no need to fix whatever strain lies between me and him before then."

Tariq gives me a sympathetic look, and I stiffen under the compassion he offers me. I know I don't deserve it.

"I can't imagine what you've been through. Or what you've been forced to do." He sighs, taking a minute to find the words. "What I do know is that I understand. You see, my aunt—" His voice breaks, so softly I barely notice it. He lets out a breath and offers me a smile that reaches the corners of his soft brown eyes. "The world was not kind to her, not for any part of her life. Yet, my aunt faced it without fear or hesitation. She knew who she was, and she knew *what* she was to the people who couldn't look past her marks. But still, she treated every day as if it were a gift. Against it all, the fighting, the threats, the hate—she lived and she loved. But most importantly, she surrounded herself with people who cared for her."

The way Tariq looks at me makes me feel too small, too seen. The warmth he offers seems to seep into my very soul, squirming around in my own darkness as if attempting to take root there. I look away quickly, burying my teeth into my cheek.

"All I'm trying to say," he offers, "is that you don't need to walk through this life on your own. If you allow it, you can find people who care for you, too."

My anger flares as soon as I feel the unwanted tears prick my eyes. "And I'm expected to find that here?" I snarl. "I saw the way he looked at me last night, felt the way Savi treated me this morning." I temper my voice before it can echo across the canyon and pull everyone's attention. "Though I'm sure your aunt suffered difficulties due to her mark, we are not the same," I rasp. "I have lived the life you speak of. I have had people look after me, and I them. And do you know what that life got me?"

I tear at my clothes, startling Mirage as I yank at the hem of my tunic to reveal the bare skin there. Tariq's eyes widen then grow solemn at the seven-inch scar that runs across my stomach, blemishing the skin. When I know he's seen enough, I drop the fabric back into place.

"Trusting that others have my best intentions at heart has only left me bloody and scarred," I stress. "So save me this talk of love and care. I will not find it in this lifetime, nor do I expect to."

Tariq winces at my words but doesn't meet my fury with his own. He simply reaches across Mirage and squeezes my hand. "I'm sorry."

He's released me before I can think to shrink from the affection. My throat grows heavy with ache, and I grit my teeth as my emotions betray me once more.

"I'm sorry this life and its people haven't been kind to you," he offers. "But it doesn't mean you still can't—"

Shouting up ahead severs the moment between us. My eyes rip toward the front of the caravan where Hassan's horse rears up, almost bucking him from the saddle. Sand sprays, and a hazy cloud of dust fills the air. It blocks everything from view.

"Stay here," Tariq orders before dismounting from his camel and rushing toward the fray.

As I'm lost in the chaos, Vish sidles up next to me. His brows pinch together tightly as his camel rests next to Tariq's abandoned one. "What's going on?" he asks.

"I'm not sure…"

The dust settles, and I strain my eyes to see through the sun's harsh glare. My heart rate picks up as I spot two men standing in front of Hassan's horse. It's only seconds later that Hassan dismounts, withdrawing the blade from his back.

"We have company," I utter, my hands gripping the reins too tightly.

Just as Vish inches his camel ahead of me to see for himself, muttered curses spill from his lips. Then, one word. "*Tofá.*"

He whispers the name so quietly I almost miss it. Vish kicks his boot against the camel's side, driving the animal forward. "Hassan, stop!"

He barrels toward the men, kicking up dust in his wake. Hassan barely glances at Vish as he approaches, nor does Hassan lower the blade. Vicious words fly from Hassan's lips. He steps closer, leveling the point of his sword toward one of the men. The man just smirks, eyes flickering down to the blade, then back up at Hassan. He mumbles something I don't catch.

Ignoring Tariq's order, I prod Mirage forward. When I reach them, Hassan is swinging his sword back and forth, not knowing which of the men is the greater threat. As I look at our visitors, I understand Hassan's agitation.

"Hassan, please," Vish demands. "Lower your weapon."

"Not until they tell me what they're doing here," he barks back. "And what they are."

"We're travelers, just like you," one of the men offers, cheeky grin plastered across his face.

I don't miss the amusement flecking his eyes, nor the columns of markings racing down both arms. I quickly size him up, feeling the hairs on the back of my neck rise as I do. He's tall, towering over his companion. Lean muscle covers his body, and I glimpse more markings peeking from the collar of his sleeveless tunic. His curly brown hair blows in the soft breeze, curls falling like curtains over his dark blue eyes.

"Travelers?" Hassan scoffs. "I—"

"As to what we are," the other man says, his smile masked with something darker. "I think you know."

I glance over him quickly. He may be shorter, but his body is stacked with thick, coiled muscle. Markings decorate his shoulders like armor and trail up the center of his throat. But it's not his marks that make my eyes grow wide. His pale skin is marred with rough, pink scars. The dense, web-like scarring runs down the right side of his face and neck. It pulls at his skin as he talks. My mouth grows dry at the sight. I may have never met a Torch, but I know their handiwork when I see it.

"If you're wanting the details," the burned man continues. "He's a Berserker. And so am I."

"Brothers by the gods." Silas laughs. His chains clank wildly as he raises his hands as if to welcome them. "Care to lend a hand?"

The two daemons pass each other curious looks, though they don't move to help Silas. Instead, they turn to Vish, ignoring the sword Hassan still has leveled between them.

"Why have you restrained the Berserker?" the taller man asks. "Is he one of—"

The man stops speaking as his eyes catch on me. He looks me over, brow raising slightly. His eyes widen for the briefest moment before his gaze grows sharp and piercing. It's then that I feel the breeze tickle my neck. As my headscarf flutters loosely against my skin, I understand my mistake.

"You have a Seer with you," the man states. His face contorts in confusion as he turns back to Vish. "Does this mean she's the—"

"Please," Vish urges. "Let us speak in private."

As he mumbles something indistinguishable to the two men, Hassan's sword wavers in his hand. He stares at Vish, brows bunching tightly before that gaze snaps to me. I only have a moment to take in his puzzled look before Vish steps in front of him and breaks my line of sight.

"Savi, Riat," Vish calls. "Watch the bounties."

Everyone grows still around me. Hassan steps up to Vish, whispering harshly in his ear. Whatever is said is quickly dismissed by Vish's raised hand. Savi shifts uncomfortably where she stands next to her horse. Tariq and Kai exchange hesitant glances. Riat's mouth has dropped open, like he's waiting to catch flies. In all the time I've been with them, Vish has never given an order, never opposed Hassan so openly. Vish mutters something to Hassan before turning toward the rest of us.

"Kai, Tariq," Vish continues, seemingly unconcerned with the way Hassan is gripping his shoulder and muttering in his ear. "Watch the Berserker."

As Vish turns to me, I watch his momentary control slip. Something hesitant spills into his eyes and sets his mouth into a firm, unsteady line. "Stay close," he orders. "We will only be a moment."

As he ushers Hassan and the two men further away, I can't help but think that last order was meant just for me. Murmurs pass between Riat and Kai before they split up to do as told. Tariq watches Hassan and Vish walk away with a steady, lingering gaze before undoing Silas's chains from the saddle and tugging him over to the rest of us. Savi can't stop staring at her cousin, as if waiting for the moment he snaps and this all goes to shit. I don't miss the way she keeps stroking the bow slung across her chest, as if reminding herself it's there. Everyone is on edge, as unsure as I am.

Something is stirring uneasily in my gut, and the constant looks from the taller Berserker aren't helping. After the third time his deep blue eyes shift to mine while mid-conversation with Vish, I can't stand it. I dismount my horse. I'm stalking across the sand, muscles tensing further with every stride. But before I can reach them, a tanned arm splays across my chest and holds me back.

"Give them some space, Ren."

I look at Savi, leveling a heated gaze at her as she continues to prevent me from going any farther. Her face is masked tightly, not even a glimmer of her old self hidden in the sharp lines of her mouth.

"Who are those men?" I prod. "Why are they asking about a Seer? About me?"

The mask slips for just a second as she swallows dryly. "I don't know."

"How can you not know?" I snap, pushing her arm away from me. "Clearly Vish—"

"I don't know, Ren," she snaps back. "Whatever is going on, trust that Hassan and Vish will handle it."

I grind my teeth together before turning my back on her. Instead of barreling toward Hassan and demanding answers, I do the one thing I know will piss him off more. On my way, I watch the conversation happening across the canyon. I study every expression, every frustrated throw of hands, and calming breath that Hassan forces himself to take. Whatever is happening over there, he's not happy about it.

When my eyes shift to the two Berserkers, I notice their earlier amusement has been stripped from them. They seem to harbor the same anger and frustration that ripples off Hassan's back. The burned one steps up to Vish, bombarding him with questions. He gestures a thumb back to Hassan before his questions turn into shouting. Hassan tries to pull the Berserker away from Vish, but the taller one steps up, leveling a black-eyed gaze at him. As Hassan goes to redraw his sword, Vish steps between them all, hands raised. His words seem to subdue the circulating anger, and the group soon goes back to their murmured conversation. I slink passed Tariq, but he barely notices. His eyes are all too focused on the others, same as mine.

The taller Berserker throws his hand in the air, seeming to let out a cynical laugh before gesturing toward the rest of us. It's only when Hassan and the others turn toward me that I realize where exactly the Berserker is pointing. Hassan's eyes lock with mine and, though I don't want them to, my footsteps slow. It's like his gaze is pinning me to the sand, his hesitation seeming to mix with my own. His jaw is rigid, set tightly like the tension wound through his body. There's a flicker of regret—of worry. It all but cuts me down as he pulls those hazel eyes from me and looks away.

"Curious, isn't it?"

My heart jumps in my chest. I glare at Silas as if he snuck up on me, as if it wasn't his presence I sought when I came over here. My eyes flicker over his shoulder to where Tariq and Kai are having their own whispered conversation. Silas steps closer to me, chains clinking faintly.

"What do you want?" I huff, pulling my attention back to him.

"It's curious that we took this path and just so happened to run into two daemons... Ones that obviously have business with the tracker, is it not?" His gestures to Vish, and the chains clank louder.

I follow his gaze just in time to see Vish placing his hand on the taller Berserker's shoulder. The man grits his teeth, not at all comforted by what Vish has to say. But still, he doesn't brush him off.

"Are you saying Vish planned to meet them here?"

My eyes flicker back to Silas and find him standing closer than he was before. His hip brushes against mine as he leans in to me. "All I'm saying is that choosing to go through this gorge adds two days to our journey. We not only have to get through it, but now we must flank the entire thing before trekking around the northeastern rim to get to Hira."

My mind spins as his words take meaning. The heat presses in on me, seeming to bake me against the canyon walls.

"Why take us to Hira instead of Varhit?" Silas presses. "From where we were camped this morning, it couldn't have been more than a day's ride to the outpost. But to extend the trip and risk running into trouble by taking the longest route possible?" His eyes widen at me knowingly. "It doesn't bode well for either of us, love."

"What are you—"

Shouting up ahead shatters my focus, striping the lingering questions from my mind. As my gaze swivels away from Silas, my stomach drops. Hassan hits Vish. It seems to play through my eyes in slow motion when the force sends the smaller man stumbling back into the sand.

The desert grows silent. Blood drips from Vish's lip, and before he can even steady himself, Hassan has his sword drawn. My heart pounds as I watch Hassan lean over him. The silver blade gleams against the high sun. Vish raises his hands up peacefully, but it does nothing to quell Hassan's anger. He can't stop yelling, and though he's too far for me to hear, I don't miss the fury and hurt contorting his face.

Just as Hassan takes another step toward Vish, two sets of eyes pool black. The Berserkers lunge for Hassan, prying him away like a wild animal. He thrashes against their hold, but it's no use. The burned one pins Hassan's arms behind his back while the other picks up the fallen sword. He stares at Hassan, eyes no more than empty bottomless pits as he snaps the steel in half with his bare hands. The blade splinters like a twig, and its *twang* echoes through the canyon. The Berserker spears the broken tip into the sand before tossing the rest at Hassan's feet.

My heart is a vicious drum in my chest. Sweat pools in my palms as my hands tingle for a dagger. The tension around me is as palpable as a rotting carcass. I can feel Silas next to me, hot with the destruction brimming in his blood.

Before either of us can act, Vish scurries up from the sand. He quickly mutters to the two Berserkers, conversation passing harshly while Hassan thrashes against the burned daemon's hold. Across the canyon, Savi takes a step closer. Her hand splays across the bow that rests against her chest. She's on edge—twitchy—but despite the adrenaline I know runs through her now, she doesn't intervene.

My eyes flicker to the rest of the group and find them equally agitated. Riat is gritting his teeth, eyes seeming to burn with fury. Kai is pacing. His boots track grooves through the hot sand. Tariq's brow is pursed tightly, though he makes no move for his weapon. We all watch and wait, bated breath the only thing that slips from our lips.

Our unrest isn't missed. The taller Berserker flickers his gaze across each and every one of us. But as he locks eyes with me, he stops. Just as he takes a step forward, Vish tugs on his arm. He's whispering feverishly now, words flying from his lips too fast to understand from this distance.

The taller daemon pays Vish little mind, his eyes still fixed on me. Next to him, the burned Berserker lets loose a bitter laugh. He answers Vish with a few stilted words that makes the smaller man stiffen. Finally, he releases his hold on Hassan.

Hassan instantly drops to the sand. My heart lurches, then resumes its frantic pace as I catch the determination locked in his gaze. Conversation continues around Hassan as he scrambles back up to his feet. He's panting—his body radiating the wrath he's been denied. I strain myself to hear the words that pass between Vish and the daemons, but their voices are cloaked in hushed tones. It's only by watching Hassan that I have any semblance of threat or danger.

His expression contorts in confusion, brow crumpling deeply. But it's when his mood shifts to something deeper, something raw and wounded, that I find myself holding my breath. Hassan is still—too still.

Vish says one last thing to the Berserkers before nodding. The daemons start walking away, but it's not them I'm focused on. I watch Vish approach Hassan. It's too hesitant of a gesture, one meant for strangers. The newfound caution Vish has for his old friend prickles my nerves. He raises his hands in front of him, as if warding off a potential blow or nearing an unbroken horse. His footsteps are slow—tentative. When he finally reaches Hassan, he talks quickly.

Hassan's jaw tightens as he listens. I find myself moving closer, ignoring Savi's faraway voice that tells me to stop. I'm too focused to hear any of her potential threats or warnings. My boots come to a halt only when Vish's words meet my ears in a muffled jumble.

"Take her—" Vish urges. The rest is lost to the noise around me. "...only way to be sure."

Vish places a tentative hand on Hassan's shoulder, but it's quickly brushed away.

"This wasn't the plan—" Hassan barks. "...nothing but a prisoner..." Words spit from Hassan like venom, muddling together before they can reach my ears. "—still have no idea..."

Vish tries his best to quell the anger in his friend, but his words only seem to do more damage. Hassan grabs him by the arm, fingers pushing up the sleeve of his tunic. The man scrambles against the hold, desperate to pry free. The scuffle stirs up sand, creating a dusty cloud around them. As Hassan shoves his tracker away, Vish is quick to tug down his sleeve, fitting his tunic back into place. Hassan's eyes blaze wide, and he offers one last comment to Vish before stalking off.

Anxious, trapped energy thrashes inside my chest. My feet take me back, away from the words that seek to unravel my mind. I try to make sense of everything, but my thoughts threaten to drown me. There are too many questions and not enough answers. Vish stands alone, gaze fixed across the canyon where Hassan is currently pacing. His eyes flicker to me, and it's then that I see it. Vish looks adrift, like his mind is waging war with itself. I hear Silas next to me, but his words are unimportant. My mind can only focus on what's in front of me. There's a desperation in Vish's eyes. He stares at me as if pleading me to take his burdens away.

Silas's fingers graze my arm, ripping me awake. I barely pull my gaze away from Vish in time to see the two Berserkers walking toward us.

They're close—too close. It was foolish to let myself get distracted by Vish. Somehow, I forgot the true danger here.

Savi tries to meet them head on, but uncertainly wavers her confidence. I watch her gaze hover too long on their markings. Her throat bobs. At the last second, she steps out of their way. Though she says nothing, her eyes track them like the threats they are.

Tariq, Kai, and Riat do the same. However, Riat takes it upon himself to utter a smart-ass remark as they pass, luckily only resulting in the burned Berserker rolling his eyes. They make their way through our caravan without much concern, other than the fretful whinnies they provoke from our horses. But as they approach me, the air seems to shift. Their footsteps slow, and my body shakes with adrenaline as they come to stand before me and Silas. The cool, grounding touch of my dagger's hilt is the only thing that keeps me from throwing up this morning's breakfast.

"Hm," the taller one says as his eyes wash over me. "And here we thought this scouting trip would be a waste."

My skin crawls under his predatory gaze but before I can draw a weapon, Silas has his hand wrapped around my waist. His chains clank as they press against my skin. "Sorry gents, but this pretty little thing is taken."

I go to argue, but his grip on me tightens. The burned daemon snickers, but as he opens his mouth to offer a retort, recognition flashes through his eyes. His jaw locks, and he tilts his head at Silas before taking a step forward. "I know you..."

Silas lets out a breathy laugh. "Do you, now? You don't look familiar at all."

The daemon stares at Silas for what feels like an eternity before his gaze tightens. "Kupor," he states through gritted teeth. He spits into the sand. The wet glob lands to the left of us, just missing Silas's boot. "I never forget a face."

Silas's fingers rub soothingly circles against my waist as he chuckles to himself. "Neither do I. But I'd have a hard time forgetting *that* face." He grimaces as he examines the man's burned skin. "Run into some trouble with an irksome Torch, *friend?*"

The Berserker makes to lunge for Silas, but his friend holds him back.

"Easy, Ivar," the taller one chuckles, shaking his head. "Wouldn't want Serehna to get hurt just because your ego is a little wounded."

My eyes widen at his words. The blood in my veins thrums uneasily. I can feel my heart pounding under my skin, as if threatening to burst free. Ivar walks away, mumbling curses from his lips, but the taller Berserker stays put. His focus doesn't waver from me for even a second.

"How do you know that name?" I choke out.

It's impossible. That name is lost. Forgotten. I let Serehna die in that alley in Artolen. *So how is it he knows me?*

The taller Berserker only smiles. He steps closer until he's all but breathing my air. Silas tenses behind me.

"Tofá, hurry your ass up," Ivar calls back. "I want to make it to Kriko by nightfall."

The Berserker in front of me, Tofá by the sound of it, simply waves him off before turning back toward me. His dark blue eyes flicker with amusement as he stares silently.

"Answer me," I spit, pulling free of Silas's grip.

Tofá laughs, not at all intimidated as he looks down to where my fingers are splayed against the hilt of my dagger.

"You're just as he described—though, I'm surprised I haven't yet taken a blade to the balls."

My jaw clenches as I take another step forward. "That can still be arranged."

"Easy there, love." Silas pulls me back against him. As I try to squirm from his hold, he presses his mouth to my ear. "Remember, I went easy on you. I doubt he'll offer you the same courtesy."

I shake Silas off but stay where I am. He's right. I know a bad idea when I see one. Tofá looks to me, then to Silas. He notes the chains around Silas's wrists, then the way Silas's hand slinks around my waist. Tofá tenses, something angry swirling in his gaze.

"I'd be careful with her if I were you," he offers. His attention burns into Silas, nothing friendly behind his eyes. "He just might cleave your head from your shoulders if harm comes to her."

"Who?" I prod. "Who do you speak of?" My hands shake though I clench them into fists to hide my unsteadiness. I wait to hear a name I now know too well, but it never comes.

"Though," Tofá adds, eyeing me curiously. "Who knows, she may be the one to take your head." His gaze lingers on my marks for far too long, and I feel an unsteady chill race up my back. "Time will tell."

Tofá hums to himself, seeming to consider something before letting out a deep sigh. "Well, I'll tell him you're well when I see him next. Though, I think it's best I don't mention the leech you've seemed to pick up."

He tosses a cruel look to Silas before stepping around us. Silas's grip tightens on me once more, fingers digging into my hip.

"Unless of course, you see him first," Tofá calls back, laugh lingering on his breath.

My heart hammers as violent green eyes come to mind. My lungs grow tight. I fight to get a full breath, but it doesn't feel possible.

Silas wraps himself around me, seeming to sense my agitation. "You're okay, love," he whispers in my ear.

My hands are shaking again, but as I press my back against Silas's chest, something in me steadies. I let out a deep breath and close my eyes.

"Get off her!"

Hassan's words reach my ears just before I'm yanked away from the comfort of Silas's touch. My eyes flash open, daylight streaming into them harshly.

"You could thank me, you know," Silas scoffs. "I was protecting her while you were off having a temper tantrum."

"Are you hurt?" Hassan asks me quietly.

My eyes flicker down to where Hassan's hand is circled around my wrist. The touch feels too hot against my skin, and I rip myself free.

"I'm fine," I stress. I regain my composure quickly, eyes spearing into him like daggers. "Care to tell me what the fuck is going on? Who were those men?"

"Yes, *hunter*," Silas adds. He offers Hassan a sinister smirk as he takes a step closer. "Whatever were you and those daemons talking about?"

Hassan opens his mouth to speak, but Silas isn't done yet.

"Whatever it was, it looks like you and your tracker aren't quite seeing eye to eye. You wouldn't have a Little Seer to blame for that, now would you?"

"Wha—" I start.

"It's best you keep your nose in your own problems, daemon," Hassan bites.

Hassan takes a step toward Silas, but before he can draw a blade, I push my way between the two of them.

"Tell me what's going on," I rasp. "Why did that Berserker act like he knew me? Who are they? How do they know Vish?"

Hassan says nothing, but his eyes betray him. It's then that my heart sinks. I've seen that look before—not on Hassan but on someone else. It's the same look I got that day in Artolen. I witnessed the same ache of betrayal when I lay bleeding, and those dark eyes looked at me for the last time.

Something foul rises in my chest, and I can't help the way my voice quivers. "Hassan, what aren't you telling me?"

"Move out, now," he bellows. He turns away from me quickly, looking to the others. "We're losing the day. We need to break through the canyon before we make camp." He steps forward and snags Silas's chains. He's tugging him toward his horse before I can stop him.

"Hassan!" I yell after him, though he doesn't turn to face me. "What's going on?"

The others look at me uncertainly. They lower their gazes, mumbling to each other as they load up and prod their animals forward. I'm left staring at their backs until it's only Vish and I who remain. His lip is bloody, and there's a heaviness to the way he holds himself now that I hadn't seen before. But despite any burdens resting on his shoulders, he looks at me like he always does. It's as if he thinks looking hard enough will reveal something hidden, like I'm a puzzle to be solved.

I shake away the abrasive feeling of his gaze and hoist myself up onto Mirage. She huffs underneath me, but the familiar sound brings no comfort. The sand around me stirs, blown across the wide canyon by a steady wind. I pull my headscarf tight to my face, trying to block the dust from reaching my eyes. Still, I can't escape the sand sticking to my sweat-coated skin. The wind and sun bake suffering into me as I trek down the canyon. It's a miserable feeling, but a known one. No laughter spills into the air around me. No one slows their horse's pace to match mine. Silence is my only companion. I am just as I have always been, just as I always will be—alone.

I scrub my hands over my face, brushing away the crust of sand. Just as I go to grab my canteen, I catch Vish motioning for Tariq up ahead. The man joins him, and soon, muffled words pass between them. Mirage's hoofbeats splatter against the sand as I watch on with worry wrinkling the corners of my eyes. The conversation carries on for a long time—too long. Brows furrow, heads nod, but ultimately, it ends with Tariq patting his friend on the shoulder and guiding his camel back toward the bounties.

I watch this happen over and over again. Tariq. Savi. Riat. Kai. I watch them all. Everyone meets with Vish. Everyone has their own quiet, but sober, conversation with him before they return to their place among the caravan. Everyone but Hassan. He keeps back, eyes fixed on Vish while Silas trails behind him. My heart is beating too fast. The heat is peppering sweat across my brow, but maybe it's not the heat at all.

I foolishly wait for Vish to turn around. I wait for him to motion me forward and spill the secrets he keeps. He never does.

As the others settle back into stillness and Vish guides us down the canyon, a grim tingle of intuition crawls up my skin. *I should go.* I should turn around now and leave this path. It only leads to trouble. I can feel it in every hesitant glance and hushed conversation around me.

I pull at Mirage's reins, ready to turn us both around and refuse this fate. But before I can, gray eyes clash with mine. Silas furrows his brow, setting it into deep ridges as he looks to where I've stopped Mirage. He stares at me, eyes widening slightly before he shakes his head. That's it. That's all it takes for doubt to splinter through me. I can't go. I can't leave this path.

I grit my teeth and urge Mirage forward. It's foolish, I know. But for some reason, I can't leave Silas. I see a soft smile flicker across his face. He gives me a final nod, a grateful one, and turns around. I don't understand this—any of it. *Why doesn't he use his gift to break free? How did he see my vision? What role does he play in my own fate?*

A heavy breath flutters through my lungs. The path ahead is brimming with uncertainty, riddled in risk. The inadequacy of my gift leaves me blind. I couldn't foresee what is to come even if I tried.

My hands shake against the reins as I guide Mirage down the canyon. Something uneasy tugs in my gut, urging me to choose differently. But I can't turn around. I need to find out where this path leads, what fate the gods have woven ahead. Against my better judgement, I choose the unknown.

CHAPTER 29

The canyon is endless, or at least it feels that way. The sun looms overhead, a sweltering force that seems to reach down the canyon walls and smother all it can find. I watch the rest of the caravan meander down the winding channels of rock and sand in front of us, sweat beading on their skin and panted breaths spilling from their animals' lungs.

We haven't stopped once, not since we ran into those daemons. Ever since, our pace has swiftly increased. There seems to be an urgency to our travels now, and the energy is restless. The bounties groan and fuss as the camels tug them forward by their bindings. Vish is far ahead, and I'm able to catch a rare glimpse of him before he snakes around yet another bend. He guides us forward like he's been down this canyon a thousand times, like he can see the destination in his mind's eye.

No one second guesses him. A few of the others raised their brows and cast wary glances when Vish diverted us down a split in the canyon's path an hour ago, but no one said anything.

They simply picked up their pace and followed. Whether their trust is by blind faith or shared knowledge of the destination ahead, I'm not sure. Whatever it is, it makes my palms sweat. Silas shares my unease; I can see it in every prolonged look he casts over his shoulder.

A loud *caw* rips my focus up to the sky. Black feathers strike out the sun before the crow comes into focus. It sails over the rest of the group, scouring the bodies in eager search. I watch it soar with a practiced elegance, gliding through the hot air. Finally, Coyir finds its target. Fluttering wings fill the quiet between us as the bird hovers above Silas.

Another *caw* rips Hassan's gaze overhead. The sight of the crow sends irritation rolling across his face. "Tell your pet to leave," he rumbles.

Silas says something under his breath, driving another scowl to Hassan's face. Both have little time for argument as the crow lets out a sharp call. It swoops down, aiming for Silas's waiting shoulder. It almost makes it there until Hassan waves an angry hand, shooing it away. The crow veers, barely avoiding its tail-feathers being swiped by rough fingers. Another *caw* echoes through the canyon as the bird climbs back into the sky. It swoops down again, this time trying to avoid Hassan, but it's impossible. Silas is too close. His chains are connected to Hassan's horse by a tightly coiled rope. He only has a few feet of distance to work with, and it isn't enough.

The crow beats its wings, hovering in the air as it tries to find a pocket of space between the two. With another wave of his hand, Hassan drives it away for good. It lurches back in a fuss, sending harsh cries through the canyon as it retreats. I don't see where it goes—I can't even pay attention. My focus is locked on Silas. I see the moment he plants his feet, see the swiftness with which his gift floods his eyes. His whites are gone within seconds. I hear Hassan's horse panic before chaos ensues.

Silas's feet stay planted in the sand while his strength yanks Hassan back. The horse bucks against the tug of the rope and the chains rattle in defiance. Hassan slides to the end of the saddle, almost losing his grip before he grabs the pommel to steady himself. The horse kicks against the sand, and Hassan jerks roughly on the reins in an attempt to settle the creature. It reels its head back toward Silas, eyes nothing but wide, glossy orbs filled with fright. I know what it sees, I've seen it myself. Silas's eyes are deep pits of tar. Not a flicker of that playful gray is left. There's no humanity in his eyes, only the anger of Veles himself.

If no one was paying attention before, they are now. Hassan has managed to calm his horse but as he slides off the saddle and draws his sword, I know this is far from over. Silas hasn't moved. His hands still hang in front of him, chains intact. He could split them in an instant—I'm sure of it—but he doesn't. Even as Hassan steps toward him and levels the broken, jagged sword at his throat, he doesn't so much as flinch.

"Why did you do that?" Hassan huffs.

The black still swims in Silas's eyes. My throat goes dry as I think about the fracturing grip Silas had on my wrist the other day. *What could he do if he really tried? Could he shatter Hassan's jaw with a single blow? Snap his neck?*

I slide off my horse before I can think better of it. Hassan must know he's no match for Silas. The altercation he had with the Berserkers earlier should have been proof enough. My hands hover near my daggers, shaking in anticipation.

"I don't like the way you treated my crow," Silas muses.

Hassan's face tightens, and he lets out an angry laugh. "So you thought you'd pull my horse down?"

"Your horse is fine," Silas replies. "But I no longer consent to these conditions."

"You're a prisoner, you have no say in your conditions," Hassan barks.

"Don't I?" Silas retorts, gesturing his hands loosely to Hassan's horse.

Silas's eyes stay fixed ahead as I come to stand beside him. However, the smirk that quivers against his mouth tells me he's all too aware I've joined.

"I want to travel with someone else." Silas's smirk deepens until it's nothing short of a shit-eating grin. "I want to travel with the Seer."

"No." Hassan takes a step closer, blade still aimed at Silas's throat. "I told you to stay away from her. She's doesn't need to deal with the threat of your company," he spits out.

I step between them, hand curling around the hilt of Hassan's sword. My fingers graze his skin, and the contact pulls his focus instantly.

"I can decide who is and isn't a threat," I state.

I pull the sword away from Silas, ultimately stepping in front of it myself. I can feel Silas's breath hot on my neck, and a lick of fear races up my spine. *What am I doing?* I'm exposed like this, with my back to him. My defenses are down. He can snap me like a twig if he so chooses. But on some gut instinct, whether it's right or wrong, I know he won't.

The steady grip Hassan has on his sword wavers. "What are you doing?"

His voice is hoarse, no more than a whisper. He views this as a betrayal; I can see it in his eyes. I've drawn a line in the sand between him and Silas. It's yet another divide between us, and like last night, I don't know if I can bridge it.

"He's under my watch until we get to Hira."

Hassan scoffs. "What?"

"Look." I sigh. "You don't like him. He doesn't like you. The journey is going to be a nightmare for all of us if you two are constantly at each other's throats."

"And what makes you think that traveling with you will be any better?" Hassan quips.

"Because he's going to promise to behave." I turn around and find that Silas's gift no longer pulses through him. His eyes are back to their mischievous gray hue. "Right?"

He grins. "Define *behave?*"

I cross my arms over my chest and level a stern look on him.

"Fine." He laughs, then turns to Hassan. "Let me walk with the Seer, and I'll *behave.*"

He chews on the word in a way that tells me he has a different understanding of it, and I don't expect I'll like it. My brow arches disapprovingly. He laughs before dragging his thumb across the marks on his cheek. The shackles pull and clank against the movement. As his thumb leaves his skin, he gestures to the earth, deep down to where the baneful god himself rests.

"Swear to Veles," he says with a wide grin.

Hassan lets out a deep sigh. "Tariq," he all but groans. "Get the prisoner bound to Ren's horse." He shakes his head and resheathes his sword. As I begin to walk back to Mirage, his voice stops me.

"But Ren—" he calls.

When I look over my shoulder I don't see Hassan—at least, not the version I've come to know. The guarded tension I saw the first day we met is masked firmly across his face once more. He's hidden himself away from me, just as Savi has. The realization aches inside me, and I feel a flicker of regret like a blade wiggling in the flesh beneath my ribs.

"—if he does something that puts anyone at risk..." Hassan's gaze tightens on me in a way that feels like ants across my skin. "You're the one I'll hold responsible."

I nod and step away, quickly settling atop my horse. I don't look at Silas as his bindings are secured to my saddle. I don't meet Tariq's gaze or any of the others. My eyes are locked on the back of Hassan's head. He hoists himself up on his horse and carries forward without so much as a backward glance. He's a dozen paces away before Tariq finishes what he's doing and leaves Silas with me.

As the others begin the journey once more, I'm left sifting through my own dumb decision. Silas is my responsibility. I may have well just tied his fate to mine. The outcome of where this leads is unclear, but I feel an unease stirring inside me. I wish for nothing more than control over my gift right now, want so desperately to see what I've done.

My thoughts are like silk running through my hands. Slippery. Unmanageable. Silas looks up at me with a smirk so loud I can practically hear his satisfaction. Clearly, this is exactly what he wanted, and somehow, I let myself play right into it. I curse the gods under my breath as I nudge Mirage forward.

The familiar sound of rocks and hooves shuffling against the canyon floor fills my ears, but it does little to distract me. My eyes drift to the front of the caravan, searching for a hint of Hassan's hesitation or concern—something to make me feel better. I find none. His feelings about the situation I've gotten myself into are clear. Silas is my problem. I'm on my own.

Before I have time to stew in my regret for any longer, a loud *caw* erupts from above. Black floods my peripheral vision. Coyir lands quickly and without concern. Silas chuckles to himself as the crow takes its time settling onto his shoulder like it's a worn-in perch. Feet tippy-tap and feathers fluff happily. Silas's bound hands barely reach high enough to stroke the bird's beak, but when they do, a *caw* echoes through the heat of the day.

The sight is absurd. I can't help but stare. My face contorts into an asinine smile as I watch the man—a man whose very existence is feared by the world—pet a crow. The bird leans into Silas's hand like a street dog eager for scratches. Before I know what I'm doing, I'm laughing. At first, it's a breezy thing that slips from my lips and crinkles the corners of my eyes. But it grows. It grows into something deep in my belly until it has me leaning over the saddle in a dizzying spell of glee and strung-out emotions. It's outrageous. To see the hands that threatened to snap my bones—the hands covered in so many markings they almost bleed together—being so gentle and loving is a sight that threatens to unravel me.

When I finally manage to catch my breath, I find Silas watching me. His brow raises curiously. "I didn't know you could laugh."

I roll my eyes but can't stop the color that floods my cheeks.

"I like to see you happy," he adds. "I could get used to that."

His eyes dart to my lips, and the thought of the kiss we've both felt but have yet to experience betrays me. I pull my gaze away quickly.

"Don't," I force out. "Once we get to Hira, our fates split to different paths."

"Hm. Is that so?"

I nod, refusing to say more on the matter.

A *tsk* slips from behind his teeth. "Shame, I was just getting used to being around another daemon."

The idea buries itself in my head before I can stop it. I think of Mikel and my heart aches. *What is he doing right now? Is he safe?*

I stare ahead, letting my eyes unfocus against the monotony of the canyon walls. I hope Mikel is far from here. I hope they all are. As much as the thought of never seeing them again makes my chest burn in anguish, I know they're better off without me. Fate has always ridden my back with a hangman's purpose. The gods have always toyed with me. Since the moment Hael's markings stained my skin, I knew they had woven suffering into the very fabric of my life. As the years passed, I grew accustomed to it all. Pain. Loss. Betrayal. Leaving friends behind. Finding myself alone with nowhere to go but ahead. I know the rest of my years will bring more of the same. *Why would I let anyone join me for that?*

"Who was the daemon you traveled with?"

Silas's voice rips me from my thoughts. I blink against the sun's glare as the moment comes back to me.

"What?"

I turn down to look at him but not before noticing we've fallen back from the others. Somehow, I let Mirage slow to a leisurely pace. We're a good twenty paces behind Riat and Kai, who keep their animals prodding at the bounties' heels. *I'm alone with Silas.* If he wanted to, he could snap his bindings, then snap my neck without anyone stopping him. He could kill me.

The realization doesn't worry me like it should. That's what worries me most of all.

"You were traveling with a daemon when you were captured," Silas adds. "How long did you know him?"

"A few years," I mumble.

The crow on Silas's shoulder squawks before taking flight. I watch it climb high into the sky until it's nothing but a black spec against the cloudless blue.

"He was a Mender, yes?"

I nod, but my focus has shifted yet again. Up ahead, Riat and Kai slip into single file formation. We're heading into another slot in the canyon; this one tighter than the one before.

"Have you known others?"

"Menders?" I ask.

"Other daemons," he says. "Ever met another Berserker? Besides those two oafs earlier, I mean."

"A few. I knew one growing up"

"But I'm your favorite, right?" Silas coos.

I scoff and nudge Mirage forward. We're too far behind, especially since I have no idea where we're going. The route we're taking feels like a maze. *Surely there's an easier way to get through the canyon?*

"What about others? A Torch, maybe?"

I shake my head. My eyes catch on Vish before he disappears once again. *Why are we cutting through slot canyons? What do they know that I don't?*

"What about a Seeker?"

I flash Silas a sideways glance as I grab my canteen. "Doesn't exist," I mutter before taking a deep swig of water. Liquid beads down my chin, and I wipe it away with the sleeve of my tunic. "It's just folly woven from Bair's Prophecies."

He only smiles. "So you don't believe in the Prophecies, then?"

"Of course not. Why would I believe the ravings of a mad man?"

"What do you believe in?" he asks.

I drop my gaze to him, eyes hardened and cold. "Myself."

He lets out a breathy laugh. "You and me both, love."

Silence beats between us. Just when I think I've escaped more of his questions, he opens his mouth again. "You're not even the least bit curious about the Prophecies? No sliver of doubt in your disbelief?"

I shoot him a sideways glare. "Bair was unwell. He pushed his gift too far, and it drove him mad. It's been told that his marks bled across every inch of his skin. I've heard some say the marks even colored the whites of his eyes, leaving no part of him unclaimed by Hael."

"Some would call that power," Silas notes. "Not madness."

"You're telling me you believe there's three daemons out there with gifts no one has seen before?"

"Technically, there would only be two." He shoots me a wide grin. "But I do."

I all but roll my eyes. "You're as crazy as Bair then."

Silas quickens his pace, coming to the front of my horse. He blocks my path, hands raised to calm Mirage's already impatient huffs.

"The Seeker. The Durit. And the Born."

I offer a glare before maneuvering Mirage around him. He falls into step with me once more and continues. "The Seeker. A daemon who the knowledge of Hael, able to see what he—"

I shoot him a hot look.

"—or she," he corrects himself, "wishes. Nothing is lost or unknown to the Seeker as long as they know what they look for. Which leads us to—"

"The Durit," I huff. "The two-in-one. The one whose blood runs with both Hael and Veles. One who is driven by sight and cloaked in shadow. Light and dark. Yeah, yeah, yeah." I level a bored look at Silas. "It sounds like Bair got high off merchen root and made it all up. I'm surprised he didn't name himself as the Durit. The only thing crazier than the Durit is th—"

"The Born," he finishes. "A godless human. Blood untouched by Hael or Veles but bestowed a gift by the Durit. The Born's power is the will of the gods. The ability to pluck the minds of men like a harp, guiding them by his—"

My brow raises.

"—or her will. Total control."

"Like I said, absolute rubbish," I scoff.

"Not all think so," Silas adds. He quirks a brow before stepping closer to my saddle. "Many have searched for both the Seeker and the Durit, and *many* would kill for a chance to be the Born."

"Only a fool would lust for such power," I mumble. "For it would surely plunge the Continent into greater chaos that it already faces."

Silas laughs. "The Continent is full of fools just like it is grains of sand." He flashes a dazzling smile at me. "Besides, I tend to like a bit of chaos."

He winks and I scoff in return. As I look ahead to where the slot canyon curves, my stomach knots. Everyone has disappeared behind a bend, leaving only emptiness stretching before me. *Shit.* We're much further back than I realized. My boots dig softly into Mirage's side, urging her forward. Silas is pressed against my leg as we navigate the narrow pass. His hands reach up to the saddle, gripping the straps in an effort to squeeze himself tighter to Mirage's flank. The horse chuffs loudly, but to my relief, she doesn't try to kick him.

The slot grows tighter still. Red dust flakes from the walls as we squeeze through. I can feel Silas's body hot against mine. I try to ignore the stirring in my stomach as his fingers brush against my thigh as we squeeze through the narrowest part. His eyes flicker up to mine, but I don't dare meet his gaze. I swallow dryly as we pass through. The second the canyon widens, I shove his bound hands off the saddle, creating space between us. Only then do I feel like I can take a deep breath.

"Have any more visions?" He smirks. "Or do you need to straddle me to kick things off?"

I ignore him, my gaze fixed rigidly ahead. The path is empty. My gut tightens at the sight. *We should have caught up with the others by now.*

"I wonder what your next vision will be," he taunts. "Think I'll be in it?"

"Not if I'm lucky."

I nudge Mirage to pick up the pace, and she lets out a shrill whinny in response. She needs a break, we both do, but every moment that passes without finding the others makes my heart pound in my chest. *Something isn't right.*

We take another bend, and when the path opens up again, it's just as empty as before. Tracks rake through the sand, but that's all that remains of the others.

"You'd tell me if you had another vision about me—right?" Silas prods with a devilish smile. "I'd hate to find out I can't trust—"

I pull back on the reins, bringing us to a sudden halt. My eyes scan ahead but find nothing. *They're gone.* The thought has my skin prickling with heat.

"What is it?"

I stay silent, my fingers hovering over the hilt of my dagger. I watch and wait. The path ends up ahead, widening into the mouth of the canyon. All that's left after that is the desert itself. I can see the edge of the horizon where the haze of sand and sun blends together, but I don't see anyone. All is still—unnervingly so. My gaze is so focused, so locked on every shadow and crack in the canyon walls, that I feel the dry heat prickling my eyes.

"Come on, love. What are you so worried about?"

I barely hear Silas's words. He's miles away, drifting further into the background as my focus burns into the empty scene in front of me. *Did they leave us? Or is this something worse?* My mind is reeling, nerves shuddering across my body in anticipation.

"Ren!"

My body jerks, startling Mirage. Up ahead, just past the mouth of the canyon, slipping around a bend I couldn't see, is Savi. She waves us over, and although I should be relieved, something inside of me is still buzzing.

"We found a place to set up camp for the night," she continues to yell over to us.

She gestures once more for us to join her, then slips back around the bend. Tension crawls across my shoulders as I stare at the mouth of the canyon, my mind painting pictures of what could lie in wait. There's been an air of disquiet stirring through the caravan all day; crossing paths with those Berserkers only made it worse. Everyone is on edge. And while I know I should learn to be more trusting, I just can't seem to shake the feeling that this is a bad idea.

"We going or what?" I hear the chains clank against each other as Silas scratches his chin. "I doubt they'll give me a mat to sleep on but food seems likely," he rambles. "And I'm starving."

I roll my eyes and nudge Mirage forward. "We both know you could break out of those chains anytime," I chastise him. "So why don't you?"

My eyes slide to him, finding a smug grin spread across his face. His tongue drags across his teeth, like he's thinking long and hard. Finally, he answers. "Maybe I'm sticking around for you."

My heart drops at his words, but I play it off with a shake of my head. "Oh yeah?" I scoff. "So you can do what exactly? Attack me again? You sure seem fond of my blades. Maybe you'll sneak into my tent tonight and steal them while I sleep."

I know I've said the wrong thing when his smile widens wickedly.

"When I end up in your tent, it won't be because I was thieving." His eyes drop to my lips before meeting my gaze once more. "It'll be because I was invited in."

I grit my teeth and look away as a blush unwillingly reddens my cheeks. I urge Mirage forward, the looming uncertainty of what lies ahead all but forgotten. Silas's words churn the treacherous waters of my mind. As much as I hate to admit it, he's right. At some point, he will end up in my tent. I've already foreseen as much. I ignore the uneasy fluttering the thought brings to my stomach and keep my gaze from slipping to him.

"The gift of the Seer is a poison-tipped blade," I utter. "Wield it without caution, and it'll be your own undoing." The words slip from my lips in a rhythmic twang. Out of the corner of my eye, I see Silas shoot me an amused look.

"You've read the Book?"

I nod.

"So you've read the Book, can recite its contents from memory, but you don't believe in Bair's Prophecies?" He lets out a breathy laugh and shakes his head. "You're either the strangest daemon I've ever met or a liar."

My head whips toward him so quickly I almost yank at the reins. "I read the Book when I was young, after I was exiled from my home for the very existence of my gift," I snap. "It was the only thing I had to truly understand who I am—*what* I am."

"It's rare to have a copy of the Book," he notes. There's a mischievous gleam in his eyes as he takes his time considering me. "How'd you steal it?"

I pull my gaze away as a restlessness stirs in my bones. The memory sweeps through my mind like a swell of shadows. I can almost feel the chill of that night.

I keep my face blank, taut and guarded against any flicker of emotion, knowing Silas is watching. We hadn't planned to steal the Book. That night, we'd decided to sneak into the shop of a local merchant. Coins and jewels had been our prize—anything to barter for food and weapons. We'd shattered the second-story window with a rock, and I'd climbed up on my accomplice's shoulders to reach the jagged opening. After scouring for as much gold as I could find, I'd felt it. The Book had called to me, urging me toward it like a moth to a flame. Before I had known what was going on, it was in my hands. Even now, after all these years, I still remember the feel of its worn leather binding and old, crinkled pages. I close my eyes and let the memory drift back to the shadows where it belongs.

"It doesn't matter," I finally reply. "All that matters is that the Book tells of many things. Yet others, it leaves cloaked in obscurity."

I shoot a guarded look at Silas, studying the markings that cover his face. For a fleeting moment, regret flickers in my chest. *Would my markings bleed across my skin in great swathes like his if things had turned out differently? Or was my gift always meant to rule me instead of me it?* I bite down against the swell of grief and mask the emotions from my face.

"You never said what it means to you," Silas prods. "The parable of your gift."

I swallow harshly and keep my gaze fixed on the horizon. "It means all is not what it seems."

CHAPTER 30

All eyes are on me as I emerge from my tent. I'd sensed something earlier when Silas and I joined the others at camp. It was the same feeling that itched at me this morning. *Distrust.*

Savi has continued to keep her distance, and Hassan has gone back to ignoring me. Luckily, the bite of Savi's coldness has worn off. It's expected, considering Hassan has clearly shared whatever secret he keeps with his cousin. But what I hadn't expected, what is currently stirring every emotion in me like a swarm of flies, is the others. No one asked me to start the fire. No one sauntered over to help with my tent. Everyone kept to themselves and their chores. I would have almost believed they were truly too busy if not for Kai and Riat's lingering looks. Every stolen glance made my skin buzz with nervous energy. Their faces were hesitant—conflicted. The looks confirmed everything foul that's been growing deep inside my stomach. Something is happening. Whatever happened with the Berserkers earlier, it changed things. Whether it involves me or not, they're not about to tell me. Once again, I'm an outsider in all of this.

I join them in the center of camp, and for the first time all day, their gazes don't shy away. They watch me carefully, conversations falling silent as I pass. It's almost more than I can bear. With a clenched jaw, I stalk over to where Silas is staked to the sand and plop down. Hassan's brows pinch together tightly as he watches me. I wait for him to say something, but he never does.

My legs stretch out across the sand as I massage a knot in my calf. I've never gotten used to such long days without any breaks from the saddle. It feels like every part of my body needs to be popped back into place.

I grumble under my breath as a new pain aches in my shoulder. What I wouldn't give for a warm bath. I wonder what a night costs at the inn in Hira. I wonder if there's enough coin in my pack for blades *and* a bath. *Mm.* My mind lulls at the thought of a bath and a warm bed. A moment without running or fighting. A night without the sand creeping up the corners of my blanket and scratching at my skin. That's all I need. After that, I'll return to the isolation of the desert where I belong.

My brow furrows as I look to the endless sands ahead. *But where to next?* Before I can stop myself, I think of the Weaver dream—of the canyon that plagues me. *Do I still go north? Or do I search for that place? For him?* The scar across my abdomen twinges with a phantom ache. My thoughts slip away like night into day as I feel Silas's eyes on me. It's like pin pricks against my skin, and I fight the urge to look at him.

"What?" I snap.

He leans back against the sand, chains clanking lightly as he does. "You're in a good mood."

I shoot him a sideways glance, eyes burning hot, but say nothing.

He chuckles under his breath. "Friends not being so friendly?" Silas taunts.

I continue ignoring him as my eye catches on Vish. He crosses camp, his leather journal tucked tightly under his arm. There's a hesitancy to his steps. Tension hunches his shoulders. When he gets to Hassan, his pace slows. He flips the journal open, finding a certain page before offering it to Hassan. The uneasy trill of Vish's voice carries across the desert, though I can't hear what he's saying.

Hassan shoves the journal away, not even bothering to meet his tracker's eyes. Vish's hands push the journal to him once more. His words spit out in hurried, desperate tones. Hassan's jaw clenches. He steps closer, looming over Vish with anger in his eyes. His voice is quieter, muffled against the chatter of camp, but I don't miss the way he lays a hand on Vish's shoulder and pins him to the spot.

Quiet words tumble from Vish's lips. His brow furrows, and something contrite and pleading slips across his face. Hassan forces a ragged breath from his lungs and relents. He snatches the journal from Vish's hands and begins reading. As he turns the page, his eyes drift over the journal, across the sands. His expression hardens as soon as he notices me. His mouth twitches around words I can't hear, and Vish quickly turns to follow his gaze. Where Hassan's is as unwavering as stone, Vish's face reveals much more. His eyes are wide and more panicked than I've ever seen them. His hand curls like a claw around his journal as he takes it back. He fidgets under my gaze, tugging the sleeve of his tunic down from where it had risen up his forearms. He mumbles something to Hassan before stalking off toward his tent. My brows are pulled in a deep furrow by the time he disappears.

"Why do you think we're going to Hira?" I ask.

I turn to Silas, and the curiosity I see plastered across his face tells me he was watching them, same as I. He takes his time replying, dropping his chin into his hands like the question is deeper than it is. "More chains," he offers dryly. "It doesn't bode well for you. For either of us."

Something nervous and feral flutters in my chest. "What do you mean by that?"

He raises a brow at me. "Have you been to Hira?"

I shake my head and he lets out a puff of air from his lungs. "It's a big city, much larger than Denheir," he states.

"So? What does that have to do with us?"

He sighs, amused. "How much do you know about bounties?"

"Maybe instead of asking questions you could answer them," I retort.

Silas smirks and scoots closer. His hand brushes my knee, and strangely, I don't find myself pulling away.

"Bounties can be ordered by anyone with cause, anywhere across the Continent. Whether it originates in an outpost or city, it doesn't matter," he starts. "But that means if someone issues a bounty on you up north, the news might not have made its way to some small outpost on the southern coast by the time you get there."

My face pinches tightly as I begin to understand. "But the bigger cities..." My voice fades as the final pieces fall into place.

He nods. "The bigger cities are hubs of the Continent. With so much trade passing through day after day, word travels quickly."

My eyes dart across camp. Tariq and Riat are watching the bounties. Vish hasn't reappeared from his tent. I see Kai just before he slips into his own with a hunk of bread between his teeth. When my gaze lands on Savi and Hassan, my chest grows tight. They're arguing, hands gesturing furiously between them. They don't stop to notice they're being watched; they're much too wrapped up in the vicious words that fly back and forth between them.

Silas leans in closely, and his breath is a soft breeze against my neck. "If there's an especially big bounty, you can't outrun how fast word travels. Especially when that word comes from Denheir."

I whip my head around quickly. As I turn to face him, I realize he's closer than I thought. My skin prickles with heat, and my gaze drops to his lips before I can stop it. He lets out a heavy sigh and smiles.

"If you're running from the world, love," he murmurs. "Hira is the last place you want to go."

I feel my pulse pick up under my skin. There's a clammy heat to my palms. "So what do we do?"

A devilish smile spreads across his face the second the words leave my lips. "We?"

"No, I mean, I just—"

He laughs. "Don't worry, love." Chains clank between us as he reaches for me. "Stick with me, and I'll make sure you get—"

The moment Silas's hand slips over my own, I feel fate pull me under its icy waters like it has countless times before. I fight against it, banging against the confines of my own mind, but I know there's no stopping it. I'm gone before I can blink.

I fall to the sand, knees sinking down as a firm hand shoves at my back. I lift my head up, breath panting, and gaze upon a devil I never wished to meet again. Blond hair glints in the sun and I stare into a smile so wide it feels like a threat to eat me whole.

"Little Seer," Olen coos. "I knew we'd be seeing each other again."

My hand darts to my blade, but before I can draw it from its sheath, heat sparks against my cheek. I still instantly. My eyes dart to the side and track the dancing flames that curl into a calloused palm hovering too close for comfort. Black crawls up her fingertips, like her dark skin has been dipped in ink. I take in the white markings that snake around her wrist, then look up at her hardened face.

She would be beautiful if not for the utter hate seeping from her gaze. Her eyes are cold. There's no mercy there. Was she always like this—hunting her own kind? Or is this what happens when Rohan breaks you fully? I hope to never know.

"Easy, Asha," Olen scolds. "Boss wants her in one piece."

He leans down and snatches my face in his hand. His grip on my jaw is too tight, and the fire next to my face only burns hotter as I try to pry free from it.

"He's eager to get you back," Olen says. "Especially since someone was a devious little thing and stabbed him with his own blade."

His eyes light up as he leans in closer. "Speaking of blades..." His other hand drops to my thigh and rips the dagger from its sheath. He brings it up to my face, teasing my skin with the cool metal. "I believe this one is mine," he whispers.

From behind me, someone clears their throat. Olen's eyes flicker above my head, and an impatient look rolls across his face.

"Yes, yes," he offers. "You did good bringing the girl to us."

He pulls away from me and digs into his pocket to retrieve a small pouch. There's no mistaking its contents as he tosses it through the air. It lands to my left with a loud clink as the gold coins rattle around. The sound is like a weight dropped on my chest. My body is all but shaking, stirred by a potent mix of rage and heartbreak.

"You're lucky the other daemon didn't get in the way," Olen remarks. "But your pay would have been double if you'd have brought him to us as well. Remember that, next time you're tasked with a job."

Out of my line of sight, a hand reaches down to snatch up the sack of coin, quickly tucking it away. Pain rips through my heart as he leans down and brushes that same hand across my cheek.

I reel back, breath sputtering in my lungs like I've been pulled from the depths of a lake. My hands reach for my daggers blindly.

I'm panicking. It's all a blur as the hazy white fades from my eyes, replaced by the setting sun's blinding glare.

Suddenly, I'm on my feet, flailing around as my dagger-clad hands swipe against the empty air like it's an onslaught of twenty men. Voices shout around me, but it's all a jumble against the fear coursing through my blood. My foot catches on something, sending me stumbling forward. Everything snaps awake the moment my body hits the sand. Air leaves my lungs in a pained blow, and my eyes water against the harsh slap of impact. The world spins. I'm curled up into a tight ball, panic overtaking every inch of my mind, body, and soul.

I can't go back to him.

Hands tug at my arms, and I find myself slipping further into hysteria. I've dropped my daggers, but my hands lash out on their own accord. Everything is unclear. My mind replays the vision, but I'm stuck on the parts that promise to shatter me again and again.

He traded me for a bounty.

The *clink* of coins echoes through my head, and I close my eyes in an effort to tune it out. My mind doesn't still though, the thoughts only grow louder. My throat is raw before I realize I'm screaming.

"Ren!"

Silas yanks at my arms, but there's no *clank* of chains. I look up at his face just in time to see the inky pools bleed from the whites of his eyes. Chains lay broken on the ground, metal fractured in unearthly splinters. His freed hands cup my face. I feel the wetness on my cheeks slip against his fingers. I want to get up but I can't. Devastation is a landslide, its hearty weight pinning me to the sand. I'm not even here, at least not in any way that feels real. My mind hovers in that vision, searching for an explanation. But with every replay, every clink of the coins and caress of his hand—I realize there is none. He betrayed me. He's *going* to betray me. I want to scream, but I can't find the energy anymore.

It's only when Silas's hand grazes my arm, touching my bare skin, that I'm shoved back into my body. The feeling of his fingers on the ruined flesh is not only a reminder of what happened in Denheir, but now of what's to come in Hira.

I shove Silas away, reeling until my back hits the sand. My breath heaves in and out of my lungs, but I don't have time to rest as movement flickers in the corner of my eye. I ignore the figure as he rushes over, instead scrambling toward the glint of metal I spy in the sand. Hassan's voice is a distant call as he bears down on us. I barely register the look of concern on his face or the anger in his eyes as he points his sword at Silas. All I can do is stare and search for something I missed before. Something that shows me the monster who's always been hiding deep inside.

When I don't find it, my anger breaks me.

"What did you do to her?" Hassan yells. "I swear to the gods if you laid a hand on—"

His words slip into nothing as I tackle him to the sand. His sword goes flying, and our bodies land in a heavy splash. I don't notice I'm crying until the tears blur my vision, obscuring the look of pure shock on Hassan's face. Fury and pain drives my hand into his throat. I make contact with his windpipe in a swift blow. He gasps and squirms underneath me, breath stolen from his lungs. He wraps his legs around my hips, but before he can flip me over, I stab one of my daggers through the sleeve of his tunic. It fails to strike flesh. I'm too overwhelmed by my emotions to know whether I meant to miss or not. The blade pins him to the sand by his tunic, and my mind spins.

As he struggles, I raise my other dagger high in the air. *I won't miss this time. I won't let this vision come true.* My hand shakes, ready to strike, but the world around me stills. An arrow buzzes by my face. It's so close I can feel the air whip across my cheek as it passes. My hand halts mid-strike, freezing as I hear another arrow nock against a bow.

"That was a warning shot, Ren."

I look up to see Savi, anguish drawn across her face as she aims her next arrow at my heart.

"Make a move for him again, and I promise I won't hesitate."

I'm distracted just long enough for Hassan to slap the dagger from my grip. He bucks me off him and yanks at the dagger pinning him to the sand. "Why are you trying to kill me?" he demands.

I scurry up to my feet at the same time he does, curling my empty hands into fists. My eyes burn into him with hate. How I could have been so naive, I don't know.

I go to take a step forward, then stop. Savi advances, arrow still held level with my rapidly beating heart. Breath rasps in my lungs as my gaze snaps back and forth between the pair of cousins.

"You're not taking me back to him," I state.

Hassan's gaze tightens on me. "What are you talking about?"

My fists clench tighter, turning the knuckles bone-white. "I saw it," I spit at him. "I saw him toss you payment for a job well done. Though he's disappointed you only brought me."

Hassan's brow pinches. "I don't know what you're—"

"I saw it!" I scream. "The vision showed me what I am to you. Nothing but a payday. A *witch* worth a good bounty." My voice cracks, and I force down the emotions that threaten to be my undoing. "I saw it."

Hassan stills. He shoots a look to his left where Vish has slipped from his tent. The two lock eyes, conversation passing between them silently. Savi has stalked closer, and while her bow is now lowered, she looks at me with the same caution I was given that first day. Hassan grabs his cousin by the shoulder, pulling her back gently. He looks at me with a feigned innocence that makes me want to ram a blade into his heart so he knows what it feels like.

"Ren," he says. "It's not what you—"

"What did you see?" Silas prods.

He sidles up next to me, but my focus doesn't waver from Hassan when I respond. "I saw myself being handed over to Rohan's men."

I clench my jaw as the vision plays out in a slow succession. The heat of the Torch's gift against my cheek. The wide smile on Olen's face. The caress of the betrayer who caused it all.

"He wanted both of us," I tell Silas.

I keep my eyes locked ahead. I want to see the flicker of guilt flash across Hassan's face. I need to see the real him—the version who never viewed me as anything other than an opportunity.

"But it seems even alone, Hassan thought I was reward enough."

"Ren, you know he wouldn't do that."

Savi's words tug at my heart, but I ignore it. My focus is locked on one person—and that person is quiet.

"Do I?" I quip. "He's wanted me gone since I got here. Seems he finally found a chance to be rid of me."

Silence beats between us. Hassan's jaw is locked down tight. He looks at Vish for too long, and the tracker's eyes widen in response.

"Say something," I snap at Hassan.

He says nothing. He doesn't let his guard down, doesn't let me see the real him. But he doesn't deny anything either. He simply stares at me like he can't believe I've figured it out.

As silence brews between us, so does my agitation. I replay every second with him, every shared glance and stilted word. *He never liked me, that was obvious from the start. But something changed along the way, didn't it?*

My heart beats too fast as my thoughts shift to the last few days. We had been getting closer, but then he pulled away again. My mind flickers to that night on guard duty, of the truths I revealed. Then to earlier today, to the Berserkers and the words they whispered. The regret on Hassan's face. The anger with Vish. The comments the taller Berserker made. As I stare at Hassan's face, waiting for answers, I decide I don't need anything more than what I already know.

I lunge forward, not caring anymore that I'm unarmed, no longer worried about Savi's arrow piercing my heart. It would be a better death than the one that certainly awaits me in Hira. But before I can meet that fate, Silas's hand snakes around my arm and tugs me back. He leans in close, his words only for me.

"This doesn't end how you think it does," he whispers gruffly. "There are too many of them."

My eyes dart over Savi's shoulder. I spot Tariq and Riat standing with mouths agape. They don't approach, but I can see Tariq's hand hovering above the dagger at his side. Kai stands a good distance away, both swords drawn from the sheathes at his back.

Silas is right.

Despite the fire burning through me, I somehow mange to unclench my fists and take a step back. I quickly stalk across the sand, retrieving my daggers from where they rest half-buried in the sand.

Savi's voice fills the heavy silence in the air. "Ren, please," she pleads.

She takes a step closer, and I tense. My hands tighten around my daggers, but I don't make a move for her, not yet. My body is buzzing with rabid energy. The second she shows her intentions, I'll show mine.

"This isn't what you think it is. Hassan, please tell her—"

"How much is it?" I snap, eyes locked on Hassan. "How much did those daemons tell you I was worth?"

There's a long silence that seems to stifle the air between us. He simply looks at me, expression heavy with things I can't seem to understand. "More than you'll ever know."

My breath catches in my throat. Those hazel eyes burn into me with a pain so deep it feels like my own.

"So, there it is," I bite. "The truth at last."

"You don't know what you speak of," he utters through clenched teeth.

"Then tell me," I growl. "If that's not the truth, tell me what news they brought. Tell me why Vish has been restless ever since, why you all but killed him earlier. Tell me why we're really going to Hira."

He looks at me steadily, emotions hidden behind his high walls once more. His eyes flicker to Vish, and as I follow his gaze, I see the panic drenching the tracker's face. Hassan opens his mouth to speak, but Vish steps up abruptly.

"Hassan, *please*. The danger this will cause…" Vish stresses.

Vish turns to me, eyes darting to Silas in the process. His throat bobs as he takes in the Berserker. Silas wraps his other arm around me, pulling me in by the waist. His fingers tease my hipbone, and for a second, I'm lost to the dizzying feel of it.

Vish's brow furrows at the sight before he raises his eyes to me, pleading. "We can resolve all of this in Hira, please just—"

"Just, what?" I bellow, pulling myself free of Silas. "Follow you to my own grave? I will not allow such a thing to happen."

"Nothing will befall you in Hira," Hassan urges. He takes a cautious step toward me, hands raised peacefully. "You have my word."

"Your word?" I laugh bitterly. "You cannot even utter a word of truth. Trusting you is a fool's errand." I shake my head and step back. As I do, I feel Silas's hand slide around my waist once more. I brush his hand away only for it to find its way back to my skin.

"Hassan," Savi starts. She looks to me, then back to her cousin. I've never seen her so uncertain, so lost in her own convictions. "She should know. She might—"

"Vish is right," Hassan barks. "This is too important. I won't put lives at risk because of some daemon we can't trust."

His words hit me like a blast of sand. I dig my teeth into the inside of my cheek, desperate to replace the anguish I feel with the biting ache of pain. It doesn't work. All I can do is stare at Hassan. He's turned his back on me. Despite the words he just uttered, he doesn't see me as a threat. Maybe he thinks I'm too noble to hurl a blade into his spine. I want to believe that I am, but the hate burning in my chest tells me I would have already delivered the blow if not for Savi. She watches me hesitantly, pain stretching lines around her eyes. The sight deepens the ache within me. As much as I want to hate her, I can't. She opens her mouth to speak, but I've already heard enough.

I stalk toward my tent, throwing the flap open wildly as I slip inside. My blood feels like it's on fire—like it's going to consume me. Breath heaves in and out of my chest as I chuck my daggers to the ground. I want to scream. I want to take everything in here and destroy it.

Somehow, I resist. I force myself to stand still and think. I drag my eyes down the far wall of my tent as rage and something I refuse to name claws inside my chest. It's too much, and I can feel every ounce of it coursing through me. I close my eyes and breathe. All the pent-up emotion I've been forcing down over the past few days is ready to burst. And when it does? I don't know if I can handle it.

How did this happen? How did I let this happen?

I open my eyes and let my gaze unfocus. I know better than to get close to anyone. I know better than to trust. But still, I did. My hands tremble at my sides. I try not to feel anything. It's a wasted effort, but I try anyway.

It's then that I hear someone step inside the tent. My hands tighten into fists, and every ounce of restraint I have left snaps. "Get out," I seethe.

"Not until you talk to me," Silas shoots back.

I spin around to face him and immediately realize it was a mistake. I ran into this tent for a reason. I need to be alone. I need to think. Seeing him in front of me—it only makes my mind spin more.

"I don't want to talk to you."

He scoffs and steps forward. Something flutters through me as he closes the distance between us. I look away, but his hand quickly finds my jaw and pulls my gaze back to him. I try to shake away from his grip, but he tightens it.

"I'm the only one you can talk to."

I grit my teeth as I stare up at him. He's right and I hate it. "What do you want, Silas?" I snap.

He cocks his head at me, a ghost of a smirk slipping across his lips before he leans down. "You."

His lips meet mine, and the fire in my veins burns hot. For a moment, I succumb to it. I let myself dance in its flames. I tug him closer, breathing in his earthy scent. His tongue presses against my lips before I surrender to desire and let him slip inside my mouth. I feel dizzy yet alive. Silas pulls me tightly against him. A breathy moan leaves my throat as his hand cups my ass. As soon as the sound hits my ears, I snap out of it and shove him away.

"Stop." I comb a hand through my tousled hair and try to steady my breath. "For Hael's sake, Silas," I pant. "Stop. I need to think."

He wipes a finger across his wet lips and smirks. "You taste as good as I remember."

I swear under my breath and turn away from him. My face feels as hot as the sun, and something unruly and wanting stirs within me. I ignore it, forcing myself to focus. I grab my pack, stuffing the few things I'd unpacked back into it swiftly. *I'll head back through the canyon, head deep into the desert. There's a chance I may run into some of Rohan's men out there, but it's better than waiting to be handed over like goods to be bartered. Maybe I'll even find Mikel.*

Just as I'm securing the pack over my shoulder, I feel Silas step up behind me. His lips find the curve of my shoulder, and my body responds without thought. I lean back into him as he whispers against my skin. "Don't worry, love," he coos. "I have a plan."

I pull myself away. With gritted teeth, I collect my daggers from where I tossed them. I slide the first one across my chest, securing it in the harness. As I lift the second one, I pause. My throat grows thick and heavy. My eyes sweep across the blade, taking in every part of it. *He's not getting this back.* I let the false truth sink into the recesses of my mind. I don't need to remind myself that there's no changing the future. I know that all too well. With one last glance, I tuck Olen's blade away. It sheathes against my thigh with a shrill whine.

"The only plan is me getting out of here," I snarl. "Now."

I push past him, barreling out of the tent. The others are huddled at the center of camp. Their voices slip into nothing as they turn to look at me. My eyes gleam with anger as I stalk past them and head for the horses. Part of me dares them to stop me, like maybe a little bloodshed would quell this ache in my chest. But no one makes a move for me, and the ache remains.

"It's best if we stick together," Silas offers.

He's snuck up on me, and I almost pull a dagger at the shock. I shoot an irritated look over my shoulder as I fling my pack onto my saddle. "Best for who?"

He smiles at that. "Come on, love. I said I have a plan. Aren't you the least bit curious?"

I turn away and finish settling in for the long journey ahead. Mirage whinnies and huffs, stirring the air with dust as she pounds a hoof into the sand. I shoot a look across camp as I hoist myself up onto the saddle. None of the others have come to stop me. No one, that is, except Hassan.

He strides across the sand, and by the time he reaches us, my nerves are tingling with anticipation. My hand hovers at my hip, ready to pull a dagger, and my mind spins with where to hurl it. But he doesn't draw a weapon. He simply stops a few paces away and looks at Silas. The Berserker is sitting atop his own horse, leads cut from Hassan's saddle. I don't need to turn to see the wicked grin I know rests on his face.

Hassan grits his teeth but pulls his focus back to me. When our eyes lock, something almost like regret slips across his face. "We're on the same side, Ren. I hope you can see that one day."

I don't understand, but by the time I open my mouth to speak, he's already gone.

A strange feeling hits me like a blow to the chest as I watch Hassan stalk away and disappear into his tent. Something deep inside me is clawing, desperate to get to the surface. I want to demand he explain himself. I want to curse the gods for choosing this fate for me.

It's only when Silas's voice breaks my focus that I find control amidst the fury.

"Ready to go, love?"

I grit my teeth and pull on Mirage's lead. "Already gone."

CHAPTER 31

We don't say anything for a while. At least—I don't. Every time Silas tries to talk to me, I offer nothing back. I don't have the words to answer his questions or rival his banter. It's only when the sun dips below the horizon that I finally turn to him and speak. "We should keep going."

He lets out a breathy laugh. "Afraid they'll change their minds about letting us go?"

I shoot him a fiery look before urging my horse ahead of his.

"Fine." He sighs. "There should be enough moonlight for us to travel through the night. If we don't make camp until tomorrow, we should be there in two days' time."

"What?" I tug on the reins, halting Mirage's pace. "I never said I was going anywhere with you."

He circles his horse around mine, wide smile gleaming on his face. "But yet, you've come this far."

I watch him with tracker-like focus as he makes another circle around me before blocking the path ahead. Mirage stomps and huffs at the other horse, but it doesn't budge.

"Admit it," Silas says. "You have nowhere to go but with me."

A scowl slips across my face as I guide my horse around his. I don't deny it. I could have ridden back into the canyon when I left camp. Or ventured north into the desert alone. But I hadn't. I had stuck with Silas without a word or a second thought.

He smirks as I pass him. It's like he can see right through me, like he knows that kiss keeps replaying through my head just as much as the vision of Olen does. It's a dizzying contrast between desire and fear that has my thoughts unmoored.

I lead Mirage forward, trudging through the heavy sands. The desert is cloaked in darkness, empty except for the orange glow of the moon. I hear Silas urge his horse onward, following once again, but I don't turn to face him.

"You said you had a plan," I offer crisply. "What is it?"

A breathy laugh fills the cold night air. "I have a friend in Letka. She can help us out."

Something foul stirs inside me, but I dampen it through the clench of my jaw. "A friend, huh?"

Silas sidles up next to me. "Unless you'd rather go back to your old ones?"

I make the mistake of looking at him. The cocky look cemented on his face sends a scowl across mine.

"And how is this *friend* going to help?"

A flurry of wings erupts in the dark, sending my heart jumping in my chest. Silas's crow appears like a phantom in the night. Its obsidian wings are tinged orange under the moonlight, and I watch as it gracefully swoops down onto Silas's shoulder.

Silas smiles deeply, stroking the bird with the back of his finger. "I'll send word to her in Letka."

Silas pulls a roll of parchment from his saddle. I watch him write something with a bit of charcoal before rolling the message into a tiny scroll and securing it to the crow's foot. The bird squawks as Silas ties off the knot.

"She'll procure supplies, weapons, food—whatever we need."

He gives the bird another loving stroke before it flies off into the night once more. I watch it go, letting my eyes prod the dark long after it disappears.

"Why?"

Silas regards me curiously, brow raised high on his face.

"Why help me?" I prod. "What could you possibly gain?"

"Maybe I like having you around." His eyes flicker with heat, offering me a look that has me squirming in my saddle. "Or maybe one kiss wasn't enough."

My mouth snaps shut as I turn to face forward. We ride in silence, nothing piercing the chilled night air except for the huff of our horses and the sand sifting against the wind. I try to think, to sort through the chaos in my own mind, but it's no use. All I can think of is the upcoming days and what they might bring. It's been too long since I tied my fate to someone else's, and there's a nervous energy buzzing in my chest. Things were different with Mikel. Despite the friendship we found after I joined Zoah's caravan, he never pushed me on how long I planned to stay. He didn't bat an eye when I left to work in the west. Even when I disappeared for days—whether to catch our next meal or merely settle my nerves— he never questioned me. It's like he always knew that eventually I'd go my own way, that I'd run from this life to start the next. But with Silas...

This is different—it *feels* different.

I sneak a glance at him as he rummages through his bag. I take in the markings covering his arms—the abundance and skill of his gift, forever marred across his flesh. I let myself wonder what it would be like to call on the tinge of Hael running through my blood and urge it to bloom inside me. *Was it too late? Or would my markings spread across my skin like Silas's if only I welcomed it?*

I pull my gaze away quickly as he turns. I spy the shell of a smile growing on his face, but he stays silent. He takes a bite of bread before reaching across the empty space between us and offering it up. I take it with a silent nod, breaking off a piece. A hunger I didn't know was there gnaws ravenously as the first bite slips down my throat and into my empty belly. I take another and hand it back before I devour the entire thing.

Silas hums to himself as we carry on into the night. At first, it's no more than an annoying buzz in my ears. I open my mouth to demand him to stop, but before I can, something awakes from the depths inside of me. Memory pulses against the blackness of night like a living thing. The tinges of nostalgia and ache have me clutching the reins tighter. I have to stop myself from humming along with him, the habit carved too deeply within me. The past floods my mind and seems to hold me under its tempestuous surface.

I struggle to get the words out, breath trapped like there's a stone lodged in the back of my throat. "Where did you learn that song?"

"Hm?" Silas snaps out of his own daydream as he turns to look at me.

"That song," I repeat. "Where did you learn it?"

He grins, his canines no more than a predatory glisten of bone against the dark. "From an old friend," he notes. "He gave me this…"

I watch him pull at the collar of his tunic. The moonlight reveals a large black scar cutting down the center of his chest. Something knowing tightens in my gut as I look at the healed Shade's cut marring his smooth skin. His fingers tap the damaged flesh before letting his tunic slide back into place. A silence hovers in the air, seeming to grow heavier with each breath he takes.

His eyes darken as he looks toward the horizon. "I hope to repay the favor one day."

Chills run up the back of my neck. Curiosity prickles my tongue, and though I want to ask, I don't. The Continent is a big place, but I don't think I could handle a familiar description rolling from Silas's lips if I asked what Shade left such a parting gift.

My fingers fidget with the reins, desperate for a distraction. The *shhh* of sand fills the night as we trek down a small dune. Mirage chuffs, and I give her a scratch right behind the ears. I try to find comfort in the living silence around me, but it only makes me uneasy. My gaze flickers to Silas. He's far more quiet than I'm used to.

I wait for him to notice my attention, to shoot me a playful grin, but he never does. His gaze is still pinned ahead, and his brow is crumpled in thought. Though I know I shouldn't, I let my eyes wander. Even against the glow of the moon, Silas's markings are unmistakable. The splotches and lines that run up and down his neck are nothing short of chaos. Harsh scrawls of ink-like marks are surrounded by soft lines and splotches. My eyes drift up to his face, to where markings shape the sharp lines of his cheekbones and nose and contrast the pale rose hue of his skin. I feel my lips part, sucking in a soft breath against my will. It's then that I realize he's beautiful.

The flicker of his eyes to mine has me turning away too quickly. "I— uh." I stumble on my words as he shoots me a knowing look. "Your markings."

He raises a brow, and embarrassment churns in my stomach.

"When did they first show up?" I ask.

He chuckles under his breath, and I can only hope he can't see how red my face is in the dark.

"When I was six," he replies. "Though I was able to keep them hidden until I was seven."

I nod, knowing all too well how and why he did such a thing. "And after that?"

Silas clicks his teeth and shrugs. "My parents were kinder than most. My mother's cousin had been a Weaver, so I was allowed to stay as long as I kept out of trouble."

"You? Trouble?" My brow arches as a smile slips across my lips. "Let me guess—that didn't last long?"

He chuckles, but it falls flat. I watch his jaw tick before his eyes sweep back to mine. "My parents were killed by Turidens when I was fourteen," he states, far calmer than I could have. "I took my younger brother and headed south. Everything after that was what you'd expect."

The silence between us is sharper than any blade I've owned. I stare at him, hoping to see a glimmer of his usual self but all I'm met with is a heavy disquiet. His shoulders are tightly bound, and his gaze is locked ahead.

Our horses carry us forward for what feels like ages before I manage to open my mouth. But before the words can come out, I stop them. He doesn't need my sympathy, nor does he want it.

My eyes roam over him, as if trying to unearth the pieces he's clearly hidden. The sight of Silas so guarded and shut down stirs something wounded in me. *Is this what people see when they look at me?* The mere thought tightens my chest.

Finally, I swallow the lump in my throat and speak. "And your brother?" I ask softly. "Where is he?"

For a while, Silas says nothing. I watch his hands knot against the reins in his lap, watch his jaw clench and unclench. Just as I turn away to give him space, he speaks.

"Tol Dena."

I can't help the way my gaze snaps to his, but when it does, my stomach drops. Silas's eyes are cold and severe. The look chills me more than the violence of his gift, more than the deep black of his eyes when Veles fills him. I'm lost in the brutality carved into his face, and only when he forces in a deep breath do I manage to take my own. I open my mouth to speak but he cuts me off.

"Don't worry," he utters through clenched teeth. "I'm going to get him back."

CHAPTER 32

My gaze feels as heavy as the heat that bears down on us. I relish the brief respite as my eyelids flutter closed, only to face the onslaught of the sun once they open again. My body slumps deeper into the saddle with every step Mirage takes across the sand. We should have made camp last night.

The sun rose hours ago, and there's yet to be a sign of anyone following us. It's good—I kept telling myself—that Hassan and the others let us go. I have no place with them, and they no place with me. But still, my mind wanders aimlessly in the space between sleep and the living. Remnants of the past few days play in my head while the sprawling land ahead holds my gaze. I think of Savi, the conflict and anguish splayed across her face as she aimed that arrow at my chest. Or Kai, both blades drawn like I was going to kill Hassan.

If the others hadn't been there, would I have?

My body teeters, then snaps awake as I feel myself slipping off the saddle. I inhale sharply and grip the reins tighter. Mirage looks back at me and chuffs as if all she needs this morning is me falling off her back like a distracted child. I shake my head, trying to dislodge the threat of sleep but its enticing lull quickly returns. My eyelids droop heavily until, finally, they close. I see Hassan's face underneath me, pinned below my blade while the other aims for his heart. He's surprised. His hazel eyes are filled with concern and hesitation. The look puzzles me, freezes me to the spot. *Did Savi's arrow stop me or was I about to stop myself?* I sink deeper into the memory, grasping for the truth when my body jolts awake.

I'm gasping, sputtering against the river that seeks to drown me. But I'm not drowning. My eyes shoot open, and I'm met with an amused grin.

"Thought that would wake you up."

My eyes dart from Silas to the open canteen he's holding. All I can manage to do is stare as my face drips with water. "Did you just…"

His face is stretched into utter amusement, and though I'm mad at him, it's a welcome return after last night's heaviness. He takes a sip from the canteen before pouring some water on his neck. It trickles down his skin, wetting his tunic. The fabric clings to his muscular chest, and for a second, I forget why I'm angry in the first place.

"You can't tell me you don't feel better," he says smugly. "It helps with the heat, too."

"I'm soaking wet," I retort, regaining my resolve. "Surely there was a better way to wake me."

He leans back in his saddle, resting comfortably while he looks me up and down.

"Yes, but it's adorable when you're angry."

"Gods. You're so…" I start, my hands waving in the air as I try to find the words.

"Charming?" He grins.

"Obnoxious."

I unwrap my headscarf, using it to mop up the water that's still streaming down my skin. "Dare to try something like that again and Veles help me..."

I mumble curses under my breath as I strip off my wet tunic. I lay it and my damp headscarf across the saddle to dry. Thankfully, today's heat has its upsides. I pat at the thin fabric of the sleeveless tunic I layered underneath my longer one. The few splashes that soaked through are already disappearing under the sun's harsh rays. I'm still shaking my head and muttering when Silas reaches for me.

"You never told me how he did this."

I flinch away as his fingers graze the cuts that have barely closed over the past few days. It doesn't hurt anymore, thanks to Mikel's salve. But while the physical pain is gone, the memory still remains.

"It doesn't matter how," I grit out.

His gaze roams over my skin. The examination is so intense that I almost slip my wet tunic back on just to escape the heat of it. I swallow harshly as his eyes rise back to my face.

"He must want you something bad." Silas tilts his head to the side, gray eyes piercing into mine. "For more than one reason now, I suspect."

My jaw clenches, but I offer nothing more. Silas lets out a breathy laugh as I snap the reins and urge my horse far ahead of his.

"You're tough, love," he calls after me. "I can't wait to see the kind of fight you put up when it really matters."

"Are all Berserkers this annoying, or just you?" I shout back.

His response doesn't reach me as I put some distance between us. Silence falls over the desert, only broken by my deep sigh.

"Gods above," I mutter to myself. *I don't know how I'll endure another day with him.*

Rolling my shoulders, I stretch my back where it feels too tight from sitting for hours on end. A soft groan leaves my lips as I hear a gratifying pop. I stare ahead, into the hazy expanse of nothing. I've never been to this part of the Continent, in the barren space between the Jahaer Desert and the coast. But there's no greenish-blue shimmer of the sea waiting on the horizon. It's only endless sand and a cloudless sky. I have no idea if we're even going the right way.

My map is rolled up in my bag, but I don't bother getting it out. It's more of an idea of the Continent than a chart. I won it from some merchant in a game of cards long ago. *Or maybe I stole it from him? I can't remember.* But the landmarks and cities dotted across the worn parchment are hand drawn and crude. They're nothing more than a personal account from myself and the owners before me. Much is missing, both from the map and my own knowledge of the land I've lived on my entire life. There's not a place called Letka known to myself or the map yet. But there will be.

I take a deep breath and press my heels into Mirage's side. The faster we get there, the sooner I can figure out what to do next.

As I turn around to see how far back Silas has fallen, an uncanny feeling I've felt so many times but can never get used to washes over me like oil mixing into water. For a second, I forget where I am. I blink slowly, but the image in front of me is shifting, moving. My hands trace over a bundle of honey-white hair. It's the color of my hair, but it's not my hair. My eyes blink and refocus. I'm on the back of a mare. *Mirage.* Although I recognize the animal, could recognize the huffed breath that comes from her, it feels foreign now. Her hooves sift through the sand and breath spills from her nose in heavy bouts. I know I've lived this moment before but somehow it still feels like the first time.

The horse carries me up the dune until we're resting on top of it. The sun is high above the horizon, blanketing the endless sands in a lush, orange glow. I stare at it, revel in its beauty before another horse comes alongside and pulls my focus. My eyes trace over the black stallion. Something about the sight of its dark coat, black like the night flecked with white stars, churns in my gut uneasily. It rears its head back as its rider brings it to a halt. The horse stares at me through glossy, black eyes like I'm a threat to be watched.

I shake off the feeling and look up to see its rider. But I don't see his face. All I can focus on are the markings running down the center of his throat. *Danger. Threat,* my instincts scream at me. But I don't reach for my daggers. My eyes raise slowly until the uncanny feeling lifts, and I remember why.

Silas looks back at me, head tilted curiously. "You all right?"

I nod quickly and urge Mirage forward. "Fine," I spit out, though my voice sounds more uneasy than I'd like it to.

He chuckles, mumbling something under his breath as he follows. I run my hand across my arm, pinching the skin. I wince, then relax. *I'm here. This isn't a vision.*

I swallow harshly. My throat is beginning to scratch, as dry as the sand around me. The urge to drink from my canteen is overpowered by the reminder that I should ration it. Who knows how long it'll truly take to get to Letka or if we'll stumble upon an outpost along the way. A knot forms in my stomach at the thought. Once again, I'm letting someone else lead me toward a destination I'm unfamiliar with. Once again, I'm taking the word of someone I don't know.

My eyes sweep over Silas, looking for something I should have seen in Hassan, but all that stands out are his markings and the way his eyes seem to brighten when he looks at me.

"You sure you're okay?"

I nod and look away.

"Hm." Silas gives me a look that tells me he doesn't believe me.

He turns away, and for a second, I think he'll grant me a moment's respite. It's not peace that I find in the brief silence, however. There are too many questions and not enough answers swirling through my mind. Just as I turn to ask one, the deep pop of a cork dismisses my thoughts. Silas lifts the bottle to his lips and takes a long swig of whatever resides inside the amber glass before holding it out to me.

"What is it?"

He smirks and shakes the bottle. "Something to settle your thoughts."

"How do—"

"You get this stern look on your face when you're thinking too much," he offers. "Right here..."

He leans across our horses, and I still as he presses his fingers into the space between my brows. His touch is gentle as it rubs the furrow away. My eyes meet his hesitantly. We hover there, too close but not close enough, until Mirage whinnies. She snaps her teeth at the other horse before finding space between us once more.

Silas chuckles as he reaches over and hands the bottle to me. "It's honeyed rum," he says. "From the market in Kupor."

I lift it to my nose and inhale. I'm immediately met with a spicy yet sweet smell that makes my mouth water. I look at him curiously, and he nods. I take a sip. The flavor bursts across my tastebuds, and I have to stifle the pleased groan it elicits.

"It's delicious," I murmur, taking another sip before handing it back to him.

He takes another as well before swirling the bottle in his hand. I watch as the liquid sloshes around the inside of the glass like a whirlpool.

"You've been to Kupor?" I ask.

"Yes."

Suddenly I remember the Berserker, the one with the burns. *Ivar.* His words come back to me and tug at my tongue. "Did you know that daemon?" I ask Silas. "The one who mentioned Kupor?"

"No." He takes another sip, mumbling his words into the bottle. "Must have confused me with another roguishly handsome Berserker."

I scoff and shoot him a glare. He's cocky, but he's not wrong. My eyes run over his sharp cheekbones and cut jaw, then down to the markings that cover his throat and slip down underneath his tunic. My eyes hover there for far too long, but luckily Silas hasn't noticed. The liquid sloshes in the bottle as he takes another sip. I watch a drop slip down his lips, and suddenly I need another taste. Of what, I'm not sure.

He offers it back to me, and I snatch the bottle from him quickly before I do something I'll regret. Two gulps of the sweet rum slide down my throat before I push the bottle back toward him. He chuckles but manages to keep his thoughts to himself.

A comfortable silence settles between us but this time, I'm the one to break it. "Have you been many places?"

He corks the bottle, turning away as he stuffs it back into his pack. "I've seen enough of what the Continent has to offer."

"Ah," I utter, noticing the way his usual charm has shifted into something cautious. "I'm sure the Continent has shown you quite a lot with how Veles is spread across your skin."

"And you?" he prods. "What life have you lived that keeps your marks so small?" His gaze narrows on me before his smile grows wider. "Or are there more hidden from prying eyes?"

"The depth of my gift is of no concern to you." I scoff. "And if I have more markings under these clothes, you certainly won't be the one to find them."

"I'll remember you said that when we make camp tonight."

"Oh yeah?" I laugh. "And why's that?"

He leans out of his saddle, lips hovering dangerously close to my ear. "Because you'll be begging me to find them."

I shove him away, groaning in frustration. "The only thing I'll be begging for is you to be silent."

I snatch my tunic off the saddle and tug it over my head. It's still damp, but I don't care. Anything to keep his lingering gaze off my flesh. I look at him from the corner of my eye as I grab my headscarf. He's grinning like a madman, well aware just how deeply he can get under my skin.

A loud *caw* slices through the air and before I can finish wrapping my headscarf, Silas's crow sits on his shoulder.

"Good boy, Coyir," he whispers, untying the bit of rolled parchment from its leg.

As he unravels it, I see that it's not the same message he sent off earlier. This one is written on clean, pressed parchment, and I spy the stain of ink before Silas pulls it out of view.

He grins, quickly tucking the slip into his pack. "They'll be waiting for us in Letka."

"They?"

His horse huffs as he spurs it forward.

"What? You thought I only had one friend?" he teases.

I roll my eyes, but as I start to speak, he stops me.

"Don't worry, love," he coos. "Play nice and we'll be in and out of the city before you know it." He lets out a breathy laugh. "Just be a good girl and behave. You can do that for me, right?"

"Behave?" I rasp, nearly choking on his words. "That's rich coming from someone with the manners of a dog in heat."

He maneuvers his horse away as I try to swat at him. Coyir crows loudly atop Silas's shoulder, flapping its wings in an attempt to stay put.

"Oh, come now," he laughs. "Don't tell me you'd prefer me any other way. I've seen that look in your eyes…" His gaze grows heavy as those gray eyes bear into mine. He drops his voice to a low, gruff whisper. "You know, the one you think I don't notice."

I *tut* under my breath as I relent my assault. There's a permanent grin spread across his face, and I'm annoyed just looking at it. "You do know I'm going my own way once we get to Letka, right?"

My words are harsher than needed and they taste bitter on my tongue. He says nothing, but I watch the way his jaw tenses oh-so-slightly. The sight stirs something unwanted in my chest—something best left untouched and ignored.

I shake my head and follow the line the sun is taking across the horizon. We're well past midday now. It will be dark within the oncoming hours. "How much longer will the journey take?"

"Less than a day," he says. "We should rest tonight. Then carry on in the morning."

I want to argue, but my body aches, desperate for sleep and a few hours off the saddle.

"Fine. But just so you know," I state, "I sleep with my daggers."

He pets the crow on his shoulder as his brow arches curiously. "Is that an invitation or a threat?"

"Thre—"

The word stills on my lips as my body goes cold. Panic takes root before I can stop it. *No, not again. Surely, I can't be having another so soon?*

I watch Silas's eyes widen as my own flood with a milky white haze. Before everything disappears from view and I slip underneath the depths of my own mind, he reaches for me. Panic has me yanking at the reins, driving Mirage away from his touch. Whatever this vision brings, it's not for him to see. Silas's voice fades into the background as the gods hold me under the swell of fate's tides.

Sand sprays around me. It's all a blur as I sprint across the desert, eyes flickering back and force across the turbulent surface before me. I'm down to one blade, and it trembles in my wary hand. Yells erupt from my right, but I don't dare turn, afraid I'll see a flash of red against the snap of shiny, black claws. Overworked breath mixes with panic in my chest. I try to draw it in deeply, try to find the energy to push myself harder, but my adrenaline has all but run its course. The cluster of rocky hoodoos ahead is a beacon of hope but it's too far. I won't make it.

The tug on my boot sends my heart into my stomach. This is it.

The sand explodes behind me as the creature breaches the surface. I wait for the burn of its stinger, the snap of its pincers, but it doesn't come. A shadow slips up my leg, yanking me across the sand. I hear the snap of exoskeleton, the shriek of the beast itself.

My chest heaves as I lie in the sand, heart pounding dangerously fast. As I look up, blinking the harsh sun from my eyes, I'm met with the dark hue of an all-too familiar gaze. He smirks down at me, sweat beading off his brow and black blood splattered across his face.

"You were never good at running," he taunts. "Good thing you still have me."

I'm ripped from the vision in an instant. My hands are clutched tightly against the reins, body pressed flat against Mirage's back. She's stopped dead in her tracks, hair bristled on her neck. I blink feverishly, desperate to clear the last of the white from my eyes and rejoin the world here as I know it.

When I finally do, I'm met with Silas's wild stare. "Are you okay?"

His voice is much too soft for my liking. I watch his throat bob nervously as his eyes roam over me. My spine feels like it's been arched like a cat's, and my fingernails have drawn blood from my palms.

"Fine," I grunt.

I try to relax, fighting through the rigid clench of my muscles as I sit up in the saddle. Every part of me feels battered. I kick my heels against Mirage, shaking her from the fright I myself caused.

It's not long before Silas spurs his horse forward to catch up. "Are they always that bad?" he presses.

I stare straight ahead, but emotion ebbs like a wave in my chest. I can feel the last of the adrenaline pumping through me—like I'm still running for my life. I've never seen a ricsin, nor did I ever plan to. My skin crawls as I think about the few glimpses the vision showed me of those giant scorpions said to inhabit the Continent's gods-drenched north.

"I mean—gods above," Silas continues. "You were practically writhing, pitching against the saddle, murmuring like a woman possessed."

I can't bear to look at Silas. My mind is still stuck in that vision. I knew eventually the past would catch up to me—that we would find each other. Though a part of me, a foolish one at that, thought I might escape the Weaver's influence. It seems the gods have other plans.

"Love, are you okay?"

I push the last twinges of fear and heartache away as I meet Silas's gaze. "I said I'm fine," I snap. I spur Mirage on, desperate to find space away from Silas's fretful gaze. He looks at me like he actually cares, and the sight stirs things best left buried.

"Come on," I utter. "We need to find somewhere to rest for the night."

CHAPTER 33

My boots drag across the sand, and already I can feel my heart pattering in my chest. It beats uneasily, every step forward seeming to spike the thumping to a violent peak. I don't know how I made it this far, don't know how long I've been here or what happened the moment before. All I know, and all I can discern, is what is right in front of me. The chasm. The doorway. It towers over me, a deep black hole amidst the bright, sweltering day.

The wind whips harshly around me, but somehow, I keep my hair out of my eyes. I study the markings that run up and down the sides of the worn cliffside. Some look like my own. Some look like those I've seen on Mikel or Silas. Their presence seems to hum against my skin. It's different than it was. Where there was an urge before, there's now a force yanking at my bones. It calls to me. It wants me.

I step closer, pulled by an innate knowing that this is inevitable. The gods want this. But do I want this?

I blink through the spray of sand as it swirls through the canyon. Through the flutter of my lashes, I see something.

The shadow.

My stomach drops. My heart rate picks up, trilling through me.

As I take another step and look closer, the slink of shadow slips from the doorway. It curls and rolls against the air, as if beckoning me closer. The sight is eldritch and untethered, but I don't back away. Where the shadow was wild and unkept last time, it's now patient and cautious. It's familiar—this darkness. It calls to me more than the canyon, more than the doorway carved in markings. It drives me forward, hastens my steps.

I walk without thinking, without care or concern. My feet trudge across the heavy sands until I feel the unmistakable pull on my boots. My heart lurches in my chest. I race forward, desperate to make it this time. Desperate to see what lies beyond the door. Desperate to reach that darkness that feels so familiar but so lost to the past. I know it's him, it has to be.

My boot sinks, sending my body sprawling against the sand. I crawl forward, every part of my body screaming to break free. The pull is inescapable now, so close I can feel it swimming through my blood. My veins burn. I look down and see the black flowing underneath my skin, flooding my system. I thrash and scream.

An answering yell rips through the canyon. A voice reaches me through the whipping wind. It's familiar, but not like the darkness. Fear picks up in my chest in a heavy rhythm. Silas's voice calls out to me again, but something tells me not to go toward it. Something inside me is screaming, pleading for me to move forward, to reach the doorway. But I can't.

I'm yelling, clawing to find a way out of the sand that only seeks to drag me deeper. The shadows race for me. Tears spill down my face, mixing with the harsh grit of sand against my skin. I want to reach it. I need to make it there this time.

The darkness reaches out a hand, a tendril of shadow that swirls like smoke. I stretch toward it, fighting against the vicious pull of what lies below me. But I don't make it forward. The shadow slips through my fingertips.

My stomach pitches as a tug reaches up my legs, yanking me into the earth. I cry out, but the sand swallows me whole. It presses down over my body like the crush of a mountain. I barely glimpse the face amidst the shadows as all fades away. I barely have time to see the piercing brown eyes, so dark they almost look black. My mouth opens to scream. But I'm already gone. And so is Malachi.

"Ren."

My blood runs cold at the sound of his voice as if I'm still in that dream.

"Ren!"

I'm gasping for air, clawing at my throat like I can still feel the sand pouring down it.

Strong hands clutch me, their grip too tight. "For the love of the gods!" Silas shouts. "It's okay. You're okay."

My heart is an untamed beast in my chest. I'm fighting for breath, still reeling from what the Weaver sent tonight. My eyes flutter open, only to find the dark. I panic again, lashing out against Silas. I feel his grip tighten, feel my bones squeeze and shudder under his strength. My body feels like an old tree ready to splinter.

"Just breathe," he urges me. "Breathe, love."

That voice echoes in my head like it did in the canyon. I turn to look up at him and see his eyes are black, darker than night. Adrenaline floods my chest. I'm frantic, tugging and thrashing in his grip. I squirm desperately but he only holds me tighter.

"Breathe," he orders. "Godsdamnit, Ren. *Breathe.*"

His arms pin mine to my sides so that I can no longer move. My hands are shaking. I force a shuddering breath into my lungs. "Silas," I rasp.

"I've got you," he mutters. "I've got you."

I swallow the quiver of emotion in my throat and give in. I fall back against him and breathe. We stay there, no words passing between us, as we pant against each other. My eyes adjust to the dark and time slows, along with the frantic beat of my heart.

Though my body grows still, my mind cannot rest. I think of the canyon. Its pull. The shadow. Silas's voice breaking through the Weaver's dream. Remembering it now pebbles my skin in goosebumps, raising my hackles like a cat. Something is telling me to abandon this path, to seek a different fate. I don't know why or to what end. It's the stress. It's the last few days. The last week of my life. My body and mind can't take anymore.

Silas's fingers rub soothing circles on my skin, and I welcome the distraction. His touch is gentle, loving. Suddenly, I'm aware of every breath he takes. I feel every beat of his heart against my back. My gaze flickers up to him and finds that the playful gray of his eyes has returned. Without thought, I'm leaning into him, pressing myself closer. His focus hovers on my lips.

He drags his gaze up my face with a brutal slowness, and it's only when he meets my eye that I see the hunger there. His fingers dig into my skin just as I crash my lips into his. Gone are the shadows. Gone is the canyon. Silas pulls me closer, and I turn to straddle his lap. His mouth doesn't leave me for a breath, devouring me as if desperate for every taste. I grind against him, fingers tugging at his hair.

It's only when his hand slides under my tunic—fingers ghosting over the scar that mars my stomach—that my eyes snap open. I shove him away, sucking in a quick breath. His eyes are wide and uncertain as I climb off him and go back to my own bedroll. I lie down, turning away from him before he has a chance to say anything. The only things I hear are the pounding of my own heart and his panting breath. Though everything feels hot, I pull the blanket over me, shielding myself from his view.

He lets out a breathy laugh before I hear him go back to bed. As I stare off into the dark, my mind goes to familiar places.

I can practically feel my blood pulsing under the scar on my stomach, can practically feel the blade slip through my skin and tear. My jaw clenches, but it does nothing to stave off the slurry of memories ravaging me. A lump forms in my throat as I blink back silent tears. *He left me.*

Life in Artolen had been reckless—one bad decision after the other. We had thought ourselves untouchable at that age. But getting cornered in the alley had proven us wrong. That was my first encounter with the Turidens, the people that want nothing more than my blood returned to the earth, and it had changed everything.

I press my hand against my stomach like I had that day, trying to stop the bleeding. I clamp my eyes shut, but it only brings me more horrors. The two men had caught us off guard. Chani stood no chance. Her marks bled across her arms at that point, and she hadn't cared to hide them. They slit her throat before we had even truly noticed. Our numbers had dwindled to three that year. The twins had left the city, heading south in search of something better. So after Chani's eyes had faded lifelessly, it was just me and Malachi.

The men had been ruthless. One for each of us, but their age and skill greatly outmatched our own. I saw the blood before I felt it seep from my skin. But once I did, it was all too much. Pain ravaged me, and blood poured freely. Shadows had exploded through the alley, much too late, as my vision darkened at the corners. The last thing I saw before I passed out was the person I cared for more than anything, and he was leaving me to die.

My throat clenches as yesterday's vision replays in my mind. *I'm not ready to see him again, to face what he's done.*

Against my wishes, Malachi's eyes flash in my mind. He could stir so much in me with just one look. Even now, the thought of that dark gaze makes my heart beat a little faster. I still remember the way his shadows would swirl around his wrist as he brushed the hair from my face. The way he would bump my chin playfully when I failed to keep my defenses up while sparring.

The thought of that silver ring sitting in the bottom of my pack, the one marked by his very gift, is too much to bear. I bite the inside of my cheek until blood fills my mouth. Memories are too dangerous to revisit, whether they be good or bad.

I burrow deeper into the bedroll. The nightmares the Weaver sends are getting worse, happening more often. Whoever they are, they won't let me rest until I give in—until I find that place. And maybe, neither will Malachi.

The urge to toss and turn plagues me all night, but I force myself to keep still. I can't wake Silas. The desert's chill is harsh, like it knows my wickedness and seeks to punish me. I beg the gods for a sleep that never comes. Every sound across the desert has me on edge. Every flutter of the dry breeze startles me from my sleepless haze.

When the sun finally rises, all I'm left with is the heavy tug of exhaustion in my bones and memories that haunt me.

CHAPTER 34

I chew the inside of my cheek as I shake sand from the thin bedroll. Silas douses the fire next to me, sending up a climbing waft of smoke. We're both silent as we pack up, though his gaze lingers on me far too often. I do what I can to ignore him, but my skin seems to prickle in goosebumps every time he passes. Last night is a burden on my thoughts. It's too close to the present to be so easily forgotten. I can still feel the panic rooted deep in my chest. It hovers there, silent and waiting, like it knows it'll be of use today. But stronger than that, I still feel Silas's arms tightening around me, protecting me from the torment of my own mind.

Gods. I would have preferred if he'd killed me instead.

I wince as my teeth slice through my cheek, drawing blood. The coppery tang spoils in my mouth as I tie my things to the saddle. The crunch of Silas's boots has me lurching where I stand. My hands work quickly to strap my pack next to the bedroll. I make sure to keep my head down all the while.

As Silas walks by with his own pack slung over his shoulder, I swear I hear him laugh under his breath. He lingers by his horse like he's waiting to say something, but I don't turn to face him. Instead, I tighten my saddle for the third time. Mirage huffs, and I relent. I've harassed her enough with my restlessness.

The pangs in my body are a quick distraction. I twist to the side. My back aches, both from the long ride and the stiffness of the ground. I know it will only get worse. *Who knows how many more hours in the saddle lay ahead of us?*

A soft groan spills from my lips as my spine pops. I hold the stretch and close my eyes. The release is a sweet burn of overused yet stiff muscles. I miss the plush cushion of bedding, miss having a tent overhead to keep the desert at bay while I sleep. I crack my neck to the side, relishing the pop there, too. There won't be any small luxuries like tents and bedding for a while. I need to lay low— stay on the move. I can't risk growing comfortable and letting my guard down. Not again.

Silas clears his throat, unwillingly pulling my attention. I stop chewing my cheek to pieces long enough to look at him.

"You look like you didn't sleep," he muses. "Care to share what's on your mind?"

Silence is all he gets from me. I hoist myself up into the saddle without a word. I'm fidgeting with the straps when Silas slinks up beside me. Mirage huffs her disapproval.

"About last night..." he starts.

My hand tightens around the saddle's pommel. "Last night was nothing."

He pauses, then shoots me a smug look that makes me want to bury my face in the sand. "Which part?"

My mouth drops before I pull a stern look across my face. "I had a nightmare, that's all."

The lie is sweet on my tongue. Silas lets out a soft chuckle, but his eyes don't meet mine. His gaze sweeps low across my neck, then to my chest, then to my thighs. He runs a hand across Mirage's shoulder, fingers too close to grazing my knee. Mirage stomps, breath chuffing as I squirm in my seat.

"And what about what happened after that?" he prods.

I'm chewing on the inside of my cheek, not knowing how to answer and not wanting to. Instead, I grab the reins and pull away from him. "We should go before the day gets ahead of us."

I'm heading across the sand before he can object. One look over my shoulder confirms what I already know—he's smirking. It's a devious grin that proves he can see right through me.

I bite back a scowl as I pull my gaze away. Last night was a mistake, clearly. My mind wanders without permission to those moments after he woke me. The feeling of sinking back against his chest. The powerful hold of his arms around me. The wanting tug of his lips. The heat shimmering in the gray of his eyes. I shake the thoughts away as something hot pools in my core. It was a mistake. A moment of weakness. Nothing more.

I swallow harshly, trying to keep the flurry of lies down. As his horse catches up to mine, the fluttering in my stomach makes it all too clear that I'm a poor liar. My gaze stays locked on the horizon as he finds pace next to me.

We're both quiet for a while, settling into a natural silence. Letka is only a few hours from here; Silas told me as much last night once I prodded for more details. But his vague answers left much to be desired. As I squint toward the horizon, against the newly risen sun that glares into my eyes, I swear I can see a hint of something. I imagine a city there, eagerly awaiting me. I wonder how big Letka is. Wonder what wares I might find, what daggers I might be able to refit my lost collection with.

As I'm dreaming of the day to come, Silas's voice shatters the peaceful silence. "You know, this would be a lot easier if you just admitted it."

I shoot him a sideways glare. "Admit what?" I huff.

"That you want me."

My heads whips toward him so fast I almost crick my neck. "Excuse me?"

"It's okay" —his teeth dig into his bottom lip as he smiles— "the feeling is more than shared."

The words catch in my throat as a blush reddens my cheeks. "No, it's not," I stammer.

He does a poor job biting back the smirk that creeps up the corners of his mouth. "You sure about that, love? Last night's kiss says differently."

"That was a mistake," I snap. "I wasn't thinking straight."

"You weren't thinking at all." He looks me up and down slowly. "You should try it more often. Maybe then you could kiss me without having a tizzy."

"I did *not* have a tizzy," I insist.

Silas only shoots me a wicked grin.

"The kiss was a mistake," I repeat. "It won't happen again."

"Even though you want it to?"

"I don't want—" I hold my tongue; there's no point in arguing. The mischievous flash of his eyes tells me he's enjoying this too much. He's only trying to get me flustered, and by the gods, it's working. I turn back toward the horizon and let silence brood between us. Sand blows across the emptiness in front of our horses. I lock my eyes on the back of Mirage's head, forcing myself to think of anything but that kiss.

The silence is quickly replaced by the prodding of his voice. "You're good at it," Silas muses.

"Good at what?" I snap.

As my gaze reluctantly pans over to him, I wish it hadn't. His eyes pierce into me so fiercely that I forget I'm supposed to hate him for a moment.

"Pretending you don't need anyone," he states.

I turn my gaze back on the horizon. "I don't know what you're going on about."

"Mm," he mutters under his breath. "I think you do."

My teeth grind against each other, stifling the retort I want to hurl his way. But he wants that. He wants me to lose my head, wants me to argue until he tricks me into saying something I'll regret—into *doing* something I'll regret. But that's not going to happen. My jaw aches from how tightly I'm clenching it.

"You don't trust people."

An indignant laugh spills from my lips. "Trust is an indulgence I can't afford. I would assume you, of all people, can understand that."

"I can," he says. "It's hard to trust the world when it's constantly trying to capture, control, or kill you." Though they're covered, he stares at my arms. "I'm sure you've seen your fair share of that, love. The fight in you is proof enough."

I don't appease him with an answer. He's watching me like I'm a bard at a tavern, just waiting for me to provide entertainment.

"Where did you learn how to fight?" he asks.

Pain blooms in my throat, but I choke it back. "I lived on the streets growing up. You either learn to fight or get good at running." A deep ache fills my chest, lingering with memories of things to come. My eyes cut across the desert to meet Silas's gaze. "I was never good at running."

"The streets, huh?" He hums to himself, stroking his chin thoughtfully. "I guess we all end up there one way or another. How did you get by?"

I shrug. "The usual. Begging, stealing, bartering with whatever we stole. I lived with four others—three of them daemons—so we looked out for one another."

He watches me for a minute, like he's trying to find some secret carved into my face. "Where are they now?"

I stare straight ahead, grip the reins a little tighter. "Gone."

"Dead?"

"Gone," I repeat, firmer this time.

He lifts his brow curiously. "Hm."

"And you?" I quip. "Does the Berserker with a bounty waiting on him back in Piro have a story?"

"Other than the one you just wrote for me?"

I roll my eyes, muttering under my breath.

"I grew up in Malneis, up north."

Uneasiness churns inside of me as I remember the story he told me the other night. About his family—his brother.

"I know Malneis," I say quickly. "It's a few days journey from Artolen."

Recognition flashes through his eyes. "You're from Artolen?"

I nod.

"Interesting," he utters. "Not the easiest place to grow up."

"Like I said," I grit out. "Learn to fight or get good at running."

"It makes sense now." He chuckles. "Why someone touched by Hael would attack me with two measly daggers." His eyes flash wildly as he looks me over. "What kind were they?"

"What?"

"The Veles-cursed you grew up with. The ones who taught you to fight like your life depended on it. What were their gifts?"

My brow furrows. "How did you know they were touched by Veles?"

He smirks and leans back in his saddle, hands resting lazily in his lap.

"Artolen is not for the weak," he states. "I wouldn't expect a Hael-blessed daemon to make it out alive without help. And if one did, their gift wouldn't be as untouched as yours."

"Is that what you think?" I scoff. "That those touched by Hael are weaker than those touched by Veles?"

"Not all." His eyes wash over me slowly. "But most."

"Why?" I pry. "Because we don't destroy everything we touch?"

He's holding back a smirk, but the arrogant look on his face has me enraged all the same. I dig my fingers into my palms to keep from reaching for my daggers.

"You seem to have strong feelings about us," he muses. "But yes, love. Veles's gifts allow us to do things you lot simply cannot. Until you find a way to slay me in one of your little visions, you're no match."

My breath catches in my throat before rage forces it out in a huff. "Is that why you didn't use your gift when we fought?" Words spew from my lips in a way I cannot seem to control. "Because you figured me outmatched?"

The smirk is spread across his face now, pulling the corners of his mouth into a sickly-sweet grin. "Don't get me wrong, you're good enough with those blades. But you stand no chance in a fight against me or any other Veles daemon."

My daggers unsheathe with a slick *swish* against the leather. "Let us see then," I rasp, holding one of the blades toward him. "I call for a rematch. Right now. No holding back."

"Oh, Little Seer," he coos. "I can't risk you getting hurt. You're much too precious."

"Coward." I laugh. I yank the reins, driving my horse against the flank of his. Before he can react, I've raised one of my blades to the exposed flesh of his throat. "Don't hide behind the virtue I know you lack. Fight me."

I'm off my horse before I see his eyes pool black. Breath heaves from my lungs in a violent huff as I hit the ground. Sand spills all around me as Mirage spooks, stomping too close to where my hands are splayed out. As she settles and I pull myself from the ground, Silas's empty gaze bears down on me.

The black vanishes from his eyes in a slow, lethargic flow. "Like I said." He grins.

"Is that the only way you can win?" I growl, quickly brushing the sand from my clothing. "Fighting dirty?"

"There's no other way to fight when it comes to survival, love." He smiles like he didn't just shove me off my horse. "You know that."

"This is hardly—" I take a breath, trying to stave off my fury but it doesn't work. As I resheathe my daggers and hoist myself back into the saddle, I refuse to look at him.

"You Veles daemons are all the same," I snipe. "Too eager to flaunt your gifts rather than use them for anything good." I urge Mirage forward, continuing our journey ahead. "Rather bleed your problems dry than face them. You only care for yourselves. Fucking cowards, the lot of you."

Silas gives me a curious look. He holds his gaze on me, the smile on his face deepening with a keen knowing. I pull away as his unrelenting focus itches across my skin.

"What was his name?"

"Who?" I ask.

He leads his horse closer until our legs practically brush against each other's. "The Veles daemon who betrayed you."

My heart seems to stop for a breath, frozen in my chest like a cold, dead thing. When it starts again, it feels too heavy, too much of a burden to keep trapped inside. The ache radiating from it makes me want to cut it from my chest.

I yank the reins, pulling away from Silas. "You don't live on the Continent this long without having someone betray you," I utter through clenched teeth. "Some daemon is of no consequence."

"But this wasn't just *some daemon*, was it?"

My gaze snaps toward him. "You know nothing of me. Stop acting like you do."

"Don't I?" He smiles. "You're just like me. Alone. *Othered.* We may be different, but we're two sides of the same coin, Ren. The blood that flows through our veins is like gold to some but a menace to all. I know, just like you, that there is no kin among daemons. We'll all gladly lie and cheat our way around each other if it means another day alive."

A *tsk* snaps across the back of Silas's teeth as he locks a heavy gaze on me. "It's a good thing you have me around, love," he coos. "Who knows what another Veles daemon might do if they had you in their grasp."

I shoot him a sidelong glare but continue to guide my horse forward. He lets out a soft chuckle, though he says nothing else. I can practically feel the anger pulsing through my veins with every step Mirage takes through the sand. Something deep within me is rabid, awakened by his words with a vicious hunger. *He's wrong about my gift. I'm not weak.*

The very thought sends a molten rage through me. I close my eyes against the persistent blaze of the sun. *I am more than the markings on my skin. I am stronger than the limits of my gift.*

I force a deep breath and lock my gaze on the horizon. Things will change once I get to Letka. No more hiding. No more pushing my gift deep into the darkest corners of myself. It's time to see the hand Hael has truly dealt for me.

My body stills as Silas catches up to me. "Have you cooled off, or are we still fighting?"

I glare at him but say nothing.

"Maybe another kiss will fix it. What do you say?"

"Maybe a gag in your mouth will rid me of the headache of your voice," I hurl back.

His grin deepens at that. "Gag me if you must. There's more than one way to rile you up, and I much prefer using my hands."

I swat him away like the pesky fly that he is. "So much as flick a grain of sand from my shoulder, and you'll find a blade somewhere rather unfavorable."

He smiles like a devil, muttering suggestions for how we might improve my mood. I ignore the stirring in my stomach and let my gaze focus on the growing silhouette of the city that awaits us. It's the promise of the unknown—a fresh start. I swallow the uneasiness I feel and nudge Mirage onward. Everything will change in Letka. It has to.

CHAPTER 35

The crow launches itself off Silas's shoulder, heading for Letka with a tiny piece of parchment wrapped around its foot. I watch until black wings disappear into the hazy, hot air. My eyes flicker to Silas though I don't say a word. We've barely spoken in the past hour, but I can feel his restlessness growing the closer we get to our destination. Even now, his hands fidget against the reins as he hums to himself.

The familiar tune grates my nerves, but I ignore it the best I can. Instead, my focus homes in on the silhouette of looming buildings carved from sandstone in front of me. The high sun casts a vibrant glare across the city, making it seem like a mirage against the barren desert. It's much different than Denheir, but I still can't stave off the nervous shiver that runs down my spine like I'm a rodent approaching a hungry cat. This might not be the same place that broke me, but I'm much safer in the desert than in any city.

My body seems to know it, too. I try to relax, dropping my tightly bound shoulders with a heavy breath. The skin prickles on the back of my neck; luckily, my hands haven't started shaking.

Whether Silas seems to notice my unease, he doesn't say. He's distracted, looking everywhere but me. The tune he hums fades into nothing, like it's competing with his thoughts, and silence overtakes the space between us. Soon enough though, his humming resumes, as incessant and annoying as ever.

It's not long before we're there. The city greets us like a sleeping giant. Tall monoliths loom like sentries guarding the city within. My eyes drift up to admire the old carvings that run down the stone faces as we pass. A familiarity sinks deep into my bones at the sight. I clench my hands against the reins as the doorway from the Weaver's dream swirls in my mind. The monoliths don't have the same energy as the canyon, but as my gaze sweeps higher, I can't help but feel nervous.

This place lacks that overwhelming pull, but the markings are identical. Not the order in which they appear, however. These markings are set in a pattern I don't recognize, seeming to tell their own story. My gaze tightens on the stone slabs, but try as I might, none of it makes any sense. Other than recognizing the different markings of Veles and Hael daemons, it means nothing to me. I give the monoliths one final look as we pass into the city, and as I do, something churns uneasily in my blood.

Mirage huffs under me as we keep pace with Silas. I give her a reassuring pat before raising my gaze ahead to the city's interior. Breath pulls into my lungs in an airy gasp. I almost can't believe my eyes. *It's beautiful.*

Stone buildings rise from the sand, leveled with wide, flat roofs and pocketed with deep windows. Bright fabrics, hued in oranges and reds, flow in the breeze, shading market stalls and covering doorways. There are carvings everywhere, decorating buildings and columns throughout the city. It's a maze of creamy stone and vibrant life. People of all kinds flood the streets. Merchants coax buyers closer. Many barter for goods. Keeps toss water against the stone steps of their shops. Mothers lead children while men maneuver donkey-drawn carts through the masses. There's an ease to the chaos, a liveliness that almost calms you.

Something aches deep in my chest, but it's not the numbing, dull ache I'm used to. I look over at Silas and actually smile.

His hesitant expression is loosened by a breathy laugh, as if the delight brightening my face is too much to ignore. "I was hoping you'd like it."

As he urges his horse onward, I quickly pull myself together and do the same. We wind through the crowds, and I find my eyes drifting aimlessly. There's so much to take in it's almost overwhelming. Hand-woven carpets hang from market stalls, their rich tapestries baking against the sun. The smell of freshly cooked meat slips into my nose as we pass a man turning a hunk of lamb over a stone fire pit. My mouth waters, and I consider asking Silas to stop.

Just as the question forms on the tip of my tongue, my blood runs cold. A child watches me pass by, wide-eyed and all too focused. The small-eyed stare douses all excitement within me. I quickly pull at the fabric that's loosely draped across my shoulders.

Foolish. Will I ever learn?

I wrap the excess over my head and tuck the tail tightly around my neck. My markings are covered now, I'm sure of it, but still the child stares. His mother appears, tugging the boy away without so much as a glance at me, or at Silas. It's only when the child looks over his shoulder before disappearing into the crowd that I see it—a small bit of black. Three marks edge the boy's hairline, but I'm too far away to distinguish what gift the child revealed. My worry stills, only to be replaced by something stronger. With a furrowed brow and eyes searching for answers, I survey the busy street.

More markings greet me. We pass two daemons—a Mender and a Weaver. For a second, my heart stops, wondering if it's the same one that plagues me; but as their eyes wander to me aimlessly, I sense no recognition there. My anxiety lulls back into wonder. Both daemons chat happily, unbothered that their markings peek out from sleeves and collars. My lip wobbles, but I bite it to stifle the feeling the sight pulls out of me.

As we go deeper into the city, more people fill the streets. Eyes sweep over us without any importance. No one is hostile. No one glares at me like I'm a blight on the earth. No one gives us a second glance except for a large, bald man who spots Silas's markings from up the street and quickly slips back inside a tavern. I urge Mirage forward, not relenting until I'm side by side with Silas.

"What is this place?"

He turns and gives me a curious look. "What do you mean?"

I look around once more, overwhelmed and unsure whether this is the same Continent I grew up on. It's almost peaceful. These people are happy.

"Everyone..." My voice trails off, lost among the sight in front of me. "This place is different."

Silas stares at me for a moment, amusement curling his lips before he understands. Something almost solemn slips across his face then. "Ah," he says. "You're wondering why they haven't chased us out of town yet."

He lets out a sigh. "Letka is much different than Denheir. Different from even the northern cities like Artolen and Malneis."

Silas leads his horse to the front of an inn and quickly slips from his saddle. He ties his reins to a post and gestures for me to do the same. Uneasiness flitters across my skin as I dismount. My hand hovers over my dagger instinctively but no one comes for us. No one is even watching.

I swallow harshly and look up at Silas. "Are there other places like this? Places where daemons live among others with no difficulty?"

Tsk. He shrugs and crosses his arms over his chest. "Letka is the only place like this I have found that has no apparent strife between daemons and those without gifts. The people in Hira are tolerable, but the deeper into the desert you go, the further north or south… things change."

Something stirs in my stomach as I look at him. He leans against his horse, as carefree as he always seems. My eyes linger on his skin. Every inch reveals him for what he is. There's no way he could ever cover his markings, ever hide the touch of Veles from unfriendly eyes. But he doesn't even try. He wears his marks like a badge of honor. He doesn't hide who he is, he embraces it. The sting of jealousy is a raw wound in my chest.

"How do you do it?" I blurt without thinking.

His gaze tightens on me playfully.

"How do you navigate the Continent so freely as a daemon when there are so many who would seek to end you?"

"Oh, Ren." Silas runs a hand through his hair and sighs. "If you only embraced your gift, you would find the world is more scared of you than you are of it."

"I'm not scared—"

"You should do your best to conquer that fear before it's too late," he interrupts. "Only those brave enough to take what they're due will survive what's to come."

"What are you talking ab—"

The flurry of wings shakes my focus, and before I know it, a familiar crow is perched atop Silas's horse. The stallion huffs and shakes its head. A shrill *caw* is the only rebuttal.

I watch Silas unwrap the parchment from the bird's foot, watch his mouth twitch as he reads. He tucks the message into his pocket before turning back toward me. "They'll meet us first thing in the morning."

My face pinches as I take in his words. I look over his shoulder at the bustling inn at his back. "We're to stay here tonight?"

He grabs his pack from the saddle, and before I can protest, he's untied mine as well. "Figured you'd like one night of peace before..."

Before I leave and don't look back. Before I scurry off into the desert where no one can find me. Before you never see me again.

He doesn't need to finish the sentence. The hesitant, solemn look on his face tells me everything I need to know.

"A bed sounds good."

Silas quirks his brow, as if expecting me to put up a fight. "Good," he states.

He gives me a long, lingering look before shouldering our packs and leading the way. The front steps creak under our weight, and I feel my body respond in turn. Suddenly, the promise of rest—true rest—has my legs barely able to hold me upright. Exhaustion has me in a daze, and I trail after Silas like a walking corpse. All I can think of is clean bedding swaddling me like a babe. And a bath. *Yes, a bath.* I can practically feel the water washing away the grime and the pain that still clings to my body.

As we step inside the inn, I'm immediately met with an overwhelming onslaught of sights, sounds, and smells. People maneuver around us, carrying pints of ale in hand. I clench my throat to stave off the memory the smell brings. I see people sitting at tables—eating, drinking, and laughing. Marks pepper the skin of a few patrons. There's a Berserker in the corner, playing a hand of cards with two others. I spot Torch markings on dark skin before the person slips from view. I see drinks spill and hands wave wildly as stories pass between lips. Something aches in my chest as I see two men roughhousing with each other. A larger man slaps them both upside the head, settling the fray. My heart feels heavy like stone, and I rip my gaze away.

The smell of food quickly pulls me from my thoughts. My stomach aches, rumbling for just a taste. Lamb. Fresh baked bread. Stew. Delicious smells waft toward me until it's all I can think about. I want it all. My mind is still floating, dreaming of all the comforts I've been deprived of for so long when Silas finally turns back toward me.

"We're set. Ours is the third room upstairs."

His words snap me out of my ravenous stupor. "Ours?"

"All but one room was taken." He tries to shoot me a sympathetic look, but I can see the mischief gleaming behind his eyes. "Guess we'll have to share."

"No." I laugh in his face and wait for him to tell me he's joking.

He only dangles the key in front of my face and smiles.

"No. *Absolutely* not." I stammer.

"I thought you wanted a bed?" he muses. "You won't find anywhere else in the city to sleep tonight. Traders are in from Torlena. But I guess if you want to sleep in the stables with—"

I snatch the key from him before he can finish his sentence. "You're sleeping on the floor."

He chuckles under his breath before passing our packs to me. "Go upstairs and take a bath," he tells me. "I'll get the horses settled and bring us something to eat."

I open my mouth to argue, but he stops me.

"Unless you'd rather I be in the room while you bathe?"

It's with a sneer and heat flushing my cheeks that I turn my back on him and stomp up the stairs. "I want lamb and bread," I shout over my shoulder. "And wine. No ale."

I hear him laugh before I disappear down the upstairs hallway. I count the rooms as I go and almost sigh in relief when ours comes into view. With a quick turn of the old brass key, the door opens. It's hard to keep my jaw from dropping when I step into the room. A four-poster bed rests against the wall, framed by two small windows. To the left, around a small stone wall, is the bathroom.

I dump our packs onto the floor, and practically race toward it. My clothes are discarded in a heap as soon as I see the bath. The copper tub gleams against the room's soft candlelight. A deep sigh leaves my lips as my hands graze across the assortment of oils and soaps at my disposal. I quickly get to work, knowing my alone time is limited. Hopefully, it takes Silas longer than expected to get the food.

The tub fills with water, and though it's lukewarm, I don't care. No sooner than I lower myself in do I let out a soft moan of relief. I close my eyes and let myself sink below the surface. My breath spills in and out of my lungs in rhythmic slowness. I can hear the clamor of drunken men and card games downstairs, but if anything, it grounds me further. *Is this what it's like to truly live on the Continent? Not on the outskirts but as someone within the thick of it all?*

Bubbles soon fill the tub, thanks to oil from a pink-hued glass bottle. It smells divine, and I dump the rest in for good measure. I grab another bottle from the shelf, inhaling the rich fragrance before washing my hair with it. I dunk my head under the water, massaging my fingers into my scalp. The feeling is heavenly and I don't bother withholding the groan that leaves my throat.

My body relaxes, as does my mind. I can't remember the last time I had a moment's peace, a moment without looking over my shoulder or worrying about what the next day would bring. I let myself settle into that peace now, no matter how fleeting it might be.

I hum to myself as I grab a bright smelling lily soap and lather up my body. As my hands drift across my skin, across the scars that taint it, I don't feel pain. I close my eyes and let the water cleanse me of everything that has happened. Nothing matters except the sweet fragrance surrounding me and the cool water lapping at my skin. Before I know it, a tune I'd hoped to forget passes across my lips in quiet murmurs.

Shadows slip into the night.
What mischief they will incite.
Treacherous dark. Oh Veles sinned.
Tell us, why that devil grinned?
Hael knows not what he has done.
Weaving fates we can't outrun.
Blood flows heavy in the land.
Tell us, what lies in the sand?
Creatures slither. Beasts they bite.
Pooled black eyes withstand the fight.
Flames grow hot and brighter still.
Tell us, who's the first they kill?

My breath hitches as memory crashes down around me without warning. I remember the first time he sang that to me. I can't forget, as much as I want to. I'd only been in Artolen for a few months, barely getting by with whatever scraps I could find or beg for. My marks were small and easily hidden then. At first, I had been okay. But I had been young, too young. A child of twelve who had little knowledge of how to navigate the Continent on her own.

It had been a miracle I'd survived so long in Merket and even withstood the journey to Artolen.

Of course, that luck didn't last. I had unknowingly wandered into the wrong part of the city, starving and dirtier than I had ever been in my life. I didn't know what it meant to stick to the shadows back then. I drew too much attention. The three men had surrounded me before I knew what was going on.

I remember crying, afraid of dying though I now know there were far worse things to fear. One of the men had stepped toward me, eyes gleaming bright against the night. He looked like a monster, like the ones my mother had told me stories about. The monster took another step, but then, that vicious gleam in his eyes faded. The life seeped out slowly.

I barely saw the boy, or the erratic, undisciplined flurry of shadows that followed. It had all been a blur. All I remember are the bodies—the men that lay groaning in puddles of their own blood. There was a gentle brush of a shadow against my wrist. And then, his eyes. Wild brown eyes, so dark they almost looked black. He had taken my hand, slowly as if to not spook me, and walked me to what would be my new home.

I had cried and cried and cried that night, somehow knowing I had escaped an unspeakable fate. He had held me, distracted me with the shadows he twirled along the dirt in front of us. The sound of his voice stilled me. The tune he sang should have warned me, should have taught me what Veles-cursed daemons were truly capable of. But I had only felt safe and loved. We were both just children, victims of the Continent's cruelty, and that night fate had brought us together.

Malachi had sung that tale often during our years together. Every time he did, I was swept back to that night. It was a feeling that everything would be okay. Though, I know now that sentiment was far from true.

The bath is cold, but I find myself unable to move. I'm floating against the pain of the past and the gentle caress of the water around me. My eyes flutter, and I don't stop them. I breathe in deeply, letting the rich, floral scents lull me to sleep.

Exhaustion takes hold before I can remember where I am. As I drift off, I forget that though I'm alone now, I won't be for long.

CHAPTER 36

"I'm disappointed. I expected you to have a weapon in there with you."

I gasp awake. My arms flail against the chilly water as I blink the sleep from my eyes and remember where I am. *Shit.*

I quickly reach for a towel, stretching across the edge of the tub. As my fingers graze the plush fabric, my eyes flicker to Silas. He rests against the stone wall, staring at himself in the bathroom mirror. He runs a hand through his hair, pushing the white strands out of his eyes. Somehow, he's managed to be a gentleman and keep his gaze from sweeping to mine. But then again, he still walked into the bathroom to begin with.

"Get out," I seethe.

A cheeky grin pulls against his sharp cheekbones. "Easy there, love," he coos. "Is that any way to speak to the person who brought you dinner?"

I quickly stand, wrapping the towel around my body before he can even think to steal a peek.

"I'm naked," I retort. "Get out before I find something in here to stab you with."

Finally, he looks at me. He assesses the towel, his gaze hovering far too long on where it skims the top of my soft thighs. "Not quite naked," he muses. "Though I'm not complaining."

My hand lashes out, snatching a perfume bottle off the counter. He scrambles out of the room, laughing under his breath, before I have a chance to throw it.

"Put on some clothes, you heathen," he taunts from the bedroom. "I'm trying to feed you."

I roll my eyes as I step out of the bath. "Toss me my—"

My pack lands in the bathroom with a muffled *thud*. I bite the inside of my cheek to keep from smiling. "Thank you," I grumble under my breath.

"What was that?" he calls from behind the wall.

I can practically hear the cocky smirk growing on his face. My lips purse, once again fighting the smile that wants to stay there. I shake my head and pull my pack toward me. As I'm digging through my things, the smokey scent of meat hits my nose. I close my eyes and salivate at the smell. The sound of a fork scraping across a plate has me ripping things out of my pack haphazardly.

"You better save me some!" I shout.

I quickly dry off and bind my chest before slipping a thin tunic over my head. My foot slips down the wrong pant leg, and I curse and tug the fabric into place, nearly toppling over.

Breathy laughter spills out from the bedroom as I struggle to dress in my haste. "Hurry up, love. My patience only goes so far."

I squeeze the water from my hair, leaving the long strands damp as they cling to my neck and shoulders. When I round the corner into the bedroom, my eyes go wide.

"You're gonna eat it all," I wail, rushing over and pulling the second plate toward me.

He only grins as I sit across from him at the small table.

I open my mouth to complain but something stops me. *Lamb. Bread.* I look up as he pushes a cup of wine my way.

I'm still staring as he digs back into his own meal. My eyes drift over his face—over the markings that trail down his cheeks and bridge his nose. His lips press against his cup, and I watch as a bead of dark wine slips to the corner. The urge to lick it from his lips is too strong, only subdued when he does it himself. I let myself think of things that aren't allowed.

What if I didn't leave tomorrow?

It's only when his eyes flicker to mine that I break away from my thoughts.

"Food okay?" he asks.

I look down but not before the flush of my cheeks gives me away. "Fine," I answer, mumbling into my cup. "Thanks."

He smirks. "If you're hungry for something else" —his eyes drop down to my lips before meeting my gaze once more— "Just say the word."

I wave him off with the flick of my hand and curse the gods for how red my face is. "I said it's fine."

He hums, gaze lingering on me for a while before he returns to his food. We finish the meal in silence. I savor my wine, drinking it slowly to prolong the inevitable. My eyes flicker to the bed, and my heart pounds a little faster in my chest. Silas follows my gaze, a breathy laugh escaping his throat as he turns back to me. I look away, trying to hide the sheepish flare of my eyes.

"Don't worry. I'll take the floor," he assures me.

Silence beats between us, and I nibble at my bottom lip. I open my mouth before I can think better of it. "The bed is big enough for two." *Gods, I'm an idiot.*

His brows pull together tightly before amusement flecks his face. "If you wanted to cuddle, you could have just said so, love."

"*Please.*" I scoff. "The last thing I want is for you to be anywhere near me." My voice pitches against the lie. I quickly clamp my mouth shut.

"Mm. I'm sure."

He slips off into the bathroom with his pack before I can say anything else. As soon as he disappears behind the wall, I chug the rest of my wine. I slam the cup on the table, making the old wooden legs creak. The heat won't leave my cheeks but maybe I can blame the drink.

I pace the room, bare feet padding softly against the floor. I hear water splash in the basin, hear Silas rummaging through his pack. But when the candlelight flickers out in the bathroom, I panic. I find my way to the far side of the bed and quickly slip under the sheets. Shame and anticipation mix violently in my stomach. I've fought plenty of men, killed more than a few, but somehow, the idea of sleeping next to Silas has me rattled. *Veles smite me. This is pathetic.*

As his footsteps trudge against the floor, I roll over to face the wall. I hear him drop his pack and his boots, feel him climb onto the other side of the bed. The mattress shudders under his weight. My breath stills in my chest and I listen to every noise, every breath coming from his side of the bed.

He sighs and blows out the candle on the bedside table. "Goodnight, love," he coos.

I grumble a goodnight before curling deeper into the edge of the mattress. My heart is a fluttering bird in my chest. I can't seem to calm it. I lie there for what feels like hours, unsteady in my own body. The chatter below us is the only thing that keeps me tethered. Occasional shouts rip through the night. Men laugh and yell. Pints of ale clatter on tabletops. Doors slam and chairs scoot across the floor with a rough rumble.

But too soon, even those noises drift away until I'm left with only Silas's steady breathing filling the space around me. While the rhythmic lull of it should soothe me, it does the opposite. *How can he be so calm? Sleeping soundly while I'm lost to thoughts that ravage me?*

I grit my teeth as I toss and turn. I don't care if I wake him. It would serve him right. He's the one doing this, torturing me so.

When I roll over for what feels like the hundredth time, a voice cuts through the dark.

"Something bothering you?" The smirk is palpable in his tone.

I bite down my frustrations and roll away from him. "No," I quip.

"Hm. Seems to me like there is."

I feel the mattress shift. My breath heaves in my chest as he moves closer. Chills race across my skin. My heart thumps too loudly. I want so desperately to turn to face him, but I won't. I can't let him win so easily.

"Tell me, what has you so worked up?"

I wait for the touch of his fingers somewhere—anywhere on my skin—but it doesn't come. My teeth dig into my bottom lip, quelling the desperate whine that wants to spill from me.

He leans in close, breath hot on my neck. "That afraid of me?"

I roll to face him, irritation spiking my blood and curses beading on my tongue. But when I do, all my resolve fades. He's close. Closer than he should be. His gray eyes are bright, piercing into me through the dark of the room.

My gaze drops lower and molten heat floods my core. He's not wearing a tunic. *Gods. This is bad.* His torso is covered in markings, the black seeming to melt into every muscle lining his lean body. Scars pepper his skin. The Shade's cut is brutal, but the sight of it only flushes my cheeks. My throat grows dry. My heart rate is so high, I'm surprised the thing hasn't burst.

"Use your words, Ren. Before I decide to go back to bed."

I scoff, desperate to reclaim some of the control I've so easily lost. "Goodnight, then," I quip.

I start to roll over, but a firm grip latches onto my arm. He pulls me back to him, eyes feral. My lips part as I feel his hand snake around the soft curve of my waist.

"No more games, love." He smirks. "Tell me what you want before I stop being so nice."

I roll my eyes, though my pulse pounding under his fingertips surely gives me away. "Is that a threat?"

His grip on my waist tightens, and I can't help the sharp breath that sucks into my lungs.

"It's a promise," he growls.

He rolls on top of me, pinning me down as his eyes fill with black. His mouth drags across my neck, sucking and biting at the marks there. I moan as his fingers trail down my center, brushing over the thin fabric of my pants. My eyes close, and my head falls back as he trails kisses down my throat. Every touch of his lips feels like it was sent from the gods themselves.

His fingers tease me, and I roll my hips against him. His touch is nothing more than a ghosting but I'm panting, desperate.

Gods, I shouldn't have hidden away in the desert for so long.

I could have satisfied this urge weeks ago with any number of men who stalk outpost taverns looking for a single night's romp. But no, I had to stay at camp and let my body ache with need.

My mind snaps awake as Silas tugs at my bottom lip, taking it in between his teeth. As he bites and pulls, I moan into his mouth. I meet him with hungry kisses until my mind is drawn elsewhere.

His fingers rub slow circles against the one place that threatens to shatter my restraint. The fabric separating his skin from mine is nothing short of torture, and I'm desperate to be rid of it. I tug at the waistband of my pants, but suddenly, his touch is gone.

My gaze snaps to his. He kneels over me, thighs bracketing my hips. A deadly grin is plastered across his face—full of desire and mischief.

"Your words, Ren."

I groan and try to push him off me, but he doesn't budge. The black drains from his eyes, and something in me aches for it to return. I pout, gaze burning into his, but he doesn't relent. He only crosses his arms over his chest and waits. My skin tingles, desperate for the touch of him. I roll my eyes and try to pull him closer, but it doesn't work.

"Bastard," I huff.

He tilts his head, eyes wandering up and down my body. "Not having fun, love?"

I grit my teeth, but before I can curse him out, a devious idea slips into my mind. My tongue darts out, wetting my bottom lip. I lock eyes with him, tilting my head in the same condescending manner. "No, I'm not." I sigh. "It's really too bad."

I raise my hips, grinding oh-so slowly into him. "I was hoping you knew what you were doing."

His eyes darken, jaw clenching as I continue to rub against him.

"Maybe we should go back to bed," I say. My hand reaches up and tugs at his waistband. "I'm suddenly feeling tired."

I watch his throat bob as my fingers slip under the fabric. Only when I feel his hardened length do I pull away. "Bored, even—"

His hand is wrapped around my throat before I can get the words out. Black spills into his eyes as he leans over me, a wicked grin spread across his face. "*Brat.*"

His hand yanks at my pants while the other keeps me pinned to the mattress. The fabric tears, quickly discarded and leaving me bare. Fingers uncurl from around my throat, and I let out a shuddering moan as his mouth slips between my legs. He laps at my center, tongue circling around the bundle of nerves that has me bucking my hips into his face.

As moans spill from my lips, Silas laughs against my skin. "Still bored?" he taunts.

Before I can respond, his tongue devours me once more. My body jolts, but soon pleasure sparks through me like an ember catching fire. His fingers dig into my hips to hold me steady. Through the flutter of my eyelids, I see his eager grin before it disappears against my skin.

My legs tremble as sensations build deep in my core. His tongue swirls and flicks, making me twitch in his grasp. My moans fill the room as he continues to feast on me like it's his final meal. Only when the pleasure inside me snaps, leaving me moaning and writhing against his hold, does he relent.

I'm shaking, coming down from my high, as he pulls away. Just as I close my eyes and settle against the sheets, he slides two fingers inside me. A sharp breath rips into my lungs and trickles out with a floating moan.

My eyes blow wide, and I'm met with a feral grin as he looks down at me. "You thought I was done with you?"

His fingers pump in and out, eliciting a flurry of noises that has my cheeks blushing red. My heart thunders, and my skin grows hot against his touch. I drop my head back against the pillow as cries of pleasure spill into the room.

"*Gods*," I moan.

He pulls his fingers from me immediately, and when I snap my head up to look at him, there's only a smug grin waiting for me there.

"Don't call for the gods," he states. "The only name I want on your lips when you come again is mine."

My brow furrows, desperate for his touch. I squirm underneath him, but he simply sits there. I'm a ball of tension and every second he denies me what I need, I only grow more restless. As I move my hand down to ease the ache between my legs, he snatches it away.

"Words, Ren," he snarls. "Use them."

"Silas, *please*," I whine.

His mouth quirks up as my hips buck. I let out a desperate groan, but he only tightens his grip against my wrist. He's enjoying this too much, and I don't have it in me to fight him. The need he's awoken within me is destroying any control I have. I need to touch him. Need to feel him. Need to taste his lips pressed against mine.

I stare at him wide-eyed, a desperation I never knew I could feel dripping from my gaze. "I need you."

I moan as his fingers slide inside me. His other hand brushes against my cheek, holding my face roughly as he locks his eyes on mine. I whimper into his mouth as he adds another finger, stretching me further. It's too much, but it's still not enough. I stare into the dark abyss of his eyes. Begging. Pleading.

My hands fumble for his pants, fingers tugging against the buttons. It takes Silas no time at all to give me what I want. He strips quickly, ridding himself of his pants and briefs; he tosses them across the room without care.

I pull in a sharp breath at the sight of him. Even in the dark, his markings are a sight to behold. They spread across his muscular thighs and darken his knee caps. I take in the patterns on his torso once more—how the chaotic swaths of black arch over the ridgeline of his defined abdomen and trail down to where his muscles taper into a delicious v-shape. As I look lower, my gaze grows heavy.

His hand strokes the thick shaft, smearing his arousal over the tip.

My mouth parts as a whispered breath leaves my lips. "*Silas.*"

His eyes are pitch black. Time seems to slow down as he leans over me and presses closer. I wiggle underneath him, but only when my nails dig into his chest does he give me what I want. Slowly, he slides in.

I groan against the pressure. It's too much—but, still—I'm desperate for more. My back arches off the bed, pressing against him and demanding everything. When he's fully seated inside of me, he pauses. Those black eyes peer down at me, and within their hungry gleam, I see my own madness reflected.

Silas's hand slides to my throat, wrapping around it tightly. "You ready, love?"

I nod, and his smirk is the only warning I get before he pulls back and slams into me. I try to scream, but his grip on my throat allows no such thing.

Breath trembles in my lungs until it's no more. My eyes unfocus. Amidst it all, the feeling of him pounding into me has my mouth opening in a silent scream. I cling to him like he's my salvation. Maybe he is.

"Fuck, you feel amazing." He grunts as he increases his unforgiving pace.

The slap of our skin is an indecent racket in the night. I hear the room next door shout at us, urging us to quiet down, but there's no use. Silas is lost to anything and everything that isn't me; I can see it in the way his gaze bores into mine and feel it in the way his hands grip me roughly.

Silas groans as he slides in and out, eyes all but rolling back in his head. His hand tightens around my throat, stealing the last of my breath with a desperate grasp. Darkness pools against my vision as my mind floats into an empty space. Sensations overwhelm me. Everything outside of this moment is lost to me, and I thank the gods for whatever fate brought Silas and I here. *Together.*

His face comes and goes between the flutter of my lashes. My lungs burn, pleading for air. Blood beads on his skin as I dig my nails into his forearm. Everything grows foggy. I start to slip away.

His lips crash into mine just as he allows me the breath I'm so desperate to take. His hand releases my throat, and I suck in a quaking gasp of air. Pleasure rushes up my body, curling my toes against the sheets. My body shudders against him. The room fills with the sound of me, though I don't care who hears.

Silas's mouth clings to my skin as he chases his own release. The way he's sucking on my neck is wild. Frantic. The bite of his teeth and the tug of his lips draw out my breathy moans. He continues to slam into me, hitting deeper as he yanks my leg up to his shoulder.

Just as I think he's left me utterly spent, my pleasure rises. It sizzles up my body, making me scream and claw at the sheets.

"It's too much," I pant. Tears flood my waterline as the bliss reaches insurmountable heights. "Silas, I can't—"

His hand snatches my chin, demanding my focus. As I meet his gaze, I see the black has left his eyes. In place of his gift, gleaming amidst the gray, is a desperate yearning.

"Give me one more," he urges. "One for us."

I feel my body answering as he hits that spot deep inside me. He stokes that fire over and over until there's nothing left in my mind but him. I arch off the bed as the shuddering high slams through me, ripping a whimper from my throat. He kisses me through it, eating up every moan and plea that spills from my lips.

He finishes with a purring rumble in my ear. "You were so good for me," he praises. "So fucking good."

My body quakes underneath his as the last flutters of pleasure dance through me. He rolls us to the side, keeping me close. His fingers drift along my arms and raise goosebumps in their wake. The touch is tender, and as he traces every scar Rohan left, I let myself relax against it—too content to fear the reminders those scars bring. Our panting breathes are the only thing to fill the room for a long while.

All too soon, the heat of his body disappears from my back. My eyelids flutter, too tired to reveal more than Silas's silhouette. I moan softly and sink into the sheets as he pads off toward the bathroom. I'm half asleep when he comes back with a washcloth, and barely present when he cleans me up. Only when I feel his presence return to me, do I open my eyes.

As he stares at me, pupils wide and pleasure-drunk, I swear the look he gives me is almost loving. "Mm. Think you can sleep now?"

My head spins in a delirious haze as I mumble incoherent words. I pull him toward me, and the result is a chuckle that rumbles deep in his chest.

"So needy." He kisses the top of my hand as he lays down next to me.

I groan and rumble and pull him closer, eager for his touch to never leave my skin again. He curls his body against mine, and I relish the heat of his breath in the shell of my ear.

"It could always be like this, you know," he offers in a husky tone that has my back arching into him. He grips my hip and tugs me against him until there's no space left between us. "You don't need to fight your fate, Ren. We could find our own way in this world. You just need to give in."

His fingers trace circles against my hip, and I practically melt at the touch—nothing more than putty in his hands. I hum softly as I scoot back and pull his arm around me.

"Silas," I purr.

"Yes, love?"

"You owe me a new pair of pants."

His mouth lingers against my neck, as if lost in the moment, before he plants a kiss there. "I owe you so much more than that."

His voice barely reaches me as exhaustion pulls me under. Silas presses another kiss to my skin, but I don't know if it's a dream or if I'm really here. I'm floating away, warmth flooding my chest. His hand snakes around my throat, holding me close as if he, too, fears that I might disappear from this bed. His breath is steady, rising his chest against my back. I lean into the heat of his body and succumb to a much-needed sleep. My mind drifts off but not before I'm met with a single thought. *What if I stayed?*

CHAPTER 37

My brow furrows as I wake to the soft cushion of bedding against my skin. Light streams in through the windows, but I don't dare open my eyes. It's too early to face the day, or at least, it feels like it.

As I roll over and press my face into the pillow, my mind shoots awake. *What if I never left Denheir? What if I'm still in that room, waiting for Rohan to coax a vision from me?*

I shoot up in a panic, desperately clawing for daggers that aren't there. My blood thrums in my veins, and the feeling urges violence with a heavy, foreign hunger. It's only when I blink the sleep from my eyes that my heart settles.

I'm not in Denheir. I'm at the inn in Letka.

My eyes sweep the room, quickly finding the flash of gray I know will comfort me. But Silas isn't amused by the manic way in which I've greeted the day. No, he's staring at me from across the room like I appeared out of thin air.

"What's wrong?"

He says nothing. The muscles in his jaw flex against the strain. His brow pinches, eyes roaming across my arms.

"Silas, what is it?" I prod.

He still won't meet my gaze. His focus is locked on my skin, raking up and down my arms like he's looking for answers. "Nothing," he murmurs. "Thought I saw something."

I scoff. "Like what?"

He swallows harshly. "Nothing."

Something about his gaze itches across my skin. Suddenly, I feel like I'm back in the Jahaer with Vish's eyes dissecting me. I look down, but all I can see are my scars. I tug the bedding toward me, covering up as casually as I can. "What—"

"Here, I got you something," Silas interjects.

He tosses me an apple from where he's leaned up against the door. The fruit bounces on the bed, rolling toward me. My eyes flash up to him uncertainly.

"We can get you something more later but we need to go," he states.

"Okay..."

I tentatively grab the apple and take a bite. As I chew, I look him over. He's dressed in pants and a fresh tunic. His boots are on, and his pack rests at his feet. All his things are packed and ready to go. *He's* ready to go.

My mouth opens, but confusion holds my tongue. I quickly slip from the bed, but my cheeks flush when I realize I'm not wearing any pants. *Gods.* I yank a blanket toward me and take one more quick bite before setting the apple down. My gaze flickers to him, expecting some smart-ass remark about being naked, but he says nothing. His head is turned away, fingers fidgeting with something.

My mouth pinches into a flat line as I cover myself up and shuffle to the bathroom. "Sorry I didn't know we had to leave so quickly," I mumble. "You should have woken me."

I drop the blanket as soon as I'm around the corner. Clothes spill across the floor as I rifle through my pack. The leathers will do. I won't need their physical protection today, but something tells me I'll need the confidence they bring. I don't know how important these friends are to Silas or if he even cares that I make a good impression. But judging by the way he's acting, I'd say whoever these people are to him, they matter.

Something uneasy swirls in my gut. *Since when do I care about making a good first impression?*

I curse under my breath and quickly get dressed. My leathers slide on like a second skin, their presence settling me a bit. I sheathe my daggers and take a deep breath before stepping back into the bedroom. Deft fingers rake through the long, wild strands of my hair as I weave them into a loose braid.

"It's my fault," Silas explains as soon as he sees me, "that you slept in." He drags a hand through his messy white hair. "I thought you needed the rest."

A soft smirk slips across my face before I can stop it. "I did." I finish knotting the braid and toss my pack over my shoulder. "Someone kept me up late," I tease.

The playful glimmer I expect to see isn't there. No, he won't even look at me.

Silas clears his throat before opening the door. "Shall we?"

My gaze tightens on him, desperate for answers, but the only one I see is clear enough. *He regrets this.* The nagging thought is confirmed when he looks up to see if I'm coming, only to flicker his gaze away once my eyes meet his.

Anger and hurt bloom in my chest. I scoff loudly and push my way past him, bumping him with my pack in the process.

"Ren—"

I make my way out of the inn quickly, ignoring his voice as it trails after me. As soon as I'm met with sunlight and fresh air, I stop. I pull in a deep breath and tilt my head up toward the sky. It doesn't help. Something foul is still bubbling up inside me, ready to lash out at any minute.

Silas's presence behind me only aggravates it more. I stomp down the steps of the inn and find that our horses are already waiting. Mirage chuffs loudly before trying to bite Silas's stallion. He's clearly been pestering her all morning. While the sight should make me laugh, it only burns my fury hotter. *How long ago did he have the horses pulled from the stables?*

My hand runs across Mirage's flank, feeling the heat of the sun on her hair. I strap my pack on the saddle with vicious precision. But as I go to load up, the tug of Silas's hand stops me.

"We'll come back for your things," he assures me. His thumb strokes the inside of my wrist, causing my stomach to flutter uneasily.

I yank my hand away before I can be swayed by the loving touch. "Alright," I utter. "Lead the way."

Silas lets out a deep sigh before he guides us forward. We weave through side streets, past markets and taverns. The sight of daemons among non-gifted people spurs no joy in me today. With every silent step we take, my irritation grows.

Who does he think he is? My gaze threatens to burn holes into the back of his head. *It was he who ate me like a starved man last night. He who fell asleep draped across me like a needy lover.*

I scowl as I trail after Silas. The entire way, he says nothing—offers me nothing. Old habits rear up in me, and I fight the urge to draw a blade. I shake the thought away though my resentment still grows.

As we slip down another side street, the buzz of the city all but fades away. The crowds disappear. Taverns grow fewer and far between until there are none left. Stone walls flank our path, radiating heat from the harsh desert sun. The stillness of the world leaves me with no distraction. All I can focus on is the flex of Silas's back against his tunic and the fact that things have changed.

My teeth dig against my cheek, but it does nothing to stop the words from flowing. "What the fuck is wrong with you?"

Silas stops dead in his tracks, turning toward me slowly.

"Love, I—"

"No." I cut him off. "No *love*. Not today. You owe me an explanation."

"Ren, please. We can't do this right—"

"Did last night really mean nothing to you?"

"I'm sorry about last night. I shouldn't have let that happen. I—"

"Then why did you?" I snap.

The silence that hovers between us is so heavy that it threatens to choke me. It continues for far too long, so long that my heart finally lags in my chest.

"I'm such a fool." I laugh bitterly. "To think you were capable of anything greater than your own selfishness. To think I could actually stand you."

I wait for his retort, but there is none.

"Like I said," I rasp. "You Veles-cursed daemons are all the same."

I storm past him, kicking dust up in my wake. The firm grasp of his hand quickly stops me. He pulls me into him, wrapping his arms around me tightly. I try to pry myself away, but he clings to me. He buries his face into my neck as his lips press hotly against my skin. "This wasn't supposed to happen," he bites out roughly. "I'm sorry."

My heart quivers in my chest, but I shove him away before the feeling has time to take root. "Not sorry enough," I object.

I continue down the alley. I don't wait for him to lead the way, don't dare turn around to see if he follows. My jaw aches from how hard I'm clenching it. There's a throbbing mess where my heart is supposed to be. But still, I keep moving. I stomp against the earth, forcing myself away from what I foolishly thought I could have. It's only when a woman slips into view, blocking the path ahead, that my determination wavers.

My boots scuff against the earth, unearthing more dust.

The woman eyes me up and down as a smirk curls her mouth. "You must be the Seer." Her gaze passes over my shoulder. "Silas." She drags her tongue over her teeth and flashes her eyes. "Whatever took you so long?" Her words float across the alley in a taunting purr. "I almost thought you'd forgotten about me."

As the woman takes a step closer, my gut clenches. There's something about the way she looks at Silas that makes my heart stutter.

My voice is thick with uncertainty when I finally speak. "Your *friend*?" I ask Silas without sparing a glance behind me.

He mutters curses under his breath before clearing his throat. "Though I wish she weren't... yes," he confesses.

I turn back to Silas, brow raised. All it takes is one look at the pained expression pinching his face for my heart to drop. *Oh.*

He looks past me. "Asha," Silas greets her, his tone clipped.

When I look back at the woman, I really look at her. She's tall. Beautiful. Her rich, dark skin is contrasted by white hair that hangs down to her waist in tightly braided strands. I try not to care, but jealousy is the ruthless thrust of a blade in my chest. The sight of her markings only makes it worse. Her gift is impressively displayed across her arms, the white swirls bright against her complexion.

Before my mind can even begin to consider what kind of relationship Silas and this woman must have, two men fill the alleyway behind her.

"Other friends of yours?" I ask.

Silas is quiet.

I try not to tense under the scrutiny, but their sneers feel less than friendly.

One of the men leans against the wall, eyes on me as he flips the dagger in his hand. The other has no weapon on him, but it's his build that sets me on edge. He's big—arms thick with muscle and riddled in scars. He's tall, too. His bald head shines against the morning sun high above my own.

Recognition flashes in my mind as my gaze snaps back to the scar curving across his eyebrow. *I've seen this man.* He was in the city yesterday. The one who slipped into the tavern as we passed through. My brow furrows before my stomach clenches.

A light sweat breaks out across my palms. I roll my shoulders, breaking up any stiffness. As I take a step back, I see something that stills my boots against the sand.

Silas's friend. *Asha.* There's a violent smolder in her eyes—one that feels too familiar. The hairs on the back of my neck rise.

It hits me all at once—the uncanny feeling of floating outside my body, the sensation that I'm seeing everything for the second time, but through different eyes. My breath shudders in my chest as the realization finally hits.

No.

Another person steps into the alley, but I know who it will be. I don't wait to see his face. I turn and run.

I make it only a few steps before I'm yanked back by the fabric of my tunic. My feet drag against the ground, arms flailing as I struggle to keep myself upright. I reach for my daggers, but my hands are ripped away harshly. The grip against my wrists is so tight it feels like my bones might snap.

The flash of familiar, marked flesh is all I see before a firm hand shoves at my back. I fall forward, knees hitting the sand. Breath heaves in my lungs as I catch myself. My vision wavers against the eerie swell of the past repeating itself. It's dizzying, but even worse is the realization that this is far from what I foresaw.

"It's survival, love," Silas rasps behind me. "Nothing personal."

In that moment, the last whole piece of me breaks. Rage takes hold, and I can't stop myself. I'm reeling back toward him, hate hardening my heart. I withdraw one of my daggers and lunge. I cut into flesh and spill blood before he manages to pin my arms behind my back. His grip is relentless, but I don't care. I struggle. I scream. I feel my muscles flex and burn.

He yanks me back until his mouth is pressed against my ear. "Stop fighting," Silas utters. The words grate out harshly as he keeps his voice low. "I don't want to hurt you."

A brutal laugh slips past my throat. *Lies. It's all been lies.* I throw myself around in his grip like a captive animal desperate to slip free. His hold only tightens. My bones ache as I thrash and yank and tug against Silas's control.

"Godsdamnit, Ren," Silas grunts. "*Stop it.*"

His fingers curl against my biceps, pulling my arms back tightly. Desperation heaves in my lungs and churns through my mind. It's with practiced action that I press my back against his chest and lift myself up. I feel his hands try to maintain their grip, but it's too late. I launch myself downward, slamming my boot against the inside of his foot. He sputters a curse as he tries to restrain me. Amidst the chaos, his grip loosens—just as I hoped it would. He's quick to tighten it, but not before I manage to rip an arm free. I'm still clutching a dagger when I spin to strike.

His hand curls around my forearm, tugging me toward him. My blade glints against the sun. His eyes pool black. *I'll be sure to make this hurt.* But before I can deliver the blow, a deafening *pop* cuts through the air.

Suddenly, everything is red hot. Bone splinters. Agony flares. I cry out as pain races up my left arm. In my shock, the dagger falls from my grip. Tears flood my eyes, blurring my vision.

Silas forces me down, pressing my cheek against the sand. His knee rests on my back as he holds me in place. He leans down, and the feeling of hot breath against my neck sends more tears spilling.

"I didn't want it to go this way," he rasps into my ear. "Fuck, Ren. This could have gone so differently."

"Traitor," I yell. "Fucking viper!" Despite the pain blazing through me, I still thrash under his hold.

"You were supposed to bring her unharmed," an irritated voice rumbles above me.

I still as boots crunch in the sand mere inches from my face.

"I tried," Silas utters through clenched teeth.

Silas releases me, and as I lift my head up, I gaze upon a devil I never wished to meet again. Blond hair glints in the sun, and I stare into a smile so wide it feels like a threat to eat me whole.

"Little Seer," Olen coos. "I knew we'd be seeing each other again."

The nickname sinks into me like teeth, awakening me to things I should have figured out sooner. My hand darts to my thigh, desperate for the only blade I have left, but before I can draw it, heat sparks against my cheek.

The memory of things not yet occurred but already envisioned floods me. I still as my eyes track the dancing flames that curl into the calloused palm hovering too close for comfort. I take note of the markings that snake around the daemon's wrist before my gaze flickers to the hardened face I feel I already know. Hate seeps from her. Her vibrant, turquoise eyes are cold and merciless. I can't help but wonder if she was always like this or if this is what happens when Rohan breaks you. Either way, I don't want to know.

"Easy, Asha," Olen scolds. "Boss wants her in one piece."

He raises a brow, then turns his attention back on me. Before I can flinch away, Olen leans down and snatches my face in his hand. His grip on my jaw is rough, but as I try to pry free from his grasp, the fire next to my face only grows hotter.

"He's eager to get you back," Olen says, grin too wide. "Especially since someone was a devious little thing and stabbed him with his own blade."

His eyes light up as he leans in close. He smells like ale, and I stifle the nausea that curls in my stomach as I'm reminded of that cellar.

"Speaking of blades..." His other hand drops to my thigh, ripping the dagger from its sheath. He teases my skin with the cool metal as he traces the blade across my cheek. "I believe this one is mine," he whispers.

From behind me, Silas clears his throat uneasily.

Olen's gaze flickers above my head. "Yes, yes," he offers. "You did good bringing the girl to us."

"You're a lucky son of a bitch." The man behind Olen laughs. He's still flipping the dagger as he approaches. "One more day without word from you, and Rohan was going to send me to finish the job." His eyes drop to mine hungrily. "And I would have loved to see what all the fuss was about."

Silas steps up, blocking me from the man's view. "She would have eaten you alive," he grits through his teeth.

"Is that so?" The man strides around Silas, eyes darting between the two of us. "Why don't you let the girl and me have a go?" He flips his dagger into the air and snatches it with a firm grasp. "See how big and bad she truly is."

Olen chuckles. "Egan, make yourself useful and bind the girl."

"I can do it," Silas snarls, pushing the other man away from me.

"You've done enough." Olen digs into his pocket. "Here."

He tosses a small pouch toward Silas, and I shudder as past vision and current reality distort my senses. It leaves a sickly taste in my mouth, but worse is the rot I feel inside. The payment for Silas's betrayal lands to my left with a loud *clink*. As the gold coins rattle around, it feels like a weight has been dropped on my chest. My body is practically shaking, bursting with rage and heavy with heartbreak.

"You *bastard*," I curse. "After I helped you. After I *trusted* you."

As I turn my gaze to Silas, I'm met with a look that only stirs my resentment. His eyes are distant, heavy with burdens I will never know. He doesn't reach for the coins, doesn't tear his focus from me. He almost looks upset, like he thinks I'll forgive him for this if he can merely utter the words. But I won't, and he doesn't.

"You said it yourself, love." His throat bobs uneasily. "Trust is an indulgence you can't afford. You shouldn't have forgotten that."

I lunge for him, broken arm hanging limply at my side. But before my body can crash against his, my head whips sideways. I gasp, spitting blood from where the strong hand struck my face. Globs of red drip into the sand as pain radiates through my jaw. For a second, I forget where I am. My vision tunnels. My head spins. I rub a hand across my mouth and look up to see the man, Egan, staring at me with a foul grin pulling his lips wide.

"Behave." He snickers.

Silas tackles him instantly. I don't have time to see his eyes turn black. Sand splashes. Fists slam into Egan's face, sending blood and spit flying. The sound of crunching bones rips a shudder through my body. Only when the Torch sends a blaze of fire across the sand in front of Silas does he relent. His gaze snaps to her, blood dripping from his knuckles.

"Now, now, Silas." Asha smiles wickedly from across the alley. "Don't tell me you went and got attached to a job?"

The black doesn't leave Silas's eyes as he glares at her. "He had it coming," he says gruffly. "Has nothing to do with her."

Time ticks by slowly. Finally, Silas's gift fades, revealing the gray hue I thought I knew so well. He looks to me before quickly averting his gaze.

"Hm." Asha grins. "Clearly."

Egan groans, coughing blood in the sand. His face is split open. Cheekbone shattered. Orbital socket caved in. He is no more than a mess of blood and bones.

"You need to leash your dog, Olen," Egan sputters.

As he struggles to stand, Silas turns to face him with a quiver in his bloodied hands. "You can certainly try," Silas offers darkly.

"Enough." Olen sighs, gesturing Egan away. "Go find a Mender before Silas makes you any uglier."

Egan wipes the blood from his mouth with the back of his hand. He shoots one last hateful look at Silas before he stalks down the alley and disappears.

"Fres, get the Seer bound." Olen shakes his head before letting out a breathy laugh. "And try not to hurt the pretty little thing. Seems Silas is rather fond of her."

Silas's hand clenches, but he says nothing. I flail as the bald man yanks me up from the sand. I try to rip free of his hold, but the threat of fire quickly stifles any struggle. My eyes dart to Asha.

The hate contorting my face is contrasted by the smugness alight on her own.

"Curious," she muses, looking me over as she approaches. "I've never known Silas to have a heart."

I wince as Fres binds my wrists together. My broken arm hangs loosely, and I feel every jolt of pain as he pulls and tightens the rope. The entire time, my gaze doesn't leave Asha. She watches me with satisfaction, fingers playing with the fire blazing in her palm. I clench my teeth together, fighting off the pain of splintering bone digging through flesh. As Fres finishes the bindings, my hands drop limply in front of me.

Asha steps closer. The fire dies out in her palm as she reaches for me. I reel away from the touch, but Fres's returned grip on my broken arm keeps me where I am. I bite back tears as pain rips through me, and watch. Asha brushes the loose hair away from my neck, but it's not my markings she traces her warm fingers over. As she grazes the tender bite marks that line my throat and trail down my collarbone, I feel my stomach tighten in shame.

"Have fun at the inn, did we?" She smiles knowingly before her gaze flickers over my shoulder to Silas. "No wonder you're attached."

"For fuck's sake," Olen utters. He shakes his head as he turns to Silas. "Is this why you couldn't bring her yesterday?"

"Maybe he was having second thoughts," Asha adds. "Didn't want to lose his plaything. Is that it, Silas? Feeling lonely?"

My eyes blaze into Asha, but she doesn't notice. She's too focused on the way Silas's fists clench at his sides. He doesn't take the bait, doesn't submit to the pull of his gift again like Asha so clearly wants him to.

"You brought her here. I guess that's all that matters." Olen chuckles under his breath. His eyes rake over me once more before his gaze tracks back to Silas.

Olen *tsks*. "You're lucky the other daemon didn't get in the way, but your pay would have been double if you'd have brought him to us as well. Remember that, next time you're tasked with a job."

Silas finally reaches down to snatch up the sack of coin. The clank of payment is like a knife to the gut.

"I couldn't take both," he spits. "And I had orders to bring her back, not any other."

"Hm," Olen hums dismissively. As his eyes flicker to me, a hungry smile grows on his face. "Ready to see Rohan?"

"I'll be sure to finish what I started," I bite. "My aim was off. I won't make that mistake again."

"Such trouble." He laughs. "I can't wait to see what he does to you this time."

Olen's smile sends a shudder under my skin. He winks at me before turning back to Silas.

"You're sure you didn't see what his markings were? The other daemon that was with them." Olen presses.

"No," Silas states. "I only got a glimpse. His sleeves always covered his marks. He made sure of it. I suspect few of the others even knew what he was."

My gaze snaps to Silas as my mind races to catch up. *Who—*

The answer slides into place, and my throat grows dry. I try to sort through a flurry of questions, but none of the answers I have make any sense. *Vish? Vish is a daemon?*

"Fine, fine," Olen sighs. "Take a few days, and then report back to Denheir. Boss wants everyone to pair up to hunt for a Shade."

"I can come now—"

"*No*, you can't," Olen remarks. "You need a few days to cool off. Go buy a nice girl for the night. Get this one out of your system." Olen's eyes drift over me with agonizing slowness. "By the time you get back, you'll have forgotten about any *attachments*, and she'll be well-behaved for Rohan."

I don't need to look at Silas to know he's fuming. The heat radiating off him is almost palpable. He mutters under his breath, and though I don't hear what he says, it's clearly laced in violence.

Before I can reel away, Silas leans down next to me and gently brushes his hand across my cheek. The touch heats my skin and drives an ache through my heart.

"Do as Rohan says, love," he whispers. "I meant what I said last night."

"Veles damn you," I spit, hot tears sliding down my face. I fight for space away from him, tugging so hard on my bindings that I nearly shriek from the pain of my fractured arm. I collapse into the sand, breath heaving in and out of my lungs.

"Don't you dare give up, Ren," Silas orders, his voice low. He snakes his hand around my head, and pulls my chin up to look where he stands over me. "We both work for Rohan now. This isn't over." His thumb scrapes across my skin, tugging at my bottom lip.

I swallow the lump in my throat as my tearful gaze burns into him. "This was over the moment we left the inn."

Fres tugs at my bindings, yanking me forward and out of Silas's grip. There's a quick flash of a blade, then a biting cut across my skin. I yell, jerking away, but it's too late. A sliver of broken flesh has been cut across my forearm, already oozing fresh blood.

"What happened to wanting her in one piece?" Silas growls.

I fall forward into the sand. Something isn't right. My body flinches, then shudders. Before I know it, I'm panting. Sweat breaks out across my forehead, and I begin to shake.

"I figured we'd need something to keep her obedient for the journey ahead," Olen adds. "The poison will disorient her for a couple of days."

Olen's hand slips through my braided hair. I try to recoil, but I'm teetering against the unsteady current of my own mind.

"Rohan's not letting this one get away again."

For a moment, I lose myself. The anger and desperation seething through me feels like slipping below a swollen tide. The poison only helps to hold me under. I can't breathe. I can't think. My vision wavers. Panic claws at my chest. It feels like there's something swimming through my veins, itching to get out.

"So a Shade?" Asha asks, though the words seem distant. "He's really looking for it, then?"

My head lulls to the side, and I feel bile creeping up my throat. *Poison,* I consider. *What kind of poison?*

"The Durit is the only thing that matters now," Olen states. "Rohan wants every Seer and every Shade across the Continent. Eventually, we'll find it."

"And when we do?" Silas bites. "What then?"

Olen's voice snaps at him, but it's too far away. My ears fill with the rancorous pumping of blood, muffling everything around me.

"...and remember who keeps your pockets full," Olen snipes. "Last I heard, you were saving up for something *special.*"

"Get up," Fres calls through the damped clamor around me.

He grabs me, not by my bindings but by my limp, broken arm. I cry out, but the pain is tempered by something stronger. Something untamed. I thrash against his hold until he grabs me by the hair, yanking me upright.

Stumbling, I struggle to find my legs under me. As I take an unsteady step forward, it's then that I feel it again. Itching in my veins. *Thrumming.* Some wild, unfettered thing inside of me. It's the same feeling that tormented me in the Weaver's dream. It wants out. *It burns.*

I stagger forward, bumping into Fres. My head swims. My body is not my own, and my mind is too clouded in a poisoned haze to guide it.

"Ren—"

Silas's familiar tone is a kick to the stomach, a hot iron poker to the chest. The surge in my veins grows hotter. I rip through the haze, undeterred by my bindings or broken bones as I blindly tackle Fres. *I won't go back. I'll kill every last one of them before I do.*

Voices shout around me as I send the bald man and I tumbling to the sand. Arms flail against me. Hands dig roughly into my skin. My arm is throbbing, like the bone has been dipped in white-hot fire. Black eyes peer from above as I'm dragged away from Fres, kicking and screaming. My rage grows louder and louder until my whole body seems to shudder with it. Pain rips through me. My vision tunnels.

Veles, help me.

I claw at Silas's arm, kicking Fres in the face as he tries to restrain my legs. My brow is dripping in sweat. Nausea quivers through me. But still, I fight. I'm thrashing and scraping and screaming until my body starts to slip away.

My eyelids flutter, and my vision stipples with black. I'm falling, but I'm upright. Slipping away, but still present. My veins throb like they could burst.

Fres reaches for me, hand aimed at my throat. But before he can touch me, my rage rips free—choked out in a brutal sob as I scream. Black lashes toward him in a quick burst. I blink, eyes flicking open long enough to see the wispy shadow slice through Fres's neck. Blood slides down his chest in a swift flow.

My body shakes. Sickness curls in the deepest dredges of my stomach. People are shouting. So much shouting.

I reel away from the hand on my shoulder as shadows whip through the alley. Everything is happening too slow, yet too fast. Fres drops to the sand in a heavy thump. I lean over, sputtering and shaking as the poison takes hold. I look up to see Asha wielding fire against the whips of darkness. My teeth grit as I stare at that heartless face of hers.

The shadows strike faster than I can watch, blurring against my fading vision. She bellows, and my blood thrums happily as I glimpse the vibrant streak of red dripping from her arm. I watch as the edges of the cut turn black, the flesh now decayed.

Fear fills Asha's eyes as she looks up and catches my gaze. She runs. The last I see of her are the braids flying behind her back as she rounds the corner.

I blink, head spinning. My body feels too heavy. It wants to slip into the sand and fall deep into the earth, never to return. Something is calling me to the underworld—to see Veles. *I won't go.*

Everything is hazy, but shadows persist among it all. I stagger forward on my hands and knees. Sweat beads on my brow and drips into my eyes. I blink it away to see shadows swirling, stirring the dirt around me. One curls around my wrist, caressing the skin.

Olen stares at me wide-eyed, face paler than stone. But as he draws his blade and steps forward, I see no hesitation there. No, it's delight that taints his gaze. His mouth morphs into a sinister grin.

My panic flares at the sight, coaxing thoughts of that cellar to the forefront of my mind. In a great burst, darkness rushes toward him. Relief is a balm for my racing heart as the shadow strikes. It wraps around his leg, dragging him to the earth. Olen hits the ground with a harsh *thud.* His dagger flys across the sand. As his eyes flicker up to mine, it's then that I see what I desperately hoped to—fear.

Suddenly, I'm relishing it, feeding off of it. More shadows rush him, tearing into flesh and driving screams from his throat. I try to pry myself up, but the pressure on my broken arm has me collapsing into the ground. I cry out, body trembling underneath me. When I look up, the shadows are gone.

I lift my head to see who wielded them, but I cannot. Olen coughs and sputters. He bleeds from four large gashes across his thigh and abdomen. The wounds shimmer against the sun. Sticky red drips into the sand and bakes there. He breathes, but doesn't rise. *Good.*

I pull in a shuddering breath, and bite back a wave of nausea. There's no sense of up or down anymore. Everything tilts. My head pounds like I've been bucked from a horse. Black spots speckle my vision. My head teeters, then lulls to the side before I right myself. I look up to see Silas in the middle of the alley. He's standing still. His brow is furrowed deeply, and he's looking at me like he did this morning—like he doesn't recognize me.

"You're the—"

The sight of him ignites something foul in my heart. Shadows explode through the alley, knocking Silas on his back. He thrashes and yells against the flare of darkness.

My body screams in protest as I drag myself forward on my hands and knees. Sand grits against my skin, mixing with the fresh slick of blood from my arm. Once again, my gaze finds Silas. His markings gleam against the high sun—the evidence of a gift outmatched. His muscles tense and strain. Amidst the poison's haze, I see Silas's eyes pool black.

"Love, *stop*," he gasps.

He flails and tries to tug at the shadows wrapped around his throat. I watch on, urging them to tighten further still. I grit my teeth and pray Veles will lend his cruelty to me. Silas coughs and sputters, desperately trying to free himself. My hands shake as I drag myself closer. I need to see. Need to watch it happen. *He deserves this.*

The black fades from his eyes too quickly. Something in me falters as I'm met with that gray-eyed stare. The shadows quiver, losing strength.

Silas's gaze is nothing but urgent. Pleading. Desperate. He sucks in a strangled breath as his eyelids flutter. "Ren, *please.*"

The shadows swell as I remember what's true. *Nothing. It was all a lie.* Silas kicks and flails as the pressure tightens around his throat.

I watch him struggle. My body sways uneasily, but I keep my eyes on him. *He doesn't care. He never did.*

The shadows tighten mercilessly. I want to hate him—*should* hate him—but something tugs in my chest as his lips turn purple. I hesitate. I pull in a shuddering breath of air as I watch his eyes roll back. But then, I remember last night.

How he held me tightly as I fell asleep and dreamed of a better tomorrow. Worse still, how he made sure to bed me before collecting his coin today.

He showed no mercy when he betrayed me. So, it's no mercy he shall receive.

My lips quiver into a snarl. This rage is so potent, I feel it twitch in my blood. I scream, cursing the very moment I let myself grow weak for a man yet again.

Shadows whip through the air, and slice into Silas. Three large gashes appear on his chest, each violently deep and dripping blood. Silas's eyes widen before the life in them finally wavers. His hands drop from his neck, and his eyes flutter closed. With a great *thud,* he falls to the ground.

My heart seizes in my chest. *No. Wait.*

I stagger toward him, and the shadows fade into nothing. Silas is crumpled in a heap. My breath hitches as blood pours from his wounds and seeps into the sand. It coats my hands, clinging to the skin. I do nothing but stare—nothing but wait for the rise of his chest.

It never comes.

The poison lurches in my stomach, and I lean over and vomit. I gasp, choking until I pull in a full breath. All at once, the sound of groaning slaps me from my daze.

Olen.

Panic surges through me. I claw into the ground, desperate to heave myself forward. My bound hands drag against the sand, but somehow, I manage to get to my feet. I sway, then stumble into the alley wall. My body shudders. I drop my head between my knees and gag. I'm gagging and coughing and shaking as bile drips from my lips. Fear and disorientation collide inside of me. I don't look for the shadows around me, don't look for the Shade who conjured them. I just move.

My legs stagger forward, trying to move faster than they're able to. There's a splitting ache in my jaw. I can already feel the bruises smarting my face where Egan struck me. Pieces of broken bone flex under my skin and alight my arm in shattering pain. I slam against the wall, losing my balance as my vision wavers once more. The day peppers with black. My world sways, but I force myself to move again. The shaking is worse now, but I can see the end of the alley. I'm close—so close.

I reach my bound hands in front of me, desperate to be free of this nightmare. My eyes flutter closed before I feel it.

Please. No more.

My skin pebbles with chills. Amidst my fading vision, a milky white creeps in. I'm shuddering, legs shaking as I desperately stagger forward to steady myself. Then, everything stops.

The hot desert heat licks against my skin, but what I see chills me to the very bone. I can't help but stare. Mirage huffs underneath me. Her head rears up, tugging on the reins as she snorts loudly. Uneasiness tugs in my chest.

Is it me who's causing her this distress now?

It's a passing thought as my eyes snap back to the stoic figure next to me. He doesn't say anything, though I know he knows I've spotted it. The clench in his jaw and the flighty flicker in his eyes tells me enough. My throat grows dry. My breath ragged. I stare at the marred flesh on his forearm and pray it's not true, pray that what I see in front of me is only a trick of the light. It's not.

The cut is bigger than my thumb, and the damage is deep. I count ten stitches in his tan skin, sewn more tightly than my own. Though the cording is pulled taut, the wound gapes open as if fighting its own healing. I can't pull my eyes away from the black, sickly curl of decayed flesh around its edges.

"What is that?"

"It's nothing," he mutters.

He moves his arm away, but I'm quick to stop him. I drop the reins, biting back the blinding surge of pain as I reach for him. My fingers push up his sleeve, drenching his arm in sunlight. My stomach turns.

I look to his arm, then back to him more than once before I manage to find the words. "When—"

He shakes me off. "It's nothing," he repeats. "You didn't know what you were doing."

Nausea rolls through me like an unruly tide, swirled in the bitter taste of my own resentment.

"Is that to be my excuse now?" I balk. "Oh, don't blame Ren. She has no control—doesn't know how to temper the violence she—" Panic crawls up my throat, choking the words.

The wind whips my tunic, slapping the fabric against my skin. My hand curls into a fist but immediately drops as I feel something *swimming in my veins. It's a feral rage—a hum of power—and it's itching to get free. It wants out.*

I shake my head, and feel panic take root. My body tenses. Mirage feels it, too. She huffs and stomps wildly underneath me. I've lost the reins and any hope of regaining the control I so desperately need.

"How did—?" I stammer. "When did I—?"

I can't find the words, can't even find a breath. He looks at me cautiously, like I'm some breakable thing. Those deep, hazel eyes hold me with such focus that it's dizzying. My heart hammers.

"Ren—"

The minute I snap back to the present, I'm slammed against something solid. Stone digs into my shoulder blades, but it's the breath I'm unable to take that breeds panic. I gasp and flail, but I'm still lost to the world around me. The white takes too long to fade from my eyes. Fear tears through me, though it's quickly tampered by the heavy swell of poison. My head sways atop my neck like a drunkard. Nausea churns my stomach. In between the hazy flicker of my lids, I see rich, dark skin and deep, turquoise eyes. The stare is vaguely familiar, yet piercingly violent. I dig my fingers against the forearm pinning me to the wall, but the crushing pressure on my windpipe doesn't lessen.

Asha sneers as she pushes her weight against me, stifling any chance of slipping free. "You're lucky he wants the godsblood in your veins," she spits. "Or else I'd have already boiled it from your flesh until you popped."

I gasp for air, but she offers me no quarter. My fingers splay out in front of me blindly, vision lost to the peppering black of waning consciousness. I try to shove Asha away, but the world is nothing but a violent, shuddering place. The poison pumps through me, distorting my senses. Tears prick my eyes. Everything is blurry.

I blink but the picture doesn't get any clearer. Voices fill the alley, though I don't hear the words that follow. I shudder. Sweat coats my skin. The world around me spins some more.

"Give me *that*," Asha barks. Her voice seems far away.

For an instant, the strangling pressure withdraws from my windpipe, allowing me to suck in a desperate breath.

"I don't care if it's too much." She argues with someone beyond my fading awareness, and the words dwindle to nothing.

I try to blink the black splotches from my vision, but I'm greeted with nothing but the tilting of the alley. My head lulls and nausea churns once more.

"Either she gets another dose of sivken venom, or we wait for her to come to and mangle your other leg."

I stagger away from the wall as Asha leaves. *Run. Go*, my mind screams. I take no more than a single step before I'm swaying wildly. Whatever strength I had earlier, it's lost to me now. My legs buckle underneath me, but before I can fall, I'm slammed back up against the rough sandstone.

Strands of hair stick to my face, clinging to the mixture of salty tears and sweat. Through the ebbing drag of poison, I feel every part of my body yelling in pain. My arm is a limp branch in front of me, and my throat feels raw. But more than that, there's a deep ache in my chest, a reminder that this is it. This is where fate has led me.

I see the violent shine in Asha's eyes before my vision peppers with black. She digs her arm against my windpipe, choking off my air supply yet again. I barely have time to heave in a final breath.

"*Oh*, how he'll reward me." Asha's breath is hot against my ear, churning the dread in my stomach. "All these years, he's been searching for it." She cocks her head, and pushes her arm up under my jaw. "And to think it's a barely-marked one like you."

My legs kick and flail as I struggle to breath. Asha only laughs.

"*Pathetic*," she utters.

My hands curl into fists, and I thrash against her with every flicker of strength I have left. I can't breath, can barely see the world before me, but I don't stop. Not until I feel a sharp slice graze my shoulder.

I watch a small trail of red slide down my arm. In an instant, the toxic rush pumping through me intensifies, racking my body with violent shudders. Scorching agony and disorientation are all I feel—that, and the faraway thrum of my blood. My eyes flicker, then roll back.

"Unconscious," I hear Asha say.

"...pissed if we leave him," a familiar man utters—though his name is lost to me.

"You can barely walk," Asha chides.

I strain to hear the voices around me, but they get trapped among the thick fog of my mind.

"...her first. Then bring the Mender quick. Eh?"

I'm yanked from the wall, and though I can now breathe, it's like my body has forgotten how. My eyelids are heavy, refusing to open. My body shakes with uncontrollable tremors. Despite it all, I'm dragged forward by the strong grip on my neck.

"We'll take her to Denheir tomorrow."

The muffled rumble of Asha's voice is the last thing I hear before poison drags me under its unsteady surface. My body collapses into nothing but pitch black.

There's no more pain. No more fighting. Just a violent thrum in my blood, and a darkness that I fear will never leave.

At long last, I let Veles take me.

Oh Little Seer,
this is only the beginning.

Turn the page for a sneak peek into Book 2.

INTO DARKNESS

Finally, night has fallen. My fingers splay against the hilt of my sword, almost twitching in anticipation. I look to my left, and search my cousin's face for any sign of hesitation. There is none—only determination in the taut grooves of her face that tells me we're really doing this. She looks like a force of nature, and I'm glad, because I need her to be. There's a firm tension in her jaw, and a readiness set in her crouching figure. But, her eyes. Her eyes give her away.

As she glances my way, she can't hide her worry from me. The gaze that meets mine swims with unspoken questions. She doesn't need to voice them, I know her fears all too well. Not a moment has gone by while watching this day fade to night that I haven't harbored the same ones. I think about offering her some sort of reassurance, but I can't. There are no guarantees in this life. Anything I could say to alleviate her worries would be a carefully crafted lie. She doesn't need that, and I promised. *No more secrets.*

Savi swallows harshly, and voices the only question she can manage. "You sure about this?"

I grit my teeth, and tear my gaze away from my cousin. "No."

The snicker to my right stokes the unease tightening my chest and does little to ease the tension riding my shoulders.

"Oh, come on." Riat grins. "It'll be a piece of cake." He throws an arm over my shoulder—a gesture I'm quick to brush off. "How do you think she'll repay me after we rescue her?" he yaps. "A kiss?"

Riat taps his chin with one of his throwing knives before his face lights up with mischief. "I guess you could just drop us off at the closest inn and we'll see—"

My fist finds his gut before I can stop myself. "Enough," I grunt. "I need you to focus."

Riat coughs quietly as he pulls a full breath back into his lungs. "*Bollocks*," he croaks. "I was just trying to lighten the mood."

"Don't," I snap. "We need to be ready for whatever we find in there."

My jaw locks as I think back to what we already know. Vish had been right. The Berserker took her to Letka—the same city whose shadows we currently hide in. Even without the tracker by my side, it didn't take long to find a familiar, ghostly white mare in front of one of the inns. A pack was secured to the saddle, but the witch was nowhere in sight. The three of us staked out the inn for hours, and as each passed, my uneasiness grew. I know Vish's worries; he's been whispering them in my ear for the past week. Every day she remained in our presence, Vish only grew more certain. And, though I didn't want to believe in such things, the evidence is getting harder to ignore.

Vish was given a name: Serehna. There was a description, too—mere fragments of what to look for. A scar from a knife wound that should have killed her. A trail of Seer's marks down her neck. Two cities she once called home—both abandoned. There were other things—things I couldn't understand for myself. Vish said his gift was different—*fabled*. It worked in ways others couldn't comprehend. He knew things; not everything, but if he asked the right questions, the world would simply unravel for him. He said it was like the gods were whispering in his ear—slipping knowledge into his mind. It was there. Tangible, but not. Known, but unproven. *A Seeker*, he calls himself.

The word tastes bitter, even as I think it now. Almost a decade of friendship, tainted by a single omission. He said it was for his safety—and ours—but an omission is still a lie.

I shake my head, shoving away things I haven't yet come to terms with. There's only one thing that matters now. Vish asked me to get the witch back, and though I had a million reasons to say no, I couldn't bring myself to. Even before we scoured this city and tracked those men here—loud mouthed and drunk—I knew I couldn't leave her to rot. I knew it in the desert, after she'd come for my head when it was that traitorous daemon's she should have sought. I knew it when she'd tackled that bounty whose capture she had no stake in. There was no fate that didn't lead to this path, and I was foolish to deny it.

Vish told me she was important from the moment I carried her into our camp. She was the one he'd been looking for—though Vish had been sure to leave me in the dark until it was much too late. Not an omission this time. A lie. I knew he was looking for a weapon—had been looking for years. And while I had offered my help long ago to make sure his mythical weapon didn't fall into Rohan's grasp, I had never expected it to be her. I should have left Vish to deal with his own problems the moment I found out. Daemons and prophecies aren't my business to get involved in; but yet, here I am.

As I stare into the night's black, I can't help but let my mind wander. The pain I'd seen in her amber eyes as she'd hoisted her dagger high, ready to strike me down, is a memory I haven't been able to shake for days. Part of me wonders if she did manage to bury that blade in my chest then, because I surely feel the ache of it now. She had been so sure I was the one to betray her, and at the moment, I wasn't convinced she was wrong. *What would have happened if I'd only told her the truth? Would the Berserker have killed us like Vish assumed? Or would I have spared the witch the fate she now faces?*

My hand clenches around my sword. It doesn't matter. Those answers will solve nothing now.

"Savi. Riat," I utter, my voice so low it all but melts into the night's hum. "Do what you must. Honor what you can't."

Savi takes a deep breath before rising from my side. She saunters casually toward the southern edge of the house, bow draped across her back, and hips swaying in a way that almost cracks a smile onto my sullen face. She's really playing it up. Though it makes me want to roll my eyes, it works.

The two men we followed here perk up at the sight of my cousin. Time has left them sober, making this part of the plan much more delicate. They speak in low, mumbled tones, and their eyes roam over Savi in a way I should gut them for. I don't care to hear the conversation that passes between them now—I heard enough before.

Insufferable bitch was what they'd called the woman that ordered them from the tavern hours earlier—a woman Savi quickly identified as a Torch by the white flurry of markings on her dark skin. After hours of searching the city for any sign of the witch, it seemed our luck had finally won out. The men were anything but discrete, despite the way the Torch had snapped at them to keep quiet. From behind the rims of barely-touched pints of ale, we watched, and we listened. But even before the woman had mentioned a problem that left all of her men wounded or dead, there was one word that made my ears burn. *Rohan.* The mere mention of his name brought back everything I hoped to keep buried. Rage. Hate. Grief. In the blink of an eye, I was twenty-something, barely a man and faced with a devastation I had never known. It was like I was stepping foot into that outpost again, seeing the land scorched and left to rot. Bodies strewn about the sand. Ash and blood coloring the desert in a sick decay. I had never known true hatred until that day. The overwhelming pull of malice that came over me felt like it belonged to the dark god himself. I would have been lost to the pull of that righteous violence if not for Savi. It was the look on her face that grounded me. Her caring, bright light was the only thing that kept me from razing the Continent to the ground in search of those who caused her harm. I withstood that righteous pull for years until I could no longer bear it. But when the blood finally coated my hands, I realized it had changed nothing. The one who had sent his men into my cousin's home for no purpose other than greed and power still lived. Until my blade pierces Rohan's heart, I will never be sated.

Today, it's that same devil that sparks an old, vengeful fire within me. Though the Torch told the men that Rohan was waiting for his prize in Denheir, the lack of his presence does nothing to calm the simmering rage I still feel now. I'm far from the man I once was, but my hand still twitches eagerly around the hilt of my sword. The witch is the only thing that keeps me from slipping into reckless habits I've far outgrown. If there wasn't more at stake here, I would have barged into that house hours ago, impatient and eager for the slick of blood on my blade. But the mere thought of her—somewhere behind those walls—is a gnawing reminder as to why I'm here getting mixed up in things I barely understand. Rohan wants the witch, and I'll be damned if another person suffers at his hand. Revenge can wait. Some things are far more important. Some people, too.

I snap back to reality as Riat slinks against the eastern wall of the house, having slipped from my side long before thoughts clouded my focus. The scenario before me runs through my head like it has countless times before. My mind searches for a flaw—any deviation that could fuck this up. There's about a hundred different ways this could go bad. I know better than to ask the gods for help; if anything, they'd see fit to test me.

My fist tightens at my side as I watch Savi flirt with the two men. They laugh too brazenly, forget their duty too easily. They pay no mind to the weapon strapped to her back, much too interested in the front of her. Riat's shadow dances against the wall, separated from Savi and the men by only a corner of the house. I hold my breath and balance on bent legs. Watching. Waiting. My muscles twitch in anticipation—itching for the moment I allow them to spring forward. I don't dare move a hair. Instead, I sink deeper into the shadows and watch Savi step to her left. She sashays closer to the shorter man, the one who rests furthest from the house—furthest from the encroaching shadow of my knife-throwing idiot. Riat shoots me a wink, and my lips curl in response. *Veles damn him. If he blows this, I'll kill him.* But the men who guard the most valuable thing on the Continent chatter and laugh, oblivious and easily swayed by Savi's attention like I knew they would be. My eyes dart from left to right, searching the desolate street for any flicker of life. Nothing. No one. The night is calm. I take a deep, steadying breath as I watch it all play out according to plan.

Savi leans against her man, wrapping an arm around his neck playfully. Just as her lips graze the shell of his ear, and his companion is distracted by the scene unfolding before him, a knife whips silently through the air. It plunges deep into its target. The second man's eyes go wide, and his hands dart to where the blade pierces his jugular. Before his choked gasps can draw attention, Savi thrusts a dagger into the supple flesh of her man's neck. He wheezes, eyes bugging as he thrashes. Savi quickly muzzles his sputtering groans with the palm of her hand. My stomach drops as I watch it all play out, but now is not the time to doubt my cousin.

With a harsh grasp, Savi withdraws her blade and lets the man's body drop with a *thud.* Riat is at her side in an instant, silencing his man with a quick slice. Seconds tick by before I'm propelled into action. I help Riat hoist the bodies and drag them out of sight. We leave them behind a stack of opened crates; it won't take anyone long to find them, but it'll do for now.

Once it's done I plant my hands on Savi's shoulders and turn her to face me. I search her expression for any sign of regret—any flicker of hesitation. She's never taken a life, and though she made her own choice, I can't help but feel responsible for anything that might haunt her.

Her teeth are clamped down tightly, as if biting back the words she wishes to keep in. There's a slight shake in her hands and a quiver in her bottom lip that makes my chest grow tight.

"Are you—"

"They were bragging about it," she utters with a steadiness in her tone that shocks me. "Told me they worked for someone important. That they were hand-picked to guard his most prized possession."

Though it's nothing we didn't already know—aside from their boastful embellishments—dread fills my stomach.

"She—" Savi's voice shakes, but as I study the violent flare in her eyes—the vibrant hazel we both get from our fathers—I know she harbors no guilt for what she's done. Something else has spooked her, something that awaits us in this very house.

"They looked inside, couldn't help themselves," she grits out. As she takes a deep breath, I hold mine. "They thought it was funny, that they were tasked to guard such a thing."

"Is she—" Riat asks uneasily, though Savi doesn't let him get the words out.

"Alive," Savi finishes, though her gaze wanders off until she's staring at the house, at the worn wooden door that'll lead us inside. Her next words as no more than a whisper. "*Merely a lamb for slaughter.*"

I don't dare look at Riat, already feeling his eyes on me. Instead, I steel all emotion from my face, and tighten the grip of my sword. The jagged, broken blade not only reminds me of what has passed, but also what might await us. Still, the heavy weight of it in my hand is a balm to my nerves.

"We don't know what or who we'll find inside," I state as flatly as I can. "There's no telling how many men rest behind that door or where they're keeping her." My gaze tightens on the solid wood that stands between me and that which I'm not ready for. "Riat," I command, finally turning toward him. "Savi and I will clear the way for you, but once we get inside and find wherever they're keeping her, it's on you to set her free."

He nods quickly, face resolved of any ill-attempted humor he might offer to ease the tension. There's nothing there but a cold understanding of the severity of what we're doing. The sight lessens the weight in my chest by a fraction. *Good.* I need him to be focused. Our lives depend on it, and so does hers.

"Savi—" I start.

"Move quickly and take out anyone I see. In and out." She looks at me steadily, though I spy the worry that flickers through her gaze. "I know the plan, cousin," she utters. "Let's just get her out of there."

I grunt in affirmation, though I hesitate. Something rests heavy on the tip of my tongue, but I keep my words at bay. None of my men, nor my cousin, have ever followed me blindly. They always have a choice, and tonight they made theirs. We all agreed—we need to do this, regardless of the consequences. If what Vish says is true, the significance of failing is far greater than we can imagine. But it's not fear for the Continent's future that propels me forward. And I don't think it's what drives my companions either.

An earlier survey of the perimeter told us that this house—situated in a deserted part of the city and surrounded by a maze of alleyways—has only one way in and out. Wide windows pepper the western walls, and though I wanted nothing more than to peer inside earlier, it was too risky in the daylight. What had me more intrigued, then and now, is the northern and eastern sides of the house. No windows grace the walls. There are no cracks or gaps in the stone—nothing to let even a flicker of light inside. Those walls tell me everything I need to know about where they're keeping her. Leave it to Rohan to inflict the most basic of cruelties.

One nod of my head is all it takes for Riat to slink his way toward the door. He's prepared to pick the lock, but it's not necessary. The cocky bastards left it open. As my eyes sweep through the alleyways, looking for trouble, Riat shimmies the knob and pulls at the door. The hinges creak open with a whine that sounds like a yell in the night...

Can't wait to read more?

Into Darkness, Book 2 in the Blood of the Durit series, is out now!

Get your copy at angiecaedis.com

Acknowledgments

This book wouldn't have been possible without a handful of amazing individuals.

First and foremost, my friends and family who have given me endless support in this crazy endeavor of becoming an author.

To my parents, thank you for believing in me. You have no idea how much it means. To my best friends, Haley and Karisa, thank you for putting up with all of my manic group texts while I worked through this book. I can alway count on you both to wrangle my overthinking spirals, but also to cheer me on when I need it.

To my fabulous beta readers (especially, Gillian), thank you for the indispensable feedback early on in this story's creation. Your insights and suggestions helped me get out of my own head and take this book to the next level. Thank you, thank you, thank you.

To Luísa Dias, thank you so much for another extraordinary book cover. You are so talented and truly brought this story to life with your work. Thank you for always being able to take my scrambled thoughts and ideas and create something truly one-of-a-kind.

To Claire Ashgrove who edited this book, thank you for your hard work in making sure this book read as clearly as possible. Your feedback was beyond beneficial. I promise to study up, and reform my wayward comma usage.

And finally, thank you so much to my readers. Your support means everything to me—whether this is your first time reading my work or you've been tagging along this wild journey for awhile. From the bottom of my heart, thank you. I hope you enjoyed reading this book as much as I enjoyed writing it.

About the Author

Angie Caedis is a mood writer with a love for too many genres. This is her first fantasy novel, and—needless to say—she's hooked. When she's not hunkered down with her laptop and a cup of tea, she enjoys hiking, photography, horror movies, solo traveling, and reading anything she can get her hands on.

Follow her on all social channels @angiecaedis for book news and sneak peeks into her stories.

www.ingramcontent.com/pod-product-compliance
Lightning Source LLC
Chambersburg PA
CBHW022018300726
48970CB00003B/936